Born in Allegheny, Pennsylvania, on February 3, 1874, to an affluent Jewish family, **Gertrude Stein** spent her early childhood in Vienna and Paris and later grew up in Oakland, California. At Radcliffe College, she studied under William James, who remained her lifelong friend; then she attended Johns Hopkins, where she began to pursue a medical degree. But in 1903 she abandoned her studies and moved to Paris with her brother, Leo. At 27 rue de Fleurus, Gertrude Stein lived with Alice B. Toklas. In addition to being an innovator in literature and a supporter of modern poetry and art, Stein was the friend and mentor to many who sought her advice and encouragement, including Pablo Picasso, Henri Matisse, Jean Cocteau, Ernest Hemingway, F. Scott Fitzgerald, Sherwood Anderson, and Guillaume Appollinaire. Her first important book was *Three Lives* (1909), followed by *Tender Buttons* (1914) and her magnum opus, *The Making of Americans* (1925). She enjoyed huge popular success with *The Autobiography of Alice B. Toklas* (1933). Just before her death at the age of seventy-two, on July 27, 1946, she asked Alice Toklas from her hospital bed, "What is the answer?" Getting no answer, she then asked, "In that case, what is the question?"

Diana Souhami is the author of many highly acclaimed books, including *The Trials of Radclyffe Hall* (winner of the Lambda Award for biography 2000), the bestselling *Mrs Keppel and Her Daughter*, and *Gertrude and Alice*, an account of the nearly forty-year marriage between Gertrude Stein and Alice B. Toklas. Her latest book, *Selkirk's Island*, won the 2001 Whitbread biography award. She lives in London and Devon.

THREE LIVES
&
TENDER BUTTONS

GERTRUDE STEIN

*With a New Introduction by
Diana Souhami*

A SIGNET CLASSIC

SIGNET CLASSIC
Published by New American Library, a division of
Penguin Putnam Inc., 375 Hudson Street,
New York, New York 10014, U.S.A.
Penguin Books Ltd, 80 Strand,
London WC2R 0RL, England
Penguin Books Australia Ltd, 250 Camberwell Road,
Camberwell, Victoria 3124, Australia
Penguin Books Canada Ltd, 10 Alcorn Avenue,
Toronto, Ontario, Canada M4V 3B2
Penguin Books (N.Z.) Ltd, 182–190 Wairau Road
Auckland 10, New Zealand

Penguin Books Ltd, Registered Offices:
Harmondsworth, Middlesex, England

Published by Signet Classic, an imprint of New American Library,
a division of Penguin Putnam Inc.

First Signet Classic Printing, February 2003
10 9 8 7 6 5 4 3 2 1

Ⓡ REGISTERED TRADEMARK—MARCA REGISTRADA

Library of Congress Catalog Card Number: 2002030244

Printed in the United States of America

CONTENTS

INTRODUCTION

GERTRUDE STEIN was a humorous, down-to-earth woman, hospitable and wise, with a love for ordinary comfortable living. She liked good food, friendly conversation, walking the dog (Basket, a large white poodle), driving down French country lanes in Auntie (her model-T Ford), holidaying in Italy, eating wild strawberries for breakfast and honey cakes for tea. Bravig Imbs, an American writer friend, said of her that she had the most engaging and infectious laugh he had ever heard: "It began abruptly at a high pitch and cascaded down and down into rolls of unctuous merriment. It was straight from the heart."[1] In life Gertrude was grounded and pleasant. By contrast, in her writing she broke all rules of narrative progression, structure, form, style and especially sense.

She confounded her readers. Narrative mattered little to her. Her writing seemed to have some elusive implication of meaning. It was as if she was all the time asking the questions: What do we mean by what we say, and why do we say things in the way we do? Her essential interest was in her own groundbreaking style. Her concerns were the cadences of speech, impressions of non-sequential events, the essence of character, quirks of behavior, the rhythms and oddities of language, the grand philosophical conundrums of time, space and existence.

Three Lives was the third of her works. Compared with what followed it is an easy read. She began it in spring 1905 when she was thirty-one. She had already written *QED* and *Fernhurst*, but put both those manuscripts away in a cupboard without attempting to find a publisher. They were too personal, both centering on

---

[1]Imbs, Bravig, *Confessions of Another Young Man* (New York, 1936).

a fraught love affair she had in Baltimore in 1900 when she was studying medicine at the Johns Hopkins Medical School. She became caught in an unworkable triangle with two Bryn Mawr college graduates, May Bookstaver and Mabel Haynes. Her studies suffered as well as her morale. She got the lowest grades in her year.

Three Lives was less obviously autobiographical, though she imbued it with the emotional bleakness of unfulfilled love. She had moved to Paris in 1903. Her brother, Leo, found a place for her to live at 27 rue de Fleurus near the Luxembourg Gardens, a two-story apartment off a paved courtyard with an adjacent studio. They set up house together, he as a painter, she as a writer.

Gertrude wrote at night in the studio at a long oak table. Gas lamps hung overhead and heat came from a cast-iron stove. She wrote in pencil in spidery writing in children's exercise books. The "three lives" were psychological studies of unprivileged women who lead unfulfilled lives in Bridgeport — her fictional name for Baltimore. They were all passive. Men were of no help to them. All are the antithesis of the nineteenth-century fictional heroine who was rich, beautiful, upper-class and lucky in love.

Two of Gertrude's women, the Good Anna and Lena, are German immigrants to America, like Gertrude's relatives.

The Good Anna, in service from the age of seventeen, likes working for large, helpless women — like Gertrude. Her only romance is her inchoate feeling for a Mrs. Lehntman, who helps hard-done-by girls: "A certain magnetic brilliance in person and in manner made Mrs. Lehntman a woman other women loved." With reference to her own tormented love for May Bookstaver, Gertrude wrote: "Romance is the ideal in one's life and it is very lonely living with it lost."

Anna achieves nothing for herself. She is law-abiding, on good terms with the police; she finds homes for stray dogs and cats and parts with her hard-earned wages to undeserving strangers. It is not an eventful narrative. After an unremarkable life the Good Anna dies an unremarkable death. Gertrude wanted there to be no significant beginning, middle or end to her stories. She thought this closer to people's true experience of reality, a multifacetedness, a "continuous present." "Always and always. Must write the hymn of repetition," she said. So her readers are told too many times for comfort that Anna has a spinster body, a pale face and yellow skin, that her half brother is a baker, that she does not like her brother's wife. They could be forgiven for thinking that Gertrude's concentration was impaired, what with her sudden lurches of direction, the interpolation of quotidian detail and non sequiturs, the introduction and abandonment of peripheral characters: "this woman's husband's brother who was very good, worked in a shop where there was a Bohemian who was getting sick with a consumption."

Gertrude had studied psychology with William James at Radcliffe College in Baltimore and she wanted to apply his theory of the stream of consciousness to her fiction. "Consciousness is nothing jointed, it flows," James wrote in *Principles of Psychology*. "So-called interruptions no more break the flow of the thought that thinks them than they break the time and space in which they lie."

In the second of the three lives, that of Melanctha, consciousness streams, with sentences a dozen lines long and paragraphs that run to pages. Melanctha, an African-American, falls for a Dr. Jefferson, who has attended her dying mother. There follows a saga of indecision, a circumlocutory reiteration of his discursive ambivalence and her reaction to it.

Lena, the third heroine, has the saddest of the three lives. She is brought to Bridgeport by an aunt and married off to a German-American tailor who dislikes women, has no conversation and flees to New York in an attempt to avoid the wedding. He is brought back by his father: "Tuesday morning came, Herman got his new clothes on and went with his father and mother to stand up for an hour and get married."

Theirs is the emptiest of relationships, with no trace or whiff of kindness, love or basic civility. The reader is left to guess at the bleakness of their coupling. Herman does not address a word to Lena, who becomes catatonic and careless of her appearance. He feels no remorse when she dies in childbirth with her fourth pregnancy. He much prefers to be alone with his children: "He liked it better not to have a woman all the time around him."

In 1934, when Gertrude Stein was famous, convinced of her

own genius and on a lecture tour of America, she claimed that
Three Lives was "the first definite step away from the nineteenth
century and into the twentieth century in literature." A journalist
asked her, "Why don't you write the way you speak?" "Why
don't you speak the way I write?" she replied. She turned mean-
ings around. She said she wanted to smash the significance of
nineteenth-century order and structure, shuck off old habits of
seeing and describing and let a new art emerge.

She wrote with Paul Cézanne's *Portrait of Madame Cézanne*
(1877) on the studio wall in front of her. She thought the painting
revolutionary and said that it inspired her; that Cézanne built up
this picture with repetitive brushstrokes and that she built up her
characters with repetitive sentences. There was no center to
Cézanne's picture to give it an organizing principle; the composition *was* the picture. "Cézanne gave me a new feeling about composition. I was obsessed by this idea of composition. . . . It was
not solely the realism of characters but the realism of the composition which was the important thing."[2]

She and Leo bought modern paintings, not with thoughts of in-
vestment (they lived on a comfortable inherited income), but
solely because they liked them. They set themselves a limit of
three hundred francs for a picture. The artists were for the most
part poor and had gravitated to Paris out of the same desire for freedom as themselves: "Paris was where the twentieth century was,"
Gertrude said, "the place that suited those of us who were to cre-
ate the twentieth-century art and literature naturally enough."

Most of the art she and Leo acquired came from dealer Am-
broise Vollard in his musty, cluttered shop in rue Lafitte. On two
spending sprees they bought two Gauguins, *Three Tahitians* for
Leo and *Sunflowers* for Gertrude—"they were rather awful but finally we liked them," she said—two versions of Cézanne's
Bathers, two Renoirs, Matisse's *Woman with a Hat*, Picasso's *Ac-
robat's Family with a Monkey* and the Cézanne portrait of his wife,
Hortense. They discussed the pictures over honey cakes at Fou-
quet's before taking them home in a cab. The walls of 27 rue de

[2]Haas, Robert Bartlett, "Gertrude Stein Talking—A Transatlantic Interview"
(1945), *Uclan Review* (Summer 1962, Spring 1963, Winter 1964).

Fleurus became crammed with paintings. Often they did not bother to have them framed. Gertrude thought frames constraining.

She wrote *Three Lives* wanting this visual shock of the new to inform her work. But she despaired of finding a publisher. Readers found the book too unconventional and strange. "I am afraid that I can never write the great American novel," Gertrude wrote to her friend Mabel Weeks. "I have to content myself with niggers and servant girls and the foreign population generally."[3] Nor was Leo encouraging. He offended her by saying her writing was all to do with her and nothing to do with literature.

Life for Gertrude changed when she met Alice B. Toklas in 1907. Theirs became one of the happiest marriages in modern literary history. Until Gertrude's death thirty-nine years later, they were never apart. Gertrude felt low in her mind if she was away from Alice for long. And Alice, writing about their relationship at the end of her own long life, said that from the moment they met "it was Gertrude Stein who held my complete attention, as she did for all the many years I knew her until her death and all these empty ones since then."[4]

Within a year of their meeting, Alice was ensconced in rue de Fleurus as Gertrude's wife, editor, amanuensis, secretary, housekeeper, lover and friend. She called Gertrude Lovey; Alice was Pussy. Leo was ousted and went to live elsewhere.

Above all, Alice confirmed Gertrude's belief in herself as a genius. "Think of the Bible and Homer, think of Shakespeare and think of me," said Gertrude. In 1908, with Alice's encouragement, Gertrude paid for fifteen hundred copies of *Three Lives* to be privately printed in America by the Grafton Press at a cost to herself of six hundred sixty dollars. The director, Mr. F. H. Hitchcock, wrote to her: "I want to say frankly that you have written a very peculiar book and it will be a hard thing to make people take it seriously."[5] He worried that her stylistic oddities would be con-

---

[3]Gertrude Stein to Mabel Weeks, undated (Yale Collection of American Literature).

[4]Alice B. Toklas, *What Is Remembered* (1963).

[5]Gallup, Donald (ed.), *The Flowers of Friendship: Letters Written to Gertrude Stein* (1941).

strued as his firm's editorial incompetence. Alice sent seventy-eight copies to reviewers and friends and pasted the scant reviews in an album. Two of these were polite—the *Boston Morning Herald* thought it an extraordinary book and the *Kansas City Star* called Gertrude "a literary artist of such originality." Nonetheless, a year after publication only seventy-three copies had been sold.

Three Lives was groundbreaking in form and content, but straightforward compared to her later work *Tender Buttons*, which she wrote on holiday in Spain with Alice in 1912. She described it as her "first conscious struggle with the problem of correlating sight, sound and sense and eliminating rhythm." The words she used exactly related to the thing at which she was looking, she said, but "as often as not had nothing to do with what any words would do that described that thing."

She placed herself firmly in the vanguard of modernism and declared her affiliation with Picasso: "I was alone at this time in understanding him. Perhaps because I was expressing the same thing in literature."[6] She said what they were producing was beyond realism, or "things remembered," or "reconstruction from memory." They were dismantling the components of reality and reconstructing them in their own highly individual ways. She felt that this subjective expression made them into the chroniclers of the twentieth century, at a time when "belief in the reality of science commenced to diminish."[7]

Sustained reading of *Tender Buttons* engenders a feeling of having gone gaga. The prose is incantatory, repetitive, prolix and discursive. "Suppose there is a pigeon. Suppose there is." There are section headings (OBJECTS, FOOD, ROOMS) and there are ostensible definitions: "Nickel, what is nickel, it is originally rid of a cover" or "sugar is not a vegetable" or "A piece of coffee is not a detainer" or "Callous is something that hardening leaves behind what will be soft if there is a genuine interest in there being present as many girls as men."

Hers are dictionary definitions for Wonderland: "MORE. An elegant use of foliage and grace and a little piece of white cloth

[6]Stein, Gertrude, *Picasso* (1938).
[7]Stein, Ibid.

and oil." "MALACHITE. The sudden spoon is the same in no size. The sudden spoon is the wound in the decision." Her tone lurches from being exhorting to conversational, questioning to marveling, admonitory to climactic. Always it is nonsensical. "A little lace makes boils. This is not true." Or "PEELED PENCIL CHOKE. Rub her coke." It is not possible to read continuously without needing to laugh at her in self-defense. For *Tender Buttons* is an assault on reason. The reader gives up on meaning and realizes that the author is undermining assertion, questioning knowledge, opinion and authority and stripping language of sense in order to show other qualities about it. In purveying seeming nonsense Stein asks the question: What is sense?

Unlike her earlier works, *Tender Buttons* found a publisher. The friend behind her literary launch was Carl Van Vechten, writer, photographer and, in 1913, assistant music critic for the *New York Times*. He gave the manuscript to an American poet friend, Donald Evans, who had started the Claire Marie Press. He promised "New Books for Exotic Tastes":

> Claire Marie believes there are in America seven hundred civilized people only. Claire Marie publishes books for civilized people only. Claire Marie's aim, it follows from the premises, is not even secondarily commercial.

In June 1914 one thousand copies of *Tender Buttons* were printed and bound in canary yellow covers. In his promotion copy Evans wrote:

> The last shackle is struck from context and collocation, each unit of the sentence stands independent and has no commerce with its fellows. The effect produced on the first reading is something like terror.

Such publicity did little to reassure readers, however civilized. The *Chicago Tribune* reviewer puzzled over whether the *Tender* of the title meant a rowboat, a fuel car attached to a locomotive or an expression of human emotion. One reader was confused enough to think that Tender Buttons were clitorises; another

thought they were marinated mushrooms; a third, more pro-
saically, thought the book got its title because of Gertrude's liking
for mushrooms.

The critic Max Eastman compared it to the ravings of a lunatic.
The *Detroit News* reviewer said that after reading excerpts from it
he felt like going out and pulling the Dime Bank building over
onto himself. The *Commercial Advertiser* wrote:

> The new Stein manner is founded on what the Germans call
> "Wort salad," a style particularly cultivated by crazy peo-
> ple. . . . The way to make a wort salad is to sit in a dark
> room, preferably between the silent and mystic hours of
> midnight and dawn, and let the moving fingers write what-
> ever comes.

The *New York Post* reviewer wondered if Gertrude had been
eating hashish. None of the reviewers claimed to understand *Tender Buttons*, but they all thought it unlike anything else and
Gertrude was described as a literary cubist.

Gertrude's esoteric work makes no more sense now than when
it was written ninety years ago. It still disconcerts and provokes,
but it resists oblivion. Her style, like her personality, remains a
force to be reckoned with. She was there in Paris at the exhibitions
of the Fauves and the cubists. She encouraged the founders of the
innovative magazines of the 1920s and the aspirations of the ex-
patriate writers between the two world wars who met at her
Thursday afternoon salons on the rue de Fleurus. May today's civilized reader of *Tender Buttons* approach it with humor, a sus-
pended expectation of meaning and a spirit of tribute to an
architect of modernism.

—Diana Souhami

THREE LIVES

*Donc je suis un malheureux et ce
n'est ni ma faute ni celle de la vie.*

JULES LAFORGUE

THE GOOD ANNA

PART 1

THE tradesmen of Bridgepoint learned to dread the sound of "Miss Mathilda", for with that name the good Anna always conquered.

The strictest of the one price stores found that they could give things for a little less, when the good Anna had fully said that "Miss Mathilda" could not pay so much and that she could buy it cheaper "by Lindheims."

Lindheims was Anna's favorite store, for there they had bargain days, when flour and sugar were sold for a quarter of a cent less for a pound, and there the heads of the departments were all her friends and always managed to give her the bargain prices, even on other days.

Anna led an arduous and troubled life.

Anna managed the whole little house for Miss Mathilda. It was a funny little house, one of a whole row of all the same kind that made a close pile like a row of dominoes that a child knocks over, for they were built along a street which at this point came down a steep hill. They were funny little houses, two stories high, with red brick fronts and long white steps.

This one little house was always very full with Miss

Mathilda, an under servant, stray dogs and cats and Anna's voice that scolded, managed, grumbled all day long.

"Sallie! can't I leave you alone a minute but you must run to the door to see the butcher boy come down the street and there is Miss Mathilda calling for her shoes. Can I do everything while you go around always thinking about nothing at all? If I ain't after you every minute you would be forgetting all the time, and I take all this pains, and when you come to me you was as ragged as a buzzard and as dirty as a dog. Go and find Miss Mathilda her shoes where you put them this morning."

"Peter!",—her voice rose higher,—"Peter!",—Peter was the youngest and the favourite dog,—"Peter, if you don't leave Baby alone,"—Baby was an old, blind terrier that Anna had loved for many years,—"Peter if you don't leave Baby alone, I take a rawhide to you, you bad dog."

The good Anna had high ideals for canine chastity and discipline. The three regular dogs, the three that always lived with Anna, Peter and old Baby, and the fluffy little Rags, who was always jumping up into the air just to show that he was happy, together with the transients, the many stray ones that Anna always kept until she found them homes, were all under strict orders never to be bad one with the other.

A sad disgrace did once happen in the family. A little transient terrier whom Anna had found a home suddenly produced a crop of pups. The new owners were certain that this Foxy had known no dog since she was in their care. The good Anna held to it stoutly that her Peter and her Rags were guiltless, and she made her statement with so much heat that Foxy's owners were at last convinced that these results were due to their neglect.

"You bad dog," Anna said to Peter that night, "you bad dog."

"Peter was the father of those pups," the good Anna explained to Miss Mathilda, "and they look just like him too, and poor little Foxy, they were so big that she could hardly have them, but Miss Mathilda, I would never let those people know that Peter was so bad."

Periods of evil thinking came very regularly to Peter and to Rags and to the visitors within their gates. At such times Anna would be very busy and scold hard, and then too she always took great care to seclude the bad dogs from each other whenever she had to leave the house. Sometimes just to see how good it was that she had made them, Anna would leave the room a little while and leave them all together, and then she would suddenly come back. Back would slink all the wicked-minded dogs at the sound of her hand upon the knob, and then they would sit desolate in their corners like a lot of disappointed children whose stolen sugar has been taken from them.

Innocent blind old Baby was the only one who preserved the dignity becoming in a dog.

You see that Anna led an arduous and troubled life.

The good Anna was a small, spare, german woman, at this time about forty years of age. Her face was worn, her cheeks were thin, her mouth drawn and firm, and her light blue eyes were very bright. Sometimes they were full of lightning and sometimes full of humor, but they were always sharp and clear.

Her voice was a pleasant one, when she told the histories of bad Peter and of Baby and of little Rags. Her voice was a high and piercing one when she called to the teamsters and to the other wicked men, what she wanted that should come to them, when she saw them beat a horse or kick a dog. She did not belong to any society that could stop them and she told them so most frankly, but her strained voice and her glittering eyes, and her queer piercing german-english first made them afraid and then ashamed. They all knew too, that all the policemen on the beat were her friends. These always respected and obeyed Miss Annie, as they called her, and promptly attended to all of her complaints.

For five years Anna managed the little house for Miss Mathilda. In these five years there were four different under servants.

The one that came first was a pretty, cheerful Irish girl. Anna took her with a doubting mind. Lizzie was an obedient, happy servant, and Anna began to have a little faith. This was not for long. The pretty, cheerful Lizzie disappeared one day without her notice and with all her baggage and returned no more.

This pretty, cheerful Lizzie was succeeded by a melancholy Molly.

Molly was born in America, of german parents. All her people had been long dead or gone away. Molly had always been alone. She was a tall, dark, sallow, thin-haired creature, and she was always troubled with a cough, and she had a bad temper, and always said ugly dreadful swear words.

Anna found all this very hard to bear, but she kept Molly a long time out of kindness. The kitchen was constantly a battle-ground. Anna scolded and Molly swore strange oaths, and then Miss Mathilda would shut her door hard to show that she could hear it all.

At last Anna had to give it up. "Please Miss Mathilda won't you speak to Molly," Anna said, "I can't do a thing with her. I scold her, and she don't seem to hear and then she swears so that she scares me. She loves you Miss Mathilda, and you scold her please once."

"But Anna," cried poor Miss Mathilda, "I don't want to," and that large, cheerful, but fainthearted woman looked all aghast at such a prospect. "But you must, please Miss Mathilda!" Anna said.

Miss Mathilda never wanted to do any scolding. "But you must please Miss Mathilda," Anna said.

Miss Mathilda every day put off the scolding, hoping always that Anna would learn to manage Molly better. It never did get better and at last Miss Mathilda saw that the scolding simply had to be.

It was agreed between the good Anna and her Miss Mathilda that Anna should be away when Molly would be scolded. The next evening that it was Anna's evening out, Miss Mathilda faced her task and went down into the kitchen.

Molly was sitting in the little kitchen leaning her elbows on the table. She was a tall, thin, sallow girl, aged twenty-three, by nature slatternly and careless but trained by Anna into superficial neatness. Her drab striped cotton dress and gray black checked apron increased the length and sadness of her melancholy figure. "Oh, Lord!" groaned Miss Mathilda to herself as she approached her.

"Molly, I want to speak to you about your behaviour to Anna!", here Molly dropped her head still lower on her arms and began to cry.

"Oh! Oh!" groaned Miss Mathilda.

"It's all Miss Annie's fault, all of it," Molly said at last, in a trembling voice, "I do my best."

"I know Anna is often hard to please," began Miss Mathilda, with a twinge of mischief, and then she sobered herself to her task, "but you must remember, Molly, she means it for your good and she is really very kind to you."

"I don't want her kindness," Molly cried, "I wish you would tell me what to do, Miss Mathilda, and then I would be all right. I hate Miss Annie."

"This will never do Molly," Miss Mathilda said sternly, in her deepest, firmest tones, "Anna is the head of the kitchen and you must either obey her or leave."

"I don't want to leave you," whimpered melancholy Molly. "Well Molly then try and do better," answered Miss Mathilda, keeping a good stern front, and backing quickly from the kitchen.

"Oh! Oh!" groaned Miss Mathilda, as she went back up the stairs.

Miss Mathilda's attempt to make peace between the constantly contending women in the kitchen had no real effect. They were very soon as bitter as before.

At last it was decided that Molly was to go away. Molly went away to work in a factory in town, and she went to live with an old woman in the slums, a very bad old woman Anna said.

Anna was never easy in her mind about the fate of Molly. Sometimes she would see or hear of her. Molly was not well, her cough was worse, and the old woman really was a bad one.

After a year of this unwholesome life, Molly was completely broken down. Anna then again took her in charge. She brought her from her work and from the woman where she lived, and put her in a hospital to stay till she was well. She found a place for her as nursemaid to a little girl out in the country, and Molly was at last established and content.

Molly had had, at first, no regular successor. In a few months it was going to be the summer and Miss Mathilda would be gone away, and old Katy would do very well to come in every day and help Anna with her work.

Old Katy was a heavy, ugly, short and rough old german woman, with a strange distorted german-english all her own. Anna was worn out now with her attempt to make the younger generation do all that it should and rough old Katy never answered back, and never wanted her own way. No scolding or abuse could make its mark on her uncouth and aged peasant hide. She said her "Yes, Miss Annie," when an answer had to come, and that was always all that she could say.

"Old Katy is just a rough old woman, Miss Mathilda," Anna said, "but I think I keep her here with me. She can work and she don't give me no trouble like I had with Molly all the time."

Anna always had a humorous sense from this old Katy's twisted peasant english, from the roughness on her tongue of buzzing s's and from the queer ways of her brutish servile humor. Anna could not let old Katy serve at table — old Katy was too coarsely made from natural earth for that — and so Anna had all this to do herself and that she never liked, but even then this simple rough old creature was pleasanter to her than any of the upstart young.

Life went on very smoothly now in these few months before the summer came. Miss Mathilda every summer went away across the ocean to be gone for several months. When she went away this summer old Katy was so sorry, and on the day Miss Mathilda went, old Katy cried hard for many hours. An earthy, uncouth, servile peasant creature old Katy surely was. She stood there on the white stone steps of the little red brick house, with her bony, square dull head with its thin, tanned, toughened skin and its sparse and kinky grizzled hair, and her strong, squat figure a little overmade on the right side, clothed in her blue striped cotton dress, all clean and always washed but rough and harsh to see — and she stayed there on the steps till Anna brought her in, blubbering, her apron to her face, and making queer guttural broken moans.

When Miss Mathilda early in the fall came to her house again old Katy was not there.

"I never thought old Katy would act so Miss Mathilda," Anna said, "when she was so sorry when you went away, and I gave her full wages all the summer, but they are all alike Miss Mathilda, there isn't one of them that's fit to trust. You know how Katy said she liked you, Miss Mathilda, and went on about it when you went away and then she was so good and worked all right until the middle of the summer, when I got sick, and then she went away and left me all

alone and took a place out in the country, where they gave
her some more money. She didn't say a word, Miss
Mathilda, she just went off and left me there alone when I
was sick after that awful hot summer that we had, and after
all we done for her when she had no place to go, and all
summer I gave her better things to eat than I had for myself.
Miss Mathilda, there isn't one of them has any sense of
what's the right way for a girl to do, not one of them."

Old Katy was never heard from any more.

No under servant was decided upon now for several
months. Many came and many went, and none of them
would do. At last Anna heard of Sallie.

Sallie was the oldest girl in a family of eleven and Sallie
was just sixteen years old. From Sallie down they came always
littler and littler in her family, and all of them were always out
at work excepting only the few littlest of them all.

Sallie was a pretty blonde and smiling german girl, and
stupid and a little silly. The littler they came in her family
the brighter they all were. The brightest of them all was a little girl of ten. She did a good day's work washing dishes for
a man and wife in a saloon, and she earned a fair day's wage,
and then there was one littler still. She only worked for half
the day. She did the housework for a bachelor doctor. She
did it all, all of the housework and received each week her
eight cents for her wage. Anna was always indignant when
she told that story.

"I think he ought to give her ten cents Miss Mathilda any
way. Eight cents is so mean when she does all his work and
she is such a bright little thing too, not stupid like our Sallie. Sallie would never learn to do a thing if I didn't scold her
all the time, but Sallie is a good girl, and I take care and she
will do all right."

Sallie was a good, obedient german child. She never answered Anna back, no more did Peter, old Baby and little
Rags and so though always Anna's voice was sharply raised

in strong rebuke and worn expostulation, they were a happy family all there together in the kitchen.

Anna was a mother now to Sallie, a good incessant german mother who watched and scolded hard to keep the girl from any evil step. Sallie's temptations and transgressions were much like those of naughty Peter and jolly little Rags, and Anna took the same way to keep all three from doing what was bad.

Sallie's chief badness besides forgetting all the time and never washing her hands clean to serve at table, was the butcher boy.

He was an unattractive youth enough, that butcher boy. Suspicion began to close in around Sallie that she spent the evenings when Anna was away, in company with this bad boy.

"Sallie is such a pretty girl, Miss Mathilda," Anna said, "and she is so dumb and silly, and she puts on that red waist, and she crinkles up her hair with irons so I have to laugh, and then I tell her if she only washed her hands clean it would be better than all that fixing all the time, but you can't do a thing with the young girls nowadays Miss Mathilda. Sallie is a good girl but I got to watch her all the time."

Suspicion closed in around Sallie more and more, that she spent Anna's evenings out with this boy sitting in the kitchen. One early morning Anna's voice was sharply raised.

"Sallie this ain't the same banana that I brought home yesterday, for Miss Mathilda, for her breakfast, and you was out early in the street this morning, what was you doing there?"

"Nothing, Miss Annie, I just went out to see, that's all and that's the same banana, 'deed it is Miss Annie."

"Sallie, how can you say so and after all I do for you, and Miss Mathilda is so good to you. I never brought home no bananas yesterday with specks on it like that. I know better, it was that boy was here last night and ate it while I was away, and you was out to get another this morning. I don't want no lying Sallie."

Sallie was stout in her defence but then she gave it up and she said it was the boy who snatched it as he ran away at the sound of Anna's key opening the outside door. "But I will never let him in again, Miss Annie, 'deed I won't," said Sallie.

And now it was all peaceful for some weeks and then Sallie with fatuous simplicity began on certain evenings to resume her bright red waist, her bits of jewels and her crinkly hair.

One pleasant evening in the early spring, Miss Mathilda was standing on the steps beside the open door, feeling cheerful in the pleasant, gentle night. Anna came down the street, returning from her evening out. "Don't shut the door, please, Miss Mathilda," Anna said in a low voice, "I don't want Sallie to know I'm home."

Anna went softly through the house and reached the kitchen door. At the sound of her hand upon the knob there was a wild scramble and a bang, and then Sallie sitting there alone when Anna came into the room, but, alas, the butcher boy forgot his overcoat in his escape.

You see that Anna led an arduous and troubled life.

Anna had her troubles, too, with Miss Mathilda. "And I slave and slave to save the money and you go out and spend it all on foolishness," the good Anna would complain when her mistress, a large and careless woman, would come home with a bit of porcelain, a new etching and sometimes even an oil painting on her arm.

"But Anna," argued Miss Mathilda, "if you didn't save this money, don't you see I could not buy these things," and then Anna would soften and looked pleased until she learned the price, and then wringing her hands, "Oh, Miss Mathilda, Miss Mathilda," she would cry, "and you gave all that money out for that, when you need a dress to go out in so bad." "Well, perhaps I will get one for myself next year, Anna," Miss Mathilda would cheerfully concede. "If we live till then Miss Mathilda, I see that you do," Anna would then answer darkly.

Anna had great pride in the knowledge and possessions of her cherished Miss Mathilda, but she did not like her careless way of wearing always her old clothes. "You can't go out to dinner in that dress, Miss Mathilda," she would say, standing firmly before the outside door, "You got to go and put on your new dress you always look so nice in." "But Anna, there isn't time." "Yes there is, I go up and help you fix it, please Miss Mathilda you can't go out to dinner in that dress and next year if we live till then, I make you get a new hat, too. It's a shame Miss Mathilda to go out like that."

The poor mistress sighed and had to yield. It suited her cheerful, lazy temper to be always without care but sometimes it was a burden to endure, for so often she had it all to do again unless she made a rapid dash out of the door before Anna had a chance to see.

Life was very easy always for this large and lazy Miss Mathilda, with the good Anna to watch and care for her and all her clothes and goods. But, alas, this world of ours is after all much what it should be and cheerful Miss Mathilda had her troubles too with Anna.

It was pleasant that everything for one was done, but annoying often that what one wanted most just then, one could not have when one had foolishly demanded and not suggested one's desire. And then Miss Mathilda loved to go out on joyous, country tramps when, stretching free and far with cheerful comrades, over rolling hills and cornfields, glorious in the setting sun, and dogwood white and shining underneath the moon and clear stars over head, and brilliant air and tingling blood, it was hard to have to think of Anna's anger at the late return, though Miss Mathilda had begged that there might be no hot supper cooked that night. And then when all the happy crew of Miss Mathilda and her friends, tired with fullness of good health and burning winds and glowing sunshine in the eyes, stiffened and justly worn and wholly ripe for pleasant food and gentle content, were all come together to the little house—it was hard for all that tired crew who loved the good things Anna made to eat, to come to the closed door and wonder there if it was Anna's evening in or out, and then the others must wait shivering on their tired feet, while Miss Mathilda softened Anna's heart, or if Anna was well out, boldly order youthful Sallie to feed all the hungry lot.

Such things were sometimes hard to bear and often grievously did Miss Mathilda feel herself a rebel with the cheerful Lizzies, the melancholy Mollies, the rough old Katies and the stupid Sallies.

Miss Mathilda had other troubles too, with the good Anna. Miss Mathilda had to save her Anna from the many friends, who in the kindly fashion of the poor, used up her savings and then gave her promises in place of payments.

The good Anna had many curious friends that she had found in the twenty years that she had lived in Bridgepoint, and Miss Mathilda would often have to save her from them all.

PART 2

THE LIFE OF THE GOOD ANNA

ANNA FEDERNER, this good Anna, was of solid lower middle-class south german stock.

When she was seventeen years old she went to service in a bourgeois family, in the large city near her native town, but she did not stay there long. One day her mistress offered her maid—that was Anna—to a friend, to see her home. Anna felt herself to be a servant, not a maid, and so she promptly left the place.

Anna had always a firm old world sense of what was the right way for a girl to do.

No argument could bring her to sit an evening in the empty parlour, although the smell of paint when they were fixing up the kitchen made her very sick, and tired as she always was, she never would sit down during the long talks she held with Miss Mathilda. A girl was a girl and should act always like a girl, both as to giving all respect and as to what she had to eat.

A little time after she left this service, Anna and her mother made the voyage to America. They came second-

class, but it was for them a long and dreary journey. The
mother was already ill with consumption.

They landed in a pleasant town in the far South and there
the mother slowly died.

Anna was now alone and she made her way to Bridgepoint where an older half brother was already settled. This
brother was a heavy, lumbering, good natured german man,
full of the infirmity that comes of excess of body.

He was a baker and married and fairly well to do.

Anna liked her brother well enough but was never in any
way dependent on him.

When she arrived in Bridgepoint, she took service with
Miss Mary Wadsmith.

Miss Mary Wadsmith was a large, fair, helpless woman,
burdened with the care of two young children. They had
been left her by her brother and his wife who had died
within a few months of each other.

Anna soon had the household altogether in her charge.

Anna found her place with large, abundant women, for
such were always lazy, careless or all helpless, and so the
burden of their lives could fall on Anna, and give her just
content. Anna's superiors must be always these large helpless women, or be men, for none others could give themselves to be made so comfortable and free.

Anna had no strong natural feeling to love children, as
she had to love cats and dogs, and a large mistress. She
never became deeply fond of Edgar and Jane Wadsmith. She
naturally preferred the boy, for boys love always better to be
done for and made comfortable and full of eating, while in
the little girl she had to meet the feminine, the subtle opposition, showing so early always in a young girl's nature.

For the summer, the Wadsmiths had a pleasant house out
in the country, and the winter months they spent in hotel
apartments in the city.

Gradually it came to Anna to take the whole direction of

their movements, to make all the decisions as to their jour-
neyings to and fro, and for the arranging of the places where
they were to live.

Anna had been with Miss Mary for three years, when little Jane began to raise her strength in opposition. Jane was
a neat, pleasant little girl, pretty and sweet with a young
girl's charm, and with two blonde braids carefully plaited
down her back.

Miss Mary, like her Anna, had no strong natural feeling
to love children, but she was fond of these two young ones
of her blood, and yielded docilely to the stronger power in
the really pleasing little girl. Anna always preferred the
rougher handling of the boy, while Miss Mary found the
gentle force and the sweet domination of the girl to please
her better.

In a spring when all the preparations for the moving had
been made, Miss Mary and Jane went together to the country home, and Anna, after finishing up the city matters was
to follow them in a few days with Edgar, whose vacation
had not yet begun.

Many times during the preparations for this summer, Jane
had met Anna with sharp resistance, in opposition to her
ways. It was simple for little Jane to give unpleasant orders,
not from herself but from Miss Mary, large, docile, helpless
Miss Mary Wadsmith who could never think out any orders
to give Anna from herself.

Anna's eyes grew slowly sharper, harder, and her lower
teeth thrust a little forward and pressing strongly up, framed
always more slowly the "Yes, Miss Jane," to the quick, "Oh
Anna! Miss Mary says she wants you to do it so!"

On the day of their migration, Miss Mary had been already put into the carriage. "Oh, Anna!" cried little Jane running back into the house, "Miss Mary says that you are to
bring along the blue dressings out of her room and mine."
Anna's body stiffened, "We never use them in the summer,

Miss Jane," she said thickly. "Yes Anna, but Miss Mary thinks it would be nice, and she told me to tell you not to forget, good-by!" and the little girl skipped lightly down the steps into the carriage and they drove away.

Anna stood still on the steps, her eyes hard and sharp and shining, and her body and her face stiff with resentment. And then she went into the house, giving the door a shattering slam.

Anna was very hard to live with in those next three days. Even Baby, the new puppy, the pride of Anna's heart, a present from her friend the widow, Mrs. Lehntman—even this pretty little black and tan felt the heat of Anna's scorching flame. And Edgar, who had looked forward to these days, to be for him filled full of freedom and of things to eat—he could not rest a moment in Anna's bitter sight.

On the third day, Anna and Edgar went to the Wadsmiths' country home. The blue dressings out of the two rooms remained behind.

All the way, Edgar sat in front with the colored man and drove. It was an early spring day in the South. The fields and woods were heavy from the soaking rains. The horses dragged the carriage slowly over the long road, sticky with brown clay and rough with masses of stones thrown here and there to be broken and trodden into place by passing teams. Over and through the soaking earth was the feathery new spring growth of little flowers, of young leaves and of ferns. The tree tops were all bright with reds and yellows, with brilliant gleaming whites and gorgeous greens. All the lower air was full of the damp haze rising from heavy soaking water on the earth, mingled with a warm and pleasant smell from the blue smoke of the spring fires in all the open fields. And above all this was the clear, upper air, and the songs of birds and the joy of sunshine and of lengthening days.

The languor and the stir, the warmth and weight and the

strong feel of life from the deep centres of the earth that comes always with the early, soaking spring, when it is not answered with an active fervent joy, gives always anger, irritation and unrest.

To Anna alone there in the carriage, drawing always nearer to the struggle with her mistress, the warmth, the slowness, the jolting over stones, the steaming from the horses, the cries of men and animals and birds, and the new life all round about were simply maddening. "Baby! if you don't lie still, I think I kill you. I can't stand it any more like this."

At this time Anna, about twenty-seven years of age, was not yet all thin and worn. The sharp bony edges and corners of her head and face were still rounded out with flesh, but already the temper and the humor showed sharply in her clean blue eyes, and the thinning was begun about the lower jaw, that was so often strained with the upward pressure of resolve.

To-day, alone there in the carriage, she was all stiff and yet all trembling with the sore effort of decision and revolt.

As the carriage turned into the Wadsmith gate, little Jane ran out to see. She just looked at Anna's face; she did not say a word about blue dressings.

Anna got down from the carriage with little Baby in her arms. She took out all the goods that she had brought and the carriage drove away. Anna left everything on the porch, and went in to where Miss Mary Wadsmith was sitting by the fire.

Miss Mary was sitting in a large armchair by the fire. All the nooks and crannies of the chair were filled full of her soft and spreading body. She was dressed in a black satin morning gown, the sleeves, great monster things, were heavy with the mass of her soft flesh. She sat there always, large, helpless, gentle. She had a fair, soft, regular, good-looking face, with pleasant, empty, grey-blue eyes, and heavy sleepy lids.

Behind Miss Mary was the little Jane, nervous and jerky with excitement as she saw Anna come into the room.

"Miss Mary," Anna began. She had stopped just within the door, her body and her face stiff with repression, her teeth closed hard and the white lights flashing sharply in the pale, clean blue of her eyes. Her bearing was full of the strange coquetry of anger and of fear, the stiffness, the bridling, the suggestive movement underneath the rigidness of forced control, all the queer ways the passions have to show themselves all one.

"Miss Mary," the words came slowly with thick utterance and with jerks, but always firm and strong. "Miss Mary, I can't stand it any more like this. When you tell me anything to do, I do it. I do everything I can and you know I work myself sick for you. The blue dressings in your room makes too much work to have for summer. Miss Jane don't know what work is. If you want to do things like that I go away."

Anna stopped still. Her words had not the strength of meaning they were meant to have, but the power in the mood of Anna's soul frightened and awed Miss Mary through and through.

Like in all large and helpless women, Miss Mary's heart beat weakly in the soft and helpless mass it had to govern. Little Jane's excitements had already tried her strength. Now she grew pale and fainted quite away.

"Miss Mary!" cried Anna running to her mistress and supporting all her helpless weight back in the chair. Little Jane, distracted, flew about as Anna ordered, bringing smelling salts and brandy and vinegar and water and chafing poor Miss Mary's wrists.

Miss Mary slowly opened her mild eyes. Anna sent the weeping little Jane out of the room. She herself managed to get Miss Mary quiet on the couch.

There was never a word more said about blue dressings.

Anna had conquered, and a few days later little Jane gave her a green parrot to make peace.

For six more years little Jane and Anna lived in the same house. They were careful and respectful to each other to the end.

Anna liked the parrot very well. She was fond of cats too and of horses, but best of all animals she loved the dog and best of all dogs, little Baby, the first gift from her friend, the widow Mrs. Lehntman.

The widow Mrs. Lehntman was the romance in Anna's life.

Anna met her first at the house of her half brother, the baker, who had known the late Mr. Lehntman, a small grocer, very well.

Mrs. Lehntman had been for many years a midwife. Since her husband's death she had herself and two young children to support.

Mrs. Lehntman was a good looking woman. She had a plump well rounded body, clear olive skin, bright dark eyes and crisp black curling hair. She was pleasant, magnetic, efficient and good. She was very attractive, very generous and very amiable.

She was a few years older than our good Anna, who was soon entirely subdued by her magnetic, sympathetic charm.

Mrs. Lehntman in her work loved best to deliver young girls who were in trouble. She would take these into her own house and care for them in secret, till they could guiltlessly go home or back to work, and then slowly pay her the money for their care. And so through this new friend Anna led a wider and more entertaining life, and often she used up her savings in helping Mrs. Lehntman through those times when she was giving very much more than she got.

It was through Mrs. Lehntman that Anna met Dr. Shonjen who employed her when at last it had to be that she must go away from her Miss Mary Wadsmith.

During the last years with her Miss Mary, Anna's health was very bad, as indeed it always was from that time on until the end of her strong life.

Anna was a medium sized, thin, hard working, worrying woman.

She had always had bad headaches and now they came more often and more wearing.

Her face grew thin, more bony and more worn, her skin stained itself pale yellow, as it does with working sickly women, and the clear blue of her eyes went pale.

Her back troubled her a good deal, too. She was always tired at her work and her temper grew more difficult and fretful.

Miss Mary Wadsmith often tried to make Anna see a little to herself, and get a doctor, and the little Jane, now blossoming into a pretty, sweet young woman, did her best to make Anna do things for her good. Anna was stubborn always to Miss Jane, and fearful of interference in her ways. Miss Mary Wadsmith's mild advice she easily could always turn aside.

Mrs. Lehntman was the only one who had any power over Anna. She induced her to let Dr. Shonjen take her in his care.

No one but a Dr. Shonjen could have brought a good and german Anna first to stop her work and then submit herself to operation, but he knew so well how to deal with german and poor people. Cheery, jovial, hearty, full of jokes that made much fun and yet were full of simple common sense and reasoning courage, he could persuade even a good Anna to do things that were for her own good.

Edgar had now been for some years away from home, first at a school and then at work to prepare himself to be a civil engineer. Miss Mary and Jane promised to take a trip for all the time that Anna was away and so there would be no need for Anna's work, nor for a new girl to take Anna's place.

Anna's mind was thus a little set at rest. She gave herself to Mrs. Lehntman and the doctor to do what they thought best to make her well and strong.

Anna endured the operation very well and was patient, almost docile, in the slow recovery of her working strength. But when she was once more at work for her Miss Mary Wadsmith, all the good effect of these several months of rest were soon worked and worried well away.

For all the rest of her strong working life Anna was never really well. She had bad headaches all the time and she was always thin and worn.

She worked away her appetite, her health and strength, and always for the sake of those who begged her not to work so hard. To her thinking, in her stubborn faithful, german soul, this was the right way for a girl to do.

Anna's life with Miss Mary Wadsmith was now drawing to an end.

Miss Jane, now altogether a young lady, had come out into the world. Soon she would become engaged and then be married, and then perhaps Miss Mary Wadsmith would make her home with her.

In such a household Anna was certain that she would never take a place. Miss Jane was always careful and respectful and very good to Anna, but never could Anna be a girl in a household where Miss Jane would be the head. This much was very certain in her mind, and so these last two years with her Miss Mary were not as happy as before.

The change came very soon.

Miss Jane became engaged and in a few months was to marry a man from out of town, from Curden, an hour's railway ride from Bridgepoint.

Poor Miss Mary Wadsmith did not know the strong resolve Anna had made to live apart from her when this new household should be formed. Anna found it very hard to speak to her Miss Mary of this change.

The preparations for the wedding went on day and night. Anna worked and sewed hard to make it all go well.

Miss Mary was much fluttered, but content and happy with Anna to make everything so easy for them all.

Anna worked so all the time to drown her sorrow and her conscience too, for somehow it was not right to leave Miss Mary so. But what else could she do? She could not live as her Miss Mary's girl, in a house where Miss Jane would be the head.

The wedding day grew always nearer. At last it came and passed.

The young people went on their wedding trip, and Anna and Miss Mary were left behind to pack up all the things.

Even yet poor Anna had not had the strength to tell Miss Mary her resolve, but now it had to be.

Anna every spare minute ran to her friend Mrs. Lehntman for comfort and advice. She begged her friend to be with her when she told the news to Miss Mary.

Perhaps if Mrs. Lehntman had not been in Bridgepoint, Anna would have tried to live in the new house. Mrs. Lehntman did not urge her to this thing nor even give her this advice, but feeling for Mrs. Lehntman as she did made even faithful Anna not quite so strong in her dependence on Miss Mary's need as she would otherwise have been.

Remember, Mrs. Lehntman was the romance in Anna's life.

All the packing was now done and in a few days Miss Mary was to go to the new house, where the young people were ready for her coming.

At last Anna had to speak.

Mrs. Lehntman agreed to go with her and help to make the matter clear to poor Miss Mary.

The two women came together to Miss Mary Wadsmith sitting placid by the fire in the empty living room. Miss Mary had seen Mrs. Lehntman many times before, and so her coming in with Anna raised no suspicion in her mind.

It was very hard for the two women to begin.

It must be very gently done, this telling to Miss Mary of the change. She must not be shocked by suddenness or with excitement.

Anna was all stiff, and inside all a quiver with shame, anxiety and grief. Even courageous Mrs. Lehntman, efficient, impulsive and complacent as she was and not deeply concerned in the event, felt awkward, abashed and almost guilty in that large, mild, helpless presence. And at her side to make her feel the power of it all, was the intense conviction of poor Anna, struggling to be unfeeling, self righteous and suppressed.

"Miss Mary"— with Anna when things had to come they came always sharp and short—"Miss Mary, Mrs. Lehntman has come here with me, so I can tell you about not staying with you there in Curden. Of course I go help you to get settled and then I think I come back and stay right here in Bridgepoint. You know my brother he is here and all his family, and I think it would be not right to go away from them so far, and you know you don't want me now so much Miss Mary when you are all together there in Curden."

Miss Mary Wadsmith was puzzled. She did not understand what Anna meant by what she said.

"Why Anna of course you can come to see your brother whenever you like to, and I will always pay your fare. I thought you understood all about that, and we will be very glad to have your nieces come to stay with you as often as they like. There will always be room enough in a big house like Mr. Goldthwaite's."

It was now for Mrs. Lehntman to begin her work.

"Miss Wadsmith does not understand just what you mean

Anna," she began. "Miss Wadsmith, Anna feels how good and kind you are, and she talks about it all the time, and what you do for her in every way you can, and she is very grateful and never would want to go away from you, only she thinks it would be better now that Mrs. Goldthwaite has this big new house and will want to manage it in her own way, she thinks perhaps it would be better if Mrs. Goldthwaite had all new servants with her to begin with, and not a girl like Anna who knew her when she was a little girl. That is what Anna feels about it now, and she asked me and I said to her that I thought it would be better for you all and you knew she liked you so much and that you were so good to her, and you would understand how she thought it would be better in the new house if she stayed on here in Bridgepoint, anyway for a little while until Mrs. Goldthwaite was used to her new house. Isn't that it Anna that you wanted Miss Wadsmith to know?"

"Oh Anna," Miss Mary Wadsmith said it slowly and in a grieved tone of surprise that was very hard for the good Anna to endure, "Oh Anna, I didn't think that you would ever want to leave me after all these years."

"Miss Mary!" it came in one tense jerky burst, "Miss Mary it's only working under Miss Jane now would make me leave you so. I know how good you are and I work myself sick for you and for Mr. Edgar and for Miss Jane too, only Miss Jane she will want everything different from like the way we always did, and you know Miss Mary I can't have Miss Jane watching at me all the time, and every minute something new. Miss Mary, it would be very bad and Miss Jane don't really want me to come with you to the new house, I know that all the time. Please Miss Mary don't feel bad about it or think I ever want to go away from you if I could do things right for you the way they ought to be."

Poor Miss Mary. Struggling was not a thing for her to do. Anna would surely yield if she would struggle, but strug-

gling was too much work and too much worry for peaceful
Miss Mary to endure. If Anna would do so she must. Poor
Miss Mary Wadsmith sighed, looked wistfully at Anna and
then gave it up.

"You must do as you think best Anna," she said at last letting all of her soft self sink back into the chair. "I am very
sorry and so I am sure will be Miss Jane when she hears
what you have thought it best to do. It was very good of Mrs.
Lehntman to come with you and I am sure she does it for
your good. I suppose you want to go out a little now. Come
back in an hour Anna and help me go to bed." Miss Mary
closed her eyes and rested still and placid by the fire.

The two women went away.

This was the end of Anna's service with Miss Mary Wadsmith, and soon her new life taking care of Dr. Shonjen was
begun.

Keeping house for a jovial bachelor doctor gave new el-
ements of understanding to Anna's maiden german mind.
Her habits were as firm fixed as before, but it always was
with Anna that things that had been done once with her enjoyment and consent could always happen any time again,
such as her getting up at any hour of the night to make a supper and cook hot chops and chicken fry for Dr. Shonjen and
his bachelor friends.

Anna loved to work for men, for they could eat so much
and with such joy. And when they were warm and full, they
were content, and let her do whatever she thought best. Not
that Anna's conscience ever slept, for neither with interference or without would she strain less to keep on saving
every cent and working every hour of the day. But truly she
loved it best when she could scold. Now it was not only
other girls and the colored man, and dogs, and cats, and
horses and her parrot, but her cheery master, jolly Dr. Shonjen, whom she could guide and constantly rebuke to his own
good.

The Doctor really loved her scoldings as she loved his wickednesses and his merry joking ways.

These days were happy days with Anna.

Her freakish humor now first showed itself, her sense of fun in the queer ways that people had, that made her later find delight in brutish servile Katy, in Sallie's silly ways and in the badness of Peter and of Rags. She loved to make sport with the skeletons the Doctor had, to make them move and make strange noises till the negro boy shook in his shoes and his eyes rolled white in his agony of fear.

Then Anna would tell these histories to her Doctor. Her worn, thin, lined, determined face would form for itself new and humorous creases, and her pale blue eyes would kindle with humour and with joy as her doctor burst into his hearty laugh. And the good Anna full of the coquetry of pleasing would bridle with her angular, thin, spinster body, straining her stories and herself to please.

These early days with jovial Dr. Shonjen were very happy days with the good Anna.

All of Anna's spare hours in these early days she spent with her friend, the widow Mrs. Lehntman. Mrs. Lehntman lived with her two children in a small house in the same part of the town as Dr. Shonjen. The older of these two children was a girl named Julia and was now about thirteen years of age. This Julia Lehntman was an unattractive girl enough, harsh featured, dull and stubborn as had been her heavy german father. Mrs. Lehntman did not trouble much with her, but gave her always all she wanted that she had, and let the girl do as she liked. This was not from indifference or dislike on the part of Mrs. Lehntman, it was just her usual way.

Her second child was a boy, two years younger than his sister, a bright, pleasant, cheery fellow, who too, did what he liked with his money and his time. All this was so with Mrs. Lehntman because she had so much in her head and in her house that clamoured for her concentration and her time.

This slackness and neglect in the running of the house, and the indifference in this mother for the training of her young was very hard for our good Anna to endure. Of course she did her best to scold, to save for Mrs. Lehntman, and to put things in their place the way they ought to be.

Even in the early days when Anna was first won by the glamour of Mrs. Lehntman's brilliancy and charm, she had been uneasy in Mrs. Lehntman's house with a need of putting things to rights. Now that the two children growing up were of more importance in the house, and now that long acquaintance had brushed the dazzle out of Anna's eyes, she began to struggle to make things go here as she thought was right.

She watched and scolded hard these days to make young Julia do the way she should. Not that Julia Lehntman was pleasant in the good Anna's sight, but it must never be that a young girl growing up should have no one to make her learn to do things right.

The boy was easier to scold, for scoldings never sank in very deep, and indeed he liked them very well for they brought with them new things to eat, and lively teasing, and good jokes.

Julia, the girl, grew very sullen with it all, and very often won her point, for after all Miss Annie was no relative of hers and had no business coming there and making trouble all the time. Appealing to the mother was no use. It was wonderful how Mrs. Lehntman could listen and not hear, could answer and yet not decide, could say and do what she was asked and yet have things as they were before.

One day it got almost too bad for even Anna's friendship to bear out.

"Well, Julia, is your mamma out?" Anna asked, one Sunday summer afternoon, as she came into the Lehntman house.

Anna looked very well this day. She was always careful

in her dress and sparing of new clothes. She made herself always fulfill her own ideal of how a girl should look when she took her Sundays out. Anna knew so well the kind of ugliness appropriate to each rank in life.

It was interesting to see how when she bought things for Miss Wadsmith and later for her cherished Miss Mathilda and always entirely from her own taste and often as cheaply as she bought things for her friends or for herself, that on the one hand she chose the things having the right air for a member of the upper class, and for the others always the things having the awkward ugliness that we call Dutch. She knew the best thing in each kind, and she never in the course of her strong life compromised her sense of what was the right thing for a girl to wear.

On this bright summer Sunday afternoon she came to the Lehntmans', much dressed up in her new, brick red, silk waist trimmed with broad black beaded braid, a dark cloth skirt and a new stiff, shiny, black straw hat, trimmed with colored ribbons and a bird. She had on new gloves, and a feather boa about her neck.

Her spare, thin, awkward body and her worn, pale yellow face though lit up now with the pleasant summer sun made a queer discord with the brightness of her clothes.

She came to the Lehntman house, where she had not been for several days, and opening the door that is always left unlatched in the houses of the lower middle class in the pleasant cities of the South, she found Julia in the family sitting-room alone.

"Well, Julia, where is your mamma?" Anna asked. "Ma is out but come in, Miss Annie, and look at our new brother." "What you talk so foolish for Julia," said Anna sitting down. "I ain't talkin' foolish, Miss Annie. Didn't you know mamma has just adopted a cute, nice little baby boy?" "You talk so crazy, Julia, you ought to know better than to say such things." Julia turned sullen. "All right Miss Annie, you don't need to believe what I say, but the little baby is in the kitchen and ma will tell you herself when she comes in."

It sounded most fantastic, but Julia had an air of truth and Mrs. Lehntman was capable of doing stranger things. Anna was disturbed. "What you mean Julia," she said. "I don't mean nothin' Miss Annie, you don't believe the baby is in there, well you can go and see it for yourself."

Anna went into the kitchen. A baby was there all right enough, and a lusty little boy he seemed. He was very tight asleep in a basket that stood in the corner by the open door.

"You mean your mamma is just letting him stay here a little while," Anna said to Julia who had followed her into the kitchen to see Miss Annie get real mad. "No that ain't it Miss Annie. The mother was that girl, Lily that came from Bishop's place out in the country, and she don't want no children, and ma liked the little boy so much, she said she'd keep him here and adopt him for her own child."

Anna, for once, was fairly dumb with astonishment and rage. The front door slammed.

"There's ma now," cried Julia in an uneasy triumph, for she was not quite certain in her mind which side of the question she was on, "There's ma now and you can ask her for yourself if I ain't told you true."

Mrs. Lehntman came into the kitchen where they were. She was bland, impersonal and pleasant, as it was her wont to be. Still to-day, through this her usual manner that gave her such success in her practice as a midwife, there shone an uneasy consciousness of guilt, for like all who had to do with the good Anna, Mrs. Lehntman dreaded her firm character, her vigorous judgments and the bitter fervour of her tongue.

It had been plain to see in the six years these women were together, how Anna gradually had come to lead. Not really lead, of course, for Mrs. Lehntman never could be led, she was so very devious in her ways; but Anna had come to have direction whenever she could learn what Mrs. Lehntman meant to do before the deed was done. Now it was hard to tell which would win out. Mrs. Lehntman had her unhearing mind and her happy way of giving a pleasant well diffused attention, and then she had it on her side that, after all, this thing was already done.

Anna was, as usual, determined for the right. She was stiff and pale with her anger and her fear, and nervous, and all a tremble as was her usual way when a bitter fight was near.

Mrs. Lehntman was easy and pleasant as she came into the room. Anna was stiff and silent and very white.

"We haven't seen you for a long time, Anna," Mrs. Lehntman cordially began. "I was just gettin' worried thinking you was sick. My! but it's a hot day to-day. Come into the sittin'-room, Anna, and Julia will make us some ice tea."

Anna followed Mrs. Lehntman into the other room in a stiff silence, and when there she did not, as invited, take a chair.

As always with Anna when a thing had to come it came very short and sharp. She found it hard to breathe just now, and every word came with a jerk.

"Mrs. Lehntman, it ain't true what Julia said about your taking that Lily's boy to keep. I told Julia when she told me she was crazy to talk so."

Anna's real excitements stopped her breath, and made her words come sharp and with a jerk. Mrs. Lehntman's feelings spread her breath, and made her words come slow, but more pleasant and more easy even than before.

"Why Anna," she began, "don't you see Lily couldn't keep her boy for she is working at the Bishops' now, and he is such a cute dear little chap, and you know how fond I am of little fellers, and I thought it would be nice for Julia and for Willie to have a little brother. You know Julia always loves to play with babies, and I have to be away so much, and Willie he is running in the streets every minute all the time, and you see a baby would be sort of nice company for Julia, and you know you are always saying Anna, Julia should not be on the streets so much and the baby will be so good to keep her in."

Anna was every minute paler with indignation and with heat.

"Mrs. Lehntman, I don't see what business it is for you to take another baby for your own, when you can't do what's right by Julia and Willie you got here already. There's Julia, nobody tells her a thing when I ain't here, and who is going to tell her now how to do things for that baby? She ain't got no sense what's the right way to do with children, and you out all the time, and you ain't got no time for your own neither, and now you want to be takin' up with strangers. I know you was careless, Mrs. Lehntman, but I didn't think that you could do this so. No, Mrs. Lehntman, it ain't your duty to take up with no others, when you got two children of your own, that got to get along just any way they can, and you know you ain't got any too much money all the time, and you are all so careless here and spend it all the time, and Julia and Willie growin' big. It ain't right, Mrs. Lehntman, to do so."

This was as bad as it could be. Anna had never spoken her mind so to her friend before. Now it was too harsh for Mrs. Lehntman to allow herself to really hear. If she really took the meaning in these words she could never ask Anna to come into her house again, and she liked Anna very well, and was used to depend on her savings and her strength. And then too Mrs. Lehntman could not really take in harsh ideas. She was too well diffused to catch the feel of any sharp firm edge.

Now she managed to understand all this in a way that made it easy for her to say, "Why, Anna, I think you feel too bad about seeing what the children are doing every minute in the day. Julia and Willie are real good, and they play with all the nicest children in the square. If you had some, all your own, Anna, you'd see it don't do no harm to let them do a little as they like, and Julia likes this baby so, and sweet dear little boy, it would be so kind of bad to send him to a 'sylum now, you know it would Anna, when you like children so yourself, and are so good to my Willie all the time. No indeed Anna, it's easy enough to say I should send this poor, cute little boy to a 'sylum when I could keep him here so nice, but you know Anna, you wouldn't like to do it yourself, now you really know you wouldn't, Anna, though you talk to me so hard.— My, it's hot to-day, what you doin' with that ice tea in there Julia, when Miss Annie is waiting all this time for her drink?"

Julia brought in the ice tea. She was so excited with the talk she had been hearing from the kitchen, that she slopped it on the plate out of the glasses a good deal. But she was safe, for Anna felt this trouble so deep down that she did not even see those awkward, bony hands, adorned to-day with a new ring, those stupid, foolish hands that always did things the wrong way.

"Here Miss Annie," Julia said, "Here, Miss Annie, is your glass of tea, I know you like it good and strong."

"No, Julia, I don't want no ice tea here. Your mamma ain't able to afford now using her money upon ice tea for her friends. It ain't right she should now any more. I go out now to see Mrs. Drehten. She does all she can, and she is sick now working so hard taking care of her own children. I go there now. Good by Mrs. Lehntman, I hope you don't get no bad luck doin' what it ain't right for you to do."

"My, Miss Annie is real mad now," Julia said, as the house shook, as the good Anna shut the outside door with a concentrated shattering slam.

It was some months now that Anna had been intimate with Mrs. Drehten.

Mrs. Drehten had had a tumor and had come to Dr. Shonjen to be treated. During the course of her visits there, she and Anna had learned to like each other very well. There was no fever in this friendship, it was just the interchange of two hard working, worrying women, the one large and motherly, with the pleasant, patient, soft, worn, tolerant face, that comes with a german husband to obey, and seven solid girls and boys to bear and rear, and the other was our good Anna with her spinster body, her firm jaw, her humorous, light, clean eyes and her lined, worn, thin, pale yellow face.

Mrs. Drehten lived a patient, homely, hard working life. Her husband an honest, decent man enough, was a brewer, and somewhat given to over drinking, and so he was often surly and stingy and unpleasant.

The family of seven children was made up of four stalwart, cheery, filial sons, and three hard working obedient simple daughters.

It was a family life the good Anna very much approved and also she was much liked by them all. With a german woman's feeling for the masterhood in men, she was docile to the surly father and rarely rubbed him the wrong way. To the large, worn, patient, sickly mother she was a sympathetic listener, wise in counsel and most efficient in her help. The young ones too, liked her very well. The sons teased her all the time and roared with boisterous pleasure when she gave them back sharp hits. The girls were all so good that her scoldings here were only in the shape of good advice, sweetened with new trimmings for their hats, and ribbons, and sometimes on their birthdays, bits of jewels.

It was here that Anna came for comfort after her grievous stroke at her friend the widow, Mrs. Lehntman. Not that Anna would tell Mrs. Drehten of this trouble. She could never lay bare the wound that came to her through this idealised affection. Her affair with Mrs. Lehntman was too sa-

cred and too grievous ever to be told. But here in this large
household, in busy movement and variety in strife, she
could silence the uneasiness and pain of her own wound.

The Drehtens lived out in the country in one of the
wooden, ugly houses that lie in groups outside of our large
cities.

The father and the sons all had their work here making
beer, and the mother and her girls scoured and sewed and
cooked.

On Sundays they were all washed very clean, and
smelling of kitchen soap. The sons, in their Sunday clothes,
loafed around the house or in the village, and on special
days went on picnics with their girls. The daughters in their
awkward, colored finery went to church most of the day and
then walking with their friends.

They always came together for their supper, where Anna
always was most welcome, the jolly Sunday evening supper
that german people love. Here Anna and the boys gave it to
each other in sharp hits and hearty boisterous laughter, the
girls made things for them to eat, and waited on them all, the
mother loved all her children all the time, and the father
joined in with his occasional unpleasant word that made a
bitter feeling but which they had all learned to pass as if it
were not said.

It was to the comfort of this house that Anna came that
Sunday summer afternoon, after she had left Mrs. Lehntman
and her careless ways.

The Drehten house was open all about. No one was there
but Mrs. Drehten resting in her rocking chair, out in the
pleasant, scented, summer air.

Anna had had a hot walk from the cars.

She went into the kitchen for a cooling drink, and then
came out and sat down on the steps near Mrs. Drehten.

Anna's anger had changed. A sadness had come to her.

Now with the patient, friendly, gentle mother talk of Mrs.
Drehten, this sadness changed to resignation and to rest.

As the evening came on the young ones dropped in one
by one. Soon the merry Sunday evening supper was begun.

It had not been all comfort for our Anna, these months of
knowing Mrs. Drehten. It had made trouble for her with the
family of her half brother, the fat baker.

Her half brother, the fat baker, was a queer kind of a man.
He was a huge, unwieldy creature, all puffed out all over,
and no longer able to walk much, with his enormous body
and the big, swollen, bursted veins in his great legs. He did
not try to walk much now. He sat around his place, leaning
on his great thick stick, and watching his workmen at their
work.

On holidays, and sometimes of a Sunday, he went out in
his bakery wagon. He went then to each customer he had
and gave them each a large, sweet, raisined loaf of caky
bread. At every house with many groans and gasps he would
descend his heavy weight out of the wagon, his good featured, black haired, flat, good natured face shining with oily
perspiration, with pride in labor and with generous kindness.
Up each stoop he hobbled with the help of his big stick, and
into the nearest chair in the kitchen or in the parlour, as the
fashion of the house demanded, and there he sat and puffed,
and then presented to the mistress or the cook the raisined
german loaf his boy had supplied him.

Anna had never been a customer of his. She had always
lived in another part of the town, but he never left her out in
these bakery progresses of his, and always with his own
hand he gave her her festive loaf.

Anna liked her half brother well enough. She never knew
him really well, for he rarely talked at all and least of all to
women, but he seemed to her, honest, and good and kind,
and he never tried to interfere in Anna's ways. And then
Anna liked the loaves of raisined bread, for in the summer

she and the second girl could live on them, and not be buying bread with the household money all the time.

But things were not so simple with our Anna, with the
other members of her half brother's house.

Her half brother's family was made up of himself, his
wife, and their two daughters.

Anna never liked her brother's wife.

The youngest of the two daughters was named after her
aunt Anna.

Anna never liked her half brother's wife. This woman
had been very good to Anna, never interfering in her ways,
always glad to see her and to make her visits pleasant, but
she had not found favour in our good Anna's sight.

Anna had too, no real affection for her nieces. She never
scolded them or tried to guide them for their good. Anna
never criticised or interfered in the running of her half
brother's house.

Mrs. Federner was a good looking, prosperous woman, a
little harsh and cold within her soul perhaps, but trying always to be pleasant, good and kind. Her daughters were well
trained, quiet, obedient, well dressed girls, and yet our good
Anna loved them not, nor their mother, nor any of their
ways.

It was in this house that Anna had first met her friend, the
widow, Mrs. Lehntman.

The Federners had never seemed to feel it wrong in
Anna, her devotion to this friend and her care of her and of
her children. Mrs. Lehntman and Anna and her feelings
were all somehow too big for their attack. But Mrs. Federner
had the mind and tongue that blacken things. Not really to
blacken black, of course, but just to roughen and to rub on a
little smut. She could somehow make even the face of the
Almighty seem pimply and a little coarse, and so she always
did this with her friends, though not with the intent to interfere.

This was really true with Mrs. Lehntman that Mrs. Federner did not mean to interfere, but Anna's friendship with the Drehtens was a very different matter.

Why should Mrs. Drehten, that poor common working wife of a man who worked for others in a brewery and who always drank too much, and was not like a thrifty, decent german man, why should that Mrs. Drehten and her ugly, awkward daughters be getting presents from her husband's sister all the time, and her husband always so good to Anna, and one of the girls having her name too, and those Drehtens all strangers to her and never going to come to any good? It was not right for Anna to do so.

Mrs. Federner knew better than to say such things straight out to her husband's fiery, stubborn sister, but she lost no chance to let Anna feel and see what they all thought.

It was easy to blacken all the Drehtens, their poverty, the husband's drinking, the four big sons carrying on and always lazy, the awkward, ugly daughters dressing up with Anna's help and trying to look so fine, and the poor, weak, hard working sickly mother, so easy to degrade with large dosings of contemptuous pity.

Anna could not do much with these attacks for Mrs. Federner always ended with, "And you so good to them Anna all the time. I don't see how they could get along at all if you didn't help them all the time, but you are so good Anna, and got such a feeling heart, just like your brother, that you give anything away you got to anybody that will ask you for it, and that's shameless enough to take it when they ain't no relatives of yours. Poor Mrs. Drehten, she is a good woman. Poor thing it must be awful hard for her to have to take things from strangers all the time, and her husband spending it on drink. I was saying to Mrs. Lehntman, Anna, only yesterday, how I never was so sorry for any one as Mrs. Drehten, and how good it was for you to help them all the time."

All this meant a gold watch and chain for her god daughter for her birthday, the next month, and a new silk umbrella for the elder sister. Poor Anna, and she did not love them very much, these relatives of hers, and they were the only kin she had.

Mrs. Lehntman never joined in, in these attacks. Mrs. Lehntman was diffuse and careless in her ways, but she never worked such things for her own ends, and she was too sure of Anna to be jealous of her other friends.

All this time Anna was leading her happy life with Dr. Shonjen. She had every day her busy time. She cooked and saved and sewed and scrubbed and scolded. And every night she had her happy time, in seeing her Doctor like the fine things she bought so cheap and cooked so good for him to eat. And then he would listen and laugh so loud, as she told him stories of what had happened on that day.

The Doctor, too, liked it better all the time and several times in these five years he had of his own motion raised her wages.

Anna was content with what she had and grateful for all her Doctor did for her.

So Anna's serving and her giving life went on, each with its varied pleasures and its pains.

The adopting of the little boy did not put an end to Anna's friendship for the widow Mrs. Lehntman. Neither the good Anna nor the careless Mrs. Lehntman would give each other up excepting for the gravest cause.

Mrs. Lehntman was the only romance Anna ever knew. A certain magnetic brilliancy in person and in manner made Mrs. Lehntman a woman other women loved. Then, too, she was generous and good and honest, though she was so careless always in her ways. And then she trusted Anna and liked her better than any of her other friends, and Anna always felt this very much.

No, Anna could not give up Mrs. Lehntman, and soon she

was busier than before making Julia do things right for little
Johnny.

And now new schemes were working strong in Mrs.
Lehntman's head, and Anna must listen to her plans and help
her make them work.

Mrs. Lehntman always loved best in her work to deliver
young girls who were in trouble. She would keep these in
her house until they could go to their homes or to their work,
and slowly pay her back the money for their care.

Anna had always helped her friend to do this thing, for
like all the good women of the decent poor, she felt it hard
that girls should not be helped, not girls that were really bad
of course, these she condemned and hated in her heart and
with her tongue, but honest, decent, good, hard working,
foolish girls who were in trouble.

For such as these Anna always liked to give her money
and her strength.

Now Mrs. Lehntman thought that it would pay to take a
big house for herself to take in girls and to do everything in
a big way.

Anna did not like this plan.

Anna was never daring in her ways. Save and you will
have the money you have saved, was all that she could
know.

Not that the good Anna had it so.

She saved and saved and always saved, and then here and
there, to this friend and to that, to one in her trouble and to
the other in her joy, in sickness, death, and weddings, or to
make young people happy, it always went, the hard earned
money she had saved.

Anna could not clearly see how Mrs. Lehntman could
make a big house pay. In the small house where she had
these girls, it did not pay, and in a big house there was so
much more that she would spend.

Such things were hard for the good Anna to very clearly

see. One day she came into the Lehntman house. "Anna," Mrs. Lehntman said, "you know that nice big house on the next corner that we saw to rent. I took it for a year yesterday. I paid a little down you know so I could have it sure all right and now you fix it up just like you want. I let you do just what you like with it."

Anna knew that it was now too late. However, "But Mrs. Lehntman you said you would not take another house, you said so just last week. Oh, Mrs. Lehntman I didn't think that you would do this so!"

Anna knew so well it was too late.

"I know, Anna, but it was such a good house, just right you know and some one else was there to see, and you know you said it suited very well, and if I didn't take it the others said they would, and I wanted to ask you only there wasn't time, and really Anna, I don't need much help, it will go so well I know. I just need a little to begin and to fix up with and that's all Anna that I need, and I know it will go awful well. You wait Anna and you'll see, and I let you fix it up just like you want, and you will make it look so nice, you got such sense in all these things. It will be a good place. You see Anna if I ain't right in what I say."

Of course Anna gave the money for this thing though she could not believe that it was best. No, it was very bad. Mrs. Lehntman could never make it pay and it would cost so much to keep. But what could our poor Anna do? Remember Mrs. Lehntman was the only romance Anna ever knew.

Anna's strength in her control of what was done in Mrs. Lehntman's house, was not now what it had been before that Lily's little Johnny came. That thing had been for Anna a defeat. There had been no fighting to a finish but Mrs. Lehntman had very surely won.

Mrs. Lehntman needed Anna just as much as Anna needed Mrs. Lehntman, but Mrs. Lehntman was more ready to risk Anna's loss, and so the good Anna grew always weaker in her power to control.

In friendship, power always has its downward curve. One's strength to manage rises always higher until there comes a time one does not win, and though one may not really lose, still from the time that victory is not sure, one's power slowly ceases to be strong. It is only in a close tie such as marriage, that influence can mount and grow always stronger with the years and never meet with a decline. It can only happen so when there is no way to escape.

Friendship goes by favour. There is always danger of a break or of a stronger power coming in between. Influence can only be a steady march when one can surely never break away.

Anna wanted Mrs. Lehntman very much and Mrs. Lehntman needed Anna, but there were always other ways to do and if Anna had once given up she might do so again, so why should Mrs. Lehntman have real fear?

No, while the good Anna did not come to open fight she had been stronger. Now Mrs. Lehntman could always hold out longer. She knew too, that Anna had a feeling heart. Anna could never stop doing all she could for any one that really needed help. Poor Anna had no power to say no.

And then, too, Mrs. Lehntman was the only romance Anna ever knew. Romance is the ideal in one's life and it is very lonely living with it lost.

So the good Anna gave all her savings for this place, although she knew that this was not the right way for her friend to do.

For some time now they were all very busy fixing up the house. It swallowed all Anna's savings fixing up this house, for when Anna once began to make it nice, she could not leave it be until it was as good as for the purpose it should be.

Somehow it was Anna now that really took the interest in

the house. Mrs. Lehntman, now the thing was done seemed very lifeless, without interest in the house, uneasy in her mind and restless in her ways, and more diffuse even than before in her attention. She was good and kind to all the people in her house, and let them do whatever they thought best.

Anna did not fail to see that Mrs. Lehntman had something on her mind that was all new. What was it that disturbed Mrs. Lehntman so? She kept on saying it was all in Anna's head. She had no trouble now at all. Everybody was so good and it was all so nice in the new house. But surely there was something here that was all wrong.

Anna heard a good deal of all this from her half brother's wife, the hard speaking Mrs. Federner.

Through the fog of dust and work and furnishing in the new house, and through the disturbed mind of Mrs. Lehntman, and with the dark hints of Mrs. Federner, there loomed up to Anna's sight a man, a new doctor that Mrs. Lehntman knew.

Anna had never met the man but she heard of him very often now. Not from her friend, the widow Mrs. Lehntman. Anna knew that Mrs. Lehntman made of him a mystery that Anna had not the strength just then to vigorously break down.

Mrs. Federner gave always dark suggestions and unpleasant hints. Even good Mrs. Drehten talked of it.

Mrs. Lehntman never spoke of the new doctor more than she could help. This was most mysterious and unpleasant and very hard for our good Anna to endure.

Anna's troubles came all of them at once.

Here in Mrs. Lehntman's house loomed up dismal and forbidding, a mysterious, perhaps an evil man. In Dr. Shonjen's house were beginning signs of interest in the Doctor in a woman.

This, too, Mrs. Federner often told to the poor Anna. The Doctor would be married soon, he liked so much now to go to Mr. Weingartner's house where there was a daughter who loved Doctor, everybody knew.

In these days the living room in her half brother's house was Anna's torture chamber. And worst of all there was so much reason for her half sister's words. The Doctor certainly did look like marriage and Mrs. Lehntman acted very queer.

Poor Anna. Dark were these days and much she had to suffer.

The Doctor's trouble came to a head the first. It was true Doctor was engaged and to be married soon. He told Anna so himself.

What was the good Anna now to do? Dr. Shonjen wanted her of course to stay. Anna was so sad with all these troubles. She knew here in the Doctor's house it would be bad when he was married, but she had not the strength now to be firm and go away. She said at last that she would try and stay.

Doctor got married now very soon. Anna made the house all beautiful and clean and she really hoped that she might stay. But this was not for long.

Mrs. Shonjen was a proud, unpleasant woman. She wanted constant service and attention and never even a thank you to a servant. Soon all Doctor's old people went away. Anna went to Doctor and explained. She told him what all the servants thought of his new wife. Anna bade him a sad farewell and went away.

Anna was now most uncertain what to do. She could go to Curden to her Miss Mary Wadsmith who always wrote how much she needed Anna, but Anna still dreaded Miss Jane's interfering ways. Then too, she could not yet go away from Bridgepoint and from Mrs. Lehntman, unpleasant as it always was now over there.

Through one of Doctor's friends Anna heard of Miss Mathilda. Anna was very doubtful about working for a Miss

Mathilda. She did not think it would be good working for a woman any more. She had found it very good with Miss Mary but she did not think that many women would be so.

Most women were interfering in their ways.

Anna heard that Miss Mathilda was a great big woman, not so big perhaps as her Miss Mary, still she was big, and the good Anna liked them better so. She did not like them thin and small and active and always looking in and always prying.

Anna could not make up her mind what was the best thing now for her to do. She could sew and this way make a living, but she did not like such business very well.

Mrs. Lehntman urged the place with Miss Mathilda. She was sure Anna would find it better so. The good Anna did not know.

"Well Anna," Mrs. Lehntman said, "I tell you what we do. I go with you to that woman that tells fortunes, perhaps she tell us something that will show us what is the best way for you now to do."

It was very bad to go to a woman who tells fortunes. Anna was of strong South German Catholic religion and the german priests in the churches always said that it was very bad to do things so. But what else now could the good Anna do? She was so mixed and bothered in her mind, and troubled with this life that was all wrong, though she did try so hard to do the best she knew. "All right, Mrs. Lehntman," Anna said at last, "I think I go there now with you."

This woman who told fortunes was a medium. She had a house in the lower quarter of the town. Mrs. Lehntman and the good Anna went to her.

The medium opened the door for them herself. She was a loose made, dusty, dowdy woman with a persuading, conscious and embracing manner and very greasy hair.

The woman let them come into the house.

The street door opened straight into the parlour, as is the

way in the small houses of the south. The parlour had a thick and flowered carpet on the floor. The room was full of dirty things all made by hand. Some hung upon the wall, some were on the seats and over backs of chairs and some on tables and on those what-nots that poor people love. And everywhere were little things that break. Many of these little things were broken and the place was stuffy and not clean.

No medium uses her parlour for her work. It is always in her eating room that she has her trances.

The eating room in all these houses is the living room in winter. It has a round table in the centre covered with a decorated woolen cloth, that has soaked in the grease of many dinners, for though it should be always taken off, it is easier to spread the cloth upon it than change it for the blanket deadener that one owns. The upholstered chairs are dark and worn, and dirty. The carpet has grown dingy with the food that's fallen from the table, the dirt that's scraped from off the shoes, and the dust that settles with the ages. The sombre greenish colored paper on the walls has been smoked a dismal dirty grey, and all pervading is the smell of soup made out of onions and fat chunks of meat.

The medium brought Mrs. Lehntman and our Anna into this eating room, after she had found out what it was they wanted. They all three sat around the table and then the medium went into her trance.

The medium first closed her eyes and then they opened very wide and lifeless. She took a number of deep breaths, choked several times and swallowed very hard. She waved her hand back every now and then, and she began to speak in a monotonous slow, even tone.

"I see—I see—don't crowd so on me,—I see—I see— too many forms—don't crowd so on me—I see—I see— you are thinking of something—you don't know whether you want to do it now. I see—I see—don't crowd so on

me—1 see—I see—you are not sure,—I see—I see—a
house with trees around it,—it is dark—it is evening—I
see—I see—you go in the house—I see—I see you come
out—it will be all right—you go and do it—do what you
are not certain about—it will come out all right—it is best
and you should do it now."

She stopped, she made deep gulps, her eyes rolled back
into her head, she swallowed hard and then she was her for-
mer dingy and bland self again.

"Did you get what you wanted that the spirit should tell
you?" the woman asked. Mrs. Lehntman answered yes, it
was just what her friend had wanted so bad to know. Anna
was uneasy in this house with superstition, with fear of her
good priest, and with disgust at all the dirt and grease, but
she was most content for now she knew what it was best for
her to do.

Anna paid the woman for her work and then they came
away.

"There Anna didn't I tell you how it would all be? You
see the spirit says so too. You must take the place with Miss
Mathilda, that is what I told you was the best thing for you
to do. We go out and see her where she lives to-night. Ain't
you glad, Anna, that I took you to this place, so you know
now what you will do?"

Mrs. Lehntman and Anna went that evening to see Miss
Mathilda. Miss Mathilda was staying with a friend who
lived in a house that did have trees about. Miss Mathilda
was not there herself to talk with Anna.

If it had not been that it was evening, and so dark, and that
this house had trees all round about, and that Anna found herself going in and coming out just as the woman that day said
that she would do, had it not all been just as the medium said,
the good Anna would never have taken the place with Miss
Mathilda.

Anna did not see Miss Mathilda and she did not like the friend who acted in her place.

This friend was a dark, sweet, gentle little mother woman, very easy to be pleased in her own work and very good to servants, but she felt that acting for her young friend, the careless Miss Mathilda, she must be very careful to examine well and see that all was right and that Anna would surely do the best she knew. She asked Anna all about her ways and her intentions and how much she would spend, and how often she went out and whether she could wash and cook and sew.

The good Anna set her teeth fast to endure and would hardly answer anything at all. Mrs. Lehntman made it all go fairly well.

The good Anna was all worked up with her resentment, and Miss Mathilda's friend did not think that she would do.

However, Miss Mathilda was willing to begin and as for Anna, she knew that the medium said it must be so. Mrs. Lehntman, too, was sure, and said she knew that this was the best thing for Anna now to do. So Anna sent word at last to Miss Mathilda, that if she wanted her, she would try if it would do.

So Anna began a new life taking care of Miss Mathilda.

Anna fixed up the little red brick house where Miss Mathilda was going to live and made it very pleasant, clean and nice. She brought over her dog, Baby, and her parrot. She hired Lizzie for a second girl to be with her and soon they were all content. All except the parrot, for Miss Mathilda did not like its scream. Baby was all right but not the parrot. But then Anna never really loved the parrot, and so she gave it to the Drehten girls to keep.

Before Anna could really rest content with Miss Mathilda, she had to tell her good german priest what it was that she had done, and how very bad it was that she had been and how she would never do so again.

Anna really did believe with all her might. It was her fortune never to live with people who had any faith, but then that never worried Anna. She prayed for them always as she should, and she was very sure that they were good. The Doctor loved to tease her with his doubts and Miss Mathilda liked to do so too, but with the tolerant spirit of her church, Anna never thought that such things were bad for them to do.

Anna found it hard to always know just why it was that things went wrong. Sometimes her glasses broke and then she knew that she had not done her duty by the church, just in the way that she should do.

Sometimes she was so hard at work that she would not go to mass. Something always happened then. Anna's temper grew irritable and her ways uncertain and distraught. Everybody suffered and then her glasses broke. That was always very bad because they cost so much to fix. Still in a way it always ended Anna's troubles, because she knew then that all this was because she had been bad. As long as she could scold it might be just the bad ways of all the thoughtless careless world, but when her glasses broke that made it clear. That meant that it was she herself who had been bad.

No, it was no use for Anna not to do the way she should, for things always then went wrong and finally cost money to make whole, and this was the hardest thing for the good Anna to endure.

Anna almost always did her duty. She made confession and her mission whenever it was right. Of course she did not tell the father when she deceived people for their good, or when she wanted them to give something for a little less.

When Anna told such histories to her Doctor and later to her cherished Miss Mathilda, her eyes were always full of humor and enjoyment as she explained that she had said it so, and now she would not have to tell the father for she had not really made a sin.

But going to a fortune teller Anna knew was really bad. That had to be told to the father just as it was and penance had then to be done.

Anna did this and now her new life was well begun, making Miss Mathilda and the rest do just the way they should.

Yes, taking care of Miss Mathilda were the happiest days of all the good Anna's strong hard working life.

With Miss Mathilda Anna did it all. The clothes, the house, the hats, what she should wear and when and what was always best for her to do. There was nothing Miss Mathilda would not let Anna manage, and only be too glad if she would do.

Anna scolded and cooked and sewed and saved so well, that Miss Mathilda had so much to spend, that it kept Anna still busier scolding all the time about the things she bought, that made so much work for Anna and the other girl to do. But for all the scolding, Anna was proud almost to bursting of her cherished Miss Mathilda with all her knowledge and her great possessions, and the good Anna was always telling of it all to everybody that she knew.

Yes, these were the happiest days of all her life with Anna, even though with her friends there were great sorrows. But these sorrows did not hurt the good Anna now, as they had done in the years that went before.

Miss Mathilda was not a romance in the good Anna's life, but Anna gave her so much strong affection that it almost filled her life as full.

It was well for the good Anna that her life with Miss Mathilda was so happy, for now in those days, Mrs. Lehntman went altogether bad. The Doctor, she had learned to know, was too certainly an evil as well as a mysterious man, and he had power over the widow and midwife, Mrs. Lehntman.

Anna never saw Mrs. Lehntman at all now any more.

Mrs. Lehntman had borrowed some more money and had

given Anna a note then for it all, and after that Anna never saw her any more. Anna now stopped altogether going to the Lehntmans'. Julia, the tall, gawky, good, blonde, stupid daughter, came often to see Anna, but she could tell little of her mother.

It certainly did look very much as if Mrs. Lehntman had now gone altogether bad. This was a great grief to the good Anna, but not so great a grief as it would have been had not Miss Mathilda meant so much to her now.

Mrs. Lehntman went from bad to worse. The doctor, the mysterious and evil man, got into trouble doing things that were not right to do.

Mrs. Lehntman was mixed up in this affair.

It was just as bad as it could be, but they managed, both the doctor and Mrs. Lehntman, finally to come out safe.

Everybody was so sorry about Mrs. Lehntman. She had been really a good woman before she met this doctor, and even now she certainly had not been really bad.

For several years now Anna never even saw her friend.

But Anna always found new people to befriend, people who, in the kindly fashion of the poor, used up her savings and then gave promises in place of payments. Anna never really thought that these people would be good, but when they did not do the way they should, and when they did not pay her back the money she had loaned, and never seemed the better for her care, then Anna would grow bitter with the world.

No, none of them had any sense of what was the right way for them to do. So Anna would repeat in her despair.

The poor are generous with their things. They give always what they have, but with them to give or to receive brings with it no feeling that they owe the giver for the gift.

Even a thrifty german Anna was ready to give all that she had saved, and so not be sure that she would have enough to take care of herself if she fell sick, or for old age, when she could not work. Save and you will have the money you have saved was true only for the day of saving, even for a thrifty german Anna. There was no certain way to have it for old age, for the taking care of what is saved can never be relied on, for it must always be in strangers' hands in a bank or in investments by a friend.

And so when any day one might need life and help from others of the working poor, there was no way a woman who had a little saved could say them no.

So the good Anna gave her all to friends and strangers, to children, dogs and cats, to anything that asked or seemed to need her care.

It was in this way that Anna came to help the barber and his wife who lived around the corner, and who somehow could never make ends meet. They worked hard, were thrifty, had no vices, but the barber was one of them who never can make money. Whoever owed him money did not pay. Whenever he had a chance at a good job he fell sick and could not take it. It was never his own fault that he had trouble, but he never seemed to make things come out right.

His wife was a blonde, thin, pale, german little woman, who bore her children very hard, and worked too soon, and then till she was sick. She too, always had things that went wrong.

They both needed constant help and patience, and the good Anna gave both to them all the time.

Another woman who needed help from the good Anna was one who was in trouble from being good to others.

This woman's husband's brother, who was very good, worked in a shop where there was a Bohemian, who was getting sick with a consumption. This man got so much worse he could not do his work, but he was not so sick that he could stay in a hospital. So this woman had him living there with her. He was not a nice man, nor was he thankful for all the woman did for him. He was cross to her two children and made a great mess always in her house. The Doctor said he must have many things to eat, and the woman and the brother of the husband got them for him.

There was no friendship, no affection, no liking even for the man this woman cared for, no claim of common country or of kin, but in the kindly fashion of the poor this woman gave her all and made her house a nasty place, and for a man who was not even grateful for the gift.

Then, of course, the woman herself got into trouble. Her husband's brother was now married. Her husband lost his job. She did not have the money for the rent. It was the good Anna's savings that were handy.

So it went on. Sometimes a little girl, sometimes a big one was in trouble and Anna heard of them and helped them to find places.

Stray dogs and cats Anna always kept until she found them homes. She was always careful to learn whether these people would be good to animals.

Out of the whole collection of stray creatures, it was the young Peter and the jolly little Rags, Anna could not find it in her heart to part with. These became part of the household of the good Anna's Miss Mathilda.

Peter was a very useless creature, a foolish, silly, cherished, coward male. It was wild to see him rush up and down in the back yard, barking and bouncing at the wall, when there was some dog out beyond, but when the very littlest one there was got inside of the fence and only looked at Peter, Peter would retire to his Anna and blot himself out between her skirts.

When Peter was left downstairs alone, he howled. "I am all alone," he wailed, and then the good Anna would have to come and fetch him up. Once when Anna stayed a few nights in a house not far away, she had to carry Peter all the way, for Peter was afraid when he found himself on the street outside his house. Peter was a good sized creature and he sat there and he howled, and the good Anna carried him all the way in her own arms. He was a coward was this Peter, but he had kindly, gentle eyes and a pretty collie head, and his fur was very thick and white and nice when he was washed. And then Peter never strayed away, and he looked out of his nice eyes and he liked it when you rubbed him down, and he forgot you when you went away, and he barked whenever there was any noise.

When he was a little pup he had one night been put into the yard and that was all of his origin she knew. The good Anna loved him well and spoiled him as a good german mother always does her son.

Little Rags was very different in his nature. He was a lively creature made out of ends of things, all fluffy and dust color, and he was always bounding up into the air and darting all about over and then under silly Peter and often straight into solemn fat, blind, sleepy Baby, and then in a wild rush after some stray cat.

Rags was a pleasant, jolly little fellow. The good Anna liked him very well, but never with her strength as she loved her good looking coward, foolish young man, Peter.

Baby was the dog of her past life and she held Anna with old ties of past affection. Peter was the spoiled, good looking young man, of her middle age, and Rags was always something of a toy. She liked him but he never struck in very deep. Rags had strayed in somehow one day and then when no home for him was quickly found, he had just stayed right there.

It was a very happy family there all together in the kitchen, the good Anna and Sallie and old Baby and young Peter and the jolly little Rags.

The parrot had passed out of Anna's life. She had really never loved the parrot and now she hardly thought to ask for him, even when she visited the Drehtens.

Mrs. Drehten was the friend Anna always went to, for her

Sundays. She did not get advice from Mrs. Drehten as she used to from the widow, Mrs. Lehntman, for Mrs. Drehten was a mild, worn, unaggressive nature that never cared to influence or to lead. But they could mourn together for the world these two worn, working german women, for its sadness and its wicked ways of doing. Mrs. Drehten knew so well what one could suffer.

Things did not go well in these days with the Drehtens. The children were all good, but the father with his temper and his spending kept everything from being what it should.

Poor Mrs. Drehten still had trouble with her tumor. She could hardly do and work now any more. Mrs. Drehten was a large, worn, patient german woman, with a soft face, lined, yellow brown in color and the look that comes from a german husband to obey, and many solid girls and boys to bear and rear, and from being always on one's feet and never having any troubles cured.

Mrs. Drehten was always getting worse, and now the doctor thought it would be best to take the tumor out.

It was no longer Dr. Shonjen who treated Mrs. Drehten. They all went now to a good old german doctor they all knew.

"You see, Miss Mathilda," Anna said, "All the old german patients don't go no more to Doctor. I stayed with him just so long as I could stand it, but now he is moved away up town too far for poor people, and his wife, she holds her head up so and always is spending so much money just for show, and so he can't take right care of us poor people any more. Poor man, he has got always to be thinking about making money now. I am awful sorry about Doctor, Miss Mathilda, but he neglected Mrs. Drehten shameful when she had her trouble, so now I never see him any more. Doctor Herman is a good, plain, german doctor and he would never do things so, and Miss Mathilda, Mrs. Drehten is coming in to-morrow to see you before she goes to the hospital for her operation. She could not go comfortable till she had seen you first to see what you would say."

All Anna's friends reverenced the good Anna's cherished Miss Mathilda. How could they not do so and still remain friends with the good Anna? Miss Mathilda rarely really saw them but they were always sending flowers and words of admiration through her Anna. Every now and then Anna would bring one of them to Miss Mathilda for advice.

It is wonderful how poor people love to take advice from people who are friendly and above them, from people who read in books and who are good.

Miss Mathilda saw Mrs. Drehten and told her she was glad that she was going to the hospital for operation for that surely would be best, and so good Mrs. Drehten's mind was set at rest.

Mrs. Drehten's tumor came out very well. Mrs. Drehten was afterwards never really well, but she could do her work a little better, and be on her feet and yet not get so tired.

And so Anna's life went on, taking care of Miss Mathilda and all her clothes and goods, and being good to everyone that asked or seemed to need her help.

Now, slowly, Anna began to make it up with Mrs. Lehntman. They could never be as they had been before. Mrs. Lehntman could never be again the romance in the good Anna's life, but they could be friends again, and Anna could help all the Lehntmans in their need. This slowly came about.

Mrs. Lehntman had now left the evil and mysterious man who had been the cause of all her trouble. She had given up, too, the new big house that she had taken. Since her trouble her practice had been very quiet. Still she managed to do fairly well. She began to talk of paying the good Anna. This, however, had not gotten very far.

Anna saw Mrs. Lehntman a good deal now. Mrs. Lehntman's crisp, black, curly hair had gotten streaked with grey.

Her dark, full, good looking face had lost its firm outline, gone flabby and a little worn. She had grown stouter and her clothes did not look very nice. She was as bland as ever in her ways, and as diffuse as always in her attention, but through it all there was uneasiness and fear and uncertainty lest some danger might be near.

She never said a word of her past life to the good Anna, but it was very plain to see that her experience had not left her easy, nor yet altogether free.

It had been hard for this good woman, for Mrs. Lehntman was really a good woman, it had been a very hard thing for this german woman to do what everybody knew and thought was wrong. Mrs. Lehntman was strong and she had courage, but it had been very hard to bear. Even the good Anna did not speak to her with freedom. There always remained a mystery and a depression in Mrs. Lehntman's affair.

And now the blonde, foolish, awkward daughter, Julia was in trouble. During the years the mother gave her no attention, Julia kept company with a young fellow who was a clerk somewhere in a store down in the city. He was a decent, dull young fellow, who did not make much money and could never save it for he had an old mother he supported. He and Julia had been keeping company for several years and now it was needful that they should be married. But then how could they marry? He did not make enough to start them and to keep on supporting his old mother too. Julia was not used to working much and she said, and she was stubborn, that she would not live with Charley's dirty, cross, old mother. Mrs. Lehntman had no money. She was just beginning to get on her feet. It was of course, the good Anna's savings that were handy.

However it paid Anna to bring about this marriage, paid her in scoldings and in managing the dull, long, awkward Julia, and her good, patient, stupid Charley. Anna loved to buy things cheap, and fix up a new place.

Julia and Charley were soon married and things went pretty well with them. Anna did not approve their slack, expensive ways of doing.

"No Miss Mathilda," she would say, "The young people nowadays have no sense for saving and putting money by so they will have something to use when they need it. There's Julia and her Charley. I went in there the other day, Miss Mathilda, and they had a new table with a marble top and on it they had a grand new plush album. 'Where you get that album?' I asked Julia. 'Oh, Charley he gave it to me for my birthday,' she said, and I asked her if it was paid for and she said not all yet but it would be soon. Now I ask you what business have they Miss Mathilda, when they ain't paid for anything they got already, what business have they to be buying new things for her birthdays. Julia she don't do no work, she just sits around and thinks how she can spend the money, and Charley he never puts one cent by. I never see anything like the people nowadays Miss Mathilda, they don't seem to have any sense of being careful about money. Julia and Charley when they have any children they won't have nothing to bring them up with right. I said that to Julia, Miss Mathilda, when she showed me those silly things that Charley bought her, and she just said in her silly, giggling way, perhaps they won't have any children. I told her she ought to be ashamed of talking so, but I don't know, Miss Mathilda, the young people nowadays have no sense at all of what's the right way for them to do, and perhaps it's better if they don't have any children, and then Miss Mathilda you know there is Mrs. Lehntman. You know she regular adopted little Johnny just so she could pay out some more money just as if she didn't have trouble enough taking care of her own children. No Miss Mathilda, I never see how people can do things so. People don't seem to have no sense of right or wrong or anything these days Miss Mathilda, they are just careless and thinking always of themselves and how they can always have a happy time. No, Miss Mathilda I don't see how people can go and do things so."

The good Anna could not understand the careless and bad ways of all the world and always she grew bitter with it all. No, not one of them had any sense of what was the right way for them to do.

Anna's past life was now drawing to an end. Her old blind dog, Baby, was sick and like to die. Baby had been the first gift from her friend the widow, Mrs. Lehntman in the old days when Anna had been with Miss Mary Wadsmith, and when these two women had first come together.

Through all the years of change, Baby had stayed with the good Anna, growing old and fat and blind and lazy. Baby had been active and a ratter when she was young, but that was so long ago it was forgotten, and for many years now Baby had wanted only her warm basket and her dinner.

Anna in her active life found need of others, of Peter and the funny little Rags, but always Baby was the eldest and held her with the ties of old affection. Anna was harsh when the young ones tried to keep poor Baby out and use her basket. Baby had been blind now for some years as dogs get, when they are no longer active. She got weak and fat and breathless and she could not even stand long any more. Anna had always to see that she got her dinner and that the young active ones did not deprive her.

Baby did not die with a real sickness. She just got older and more blind and coughed and then more quiet, and then slowly one bright summer's day she died.

There is nothing more dreary than old age in animals. Somehow it is all wrong that they should have grey hair and withered skin, and blind old eyes, and decayed and useless teeth. An old man or an old woman almost always has some tie that seems to bind them to the younger, realer life. They have children or the remembrance of old duties, but a dog that's old and so cut off from all its world of struggle, is like a dreary, deathless Struldbrug, the dreary dragger on of death through life.

And so one day old Baby died. It was dreary, more than sad, for the good Anna. She did not want the poor old beast to linger with its weary age, and blind old eyes and dismal shaking cough, but this death left Anna very empty. She had the foolish young man Peter, and the jolly little Rags for comfort, but Baby had been the only one that could remember.

The good Anna wanted a real graveyard for her Baby, but this could not be in a Christian country, and so Anna all alone took her old friend done up in decent wrappings and put her into the ground in some quiet place that Anna knew of.

The good Anna did not weep for poor old Baby. Nay, she had not time even to feel lonely, for with the good Anna it was sorrow upon sorrow. She was now no longer to keep house for Miss Mathilda.

When Anna had first come to Miss Mathilda she had known that it might only be for a few years, for Miss Mathilda was given to much wandering and often changed her home, and found new places where she went to live. The good Anna did not then think much about this, for when she first went to Miss Mathilda she had not thought that she would like it and so she had not worried about staying. Then in those happy years that they had been together, Anna had made herself forget it. This last year when she knew that it was coming she had tried hard to think it would not happen.

"We don't talk about it now Miss Mathilda, perhaps we all be dead by then," she would say when Miss Mathilda tried to talk it over. Or, "If we live till then Miss Mathilda, perhaps you will be staying on right here."

No, the good Anna could not talk as if this thing were real, it was too weary to be once more left with strangers.

Both the good Anna and her cherished Miss Mathilda

tried hard to think that this would not really happen. Anna made missions and all kinds of things to keep her Miss Mathilda and Miss Mathilda thought out all the ways to see if the good Anna could not go with her, but neither the missions nor the plans had much success. Miss Mathilda would go, and she was going far away to a new country where Anna could not live, for she would be too lonesome.

There was nothing that these two could do but part. Perhaps we all be dead by then, the good Anna would repeat, but even that did not really happen. If we all live till then Miss Mathilda, came out truer. They all did live till then, all except poor old blind Baby, and they simply had to part.

Poor Anna and poor Miss Mathilda. They could not look at each other that last day. Anna could not keep herself busy working. She just went in and out and sometimes scolded.

Anna could not make up her mind what she should do now for her future. She said that she would for a while keep this little red brick house that they had lived in. Perhaps she might just take in a few boarders. She did not know, she would write about it later and tell it all to Miss Mathilda.

The dreary day dragged out and then all was ready and Miss Mathilda left to take her train. Anna stood strained and pale and dry eyed on the white stone steps of the little red brick house that they had lived in. The last thing Miss Mathilda heard was the good Anna bidding foolish Peter say good-by and be sure to remember Miss Mathilda.

PART 3

THE DEATH OF THE GOOD ANNA

EVERY one who had known of Miss Mathilda wanted the good Anna now to take a place with them, for they all knew how well Anna could take care of people and all their clothes and goods. Anna too could always go to Curden to Miss Mary Wadsmith, but none of all these ways seemed very good to Anna.

It was not now any longer that she wanted to stay near Mrs. Lehntman. There was no one now that made anything important, but Anna was certain that she did not want to take a place where she would be under some new people. No one could ever be for Anna as had been her cherished Miss Mathilda. No one could ever again so freely let her do it all. It would be better Anna thought in her strong strained weary body, it would be better just to keep on there in the little red brick house that was all furnished, and make a living taking in some boarders. Miss Mathilda had let her have the things, so it would not cost any money to begin. She could perhaps manage to live on so. She could do all the work and do everything as she thought best, and she was too weary with the changes to do more than she just had to, to keep living.

So she stayed on in the house where they had lived, and she found some men, she would not take in women, who took her rooms and who were her boarders.

Things soon with Anna began to be less dreary. She was very popular with her few boarders. They loved her scoldings and the good things she made for them to eat. They made good jokes and laughed loud and always did whatever Anna wanted, and soon the good Anna got so that she liked it very well. Not that she did not always long for Miss Mathilda. She hoped and waited and was very certain that sometime, in one year or in another Miss Mathilda would come back, and then of course would want her, and then she could take all good care of her again.

Anna kept all Miss Mathilda's things in the best order. The boarders were well scolded if they ever made a scratch on Miss Mathilda's table.

Some of the boarders were hearty good south german fellows and Anna always made them go to mass. One boarder was a lusty german student who was studying in Bridgepoint to be a doctor. He was Anna's special favourite and she scolded him as she used to her old doctor so that he always would be good. Then, too, this cheery fellow always sang when he was washing, and that was what Miss Mathilda always used to do. Anna's heart grew warm again with this young fellow who seemed to bring back to her everything she needed.

And so Anna's life in these days was not all unhappy. She worked and scolded, she had her stray dogs and cats and people, who all asked and seemed to need her care, and she had hearty german fellows who loved her scoldings and ate so much of the good things that she knew so well the way to make.

No, the good Anna's life in these days was not all unhappy. She did not see her old friends much, she was too

busy, but once in a great while she took a Sunday afternoon
and went to see good Mrs. Drehten.

The only trouble was that Anna hardly made a living. She
charged so little for her board and gave her people such
good things to eat, that she could only just make both ends
meet. The good german priest to whom she always told her
troubles tried to make her have the boarders pay a little
higher, and Miss Mathilda always in her letters urged her to
this thing, but the good Anna somehow could not do it. Her
boarders were nice men but she knew they did not have
much money, and then she could not raise on those who had
been with her and she could not ask the new ones to pay
higher, when those who were already there were paying just
what they had paid before. So Anna let it go just as she had
begun it. She worked and worked all day and thought all
night how she could save, and with all the work she just
managed to keep living. She could not make enough to lay
any money by.

Anna got so little money that she had all the work to do
herself. She could not pay even the little Sallie enough to
keep her with her.

Not having little Sallie nor having any one else working
with her, made it very hard for Anna ever to go out, for she
never thought that it was right to leave a house all empty.
Once in a great while of a Sunday, Sallie who was now
working in a factory would come and stay in the house for
the good Anna, who would then go out and spend the afternoon with Mrs. Drehten.

No, Anna did not see her old friends much any more. She
went sometimes to see her half brother and his wife and her
nieces, and they always came to her on her birthdays to give
presents, and her half brother never left her out of his festive
raisined bread giving progresses. But these relatives of hers
had never meant very much to the good Anna. Anna always
did her duty by them all, and she liked her half brother very

well and the loaves of raisined bread that he supplied her were most welcome now, and Anna always gave her god daughter and her sister handsome presents, but no one in this family had ever made a way inside to Anna's feelings.

Mrs. Lehntman she saw very rarely. It is hard to build up new on an old friendship when in that friendship there has been bitter disillusion. They did their best, both these women, to be friends, but they were never able to again touch one another nearly. There were too many things between them that they could not speak of, things that had never been explained nor yet forgiven. The good Anna still did her best for foolish Julia and still every now and then saw Mrs. Lehntman, but this family had now lost all its real hold on Anna.

Mrs. Drehten was now the best friend that Anna knew. Here there was never any more than the mingling of their sorrows. They talked over all the time the best way for Mrs. Drehten now to do; poor Mrs. Drehten who with her chief trouble, her bad husband, had really now no way that she could do. She just had to work and to be patient and to love her children and be very quiet. She always had a soothing mother influence on the good Anna who with her irritable, strained, worn-out body would come and sit by Mrs. Drehten and talk all her troubles over.

Of all the friends that the good Anna had had in these twenty years in Bridgepoint, the good father and patient Mrs. Drehten were the only ones that were now near to Anna and with whom she could talk her troubles over.

Anna worked, and thought, and saved, and scolded, and took care of all the boarders, and of Peter and of Rags, and all the others. There was never any end to Anna's effort and she grew always more tired, more pale yellow, and in her face more thin and worn and worried. Sometimes she went farther in not being well, and then she went to see Dr. Herman who had operated on good Mrs. Drehten.

The things that Anna really needed were to rest sometimes and eat more so that she could get stronger, but these
were the last things that Anna could bring herself to do.
Anna could never take a rest. She must work hard through
the summer as well as through the winter, else she could
never make both ends meet. The doctor gave her medicines
to make her stronger but these did not seem to do much
good.

Anna grew always more tired, her headaches came oftener and harder, and she was now almost always feeling
very sick. She could not sleep much in the night. The dogs
with their noises disturbed her and everything in her body
seemed to pain her.

The doctor and the good father tried often to make her
give herself more care. Mrs. Drehten told her that she surely
would not get well unless for a little while she would stop
working. Anna would then promise to take care, to rest in
bed a little longer and to eat more so that she would get
stronger, but really how could Anna eat when she always did
the cooking and was so tired of it all, before it was half
ready for the table?

Anna's only friendship now was with good Mrs. Drehten
who was too gentle and too patient to make a stubborn faithful german Anna ever do the way she should, in the things
that were for her own good.

Anna grew worse all through this second winter. When
the summer came the doctor said that she simply could not
live on so. He said she must go to his hospital and there he
would operate upon her. She would then be well and strong
and able to work hard all next winter.

Anna for some time would not listen. She could not do
this so, for she had her house all furnished and she simply
could not let it go. At last a woman came and said she would
take care of Anna's boarders and then Anna said that she was
prepared to go.

Anna went to the hospital for her operation. Mrs. Drehten was herself not well but she came into the city, so that some friend would be with the good Anna. Together, then, they went to this place where the doctor had done so well by Mrs. Drehten.

In a few days they had Anna ready. Then they did the operation, and then the good Anna with her strong, strained, worn-out body died.

Mrs. Drehten sent word of her death to Miss Mathilda.

"Dear Miss Mathilda," wrote Mrs. Drehten, "Miss Annie died in the hospital yesterday after a hard operation. She was talking about you and Doctor and Miss Mary Wadsmith all the time. She said she hoped you would take Peter and the little Rags to keep when you came back to America to live. I will keep them for you here Miss Mathilda. Miss Annie died easy, Miss Mathilda, and sent you her love."

MELANCTHA

EACH ONE AS SHE MAY

ROSE JOHNSON made it very hard to bring her baby to its birth.

Melanctha Herbert who was Rose Johnson's friend, did everything that any woman could. She tended Rose, and she was patient, submissive, soothing, and untiring, while the sullen, childish, cowardly, black Rosie grumbled and fussed and howled and made herself to be an abomination and like a simple beast.

The child though it was healthy after it was born, did not live long. Rose Johnson was careless and negligent and selfish, and when Melanctha had to leave for a few days, the baby died. Rose Johnson had liked the baby well enough and perhaps she just forgot it for awhile, anyway the child was dead and Rose and Sam her husband were very sorry but then these things came so often in the negro world in Bridgepoint, that they neither of them thought about it very long.

Rose Johnson and Melanctha Herbert had been friends now for some years. Rose had lately married Sam Johnson a decent honest kindly fellow, a deck hand on a coasting steamer.

Melanctha Herbert had not yet been really married.

Rose Johnson was a real black, tall, well built, sullen, stupid, childlike, good looking negress. She laughed when she was happy and grumbled and was sullen with everything that troubled.

Rose Johnson was a real black negress but she had been brought up quite like their own child by white folks.

Rose laughed when she was happy but she had not the wide, abandoned laughter that makes the warm broad glow of negro sunshine. Rose was never joyous with the earthborn, boundless joy of negroes. Hers was just ordinary, any sort of woman laughter.

Rose Johnson was careless and was lazy, but she had been brought up by white folks and she needed decent comfort. Her white training had only made for habits, not for nature. Rose had the simple, promiscuous unmorality of the black people.

Rose Johnson and Melanctha Herbert like many of the twos with women were a curious pair to be such friends.

Melanctha Herbert was a graceful, pale yellow, intelligent, attractive negress. She had not been raised like Rose by white folks but then she had been half made with real white blood.

She and Rose Johnson were both of the better sort of negroes, there, in Bridgepoint.

"No, I ain't no common nigger," said Rose Johnson, "for I was raised by white folks, and Melanctha she is so bright and learned so much in school, she ain't no common nigger either, though she ain't got no husband to be married to like I am to Sam Johnson."

Why did the subtle, intelligent, attractive, half white girl Melanctha Herbert love and do for and demean herself in service to this coarse, decent, sullen, ordinary, black childish Rose, and why was this unmoral, promiscuous, shiftless Rose married, and that's not so common either, to a good man of the negroes, while Melanctha with her white blood

and attraction and her desire for a right position had not yet
been really married.

Sometimes the thought of how all her world was made,
filled the complex, desiring Melanctha with despair. She
wondered, often, how she could go on living when she was
so blue.

Melanctha told Rose one day how a woman whom she
knew had killed herself because she was so blue. Melanctha
said, sometimes, she thought this was the best thing for her
herself to do.

Rose Johnson did not see it the least bit that way.

"I don't see Melanctha why you should talk like you
would kill yourself just because you're blue. I'd never kill
myself Melanctha just 'cause I was blue. I'd maybe kill
somebody else Melanctha 'cause I was blue, but I'd never
kill myself. If I ever killed myself Melanctha it'd be by accident, and if I ever killed myself by accident Melanctha, I'd
be awful sorry."

Rose Johnson and Melanctha Herbert had first met, one
night, at church. Rose Johnson did not care much for religion. She had not enough emotion to be really roused by a
revival. Melanctha Herbert had not come yet to know how
to use religion. She was still too complex with desire. However, the two of them in negro fashion went very often to the
negro church, along with all their friends, and they slowly
came to know each other very well.

Rose Johnson had been raised not as a servant but quite
like their own child by white folks. Her mother who had
died when Rose was still a baby, had been a trusted servant
in the family. Rose was a cute, attractive, good looking little
black girl and these people had no children of their own and
so they kept Rose in their house.

As Rose grew older she drifted from her white folks back
to the colored people, and she gradually no longer lived in
the old house. Then it happened that these people went away

to some other town to live, and somehow Rose stayed behind in Bridgepoint. Her white folks left a little money to take care of Rose, and this money she got every little while.

Rose now in the easy fashion of the poor lived with one woman in her house, and then for no reason went and lived with some other woman in her house. All this time, too, Rose kept company, and was engaged, first to this colored man and then to that, and always she made sure she was engaged, for Rose had strong the sense of proper conduct.

"No, I ain't no common nigger just to go around with any man, nor you Melanctha shouldn't neither," she said one day when she was telling the complex and less sure Melanctha what was the right way for her to do. "No Melanctha, I ain't no common nigger to do so, for I was raised by white folks. You know very well Melanctha that I'se always been engaged to them."

And so Rose lived on, always comfortable and rather decent and very lazy and very well content.

After she had lived some time this way, Rose thought it would be nice and very good in her position to get regularly really married. She had lately met Sam Johnson somewhere, and she liked him and she knew he was a good man, and then he had a place where he worked every day and got good wages. Sam Johnson liked Rose very well and he was quite ready to be married. One day they had a grand real wedding and were married. Then with Melanctha Herbert's help to do the sewing and the nicer work, they furnished comfortably a little red brick house. Sam then went back to his work as deck hand on a coasting steamer, and Rose stayed home in her house and sat and bragged to all her friends how nice it was to be married really to a husband.

Life went on very smoothly with them all the year. Rose was lazy but not dirty and Sam was careful but not fussy, and then there was Melanctha to come in every day and help to keep things neat.

When Rose's baby was coming to be born, Rose came to stay in the house where Melanctha Herbert lived just then, with a big good natured colored woman who did washing.

Rose went there to stay, so that she might have the doctor from the hospital near to help her have the baby, and then, too, Melanctha could attend to her while she was sick.

Here the baby was born, and here it died, and then Rose went back to her house again with Sam.

Melanctha Herbert had not made her life all simple like Rose Johnson. Melanctha had not found it easy with herself to make her wants and what she had, agree.

Melanctha Herbert was always losing what she had in wanting all the things she saw. Melanctha was always being left when she was not leaving others.

Melanctha Herbert always loved too hard and much too often. She was always full with mystery and subtle movements and denials and vague distrusts and complicated disillusions. Then Melanctha would be sudden and impulsive and unbounded in some faith, and then she would suffer and be strong in her repression.

Melanctha Herbert was always seeking rest and quiet, and always she could only find new ways to be in trouble.

Melanctha wondered often how it was she did not kill herself when she was so blue. Often she thought this would be really the best way for her to do.

Melanctha Herbert had been raised to be religious, by her mother. Melanctha had not liked her mother very well. This mother, 'Mis' Herbert, as her neighbors called her, had been a sweet appearing and dignified and pleasant, pale yellow, colored woman. 'Mis' Herbert had always been a little wandering and mysterious and uncertain in her ways.

Melanctha was pale yellow and mysterious and a little pleasant like her mother, but the real power in Melanctha's nature came through her robust and unpleasant and very unendurable black father.

Melanctha's father only used to come to where Melanctha and her mother lived, once in a while.

It was many years now that Melanctha had not heard or seen or known of anything her father did.

Melanctha Herbert almost always hated her black father, but she loved very well the power in herself that came through him. And so her feeling was really closer to her black coarse father, than her feeling had ever been toward her pale yellow, sweet appearing mother. The things she had in her of her mother never made her feel respect.

Melanctha Herbert had not loved herself in childhood. All of her youth was bitter to remember.

Melanctha had not loved her father and her mother and they had found it very troublesome to have her.

Melanctha's mother and her father had been regularly married. Melanctha's father was a big black virile negro. He only came once in a while to where Melanctha and her mother lived, but always that pleasant, sweet-appearing, pale yellow woman, mysterious and uncertain and wandering in her ways, was close in sympathy and thinking to her big black virile husband.

James Herbert was a common, decent enough, colored workman, brutal and rough to his one daughter, but then she was a most disturbing child to manage.

The young Melanctha did not love her father and her mother, and she had a break neck courage, and a tongue that could be very nasty. Then, too, Melanctha went to school and was very quick in all the learning, and she knew very well how to use this knowledge to annoy her parents who knew nothing.

Melanctha Herbert had always had a break neck courage. Melanctha always loved to be with horses; she loved to do wild things, to ride the horses and to break and tame them.

Melanctha, when she was a little girl, had had a good chance to live with horses. Near where Melanctha and her

mother lived was the stable of the Bishops, a rich family
who always had fine horses.

John, the Bishops' coachman, liked Melanctha very well
and he always let her do anything she wanted with the
horses. John was a decent, vigorous mulatto with a prosperous house and wife and children. Melanctha Herbert was
older than any of his children. She was now a well grown
girl of twelve and just beginning as a woman.

James Herbert, Melanctha's father, knew this John, the
Bishops' coachman very well.

One day James Herbert came to where his wife and
daughter lived, and he was furious.

"Where's that Melanctha girl of yours," he said fiercely,
"if she is to the Bishops' stables again, with that man John, I
swear I kill her. Why don't you see to that girl better you,
you're her mother."

James Herbert was a powerful, loose built, hard handed,
black, angry negro. Herbert never was a joyous negro. Even
when he drank with other men, and he did that very often,
he was never really joyous. In the days when he had been
most young and free and open, he had never had the wide
abandoned laughter that gives the broad glow to negro sunshine.

His daughter, Melanctha Herbert, later always made a
hard forced laughter. She was only strong and sweet and in
her nature when she was really deep in trouble, when she
was fighting so with all she really had, that she did not use
her laughter. This was always true of poor Melanctha who
was so certain that she hated trouble. Melanctha Herbert was
always seeking peace and quiet, and she could always only
find her new ways to get excited.

James Herbert was often a very angry negro. He was
fierce and serious, and he was very certain that he often had
good reason to be angry with Melanctha, who knew so well

how to be nasty, and to use her learning with a father who knew nothing.

James Herbert often drank with John, the Bishops' coachman. John in his good nature sometimes tried to soften Herbert's feeling toward Melanctha. Not that Melanctha ever complained to John of her home life or her father. It was never Melanctha's way, even in the midst of her worst trouble to complain to any one of what happened to her, but nevertheless somehow every one who knew Melanctha always knew how much she suffered. It was only while one really loved Melanctha that one understood how to forgive her, that she never once complained nor looked unhappy, and was always handsome and in spirits, and yet one always knew how much she suffered.

The father, James Herbert, never told his troubles either, and he was so fierce and serious that no one ever thought of asking.

'Mis' Herbert as her neighbors called her was never heard even to speak of her husband or her daughter. She was always pleasant, sweet-appearing, mysterious and uncertain, and a little wandering in her ways.

The Herberts were a silent family with their troubles, but somehow every one who knew them always knew everything that happened.

The morning of one day when in the evening Herbert and the coachman John were to meet to drink together, Melanctha had to come to the stable joyous and in the very best of humors. Her good friend John on this morning felt very firmly how good and sweet she was and how very much she suffered.

John was a very decent colored coachman. When he thought about Melanctha it was as if she were the eldest of his children. Really he felt very strongly the power in her of a woman. John's wife always liked Melanctha and she always did all she could to make things pleasant. And Melanctha all her life loved and respected kind and good and considerate people. Melanctha always loved and wanted peace and gentleness and goodness and all her life for herself poor Melanctha could only find new ways to be in trouble.

This evening after John and Herbert had drunk awhile together, the good John began to tell the father what a fine girl he had for a daughter. Perhaps the good John had been drinking a good deal of liquor, perhaps there was a gleam of something softer than the feeling of a friendly elder in the way John then spoke of Melanctha. There had been a good deal of drinking and John certainly that very morning had felt strongly Melanctha's power as a woman. James Herbert was always a fierce, suspicious, serious negro, and drinking never made him feel more open. He looked very black and evil as he sat and listened while John grew more and more admiring as he talked half to himself, half to the father, of the virtues and the sweetness of Melanctha.

Suddenly between them there came a moment filled full with strong black curses, and then sharp razors flashed in the black hands, that held them flung backward in the negro fashion, and then for some minutes there was fierce slashing.

John was a decent, pleasant, good natured, light brown negro, but he knew how to use a razor to do bloody slashing.

When the two men were pulled apart by the other negroes who were in the room drinking, John had not been much wounded but James Herbert had gotten one good strong cut that went from his right shoulder down across the front of his whole body. Razor fighting does not wound very deeply, but it makes a cut that looks most nasty, for it is so very bloody.

Herbert was held by the other negroes until he was cleaned and plastered, and then he was put to bed to sleep off his drink and fighting.

The next day he came to where his wife and daughter lived and he was furious.

"Where's that Melanctha, of yours?" he said to his wife, when he saw her. "If she is to the Bishops' stables now with that yellow John, I swear I kill her. A nice way she is going for a decent daughter. Why don't you see to that girl better you, ain't you her mother!"

Melanctha Herbert had always been old in all her ways and she knew very early how to use her power as a woman, and yet Melanctha with all her inborn intense wisdom was really very ignorant of evil. Melanctha had not yet come to understand what they meant, the things she so often heard around her, and which were just beginning to stir strongly in her.

Now when her father began fiercely to assail her, she did not really know what it was that he was so furious to force from her. In every way that he could think of in his anger, he tried to make her say a thing she did not really know. She held out and never answered anything he asked her, for Melanctha had a break neck courage and she just then badly hated her black father.

When the excitement was all over, Melanctha began to know her power, the power she had so often felt stirring within her and which she now knew she could use to make her stronger.

James Herbert did not win this fight with his daughter. After awhile he forgot it as he soon forgot John and the cut of his sharp razor.

Melanctha almost forgot to hate her father, in her strong interest in the power she now knew she had within her.

Melanctha did not care much now, any longer, to see John or his wife or even the fine horses. This life was too quiet and accustomed and no longer stirred her to any interest or excitement.

Melanctha now really was beginning as a woman. She

was ready, and she began to search in the streets and in dark corners to discover men and to learn their natures and their various ways of working.

In these next years Melanctha learned many ways that lead to wisdom. She learned the ways, and dimly in the distance she saw wisdom. These years of learning led very straight to trouble for Melanctha, though in these years Melanctha never did or meant anything that was really wrong.

Girls who are brought up with care and watching can always find moments to escape into the world, where they may learn the ways that lead to wisdom. For a girl raised like Melanctha Herbert, such escape was always very simple. Often she was alone, sometimes she was with a fellow seeker, and she strayed and stood, sometimes by railroad yards, sometimes on the docks or around new buildings where many men were working. Then when the darkness covered everything all over, she would begin to learn to know this man or that. She would advance, they would respond, and then she would withdraw a little, dimly, and always she did not know what it was that really held her. Sometimes she would almost go over, and then the strength in her of not really knowing, would stop the average man in his endeavor. It was a strange experience of ignorance and power and desire. Melanctha did not know what it was that she so badly wanted. She was afraid, and yet she did not understand that here she really was a coward.

Boys had never meant much to Melanctha. They had always been too young to content her. Melanctha had a strong respect for any kind of successful power. It was this that always kept Melanctha nearer, in her feeling toward her virile and unendurable black father, than she ever was in her feeling for her pale yellow, sweet-appearing mother. The things she had in her of her mother, never made her feel respect.

In these young days, it was only men that for Melanctha

held anything there was of knowledge and power. It was not from men however that Melanctha learned to really understand this power.

From the time that Melanctha was twelve until she was sixteen she wandered, always seeking but never more than very dimly seeing wisdom. All this time Melanctha went on with her school learning; she went to school rather longer than do most of the colored children.

Melanctha's wanderings after wisdom she always had to do in secret and by snatches, for her mother was then still living and 'Mis' Herbert always did some watching, and Melanctha with all her hard courage dreaded that there should be much telling to her father, who came now quite often to where Melanctha lived with her mother.

In these days Melanctha talked and stood and walked with many kinds of men, but she did not learn to know any of them very deeply. They all supposed her to have world knowledge and experience. They, believing that she knew all, told her nothing, and thinking that she was deciding with them, asked for nothing, and so though Melanctha wandered widely, she was really very safe with all the wandering.

It was a very wonderful experience this safety of Melanctha in these days of her attempted learning. Melanctha herself did not feel the wonder, she only knew that for her it all had no real value.

Melanctha all her life was very keen in her sense for real experience. She knew she was not getting what she so badly wanted, but with all her break neck courage Melanctha here was a coward, and so she could not learn to really understand.

Melanctha liked to wander, and to stand by the railroad yard, and watch the men and the engines and the switches and everything that was busy there, working. Railroad yards are a ceaseless fascination. They satisfy every kind of nature. For the lazy man whose blood flows very slowly, it is

a steady soothing world of motion which supplies him with
the sense of a strong moving power. He need not work and
yet he has it very deeply; he has it even better than the man
who works in it or owns it. Then for natures that like to feel
emotion without the trouble of having any suffering, it is
very nice to get the swelling in the throat, and the fullness,
and the heart beats, and all the flutter of excitement that
comes as one watches the people come and go, and hears the
engine pound and give a long drawn whistle. For a child
watching through a hole in the fence above the yard, it is a
wonder world of mystery and movement. The child loves all
the noise, and then it loves the silence of the wind that
comes before the full rush of the pounding train, that bursts
out from the tunnel where it lost itself and all its noise in
darkness, and the child loves all the smoke, that sometimes
comes in rings, and always puffs with fire and blue color.

For Melanctha the yard was full of the excitement of
many men, and perhaps a free and whirling future.

Melanctha came here very often and watched the men
and all the things that were so busy working. The men always had time for, "Hullo sis, do you want to sit on my engine," and, "Hullo, that's a pretty lookin' yaller girl, do you
want to come and see him cookin'?"

All the colored porters liked Melanctha. They often told
her exciting things that had happened; how in the West they
went through big tunnels where there was no air to breathe,
and then out and winding around edges of great canyons on
thin high spindling trestles, and sometimes cars, and sometimes whole trains fell from the narrow bridges, and always
up from the dark places death and all kinds of queer devils
looked up and laughed in their faces. And then they would
tell how sometimes when the train went pounding down
steep slippery mountains, great rocks would racket and roll
down around them, and sometimes would smash in the car
and kill men; and as the porters told these stories their

round, black, shining faces would grow solemn, and their color would go grey beneath the greasy black, and their eyes would roll white in the fear and wonder of the things they could scare themselves by telling.

There was one, big, serious, melancholy, light brown porter who often told Melanctha stories, for he liked the way she had of listening with intelligence and sympathetic feeling, when he told how the white men in the far South tried to kill him because he made one of them who was drunk and called him a damned nigger, and who refused to pay money for his chair to a nigger, get off the train between stations. And then this porter had to give up going to that part of the Southern country, for all the white men swore that if he ever came there again they would surely kill him.

Melanctha liked this serious, melancholy light brown negro very well, and all her life Melanctha wanted and respected gentleness and goodness, and this man always gave her good advice and serious kindness, and Melanctha felt such things very deeply, but she would never let them help her or affect her to change the ways that always made her keep herself in trouble.

Melanctha spent many of the last hours of the daylight with the porters and with other men who worked hard, but when darkness came it was always different. Then Melanctha would find herself with the, for her, gentlemanly classes. A clerk, or a young express agent would begin to know her, and they would stand, or perhaps, walk a little while together.

Melanctha always made herself escape but often it was with an effort. She did not know what it was that she so badly wanted, but with all her courage Melanctha here was a coward, and so she could not learn to understand.

Melanctha and some man would stand in the evening and would talk together. Sometimes Melanctha would be with another girl and then it was much easier to stay or to escape, for then they would make way for themselves together, and by throwing words and laughter to each other, could keep a man from getting too strong in his attention.

But when Melanctha was alone, and she was so, very often, she would sometimes come very near to making a long step on the road that leads to wisdom. Some man would learn a good deal about her in the talk, never altogether truly, for Melanctha all her life did not know how to tell a story wholly. She always, and yet not with intention, managed to leave out big pieces which make a story very different, for when it came to what had happened and what she had said and what it was that she had really done, Melanctha never could remember right. The man would sometimes come a little nearer, would detain her, would hold her arm or make his jokes a little clearer, and then Melanctha would always make herself escape. The man thinking that she really had world wisdom would not make his meaning clear, and believing that she was deciding with him he never went so fast that he could stop her when at last she made herself escape.

And so Melanctha wandered on the edge of wisdom. "Say, Sis, why don't you when you come here stay a little longer?" they would all ask her, and they would hold her for an answer, and she would laugh, and sometimes she did stay longer, but always just in time she made herself escape.

Melanctha Herbert wanted very much to know and yet she feared the knowledge. As she grew older she often stayed a good deal longer, and sometimes it was almost a balanced struggle, but she always made herself escape.

Next to the railroad yard it was the shipping docks that Melanctha loved best when she wandered. Often she was alone, sometimes she was with some better kind of black girl, and she would stand a long time and watch the men working at unloading, and see the steamers do their coaling, and she would listen with full feeling to the yowling of the free swinging negroes, as they ran, with their powerful loose jointed bodies and their childish savage yelling, pushing, carrying, pulling great loads from the ships to the warehouses.

The men would call out, "Say, Sis, look out or we'll come and catch yer," or "Hi, there, you yaller girl, come here and we'll take you sailin'." And then, too, Melanctha would learn to know some of the serious foreign sailors who told her all sorts of wonders, and a cook would sometimes take her and her friends over a ship and show where he made his messes and where the men slept, and where the shops were, and how everything was made by themselves, right there, on ship board.

Melanctha loved to see these dark and smelly places. She always loved to watch and talk and listen with men who worked hard. But it was never from these rougher people that Melanctha tried to learn the ways that lead to wisdom. In the daylight she always liked to talk with rough men and to listen to their lives and about their work and their various ways of doing, but when the darkness covered everything all over, Melanctha would meet, and stand, and talk with a clerk or a young shipping agent who had seen her watching, and so it was that she would try to learn to understand.

And then Melanctha was fond of watching men work on new buildings. She loved to see them hoisting, digging, sawing and stone cutting. Here, too, in the daylight, she always learned to know the common workmen. "Heh, Sis, look out or that rock will fall on you and smash you all up into little pieces. Do you think you would make a nice jelly?" And then they would all laugh and feel that their jokes were very funny. And "Say, you pretty yaller girl, would it scare you bad to stand up here on top where I be? See if you've got grit and come up here where I can hold you. All you got to do is to sit still on that there rock that they're just hoistin', and then when you get here I'll hold you tight, don't you be scared Sis."

Sometimes Melanctha would do some of these things that had much danger, and always with such men, she showed her power and her break neck courage. Once she slipped and fell from a high place. A workman caught her and so she was not killed, but her left arm was badly broken.

All the men crowded around her. They admired her boldness in doing and in bearing pain when her arm was broken. They all went along with her with great respect to the doctor, and then they took her home in triumph and all of them were bragging about her not squealing.

James Herbert was home where his wife lived, that day. He was furious when he saw the workmen and Melanctha. He drove the men away with curses so that they were all very nearly fighting, and he would not let a doctor come in to attend Melanctha. "Why don't you see to that girl better, you, you're her mother."

James Herbert did not fight things out now any more with his daughter. He feared her tongue, and her school learning, and the way she had of saying things that were very nasty to a brutal black man who knew nothing. And Melanctha just then hated him very badly in her suffering.

And so this was the way Melanctha lived the four years of her beginning as a woman. And many things happened to Melanctha, but she knew very well that none of them had led her on to the right way, that certain way that was to lead her to world wisdom.

Melanctha Herbert was sixteen when she first met Jane Harden. Jane was a negress, but she was so white that hardly any one could guess it. Jane had had a good deal of education. She had been two years at a colored college. She had had to leave because of her bad conduct. She taught Melanctha many things. She taught her how to go the ways that lead to wisdom.

Jane Harden was at this time twenty-three years old and she had had much experience. She was very much attracted by Melanctha, and Melanctha was very proud that this Jane would let her know her.

Jane Harden was not afraid to understand. Melanctha who had strong the sense for real experience, knew that here was a woman who had learned to understand.

Jane Harden had many bad habits. She drank a great deal, and she wandered widely. She was safe though now, when she wanted to be safe, in this wandering.

Melanctha Herbert soon always wandered with her. Melanctha tried the drinking and some of the other habits, but she did not find that she cared very much to do them. But every day she grew stronger in her desire to really understand.

It was now no longer, even in the daylight, the rougher men that these two learned to know in their wanderings, and for Melanctha the better classes were now a little higher. It was no longer express agents and clerks that she learned to know, but men in business, commercial travelers, and even men above these, and Jane and she would talk and walk and laugh and escape from them all very often. It was still the same, the knowing of them and the always just escaping, only now for Melanctha somehow it was different, for though it was always the same thing that happened it had a different flavor, for now Melanctha was with a woman who had wisdom, and dimly she began to see what it was that she should understand.

It was not from the men that Melanctha learned her wisdom. It was always Jane Harden herself who was making Melanctha begin to understand.

Jane was a roughened woman. She had power and she liked to use it, she had much white blood and that made her see clear, she liked drinking and that made her reckless. Her white blood was strong in her and she had grit and endurance and a vital courage. She was always game, however much she was in trouble. She liked Melanctha Herbert for the things that she had like her, and then Melanctha was young, and she had sweetness, and a way of listening with intelligence and sympathetic interest, to the stories that Jane Harden often told out of her experience.

Jane grew always fonder of Melanctha. Soon they began to wander, more to be together than to see men and learn their various ways of working. Then they began not to wander, and Melanctha would spend long hours with Jane in her room, sitting at her feet and listening to her stories, and feeling her strength and the power of her affection, and slowly she began to see clear before her one certain way that would be sure to lead to wisdom.

Before the end came, the end of the two years in which Melanctha spent all her time when she was not at school or in her home, with Jane Harden, before these two years were finished, Melanctha had come to see very clear, and she had come to be very certain, what it is that gives the world its wisdom.

Jane Harden always had a little money and she had a room in the lower part of the town. Jane had once taught in a colored school. She had had to leave that too on account of her bad conduct. It was her drinking that always made all the trouble for her, for that can never be really covered over.

Jane's drinking was always growing worse upon her. Melanctha had tried to do the drinking but it had no real attraction for her.

In the first year, between Jane Harden and Melanctha Herbert, Jane had been much the stronger. Jane loved Melanctha and she found her always intelligent and brave and sweet and docile, and Jane meant to, and before the year was over she had taught Melanctha what it is that gives many people in the world their wisdom.

Jane had many ways in which to do this teaching. She told Melanctha many things. She loved Melanctha hard and made Melanctha feel it very deeply. She would be with other

people and with men and with Melanctha, and she would
make Melanctha understand what everybody wanted, and
what one did with power when one had it.

Melanctha sat at Jane's feet for many hours in these days
and felt Jane's wisdom. She learned to love Jane and to have
this feeling very deeply. She learned a little in these days to
know joy, and she was taught too how very keenly she could
suffer. It was very different this suffering from that Melanctha sometimes had from her mother and from her very unendurable black father. Then she was fighting and she could
be strong and valiant in her suffering, but there with Jane
Harden she was longing and she bent and pleaded with her
suffering.

It was a very tumultuous, very mingled year, this time for
Melanctha, but she certainly did begin to really understand.

In every way she got it from Jane Harden. There was
nothing good or bad in doing, feeling, thinking or in talking,
that Jane spared her. Sometimes the lesson came almost too
strong for Melanctha, but somehow she always managed to
endure it and so slowly, but always with increasing strength
and feeling, Melanctha began to really understand.

Then slowly, between them, it began to be all different.
Slowly now between them, it was Melanctha Herbert, who
was stronger. Slowly now they began to drift apart from one
another.

Melanctha Herbert never really lost her sense that it was
Jane Harden who had taught her, but Jane did many things
that Melanctha now no longer needed. And then, too,
Melanctha never could remember right when it came to
what she had done and what had happened. Melanctha now
sometimes quarreled with Jane, and they no longer went
about together, and sometimes Melanctha really forgot how
much she owed to Jane Harden's teaching.

Melanctha began now to feel that she had always had
world wisdom. She really knew of course, that it was Jane

who had taught her, but all that began to be covered over by the trouble between them, that was now always getting stronger.

Jane Harden was a roughened woman. Once she had been very strong, but now she was weakened in all her kinds of strength by her drinking. Melanctha had tried the drinking but it had had no real attraction for her.

Jane's strong and roughened nature and her drinking made it always harder for her to forgive Melanctha, that now Melanctha did not really need her any longer. Now it was Melanctha who was stronger and it was Jane who was dependent on her.

Melanctha was now come to be about eighteen years old. She was a graceful, pale yellow, good looking, intelligent, attractive negress, a little mysterious sometimes in her ways, and always good and pleasant, and always ready to do things for people.

Melanctha from now on saw very little of Jane Harden. Jane did not like that very well and sometimes she abused Melanctha, but her drinking soon covered everything all over.

It was not in Melanctha's nature to really lose her sense for Jane Harden. Melanctha all her life was ready to help Jane out in any of her trouble, and later, when Jane really went to pieces, Melanctha always did all that she could to help her.

But Melanctha Herbert was ready now herself to do teaching. Melanctha could do anything now that she wanted. Melanctha knew now what everybody wanted.

Melanctha had learned how she might stay a little longer; she had learned that she must decide when she wanted really to stay longer, and she had learned how when she wanted to, she could escape.

And so Melanctha began once more to wander. It was all now for her very different. It was never rougher men now

that she talked to, and she did not care much now to know
white men of the, for her, very better classes. It was now
something realer that Melanctha wanted, something that
would move her very deeply, something that would fill her
fully with the wisdom that she planted now within her, and
that she wanted badly, should really wholly fill her.

Melanctha these days wandered very widely. She was always alone now when she wandered. Melanctha did not
need help now to know, or to stay longer, or when she
wanted to escape.

Melanctha tried a great many men, in these days before
she was really suited. It was almost a year that she wandered
and then she met with a young mulatto. He was a doctor
who had just begun to practice. He would most likely do
well in the future, but it was not this that concerned Melanctha. She found him good and strong and gentle and very in-
tellectual, and all her life Melanctha liked and wanted good
and considerate people, and then too he did not at first believe in Melanctha. He held off and did not know what it
was that Melanctha wanted. Melanctha came to want him
very badly. They began to know each other better. Things
began to be very strong between them. Melanctha wanted
him so badly that now she never wandered. She just gave
herself to this experience.

Melanctha Herbert was now, all alone, in Bridgepoint.
She lived now with this colored woman and now with that
one, and she sewed, and sometimes she taught a little in a
colored school as substitute for some teacher. Melanctha had
now no home nor any regular employment. Life was just
commencing for Melanctha. She had youth and had learned
wisdom, and she was graceful and pale yellow and very
pleasant, and always ready to do things for people, and she
was mysterious in her ways and that only made belief in her
more fervent.

During the year before she met Jefferson Campbell,

Melanctha had tried many kinds of men but they had none of them interested Melanctha very deeply. She met them, she was much with them, she left them, she would think perhaps this next time it would be more exciting, and always she found that for her it all had no real meaning. She could now do everything she wanted, she knew now everything that everybody wanted, and yet it all had no excitement for her. With these men, she knew she could learn nothing. She wanted some one that could teach her very deeply and now at last she was sure that she had found him, yes she really had it, before she had thought to look if in this man she would find it.

During this year 'Mis' Herbert as her neighbors called her, Melanctha's pale yellow mother was very sick, and in this year she died.

Melanctha's father during these last years did not come very often to the house where his wife lived and Melanctha. Melanctha was not sure that her father was now any longer in Bridgepoint. It was Melanctha who was very good now to her mother. It was always Melanctha's way to be good to any one in trouble.

Melanctha took good care of her mother. She did anything that any woman could, she tended and soothed and helped her pale yellow mother, and she worked hard in every way to take care of her, and make her dying easy. But Melanctha did not in these days like her mother any better, and her mother never cared much for this daughter who was always a hard child to manage, and who had a tongue that always could be very nasty.

Melanctha did everything that any woman could, and at last her mother died, and Melanctha had her buried. Melanctha's father was not heard from, and Melanctha in all her life after, never saw or heard or knew of anything that her father did.

It was the young doctor, Jefferson Campbell, who helped

Melanctha toward the end, to take care of her sick mother. Jefferson Campbell had often before seen Melanctha Herbert, but he had never liked her very well, and he had never believed that she was any good. He had heard something about how she wandered. He knew a little too of Jane Harden, and he was sure that this Melanctha Herbert, who was her friend and who wandered, would never come to any good.

Dr. Jefferson Campbell was a serious, earnest, good young joyous doctor. He liked to take care of everybody and he loved his own colored people. He always found life very easy did Jeff Campbell, and everybody liked to have him with them. He was so good and sympathetic, and he was so earnest and so joyous. He sang when he was happy, and he laughed, and his was the free abandoned laughter that gives the warm broad glow to negro sunshine.

Jeff Campbell had never yet in his life had real trouble. Jefferson's father was a good, kind, serious, religious man. He was a very steady, very intelligent, and very dignified, light brown, grey haired negro. He was a butler and he had worked for the Campbell family many years, and his father and his mother before him had been in the service of this family as free people.

Jefferson Campbell's father and his mother had of course been regularly married. Jefferson's mother was a sweet, little, pale brown, gentle woman who reverenced and obeyed her good husband, and who worshipped and admired and loved hard her good, earnest, cheery, hard working doctor boy who was her only child.

Jeff Campbell had been raised religious by his people but religion had never interested Jeff very much. Jefferson was very good. He loved his people and he never hurt them, and he always did everything they wanted and that he could to please them, but he really loved best science and experimenting and to learn things, and he early wanted to be a doctor, and he was always very interested in the life of the colored people.

The Campbell family had been very good to him and had helped him on with his ambition. Jefferson studied hard, he went to a colored college, and then he learnt to be a doctor.

It was now two or three years, that he had started in to practice. Everybody liked Jeff Campbell, he was so strong and kindly and cheerful and understanding, and he laughed so with pure joy, and he always liked to help all his own colored people.

Dr. Jeff knew all about Jane Harden. He had taken care of her in some of her bad trouble. He knew about Melanctha too, though until her mother was taken sick he had never met her. Then he was called in to help Melanctha to take care of her sick mother. Dr. Campbell did not like Melanctha's ways and he did not think that she would ever come to any good.

Dr. Campbell had taken care of Jane Harden in some of her bad trouble. Jane sometimes had abused Melanctha to him. What right had that Melanctha Herbert who owed everything to her, Jane Harden, what right had a girl like that to go away to other men and leave her, but Melanctha Herbert never had any sense of how to act to anybody. Melanctha had a good mind, Jane never denied her that, but she never used it to do anything decent with it. But what could you expect when Melanctha had such a brute of a black nigger father, and Melanctha was always abusing her father and yet she was just like him, and really she admired him so much and he never had any sense of what he owed to anybody, and Melanctha was just like him and she was proud of it too, and it made Jane so tired to hear Melanctha talk all the time as if she wasn't. Jane Harden hated people who had good minds and didn't use them, and Melanctha always had that weakness, and wanting to keep in with people, and never really saying that she wanted to be like her father, and it was so silly of Melanctha to abuse her father, when she was so much like him and she really liked it. No, Jane Harden had no use for Melanctha. Oh yes, Melanctha always came around to be good to her. Melanctha was always sure to do that. She never really went away and left one. She didn't use her mind enough to do things straight out like that. Melanctha Herbert had a good mind, Jane never denied that to her, but she never wanted to see or hear about Melanctha Herbert any more, and she wished Melanctha wouldn't come in any more to see her. She didn't hate her, but she didn't want to hear about her father and all that talk Melanctha always made, and that just meant nothing to her. Jane Harden was very tired of all that now. She didn't have any use now any more for Melanctha, and if Dr. Campbell saw her he better tell her Jane didn't want to see her, and she could take her talk to somebody else, who was ready to believe her. And then Jane Harden would drop away and forget Melanctha and all her life before, and then she would begin to drink and so she would cover everything all over.

Jeff Campbell heard all this very often, but it did not interest him very deeply. He felt no desire to know more of this Melanctha. He heard her, once, talking to another girl outside of the house, when he was paying a visit to Jane Harden. He did not see much in the talk that he heard her do. He did not see much in the things Jane Harden said when she abused Melanctha to him. He was more interested in Jane herself than in anything he heard about Melanctha. He knew Jane Harden had a good mind, and she had had power, and she could really have done things, and now this drinking covered everything all over. Jeff Campbell was always very sorry when he had to see it. Jane Harden was a roughened woman, and yet Jeff found a great many strong good things in her, that still made him like her.

Jeff Campbell did everything he could for Jane Harden. He did not care much to hear about Melanctha. He had no feeling, much, about her. He did not find that he took any interest in her. Jane Harden was so much a stronger woman, and Jane really had had a good mind, and she had used it to do things with it, before this drinking business had taken such a hold upon her.

Dr. Campbell was helping Melanctha Herbert to take care of her sick mother. He saw Melanctha now for long times and very often, and they sometimes talked a good deal together, but Melanctha never said anything to him about Jane Harden. She never talked to him about anything that was not just general matters, or about medicine, or to tell him funny stories. She asked him many questions and always listened very well to all he told her, and she always remembered everything she heard him say about doctoring, and she always remembered everything that she had learned from all the others.

Jeff Campbell never found that all this talk interested him deeply. He did not find that he liked Melanctha when he saw her so much, any better. He never found that he thought much about Melanctha. He never found that he believed much in her having a good mind, like Jane Harden. He found he liked Jane Harden always better, and that he wished very much that she had never begun that bad drinking.

Melanctha Herbert's mother was now always getting sicker. Melanctha really did everything that any woman could. Melanctha's mother never liked her daughter any better. She never said much, did 'Mis' Herbert, but anybody could see that she did not think much of this daughter.

Dr. Campbell now often had to stay a long time to take care of 'Mis' Herbert. One day 'Mis' Herbert was much sicker and Dr. Campbell thought that this night, she would surely die. He came back late to the house, as he had said he would, to sit up and watch 'Mis' Herbert, and to help Melanctha, if she should need anybody to be with her.

Melanctha Herbert and Jeff Campbell sat up all that night together. 'Mis' Herbert did not die. The next day she was a little better.

This house where Melanctha had always lived with her mother was a little red brick, two story house. They had not much furniture to fill it and some of the windows were broken and not mended. Melanctha did not have much money to use now on the house, but with a colored woman, who was their neighbor and good natured and who had always helped them, Melanctha managed to take care of her mother and to keep the house fairly clean and neat.

Melanctha's mother was in bed in a room upstairs, and the steps from below led right up into it. There were just two rooms on this upstairs floor. Melanctha and Dr. Campbell sat down on the steps, that night they watched together, so that they could hear and see Melanctha's mother and yet the light would be shaded, and they could sit and read, if they wanted to, and talk low some, and yet not disturb 'Mis' Herbert.

Dr. Campbell was always very fond of reading. Dr. Campbell had not brought a book with him that night. He had just forgotten it. He had meant to put something in his pocket to read, so that he could amuse himself, while he was sitting there and watching. When he was through with taking care of 'Mis' Herbert, he came and sat down on the steps just above where Melanctha was sitting. He spoke about how he had forgotten to bring his book with him. Melanctha said there were some old papers in the house, perhaps Dr. Campbell could find something in them that would help pass the time for a while for him. All right, Dr. Campbell said, that would be better than just sitting there with nothing. Dr. Campbell began to read through the old papers that Melanctha gave him. When anything amused him in them, he read it out to Melanctha. Melanctha was now pretty silent, with him. Dr. Campbell began to feel a little, about how she responded to him. Dr. Campbell began to see a little that perhaps Melanctha had a good mind. Dr. Campbell was not sure yet that she had a good mind, but he began to think a little that perhaps she might have one.

Jefferson Campbell always liked to talk to everybody about the things he worked at and about his thinking about what he could do for the colored people. Melanctha Herbert never thought about these things the way that he did. Melanctha had never said much to Dr. Campbell about what she thought about them. Melanctha did not feel the same as he did about being good and regular in life, and not having excitements all the time, which was the way that Jefferson Campbell wanted that everybody should be, so that everybody would be wise and yet be happy. Melanctha always had strong the sense for real experience. Melanctha Herbert did not think much of this way of coming to real wisdom.

Dr. Campbell soon got through with his reading, in the old newspapers, and then somehow he began to talk along about the things he was always thinking. Dr. Campbell said he wanted to work so that he could understand what troubled people, and not to just have excitements, and he believed you ought to love your father and your mother and to be regular in all your life, and not to be always wanting new things and excitements, and to always know where you were, and what you wanted, and to always tell everything just as you meant it. That's the only kind of life he knew or believed in, Jeff Campbell repeated. "No I ain't got any use for all the time being in excitements and wanting to have all kinds of experience all the time. I got plenty of experience just living regular and quiet and with my family, and doing my work, and taking care of people, and trying to understand it. I don't believe much in this running around business and I don't want to see the colored people do it. I am a colored man and I ain't sorry, and I want to see the colored people like what is good and what I want them to have, and that's to live regular and work hard and understand things, and that's enough to keep any decent man excited." Jeff Campbell spoke now with some anger. Not to Melanctha, he did not think of her at all when he was talking. It was the life he wanted that he spoke to, and the way he wanted things to be with the colored people.

But Melanctha Herbert had listened to him say all this. She knew he meant it, but it did not mean much to her, and she was sure some day he would find out, that it was not all, of real wisdom. Melanctha knew very well what it was to have real wisdom. "But how about Jane Harden?" said Melanctha to Jeff Campbell, "seems to me Dr. Campbell you find her to have something in her, and you go there very often, and you talk to her much more than you do to the nice girls that stay at home with their people, the kind you say you are really wanting. It don't seem to me Dr. Campbell, that what you say and what you do seem to have much to do with each other. And about your being so good Dr. Campbell," went on Melanctha, "You don't care about going to church much yourself, and yet you always are saying you believe so much in things like that, for people. It seems to me, Dr. Campbell you want to have a good time just like all us others, and then you just keep on saying that it's right to be good and you ought not to have excitements, and yet you really don't want to do it Dr. Campbell, no more than me or Jane Harden. No, Dr. Campbell, it certainly does seem to me you don't know very well yourself, what you mean, when you are talking."

Jefferson had been talking right along, the way he always did when he got started, and now Melanctha's answer only made him talk a little harder. He laughed a little, too, but very low, so as not to disturb 'Mis' Herbert who was sleeping very nicely, and he looked brightly at Melanctha to enjoy her, and then he settled himself down to answer.

"Yes," he began, "it certainly does sound a little like I

didn't know very well what I do mean, when you put it like that to me, Miss Melanctha, but that's just because you don't understand enough about what I meant, by what I was just saying to you. I don't say, never, I don't want to know all kinds of people, Miss Melanctha, and I don't say there ain't many kinds of people, and I don't say ever, that I don't find some like Jane Harden very good to know and talk to, but it's the strong things I like in Jane Harden, not all her excitements. I don't admire the bad things she does, Miss Melanctha, but Jane Harden is a strong woman and I always respect that in her. No I know you don't believe what I say, Miss Melanctha, but I mean it, and it's all just because you don't understand it when I say it. And as for religion, that just ain't my way of being good, Miss Melanctha, but it's a good way for many people to be good and regular in their way of living, and if they believe it, it helps them to be good, and if they're honest in it, I like to see them have it. No, what I don't like, Miss Melanctha, is this what I see so much with the colored people, their always wanting new things just to get excited."

Jefferson Campbell here stopped himself in this talking. Melanctha Herbert did not make any answer. They both sat there very quiet.

Jeff Campbell then began again on the old papers. He sat there on the steps just above where Melanctha was sitting, and he went on with his reading, and his head went moving up and down, and sometimes he was reading, and sometimes he was thinking about all the things he wanted to be doing, and then he would rub the back of his dark hand over his mouth, and in between he would be frowning with his thinking, and sometimes he would be rubbing his head hard to help his thinking. And Melanctha just sat still and watched the lamp burning, and sometimes she turned it down a little, when the wind caught it and it would begin to get to smoking.

And so Jeff Campbell and Melanctha Herbert sat there on the steps, very quiet, a long time, and they didn't seem to think much, that they were together. They sat there so, for about an hour, and then it came to Jefferson very slowly and as a strong feeling that he was sitting there on the steps, alone, with Melanctha. He did not know if Melanctha Herbert was feeling very much about their being there alone together. Jefferson began to wonder about it a little. Slowly he felt that surely they must both have this feeling. It was so important that he knew that she must have it. They both sat there, very quiet, a long time.

At last Jefferson began to talk about how the lamp was smelling. Jefferson began to explain what it is that makes a lamp get to smelling. Melanctha let him talk. She did not answer, and then he stopped in his talking. Soon Melanctha began to sit up straighter and then she started in to question.

"About what you was just saying Dr. Campbell about living regular and all that, I certainly don't understand what you meant by what you was just saying. You ain't a bit like good people Dr. Campbell, like the good people you are always saying are just like you. I know good people Dr. Campbell, and you ain't a bit like men who are good and got religion. You are just as free and easy as any man can be Dr. Campbell, and you always like to be with Jane Harden, and she is a pretty bad one and you don't look down on her and you never tell her she is a bad one. I know you like her just like a friend Dr. Campbell, and so I certainly don't understand just what it is you mean by all that you was just saying to me. I know you mean honest Dr. Campbell, and I am always trying to believe you, but I can't say as I see just what you mean when you say you want to be good and real pious, because I am very certain Dr. Campbell that you ain't that kind of a man at all, and you ain't never ashamed to be with queer folks Dr. Campbell, and you seem to be thinking what you are doing is just like what you are always saying, and Dr. Campbell, I certainly don't just see what you mean by what you say."

Dr. Campbell almost laughed loud enough to wake 'Mis' Herbert. He did enjoy the way Melanctha said these things to him. He began to feel very strongly about it that perhaps Melanctha really had a good mind. He was very free now in his laughing, but not so as to make Melanctha angry. He was very friendly with her in his laughing, and then he made his face get serious, and he rubbed his head to help him in his thinking.

"I know Miss Melanctha," he began, "It ain't very easy for you to understand what I was meaning by what I was just saying to you, and perhaps some of the good people I like so wouldn't think very much, any more than you do, Miss Melanctha, about the ways I have to be good. But that's no matter Miss Melanctha. What I mean Miss Melanctha by what I was saying to you is, that I don't, no, never, believe in doing things just to get excited. You see Miss Melanctha I mean the way so many of the colored people do it. Instead of just working hard and caring about their working and living regular and with their families and saving up all their money, so they will have some to bring up their children better, instead of living regular and doing like that and getting all their new ways from just decent living, the colored people just keep running around and perhaps drinking and doing everything bad they can ever think of, and not just because they like all those bad things that they are always doing, but only just because they want to get excited. No Miss Melanctha, you see I am a colored man myself and I ain't sorry, and I want to see the colored people being good and careful and always honest and living always just as regular as can be, and I am sure Miss Melanctha, that that way everybody can have a good time, and be happy and keep right and be busy, and not always have to be doing bad things for new ways to get excited. Yes Miss Melanctha, I certainly do like everything to be good, and quiet, and I certainly do think that is the best way for all us colored people. No, Miss Melanctha too, I don't mean this except only just the way I say it. I ain't got any other meaning Miss Melanctha, and it's that what I mean when I am saying about being really good. It ain't Miss Melanctha to be pious and not liking every kind of people, and I don't say ever Miss Melanctha that when other kind of people come regular into your life you shouldn't want to know them always. What I mean Miss Melanctha by what I am always saying is, you shouldn't try to know everybody just to run around and get excited. It's that kind of way of doing that I hate so always Miss Melanctha, and that is so bad for all us colored people. I don't know as you understand now any better what I mean by what I was just saying to you. But you certainly do know now Miss Melanctha, that I always mean it what I say when I am talking."

"Yes I certainly do understand you when you talk so Dr. Campbell. I certainly understand now what you mean by what you was always saying to me. I certainly do understand Dr. Campbell that you mean you don't believe it's right to love anybody." "Why sure no, yes I do Miss Melanctha, I certainly do believe strong in loving, and in being good to everybody, and trying to understand what they all need, to help them." "Oh I know all about that way of doing Dr. Campbell, but that certainly ain't the kind of love I mean when I am talking. I mean real, strong, hot love Dr. Campbell, that makes you do anything for somebody that loves you." "I don't know much about that kind of love yet Miss Melanctha. You see it's this way with me always Miss Melanctha. I am always so busy with my thinking about my work I am doing and so I don't have time for just fooling, and then too, you see Miss Melanctha, I really certainly don't ever like to get excited, and that kind of loving hard does seem always to mean just getting all the time excited.

That certainly is what I always think from what I see of them that have it bad Miss Melanctha, and that certainly would never suit a man like me. You see Miss Melanctha I am a very quiet kind of fellow, and I believe in a quiet life for all the colored people. No Miss Melanctha I certainly never have mixed myself up in that kind of trouble."

"Yes I certainly do see that very clear Dr. Campbell," said Melanctha, "I see that's certainly what it is always made me not know right about you and that's certainly what it is that makes you really mean what you was always saying. You certainly are just too scared Dr. Campbell to really feel things way down in you. All you are always wanting Dr. Campbell, is just to talk about being good, and to play with people just to have a good time, and yet always to certainly keep yourself out of trouble. It don't seem to me Dr. Campbell that I admire that way to do things very much. It certainly ain't really to me being very good. It certainly ain't any more to me Dr. Campbell, but that you certainly are awful scared about really feeling things way down in you, and that's certainly the only way Dr. Campbell I can see that you can mean, by what it is that you are always saying to me."

"I don't know about that Miss Melanctha, I certainly don't think I can't feel things very deep in me, though I do say I certainly do like to have things nice and quiet, but I don't see harm in keeping out of danger Miss Melanctha, when a man knows he certainly don't want to get killed in it, and I don't know anything that's more awful dangerous Miss Melanctha than being strong in love with somebody. I don't mind sickness or real trouble Miss Melanctha, and I don't want to be talking about what I can do in real trouble, but you know something about that Miss Melanctha, but I certainly don't see much in mixing up just to get excited, in that awful kind of danger. No Miss Melanctha I certainly do only know just two kinds of ways of loving. One kind of loving seems to me, is like one has a good quiet feeling in a family when one does his work, and is always living good and being regular, and then the other way of loving is just like having it like any animal that's low in the streets together, and that don't seem to me very good Miss Melanctha, though I don't say ever that it's not all right when anybody likes it, and that's all the kinds of love I know Miss Melanctha, and I certainly don't care very much to get mixed up in that kind of a way just to be in trouble."

Jefferson stopped and Melanctha thought a little.

"That certainly does explain to me Dr. Campbell what I been thinking about you this long time. I certainly did wonder how you could be so live, and knowing everything, and everybody, and talking so big always about everything, and everybody always liking you so much, and you always looking as if you was thinking, and yet you really was never knowing about anybody and certainly not being really very understanding. It certainly is all Dr. Campbell because you is so afraid you will be losing being good so easy, and it certainly do seem to me Dr. Campbell that it certainly don't amount to very much that kind of goodness."

"Perhaps you are right Miss Melanctha," Jefferson answered. "I don't say never, perhaps you ain't right Miss Melanctha. Perhaps I ought to know more about such ways Miss Melanctha. Perhaps it would help me some, taking care of the colored people, Miss Melanctha. I don't say, no, never, but perhaps I could learn a whole lot about women the right way, if I had a real good teacher."

'Mis' Herbert just then stirred a little in her sleep. Melanctha went up the steps to the bed to attend her. Dr. Campbell got up too and went to help her. 'Mis' Herbert woke up and was a little better. Now it was morning and Dr. Campbell gave his directions to Melanctha, and then left her.

Melanctha Herbert all her life long, loved and wanted

good, kind and considerate people. Jefferson Campbell was all the things that Melanctha had ever wanted. Jefferson was a strong, well built, good looking, cheery, intelligent and good mulatto. And then at first he had not cared to know Melanctha, and when he did begin to know her he had not liked her very well, and he had not thought that she would ever come to any good. And then Jefferson Campbell was so very gentle. Jefferson never did some things like other men, things that now were beginning to be ugly, for Melanctha. And then too Jefferson Campbell did not seem to know very well what it was that Melanctha really wanted, and all this was making Melanctha feel his power with her always getting stronger.

Dr. Campbell came in every day to see 'Mis' Herbert. 'Mis' Herbert, after that night they watched together, did get a little better, but 'Mis' Herbert was really very sick, and soon it was pretty sure that she would have to die. Melanctha certainly did everything, all the time, that any woman could. Jefferson never thought much better of Melanctha while she did it. It was not her being good, he wanted to find in her. He knew very well Jane Harden was right, when she said Melanctha was always being good to everybody but that that did not make Melanctha any better for her. Then too, 'Mis' Herbert never liked Melanctha any better, even on the last day of her living, and so Jefferson really never thought much of Melanctha's always being good to her mother.

Jefferson and Melanctha now saw each other, very often. They now always liked to be with each other, and they always now had a good time when they talked to one another. They, mostly in their talking to each other, still just talked about outside things and what they were thinking. Except just in little moments, and not those very often, they never said anything about their feeling. Sometimes Melanctha would tease Jefferson a little just to show she had not forgotten, but mostly she listened to his talking, for Jefferson still always liked to talk along about the things he believed in. Melanctha was liking Jefferson Campbell better every day, and Jefferson was beginning to know that Melanctha certainly had a good mind, and he was beginning to feel a little her real sweetness. Not in her being good to 'Mis' Herbert, that never seemed to Jefferson to mean much in her, but there was a strong kind of sweetness in Melanctha's nature that Jefferson began now to feel when he was with her.

'Mis' Herbert was now always getting sicker. One night again Dr. Campbell felt very certain that before it was morning she would surely die. Dr. Campbell said he would come back to help Melanctha watch her, and to do anything he could to make 'Mis' Herbert's dying more easy for her. Dr. Campbell came back that evening, after he was through with his other patients, and then he made 'Mis' Herbert easy, and then he came and sat down on the steps just above where Melanctha was sitting with the lamp, and looking very tired. Dr. Campbell was pretty tired too, and they both sat there very quiet.

"You look awful tired to-night, Dr. Campbell," Melanctha said at last, with her voice low and very gentle, "Don't you want to go lie down and sleep a little? You're always being much too good to everybody, Dr. Campbell. I like to have you stay here watching to-night with me, but it don't seem right you ought to stay here when you got so much always to do for everybody. You are certainly very kind to come back, Dr. Campbell, but I can certainly get along to-night without you. I can get help next door sure if I need it. You just go 'long home to bed, Dr. Campbell. You certainly do look as if you need it."

Jefferson was silent for some time, and always he was looking very gently at Melanctha.

"I certainly never did think, Miss Melanctha, I would find you to be so sweet and thinking, with me." "Dr. Campbell," said Melanctha, still more gentle, "I certainly never did think that you would ever feel it good to like me. I certainly never did think you would want to see for yourself if I had sweet ways in me."

They both sat there very tired, very gentle, very quiet, a long time. At last Melanctha in a low, even tone began to talk to Jefferson Campbell.

"You are certainly a very good man, Dr. Campbell, I certainly do feel that more every day I see you. Dr. Campbell, I sure do want to be friends with a good man like you, now I know you. You certainly, Dr. Campbell, never do things like other men, that's always ugly for me. Tell me true, Dr. Campbell, how you feel about being always friends with me. I certainly do know, Dr. Campbell, you are a good man, and if you say you will be friends with me, you certainly never will go back on me, the way so many kinds of them do to every girl they ever get to like them. Tell me for true, Dr. Campbell, will you be friends with me."

"Why, Miss Melanctha," said Campbell slowly, "why you see I just can't say that right out that way to you. Why sure you know Miss Melanctha, I will be very glad if it comes by and by that we are always friends together, but you see, Miss Melanctha, I certainly am a very slow-minded quiet kind of fellow though I do say quick things all the time to everybody, and when I certainly do want to mean it what I am saying to you, I can't say things like that right out to everybody till I know really more for certain all about you, and how I like you, and what I really mean to do better for you. You certainly do see what I mean, Miss Melanctha." "I certainly do admire you for talking honest to me, Jeff Campbell," said Melanctha. "Oh, I am always honest, Miss Melanctha. It's easy enough for me always to be honest, Miss Melanctha. All I got to do is always just to say right out what I am thinking. I certainly never have any real reason for not saying it right out like that to anybody."

They sat together, very silent. "I certainly do wonder, Miss Melanctha," at last began Jeff Campbell, "I certainly do wonder, if we know very right, you and me, what each other is really thinking. I certainly do wonder, Miss Melanctha, if we know at all really what each other means by what we are always saying." "That certainly do mean, by what you say, that you think I am a bad one, Jeff Campbell," flashed out Melanctha. "Why no, Miss Melanctha, why sure I don't mean any thing like that at all, by what I am saying to you. You know well as I do, Miss Melanctha, I think better of you every day I see you, and I like to talk with you all the time now, Miss Melanctha, and I certainly do think we both like it very well when we are together, and it seems to me always more, you are very good and sweet always to everybody. It only is, I am really so slow-minded in my ways, Miss Melanctha, for all I talk so quick to everybody, and I don't like to say to you what I don't know for very sure, and I certainly don't know for sure I know just all what you mean by what you are always saying to me. And you see, Miss Melanctha, that's what makes me say what I was just saying to you when you asked me."

"I certainly do thank you again for being honest to me, Dr. Campbell," said Melanctha. "I guess I leave you now, Dr. Campbell. I think I go in the other room and rest a little. I leave you here, so perhaps if I ain't here you will maybe sleep and rest yourself a little. Good night now, Dr. Campbell, I call you if I need you later to help me, Dr. Campbell, I hope you rest well, Dr. Campbell."

Jeff Campbell, when Melanctha left him, sat there and he was very quiet and just wondered. He did not know very well just what Melanctha meant by what she was always saying to him. He did not know very well how much he really knew about Melanctha Herbert. He wondered if he should go on being so much all the time with her. He began to think about what he should do now with her. Jefferson

Campbell was a man who liked everybody and many people liked very much to be with him. Women liked him, he was so strong, and good, and understanding, and innocent, and firm, and gentle. Sometimes they seemed to want very much he should be with them. When they got so, they always had made Campbell very tired. Sometimes he would play a little with them, but he never had had any strong feeling for them. Now with Melanctha Herbert everything seemed different. Jefferson was not sure that he knew here just what he wanted. He was not sure he knew just what it was that Melanctha wanted. He knew if it was only play, with Melanctha, that he did not want to do it. But he remembered always how she had told him he never knew how to feel things very deeply. He remembered how she told him he was afraid to let himself ever know real feeling, and then too, most of all to him, she had told him he was not very understanding. That always troubled Jefferson very keenly, he wanted very badly to be really understanding. If Jefferson only knew better just what Melanctha meant by what she said. Jefferson always had thought he knew something about women. Now he found that really he knew nothing. He did not know the least bit about Melanctha. He did not know what it was right that he should do about it. He wondered if it was just a little play that they were doing. If it was a play he did not want to go on playing, but if it was really that he was not very understanding, and that with Melanctha Herbert he could learn to really understand, then he was very certain he did not want to be a coward. It was very hard for him to know what he wanted. He thought and thought, and always did not seem to know any better what he wanted. At last he gave up this thinking. He felt sure it was only play with Melanctha. "No, I certainly won't go on fooling with her any more this way," he said at last out loud to himself, when he was through with this thinking. "I certainly will stop fooling, and begin to go on with my thinking about my work and what's the matter with people like 'Mis' Herbert," and Jefferson took out his book from his pocket, and drew near to the lamp, and began with some hard scientific reading.

Jefferson sat there for about an hour reading, and he had really forgotten all about his trouble with Melanctha's meaning. Then 'Mis' Herbert had some trouble with her breathing. She woke up and was gasping. Dr. Campbell went to her and gave her something that would help her. Melanctha came out from the other room and did things as he told her. They together made 'Mis' Herbert more comfortable and easy, and soon she was again in her deep sleep.

Dr. Campbell went back to the steps where he had been sitting. Melanctha came and stood a little while beside him, and then she sat down and watched him reading. By and by they began with their talking. Jeff Campbell began to feel that perhaps it was all different. Perhaps it was not just play, with Melanctha. Anyway he liked it very well that she was with him. He began to tell her about the book he was just reading.

Melanctha was very intelligent always in her questions. Jefferson knew now very well that she had a good mind. They were having a very good time, talking there together. And then they began again to get quiet.

"It certainly was very good in you to come back and talk to me Miss Melanctha," Jefferson said at last to her, for now he was almost certain, it was no game she was playing. Melanctha really was a good woman, and she had a good mind, and she had a real, strong sweetness, and she could surely really teach him. "Oh I always like to talk to you Dr. Campbell," said Melanctha, "And then you was only just honest to me, and I always like it when a man is really honest to me." Then they were again very silent, sitting there together, with the lamp between them, that was always smoking. Melanctha began to lean a little more toward Dr.

Campbell, where he was sitting, and then she took his hand between her two and pressed it hard, but she said nothing to him. She let it go then and leaned a little nearer to him. Jefferson moved a little but did not do anything in answer. At last, "Well," said Melanctha sharply to him. "I was just thinking," began Dr. Campbell slowly, "I was just wondering," he was beginning to get ready to go on with his talking. "Don't you ever stop with your thinking long enough ever to have any feeling Jeff Campbell," said Melanctha a little sadly. "I don't know," said Jeff Campbell slowly, "I don't know Miss Melanctha much about that. No, I don't stop thinking much Miss Melanctha and if I can't ever feel without stopping thinking, I certainly am very much afraid Miss Melanctha that I never will do much with that kind of feeling. Sure you ain't worried Miss Melanctha, about my really not feeling very much all the time. I certainly do think I feel some, Miss Melanctha, even though I always do it without ever knowing how to stop with my thinking." "I am certainly afraid I don't think much of your kind of feeling Dr. Campbell." "Why I think you certainly are wrong Miss Melanctha. I certainly do think I feel as much for you Miss Melanctha, as you ever feel about me, sure I do. I don't think you know me right when you talk like that to me. Tell me just straight out how much do you care about me, Miss Melanctha." "Care about you Jeff Campbell," said Melanctha slowly. "I certainly do care for you Jeff Campbell less than you are always thinking and much more than you are ever knowing."

Jeff Campbell paused on this, and he was silent with the power of Melanctha's meaning. They sat there together very silent, a long time. "Well Jeff Campbell," said Melanctha. "Oh," said Mr. Campbell and he moved himself a little, and then they were very silent a long time. "Haven't you got nothing to say to me Jeff Campbell?" said Melanctha. "Why yes, what was it we were just saying about to one another.

You see Miss Melanctha I am a very quiet, slow-minded kind of fellow, and I am never sure I know just exactly what you mean by all that you are always saying to me. But I do like you very much Miss Melanctha and I am very sure you got very good things in you all the time. You sure do believe what I am saying to you Miss Melanctha." "Yes I believe it when you say it to me, Jeff Campbell," said Melanctha, and then she was silent and there was much sadness in it. "I guess I go in and lie down again Dr. Campbell," said Melanctha. "Don't go leave me Miss Melanctha," said Jeff Campbell quickly. "Why not, what you want of me Jeff Campbell?" said Melanctha. "Why," said Jeff Campbell slowly, "I just want to go on talking with you. I certainly do like talking about all kinds of things with you. You certainly know that all right, Miss Melanctha." "I guess I go lie down again and leave you here with your thinking," said Melanctha gently. "I certainly am very tired to-night Dr. Campbell. Good night I hope you rest well Dr. Campbell." Melanctha stooped over him, where he was sitting, to say this good night, and then, very quick and sudden, she kissed him and then, very quick again, she went away and left him.

Dr. Campbell sat there very quiet, with only a little thinking and sometimes a beginning feeling, and he was alone until it began to be morning, and then he went, and Melanctha helped him, and he made 'Mis' Herbert more easy in her dying. 'Mis' Herbert lingered on till about ten o'clock the next morning, and then slowly and without much pain she died away. Jeff Campbell staid till the last moment, with Melanctha, to make her mother's dying easy for her. When it was over he sent in the colored woman from next door to help Melanctha fix things, and then he went away to take care of his other patients. He came back very soon to Melanctha. He helped her to have a funeral for her mother. Melanctha then went to live with the good natured woman, who had been her neighbor. Melanctha still saw Jeff Camp-

bell very often. Things began to be very strong between
them.

Melanctha now never wandered, unless she was with Jeff
Campbell. Sometimes she and he wandered a good deal together. Jeff Campbell had not got over his way of talking to
her all the time about all the things he was always thinking.
Melanctha never talked much, now, when they were together. Sometimes Jeff Campbell teased her about her not
talking to him. "I certainly did think Melanctha you was a
good talker from the way Jane Harden and everybody said
things to me, and from the way I heard talk so much when I
first met you. Tell me true Melanctha, why don't you talk
more now to me, perhaps it is I talk so much I don't give you
any chance to say things to me, or perhaps it is you hear me
talk so much you don't think so much now of a whole lot of
talking. Tell me honest Melanctha, why don't you talk more
to me." "You know very well Jeff Campbell," said Melanctha. "You certainly do know very well Jeff, you don't think
really much, of my talking. You think a whole lot more
about everything than I do Jeff, and you don't care much
what I got to say about it. You know that's true what I am
saying Jeff, if you want to be real honest, the way you always are when I like you so much." Jeff laughed and looked
fondly at her. "I don't say ever I know, you ain't right, when
you say things like that to me, Melanctha. You see you always like to be talking just what you think everybody wants
to be hearing from you, and when you are like that, Melanctha, honest, I certainly don't care very much to hear you, but
sometimes you say something that is what you are really
thinking, and then I like a whole lot to hear you talking."
Melanctha smiled, with her strong sweetness, on him, and
she felt her power very deeply. "I certainly never do talk
very much when I like anybody really, Jeff. You see, Jeff, it
ain't much use to talk about what a woman is really feeling
in her. You see all that, Jeff, better, by and by, when you get

to really feeling. You won't be so ready then always with your talking. You see, Jeff, if it don't come true what I am saying." "I don't ever say you ain't always right, Melanctha," said Jeff Campbell. "Perhaps what I call my thinking ain't really so very understanding. I don't say, no never now any more, you ain't right, Melanctha, when you really say things to me. Perhaps I see it all to be very different when I come to really see what you mean by what you are always saying to me." "You is very sweet and good to me always, Jeff Campbell," said Melanctha. "'Deed I certainly am not good to you, Melanctha. Don't I bother you all the time with my talking, but I really do like you a whole lot, Melanctha." "And I like you, Jeff Campbell, and you certainly are mother, and father, and brother, and sister, and child and everything, always to me. I can't say much about how good you been to me, Jeff Campbell, I never knew any man who was good and didn't do things ugly, before I met you to take care of me, Jeff Campbell. Good-by, Jeff, come see me tomorrow, when you get through with your working." "Sure Melanctha, you know that already," said Jeff Campbell, and then he went away and left her.

These months had been an uncertain time for Jeff Campbell. He never knew how much he really knew about Melanctha. He saw her now for long times and very often. He was beginning always more and more to like her. But he did not seem to himself to know very much about her. He was beginning to feel he could almost trust the goodness in her. But then, always, really, he was not very sure about her. Melanctha always had ways that made him feel uncertain with her, and yet he was so near, in his feeling for her. He now never thought about all this in real words any more. He was always letting it fight itself out in him. He was now never taking any part in this fighting that was always going on inside him.

Jeff always loved now to be with Melanctha and yet he

always hated to go to her. Somehow he was always afraid
when he was to go to her, and yet he had made himself very
certain that here he would not be a coward. He never felt any
of this being afraid, when he was with her. Then they always
were very true, and near to one another. But always he was
going to her, Jeff would like anything that could happen that
would keep him a little longer from her.

It was a very uncertain time, all these months, for Jeff
Campbell. He did not know very well what it was that he really wanted. He was very certain that he did not know very
well what it was that Melanctha wanted. Jeff Campbell had
always all his life loved to be with people, and he had loved
all his life always to be thinking, but he was still only a great
boy, was Jeff Campbell, and he had never before had any of
this funny kind of feeling. Now, this evening, when he was
free to go and see Melanctha, he talked to anybody he could
find who would detain him, and so it was very late when at
last he came to the house where Melanctha was waiting to
receive him.

Jeff came in to where Melanctha was waiting for him,
and he took off his hat and heavy coat, and then drew up a
chair and sat down by the fire. It was very cold that night,
and Jeff sat there, and rubbed his hands and tried to warm
them. He had only said "How do you do" to Melanctha, he
had not yet begun to talk to her. Melanctha sat there, by the
fire, very quiet. The heat gave a pretty pink glow to her pale
yellow and attractive face. Melanctha sat in a low chair, her
hands, with their long, fluttering fingers, always ready to
show her strong feeling, were lying quiet in her lap. Melanctha was very tired with her waiting for Jeff Campbell. She
sat there very quiet and just watching. Jeff was a robust,
dark, healthy, cheery negro. His hands were firm and kindly
and unimpassioned. He touched women always with his big
hands, like a brother. He always had a warm broad glow,
like southern sunshine. He never had anything mysterious in

him. He was open, he was pleasant, he was cheery, and always he wanted, as Melanctha once had wanted, always now he too wanted really to understand.

Jeff sat there this evening in his chair and was silent a long time, warming himself with the pleasant fire. He did not look at Melanctha who was watching. He sat there and just looked into the fire. At first his dark, open face was smiling, and he was rubbing the back of his black-brown hand over his mouth to help him in his smiling. Then he was thinking, and he frowned and rubbed his head hard, to help him in his thinking. Then he smiled again, but now his smiling was not very pleasant. His smile was now wavering on the edge of scorning. His smile changed more and more, and then he had a look as if he were deeply down, all disgusted. Now his face was darker, and he was bitter in his smiling, and he began, without looking from the fire, to talk to Melanctha, who was now very tense with her watching.

"Melanctha Herbert," began Jeff Campbell, "I certainly after all this time I know you, I certainly do know little, real about you. You see, Melanctha, it's like this way with me"; Jeff was frowning, with his thinking and looking very hard into the fire, "You see it's just this way, with me now, Melanctha. Sometimes you seem like one kind of a girl to me, and sometimes you are like a girl that is all different to me, and the two kinds of girls is certainly very different to each other, and I can't see any way they seem to have much to do, to be together in you. They certainly don't seem to be made much like as if they could have anything really to do with each other. Sometimes you are a girl to me I certainly never would be trusting, and you got a laugh then so hard, it just rattles, and you got ways so bad, I can't believe you mean them hardly, and yet all that I just been saying is certainly you one way I often see you, and it's what your mother and Jane Harden always found you, and it's what makes me hate so, to come near you. And then certainly sometimes, Melanctha, you certainly is all a different creature, and sometimes then there comes out in you what is certainly a thing, like a real beauty. I certainly, Melanctha, never can tell just how it is that it comes so lovely. Seems to me when it comes it's got a real sweetness, that is more wonderful than a pure flower, and a gentleness, that is more tender than the sunshine, and a kindness, that makes one feel like summer, and then a way to know, that makes everything all over, and all that, and it does certainly seem to be real for the little while it's lasting, for the little while that I can surely see it, and it gives me to feel like I certainly had got real religion. And then when I got rich with such a feeling, comes all that other girl, and then that seems more likely that that is really you what's honest, and then I certainly do get awful afraid to come to you, and I certainly never do feel I could be very trusting with you. And then I certainly don't know anything at all about you, and I certainly don't know which is a real Melanctha Herbert, and I certainly don't feel no longer, I ever want to talk to you. Tell me honest, Melanctha, which is the way that is you really, when you are alone, and real, and all honest. Tell me, Melanctha, for I certainly do want to know it."

Melanctha did not make him any answer, and Jeff, without looking at her, after a little while, went on with his talking. "And then, Melanctha, sometimes you certainly do seem sort of cruel, and not to care about people being hurt or in trouble, something so hard about you it makes me sometimes real nervous, sometimes somehow like you always, like your being, with 'Mis' Herbert. You sure did do everything that any woman could, Melanctha, I certainly never did see anybody do things any better, and yet, I don't know how to say just what I mean, Melanctha, but there was something awful hard about your feeling, so different from the way I'm always used to see good people feeling, and so it was the way Jane Harden and 'Mis' Herbert talked when they felt strong to talk about you, and yet, Melanctha, somehow I feel so really near to you, and you certainly have got an awful wonderful, strong kind of sweetness. I certainly would like to know for sure, Melanctha, whether I got really anything to be afraid for. I certainly did think once, Melanctha, I knew something about all kinds of women. I certainly know now really, how I don't know anything sure at all about you, Melanctha, though I been with you so long, and so many times for whole hours with you, and I like so awful much to be with you, and I can always say anything I am thinking to you. I certainly do awful wish, Melanctha, I really was more understanding. I certainly do that same, Melanctha."

Jeff stopped now and looked harder than before into the fire. His face changed from his thinking back into that look that was so like as if he was all through and through him, disgusted with what he had been thinking. He sat there a long time, very quiet, and then slowly, somehow, it came strongly to him that Melanctha Herbert, there beside him, was trembling and feeling it all to be very bitter. "Why, Melanctha," cried Jeff Campbell, and he got up and put his arm around her like a brother. "I stood it just so long as I could bear it, Jeff," sobbed Melanctha, and then she gave herself away, to her misery, "I was awful ready, Jeff, to let you say anything you liked that gave you any pleasure. You could say all about me what you wanted, Jeff, and I would try to stand it, so as you would be sure to be liking it, Jeff, but you was too cruel to me. When you do that kind of seeing how much you can make a woman suffer, you ought to give her a little rest, once sometimes, Jeff. They can't any of us stand it so for always, Jeff. I certainly did stand it just as long as I could, so you would like it, but I,—oh Jeff, you went on too long to-night Jeff. I couldn't stand it not a minute longer the way you was doing of it, Jeff. When you want to be seeing how the way a woman is really made of, Jeff, you shouldn't never be so cruel, never to be thinking how much she can stand, the strong way you always do it, Jeff." "Why, Melanctha," cried Jeff Campbell, in his horror, and then he was very tender to her, and like a good, strong, gentle brother in his soothing of her, "Why Melanctha dear, I certainly don't now see what it is you mean by what you was just saying to me. Why Melanctha, you poor little girl, you certainly never did believe I ever knew I was giving you real suffering. Why, Melanctha, how could you ever like me if you thought I ever could be so like a red Indian?" "I didn't just know, Jeff," and Melanctha nestled to him, "I certainly never did know just what it was you wanted to be doing with me, but I certainly wanted you should do anything you liked, you wanted, to make me more understanding for you. I tried awful hard to stand it, Jeff, so as you could do anything you wanted with me." "Good Lord and Jesus Christ, Melanctha!" cried Jeff Campbell. "I certainly never can know anything about you real, Melanctha, you poor little girl," and Jeff drew her closer to him, "But I certainly do admire and trust you a whole lot now, Melanctha. I certainly do, for I certainly never did think I was hurting you at all, Melanctha, by the things I always been saying to you. Melanctha, you poor little, sweet, trembling baby now, be good, Melanctha. I certainly can't ever tell you how awful sorry I am to hurt you so, Melanctha. I do anything I can to show you how I never did mean to hurt you, Melanctha." "I know, I know," murmured Melanctha, clinging to him. "I know you are a good man, Jeff. I always know that, no matter how much you can hurt me." "I sure don't see how you can think so, Melanctha, if you certainly did think I was trying so hard just to hurt you." "Hush, you are only a great big boy, Jeff Campbell, and you don't know nothing yet about real hurting," said Melanctha, smiling up through her crying, at him. "You see, Jeff, I never knew anybody I could know real well and yet keep on always respecting, till I came to know you real well, Jeff." "I sure don't understand that very well, Melanctha. I ain't a bit better than just lots of others of the colored people. You certainly have been unlucky with the kind you met before me, that's all, Melanctha. I certainly ain't very good, Melanctha." "Hush, Jeff, you don't know nothing at all about what you are," said Melanctha. "Perhaps you are right, Melanctha. I don't say ever any more, you ain't right, when you say things to me, Melanctha," and Jefferson sighed, and then he smiled, and then they were quiet a long time together, and then after some more kindness, it was late, and then Jeff left her.

Jeff Campbell, all these months, had never told his good mother anything about Melanctha Herbert. Somehow he always kept his seeing her so much now, to himself. Melanctha too had never had any of her other friends meet him. They always acted together, these two, as if their being so much together was a secret, but really there was no one who would have made it any harder for them. Jeff Campbell did not really know how it had happened that they were so secret. He did not know if it was what Melanctha wanted. Jeff had never spoken to her at all about it. It just seemed as if it were well understood between them that nobody should know that they were so much together. It was as if it were agreed between them, that they should be alone by themselves always, and so they would work out together what they meant by what they were always saying to each other.

Jefferson often spoke to Melanctha about his good mother. He never said anything about whether Melanctha would want to meet her. Jefferson never quite understood why all this had happened so, in secret. He never really knew what it was that Melanctha really wanted. In all these ways he just, by his nature, did, what he sort of felt Melanctha wanted. And so they continued to be alone and much together, and now it had come to be the spring time, and now they had all out-doors to wander.

They had many days now when they were very happy.

Jeff every day found that he really liked Melanctha better. Now surely he was beginning to have real, deep feeling in him. And still he loved to talk himself out to Melanctha, and he loved to tell her how good it all was to him, and how he always loved to be with her, and to tell her always all about it. One day, now Jeff arranged, that Sunday they would go out and have a happy, long day in the bright fields, and they would be all day just alone together. The day before, Jeff was called in to see Jane Harden.

Jane Harden was very sick almost all day and Jeff Campbell did everything he could to make her better. After a while Jane became more easy and then she began to talk to Jeff about Melanctha. Jane did not know how much Jeff was now seeing of Melanctha. Jane these days never saw Melanctha. Jane began to talk of the time when she first knew Melanctha. Jane began to tell how in these days Melanctha had very little understanding. She was young then and she had a good mind. Jane Harden never would say Melanctha never had a good mind, but in those days Melanctha certainly had not been very understanding. Jane began to explain to Jeff Campbell how in every way, she Jane, had taught Melanctha. Jane then began to explain how eager Melanctha always had been for all that kind of learning. Jane Harden began to tell how they had wandered. Jane began to tell how Melanctha once had loved her, Jane Harden. Jane began to tell Jeff of all the bad ways Melanctha had used with her. Jane began to tell all she knew of the way Melanctha had gone on, after she had left her. Jane began to tell all about the different men, white ones and blacks, Melanctha never was particular about things like that, Jane Harden said in passing, not that Melanctha was a bad one, and she had a good mind, Jane Harden never would say that she hadn't, but Melanctha always liked to use all the understanding ways that Jane had taught her, and so she wanted to know everything, always, that they knew how to teach her.

Jane was beginning to make Jeff Campbell see much clearer. Jane Harden did not know what it was that she was really doing with all this talking. Jane did not know what Jeff was feeling. Jane was always honest when she was talking, and now it just happened she had started talking about her old times with Melanctha Herbert. Jeff understood very well that it was all true what Jane was saying. Jeff Campbell was beginning now to see very clearly. He was beginning to feel very sick inside him. He knew now many things Melanctha had not yet taught him. He felt very sick and his heart was very heavy, and Melanctha certainly did seem very ugly to him. Jeff was at last beginning to know what it was to have deep feeling. He took care a little longer of Jane Harden, and then he went to his other patients, and then he went home to his room, and he sat down and at last he had stopped thinking. He was very sick and his heart was very heavy in him. He was very tired and all the world was very dreary to him, and he knew very well now at last, he was really feeling. He knew it now from the way it hurt him. He knew very well that now at last he was beginning to really have understanding. The next day he had arranged to spend, long and happy, all alone in the spring fields with Melanctha, wandering. He wrote her a note and said he could not go, he had a sick patient and would have to stay home with him. For three days after, he made no sign to Melanctha. He was very sick all these days, and his heart was very heavy in him, and he knew very well that now at last he had learned what it was to have deep feeling.

At last one day he got a letter from Melanctha. "I certainly don't rightly understand what you are doing now to me Jeff Campbell," wrote Melanctha Herbert. "I certainly don't rightly understand Jeff Campbell why you ain't all these days been near me, but I certainly do suppose it's just another one of the queer kind of ways you have to be good, and repenting of yourself all of a sudden. I certainly don't say to you Jeff Campbell I admire very much the way you take to be good Jeff Campbell. I am sorry Dr. Campbell, but I certainly am afraid I can't stand it no more from you the way you have been just acting. I certainly can't stand it any more the way you act when you have been as if you thought I was always good enough for anybody to have with them, and then you act as if I was a bad one and you always just despise me. I certainly am afraid Dr. Campbell I can't stand it any more like that. I certainly can't stand it any more the way you are always changing. I certainly am afraid Dr. Campbell you ain't man enough to deserve to have anybody care so much to be always with you. I certainly am awful afraid Dr. Campbell I don't ever any more want to really see you. Good-by Dr. Campbell I wish you always to be real happy."

Jeff Campbell sat in his room, very quiet, a long time, after he got through reading this letter. He sat very still and first he was very angry. As if he, too, did not know very badly what it was to suffer keenly. As if he had not been very strong to stay with Melanctha when he never knew what it was that she really wanted. He knew he was very right to be angry, he knew he really had not been a coward. He knew Melanctha had done many things it was very hard for him to forgive her. He knew very well he had done his best to be kind, and to trust her, and to be loyal to her, and now;— and then Jeff suddenly remembered how one night Melanctha had been so strong to suffer, and he felt come back to him the sweetness in her, and then Jeff knew that really, he always forgave her, and that really, it all was that he was so sorry he had hurt her, and he wanted to go straight away and be a comfort to her. Jeff knew very well, that what Jane Harden had told him about Melanctha and her bad ways, had been a true story, and yet he wanted very badly to be with

Melanctha. Perhaps she could teach him to really understand it better. Perhaps she could teach him how it could be all true, and yet how he could be right to believe in her and to trust her.

Jeff sat down and began his answer to her. "Dear Melanctha," Jeff wrote to her. "I certainly don't think you got it all just right in the letter, I just been reading, that you just wrote me. I certainly don't think you are just fair or very understanding to all I have to suffer to keep straight on to really always to believe in you and trust you. I certainly don't think you always are fair to remember right how hard it is for a man, who thinks like I was always thinking, not to think you do things very bad very often. I certainly don't think, Melanctha, I ain't right when I was so angry when I got your letter to me. I know very well, Melanctha, that with you, I never have been a coward. I find it very hard, and I never said it any different, it is hard to me to be understanding, and to know really what it is you wanted, and what it is you are meaning by what you are always saying to me. I don't say ever, it ain't very hard for you to be standing that I ain't very quick to be following whichever way that you are always leading. You know very well, Melanctha, it hurts me very bad and way inside me when I have to hurt you, but I always got to be real honest with you. There ain't no other way for me to be, with you, and I know very well it hurts me too, a whole lot, when I can't follow so quick as you would have me. I don't like to be a coward to you, Melanctha, and I don't like to say what I ain't meaning to you. And if you don't want me to do things honest, Melanctha, why I can't ever talk to you, and you are right when you say, you never again want to see me, but if you got any real sense of what I always been feeling with you, and if you got any right sense, Melanctha, of how hard I been trying to think and to feel right for you, I will be very glad to come and see you, and to begin again with you. I don't say anything now,

Melanctha, about how bad I been this week, since I saw you, Melanctha. It don't ever do any good to talk such things over. All I know is I do my best, Melanctha, to you, and I don't say, no, never, I can do any different than just to be honest and come as fast as I think it's right for me to be going in the ways you teach me to be really understanding. So don't talk any more foolishness, Melanctha, about my always changing. I don't change, never, and I got to do what I think is right and honest to me, and I never told you any different, and you always knew it very well that I always would do just so. If you like me to come and see you to-morrow, and go out with you, I will be very glad to, Melanctha. Let me know right away, what it is you want me to be doing for you, Melanctha.

> Very truly yours,
> JEFFERSON CAMPBELL"

"Please come to me, Jeff," Melanctha wrote back for her answer. Jeff went very slowly to Melanctha, glad as he was, still to be going to her. Melanctha came, very quick, to meet him, when she saw him from where she had been watching for him. They went into the house together. They were very glad to be together. They were very good to one another.

"I certainly did think, Melanctha, this time almost really, you never did want me to come to you at all any more to see you," said Jeff Campbell to her, when they had begun again with their talking to each other. "You certainly did make me think, perhaps really this time, Melanctha, it was all over, my being with you ever, and I was very mad, and very sorry, too, Melanctha."

"Well you certainly was very bad to me, Jeff Campbell," said Melanctha, fondly.

"I certainly never do say any more you ain't always right, Melanctha," Jeff answered and he was very ready now with cheerful laughing, "I certainly never do say that any more,

Melanctha, if I know it, but still, really, Melanctha, honest,
I think perhaps I wasn't real bad to you any more than you
just needed from me."

Jeff held Melanctha in his arms and kissed her. He sighed
then and was very silent with her. "Well, Melanctha," he
said at last, with some more laughing, "well, Melanctha, any
way you can't say ever it ain't, if we are ever friends good
and really, you can't say, no, never, but that we certainly
have worked right hard to get both of us together for it, so
we shall sure deserve it then, if we can ever really get it."
"We certainly have worked real hard, Jeff, I can't say that
ain't all right the way you say it," said Melanctha. "I certainly never can deny it, Jeff, when I feel so worn with all
the trouble you been making for me, you bad boy, Jeff," and
then Melanctha smiled and then she sighed, and then she
was very silent with him.

At last Jeff was to go away. They stood there on the steps
for a long time trying to say good-by to each other. At last
Jeff made himself really say it. At last he made himself, that
he went down the steps and went away.

On the next Sunday they arranged, they were to have the
long happy day of wandering that they had lost last time by
Jane Harden's talking. Not that Melanctha Herbert had
heard yet of Jane Harden's talking.

Jeff saw Melanctha every day now. Jeff was a little uncertain all this time inside him, for he had never yet told to
Melanctha what it was that had so nearly made him really
want to leave her. Jeff knew that for him, it was not right he
should not tell her. He knew they could only have real peace
between them when he had been honest, and had really told
her. On this long Sunday Jeff was certain that he would really tell her.

They were very happy all that day in their wandering.
They had taken things along to eat together. They sat in the
bright fields and they were happy, they wandered in the

woods and they were happy. Jeff always loved in this way to wander. Jeff always loved to watch everything as it was growing, and he loved all the colors in the trees and on the ground, and the little, new, bright colored bugs he found in the moist ground and in the grass he loved to lie on and in which he was always so busy searching. Jeff loved everything that moved and that was still, and that had color, and beauty, and real being.

Jeff loved very much this day while they were wandering. He almost forgot that he had any trouble with him still inside him. Jeff loved to be there with Melanctha Herbert. She was always so sympathetic to him for the way she listened to everything he found and told her, the way she felt his joy in all this being, the way she never said she wanted anything different from the way they had it. It was certainly a busy and a happy day, this their first long day of really wandering.

Later they were tired, and Melanctha sat down on the ground, and Jeff threw himself his full length beside her. Jeff lay there, very quiet, and then he pressed her hand and kissed it and murmured to her, "You certainly are very good to me, Melanctha." Melanctha felt it very deep and did not answer. Jeff lay there a long time, looking up above him. He was counting all the little leaves he saw above him. He was following all the little clouds with his eyes as they sailed past him. He watched all the birds that flew high beyond him, and all the time Jeff knew he must tell to Melanctha what it was he knew now, that which Jane Harden, just a week ago, had told him. He knew very well that for him it was certain that he had to say it. It was hard, but for Jeff Campbell the only way to lose it was to say it, the only way to know Melanctha really, was to tell her all the struggle he had made to know her, to tell her so she could help him to understand his trouble better, to help him so that never again he could have any way to doubt her.

Jeff lay there a long time, very quiet, always looking up above him, and yet feeling very close now to Melanctha. At last he turned a little toward her, took her hands closer in his to make him feel it stronger, and then very slowly, for the words came very hard for him, slowly he began his talk to her.

"Melanctha," began Jeff, very slowly, "Melanctha, it ain't right I shouldn't tell you why I went away last week and almost never got the chance again to see you. Jane Harden was sick, and I went in to take care of her. She began to tell everything she ever knew about you. She didn't know how well now I know you. I didn't tell her not to go on talking. I listened while she told me everything about you. I certainly found it very hard with what she told me. I know she was talking truth in everything she said about you. I knew you had been free in your ways, Melanctha, I knew you liked to get excitement the way I always hate to see the colored people take it. I didn't know, till I heard Jane Harden say it, you had done things so bad, Melanctha. When Jane Harden told me, I got very sick, Melanctha. I couldn't bear hardly, to think, perhaps I was just another like them to you, Melanctha. I was wrong not to trust you perhaps, Melanctha, but it did make things very ugly to me. I try to be honest to you, Melanctha, the way you say you really want it from me."

Melanctha drew her hands from Jeff Campbell. She sat there, and there was deep scorn in her anger.

"If you wasn't all through just selfish and nothing else, Jeff Campbell, you would take care you wouldn't have to tell me things like this, Jeff Campbell."

Jeff was silent a little, and he waited before he gave his answer. It was not the power of Melanctha's words that held him, for, for them, he had his answer, it was the power of the mood that filled Melanctha, and for that he had no answer.

At last he broke through this awe, with his slow fighting resolution, and he began to give his answer.

"I don't say ever, Melanctha," he began, "it wouldn't have been more right for me to stop Jane Harden in her talking and to come to you to have you tell me what you were when I never knew you. I don't say it, no never to you, that that would not have been the right way for me to do, Melanctha. But I certainly am without any kind of doubting, I certainly do know for sure, I had a good right to know about what you were and your ways and your trying to use your understanding, every kind of way you could to get your learning. I certainly did have a right to know things like that about you, Melanctha. I don't say it ever, Melanctha, and I say it very often, I don't say ever I shouldn't have stopped Jane Harden in her talking and come to you and asked you yourself to tell me all about it, but I guess I wanted to keep myself from how much it would hurt me more, to have you yourself say it to me. Perhaps it was I wanted to keep you from having it hurt you so much more, having you to have to tell it to me. I don't know, I don't say it was to help you from being hurt most, or to help me. Perhaps I was a coward to let Jane Harden tell me 'stead of coming straight to you, to have you tell me, but I certainly am sure, Melanctha, I certainly had a right to know such things about you. I don't say it ever, ever, Melanctha, I hadn't the just right to know those things about you." Melanctha laughed her harsh laugh. "You needn't have been under no kind of worry, Jeff Campbell, about whether you should have asked me. You could have asked, it wouldn't have hurt nothing. I certainly never would have told you nothing." "I am not so sure of that, Melanctha," said Jeff Campbell. "I certainly do think you would have told me. I certainly do think I could make you feel it right to tell me. I certainly do think all I did wrong was to let Jane Harden tell me. I certainly do know I never did wrong, to learn what she told me. I certainly know very well, Melanctha, if I had come here to you, you would have told it all to me, Melanctha."

He was silent, and this struggle lay there, strong, between them. It was a struggle, sure to be going on always between them. It was a struggle that was as sure always to be going on between them, as their minds and hearts always were to have different ways of working.

At last Melanctha took his hand, leaned over him and kissed him. "I sure am very fond of you, Jeff Campbell," Melanctha whispered to him.

Now for a little time there was not any kind of trouble between Jeff Campbell and Melanctha Herbert. They were always together now for long times, and very often. They got much joy now, both of them, from being all the time together.

It was summer now, and they had warm sunshine to wander. It was summer now, and Jeff Campbell had more time to wander, for colored people never get sick so much in summer. It was summer now, and there was a lovely silence everywhere, and all the noises, too, that they heard around them were lovely ones, and added to the joy, in these warm days, they loved so much to be together.

They talked some to each other in these days, did Jeff Campbell and Melanctha Herbert, but always in these days their talking more and more, was like it always is with real lovers. Jeff did not talk so much now about what he before always had been thinking. Sometimes Jeff would be, as if he was just waking from himself to be with Melanctha, and then he would find he had been really all the long time with her, and he had really never needed to be doing any thinking.

It was sometimes pure joy Jeff would be talking to Melanctha, in these warm days he loved so much to wander with her. Sometimes Jeff would lose all himself in a strong feeling. Very often now, and always with more joy in his feeling, he would find himself, he did not know how or what it was he had been thinking. And Melanctha always loved very well to make him feel it. She always now laughed a little at him, and went back a little in him to his before, always thinking, and she teased him with his always now being so good with her in his feeling, and then she would so well and freely, and with her pure, strong ways of reaching, she would give him all the love she knew now very well, how much he always wanted to be sure he really had it.

And Jeff took it straight now, and he loved it, and he felt, strong, the joy of all this being, and it swelled out full inside him, and he poured it all out back to her in freedom, in tender kindness, and in joy, and in gentle brother fondling. And Melanctha loved him for it always, her Jeff Campbell now, who never did things ugly, for her, like all the men she always knew before always had been doing to her. And they loved it always, more and more, together, with this new feeling they had now, in these long summer days so warm; they, always together now, just these two so dear, more and more to each other always, and the summer evenings when they wandered, and the noises in the full streets, and the music of the organs, and the dancing, and the warm smell of the people, and of dogs and of the horses, and all the joy of the strong, sweet pungent, dirty, moist, warm negro southern summer.

Every day now, Jeff seemed to be coming nearer, to be really loving. Every day now, Melanctha poured it all out to him, with more freedom. Every day now, they seemed to be having more and more, both together, of this strong, right feeling. More and more every day now they seemed to know more really, what it was each other one was always feeling. More and more now every day Jeff found in himself, he felt more trusting. More and more every day now, he did not think anything in words about what he was always doing.

Every day now more and more Melanctha would let out to Jeff her real, strong feeling.

One day there had been much joy between them, more than they ever yet had had with their new feeling. All the day they had lost themselves in warm wandering. Now they were lying there and resting, with a green, bright, light-flecked world around them.

What was it that now really happened to them? What was it that Melanctha did, that made everything get all ugly for them? What was it that Melanctha felt then, that made Jeff remember all the feeling he had had in him when Jane Harden told him how Melanctha had learned to be so very understanding? Jeff did not know how it was that it had happened to him. It was all green, and warm, and very lovely to him, and now Melanctha somehow had made it all so ugly for him. What was it Melanctha was now doing with him? What was it he used to be thinking was the right way for him and all the colored people to be always trying to make it right, the way they should be always living? Why was Melanctha Herbert now all so ugly for him?

Melanctha Herbert somehow had made him feel deeply just then, what very more it was that she wanted from him. Jeff Campbell now felt in him what everybody always had needed to make them really understanding, to him. Jeff felt a strong disgust inside him; not for Melanctha herself, to him, not for himself really, in him, not for what it was that everybody wanted, in them; he only had disgust because he never could know really in him, what it was he wanted, to be really right in understanding, for him, he only had disgust because he never could know really what it was really right to him to be always doing, in the things he had before believed in, the things he before had believed in for himself and for all the colored people, the living regular, and the never wanting to be always having new things, just to keep on, always being in excitements. All the old thinking now came up very strong inside him. He sort of turned away then, and threw Melanctha from him.

Jeff never, even now, knew what it was that moved him. He never, even now, was ever sure, he really knew what Melanctha was, when she was real herself, and honest. He thought he knew, and then there came to him some moment, just like this one, when she really woke him up to be strong in him. Then he really knew he could know nothing. He knew then, he never could know what it was she really wanted with him. He knew then he never could know really what it was he felt inside him. It was all so mixed up inside him. All he knew was he wanted very badly Melanctha should be there beside him, and he wanted very badly, too, always to throw her from him. What was it really that Melanctha wanted with him? What was it really, he, Jeff Campbell, wanted she should give him? "I certainly did think now," Jeff Campbell groaned inside him, "I certainly did think now I really was knowing all right, what I wanted. I certainly did really think now I was knowing how to be trusting with Melanctha. I certainly did think it was like that now with me sure, after all I've been through all this time with her. And now I certainly do know I don't know anything that's very real about her. Oh the good Lord help and keep me!" and Jeff groaned hard inside him, and he buried his face deep in the green grass underneath him, and Melanctha Herbert was very silent there beside him.

Then Jeff turned to look and see her. She was lying very still there by him, and the bitter water on her face was biting. Jeff was so very sorry then, all over and inside him, the way he always was when Melanctha had been deep hurt by him. "I didn't mean to be so bad again to you, Melanctha, dear one," and he was very tender to her. "I certainly didn't never mean to go to be so bad to you, Melanctha, darling. I certainly don't know, Melanctha, darling, what it is makes me act so to you sometimes, when I certainly ain't meaning anything like I want to hurt you. I certainly don't mean to be so bad, Melanctha, only it comes so quick on me before I know what I am acting to you. I certainly am all sorry, hard, to be so bad to you, Melanctha, darling." "I suppose, Jeff," said Melanctha, very low and bitter, "I suppose you are always thinking, Jeff, somebody had ought to be ashamed with us two together, and you certainly do think you don't see any way to it, Jeff, for me to be feeling that way ever, so you certainly don't see any way to it, only to do it just so often for me. That certainly is the way always with you, Jeff Campbell, if I understand you right the way you are always acting to me. That certainly is right the way I am saying it to you now, Jeff Campbell. You certainly didn't anyway trust me now no more, did you, when you just acted so bad to me. I certainly am right the way I say it Jeff now to you. I certainly am right when I ask you for it now, to tell me what I ask you, about not trusting me more then again, Jeff, just like you never really knew me. You certainly never did trust me just then, Jeff, you hear me?" "Yes, Melanctha," Jeff answered slowly. Melanctha paused. "I guess I certainly never can forgive you this time, Jeff Campbell," she said firmly. Jeff paused too, and thought a little. "I certainly am afraid you never can no more now again, Melanctha," he said sadly.

They lay there very quiet now a long time, each one thinking very hard on their own trouble. At last Jeff began again to tell Melanctha what it was he was always thinking with her. "I certainly do know, Melanctha, you certainly now don't want any more to be hearing me just talking, but you see, Melanctha, really, it's just like this way always with me. You see, Melanctha, it's like this way now all the time with me. You remember, Melanctha, what I was once telling to you, when I didn't know you very long together, about how I certainly never did know more than just two kinds of ways of loving, one way the way it is good to be in families and the other kind of way, like animals are all the time just with each other, and how I didn't ever like that last kind of way much for any of the colored people. You see Melanctha, it's like this way with me. I got a new feeling now, you been teaching to me, just like I told you once, just like a new religion to me, and I see perhaps what really loving is like, like really having everything together, new things, little pieces all different, like I always before been thinking was bad to be having, all go together like, to make one good big feeling. You see, Melanctha, it's certainly like that you make me been seeing, like I never know before any way there was of all kinds of loving to come together to make one way really truly lovely. I see that now, sometimes, the way you certainly been teaching me, Melanctha, really, and I love you those times, Melanctha, like a real religion, and then it comes over me all sudden, I don't know anything real about you Melanctha, dear one, and then it comes over me sudden, perhaps I certainly am wrong now, thinking all this way so lovely, and not thinking now any more the old way I always before was always thinking, about what was the right way for me, to live regular and all the colored people, and then I think, perhaps, Melanctha you are really just a bad one, and I think, perhaps I certainly am doing it so because I just am too anxious to be just having all the time excitements, like I don't ever like really to be doing when I know it, and then I always get so bad to you, Melanctha, and I can't help it with myself then, never, for I want to be always right really in the ways, I have to do them. I certainly do very badly want to be right, Melanctha, the only way I know is right Melanctha really, and I don't know any way, Melanctha, to find out really, whether my old way, the way I always used to be thinking, or the new way, you make so like a real religion to me, sometimes, Melanctha, which way certainly is the real right way for me to be always thinking, and then I certainly am awful good and sorry, Melanctha, I always give you so much trouble, hurting you with the bad ways I am acting. Can't you help me to any way, to make it all straight for me, Melanctha, so I know right and real what it is I should be acting. You see, Melanctha, I don't want always to be a coward with you, if I only could know certain what was the right way for me to be acting. I certainly am real sure, Melanctha, that would be the way I would be acting, if I only knew it sure for certain now, Melanctha. Can't you help me any way to find out real and true, Melanctha, dear one. I certainly do badly want to know always, the way I should be acting."

"No, Jeff, dear, I certainly can't help you much in that kind of trouble you are always having. All I can do now, Jeff, is to just keep certainly with my believing you are good always, Jeff, and though you certainly do hurt me bad, I always got strong faith in you, Jeff, more in you certainly, than you seem to be having in your acting to me, always so bad, Jeff."

"You certainly are very good to me, Melanctha, dear one," Jeff said, after a long, tender silence. "You certainly are very good to me, Melanctha, darling, and me so bad to you always, in my acting. Do you love me good, and right, Melanctha, always?" "Always and always, you be sure of that now you have me. Oh you Jeff, you always be so stupid." "I certainly never can say now you ain't right, when you say that to me so, Melanctha," Jeff answered. "Oh, Jeff dear, I love you always, you know that now, all right, for certain. If you don't know it right now, Jeff, really, I prove it to you now, for good and always." And they lay there a long time in their loving, and then Jeff began again with his happy free enjoying.

"I sure am a good boy to be learning all the time the right way you are teaching me, Melanctha, darling," began Jeff Campbell, laughing. "You can't say no, never, I ain't a good scholar for you to be teaching now, Melanctha, and I am always so ready to come to you every day, and never playing hooky ever from you. You can't say ever, Melanctha, now can you, I ain't a real good boy to be always studying to be learning to be real bright, just like my teacher. You can't say ever to me, I ain't a good boy to you now, Melanctha." "Not near so good, Jeff Campbell, as such a good, patient kind of teacher, like me, who never teaches any ways it ain't good her scholars should be knowing, ought to be really having, Jeff, you hear me? I certainly don't think I am right for you, to be forgiving always, when you are so bad, and I so patient, with all this hard teaching always." "But you do forgive me always, sure, Melanctha, always?" "Always and always, you be sure Jeff, and I certainly am afraid I never can stop with my forgiving, you always are going to be so bad to me, and I always going to have to be so good with my forgiving." "Oh! Oh!" cried Jeff Campbell, laughing, "I ain't going to be so bad for always, sure I ain't, Melanctha, my own darling. And sure you do forgive me really, and sure you love me true and really, sure Melanctha?" "Sure, sure, Jeff, boy, sure now and always, sure now you believe me, sure you do, Jeff, always." "I sure hope I does, with all my heart, Melanctha, darling." "I sure do that same, Jeff, dear boy, now you really know what it is to be loving, and I prove it to you now so, Jeff, you never can be forgetting. You see now, Jeff, good and certain, what I always before been saying to you, Jeff, now." "Yes, Melanctha, darling," murmured Jeff, and he was very happy in it, and so the two of them now in the warm air of the sultry, southern, negro sunshine, lay there for a long time just resting.

And now for a real long time there was no open trouble any more between Jeff Campbell and Melanctha Herbert. Then it came that Jeff knew he could not say out any more, what it was he wanted, he could not say out any more, what it was, he wanted to know about, what Melanctha wanted.

Melanctha sometimes now, when she was tired with being all the time so much excited, when Jeff would talk a long time to her about what was right for them both to be always doing, would be, as if she gave way in her head, and lost herself in a bad feeling. Sometimes when they had been strong in their loving, and Jeff would have rise inside him some strange feeling, and Melanctha felt it in him as it would soon be coming, she would lose herself then in this bad feeling that made her head act as if she never knew what it was they were doing. And slowly now, Jeff soon always came to be feeling that his Melanctha would be hurt very much in her head in the ways he never liked to think of, if she would ever now again have to listen to his trouble, when he was telling about what it was he still was wanting to make things for himself really understanding.

Now Jeff began to have always a strong feeling that Melanctha could no longer stand it, with all her bad suffering, to let him fight out with himself what was right for him to be doing. Now he felt he must not, when she was there with him, keep on, with this kind of fighting that was always going on inside him. Jeff Campbell never knew yet, what he thought was the right way, for himself and for all the colored people to be living. Jeff was coming always each time closer to be really understanding, but now Melanctha was so bad in her suffering with him, that he knew she could not any longer have him with her while he was always showing that he never really yet was sure what it was, the right way, for them to be really loving.

Jeff saw now he had to go so fast, so that Melanctha never would have to wait any to get from him always all that she ever wanted. He never could be honest now, he never could be now, any more, trying to be really understanding, for always every moment now he felt it to be a strong thing in him, how very much it was Melanctha Herbert always suffered.

Jeff did not know very well these days, what it was, was really happening to him. All he knew every now and then, when they were getting strong to get excited, the way they used to when he gave his feeling out so that he could be always honest, that Melanctha somehow never seemed to hear him, she just looked at him and looked as if her head hurt with him, and then Jeff had to keep himself from being honest, and he had to go so fast, and to do everything Melanctha ever wanted from him.

Jeff did not like it very well these days, in his true feeling. He knew now very well Melanctha was not strong enough inside her to stand any more of his slow way of doing. And yet now he knew he was not honest in his feeling. Now he always had to show more to Melanctha than he was ever feeling. Now she made him go so fast, and he knew it was not real with his feeling, and yet he could not make her suffer so any more because he always was so slow with his feeling.

It was very hard for Jeff Campbell to make all this way of doing, right, inside him. If Jeff Campbell could not be straight out, and real honest, he never could be very strong inside him. Now Melanctha, with her making him feel, always, how good she was and how very much she suffered in him, made him always go so fast then, he could not be strong then, to feel things out straight then inside him. Always now when he was with her, he was being more, than he could already yet, be feeling for her. Always now, with her, he had something inside him always holding in him, always now, with her, he was far ahead of his own feeling.

Jeff Campbell never knew very well these days what it was that was going on inside him. All he knew was, he was uneasy now always to be with Melanctha. All he knew was, that he was always uneasy when he was with Melanctha, not the way he used to be from just not being very understanding, but now, because he never could be honest with her, because he was now always feeling her strong suffering, in her, because he knew now he was having a straight, good feeling with her, but she went so fast, and he was so slow to her; Jeff knew his right feeling never got a chance to show itself as strong, to her.

All this was always getting harder for Jeff Campbell. He was very proud to hold himself to be strong, was Jeff Campbell. He was very tender not to hurt Melanctha, when he knew she would be sure to feel it badly in her head a long time after, he hated that he could not now be honest with her, he wanted to stay away to work it out all alone, without her, he was afraid she would feel it to suffer, if he kept away now from her. He was uneasy always, with her, he was uneasy when he thought about her, he knew now he had a good, straight, strong feeling of right loving for her, and yet now he never could use it to be good and honest with her.

Jeff Campbell did not know, these days, anything he could do to make it better for her. He did not know anything he could do, to set himself really right in his acting and his thinking toward her. She pulled him so fast with her, and he did not dare to hurt her, and he could not come right, so fast, the way she always needed he should be doing it now, for her.

These days were not very joyful ones now any more, to Jeff Campbell, with Melanctha. He did not think it out to himself now, in words, about her. He did not know enough, what was his real trouble, with her.

Sometimes now and again with them, and with all this trouble for a little while well forgotten by him, Jeff, and Melanctha with him, would be very happy in a strong, sweet loving. Sometimes then, Jeff would find himself to be soaring very high in his true loving. Sometimes Jeff would find then, in his loving, his soul swelling out full inside him. Always Jeff felt now in himself, deep feeling.

Always now Jeff had to go so much faster than was real with his feeling. Yet always Jeff knew now he had a right, strong feeling. Always now when Jeff was wondering, it was

Melanctha he was doubting, in the loving. Now he would often ask her, was she real now to him, in her loving. He would ask her often, feeling something queer about it all inside him, though yet he was never really strong in his doubting, and always Melanctha would answer to him, "Yes Jeff, sure, you know it, always," and always Jeff felt a doubt now, in her loving.

Always now Jeff felt in himself, deep loving. Always now he did not know really, if Melanctha was true in her loving.

All these days Jeff was uncertain in him, and he was uneasy about which way he should act so as not to be wrong and put them both into bad trouble. Always now he was, as if he must feel deep into Melanctha to see if it was real loving he would find she now had in her, and always he would stop himself, with her, for always he was afraid now that he might badly hurt her.

Always now he liked it better when he was detained when he had to go and see her. Always now he never liked to go to be with her, although he never wanted really, not to be always with her. Always now he never felt really at ease with her, even when they were good friends together. Always now he felt, with her, he could not be really honest to her. And Jeff never could be happy with her when he could not feel strong to tell all his feeling to her. Always now every day he found it harder to make the time pass, with her, and not let his feeling come so that he would quarrel with her.

And so one evening, late, he was to go to her. He waited a little long, before he went to her. He was afraid, in himself, to-night, he would surely hurt her. He never wanted to go when he might quarrel with her.

Melanctha sat there looking very angry, when he came in to her. Jeff took off his hat and coat and then sat down by the fire with her.

"If you come in much later to me just now, Jeff Campbell, I certainly never would have seen you no more never to speak to you, 'thout your apologising real humble to me." "Apologising Melanctha," and Jeff laughed and was scornful to her, "Apologising, Melanctha, I ain't proud that kind of way, Melanctha, I don't mind apologising to you, Melanctha, all I mind, Melanctha is to be doing of things wrong, to you." "That's easy, to say things that way, Jeff to me. But you never was very proud Jeff, to be courageous to me." "I don't know about that Melanctha. I got courage to say some things hard, when I mean them, to you." "Oh, yes, Jeff, I know all about that, Jeff, to me. But I mean real courage, to run around and not care nothing about what happens, and always to be game in any kind of trouble. That's what I mean by real courage, to me, Jeff, if you want to know it." "Oh, yes, Melanctha, I know all that kind of courage. I see plenty of it all the time with some kinds of colored men and with some girls like you Melanctha, and Jane Harden. I know all about how you are always making a fuss to be proud because you don't holler so much when you run in to where you ain't got any business to be, and so you get hurt, the way you ought to. And then, you kind of people are very brave then, sure, with all your kinds of suffering, but the way I see it, going round with all my patients, that kind of courage makes all kind of trouble, for them who ain't so noble with their courage, and then they got it, always to be bearing it, when the end comes, to be hurt the hardest. It's like running around and being game to spend all your money always, and then a man's wife and children are the ones do all the starving and they don't ever get a name for being brave, and they don't ever want to be doing all that suffering, and they got to stand it and say nothing. That's the way I see it a good deal now with all that kind of braveness in some of the colored people. They always make a lot of noise to show they are so brave not to holler, when they got so much suffering they always bring all on themselves, just by doing things they got no business to be doing. I don't say, never, Melanctha, they ain't got good courage not to holler, but I never did see much in looking for that kind of trouble just to show you ain't going to holler. No it's all right being brave every day, just living regular and not having new ways all the time just to get excitements, the way I hate to see it in all the colored people. No I don't see much, Melanctha, in being brave just to get it good, where you've got no business. I ain't ashamed Melanctha, right here to tell you, I ain't ashamed ever to say I ain't got no longing to be brave, just to go around and look for trouble." "Yes, that's just like you always, Jeff, you never understand things right, the way you are always feeling in you. You ain't got no way to understand right, how it depends what way somebody goes to look for new things, the way it makes it right for them to get excited." "No Melanctha, I certainly never do say I understand much anybody's got a right to think they won't have real bad trouble, if they go and look hard where they are certain sure to find it. No Melanctha, it certainly does sound very pretty all this talking about danger and being game and never hollering, and all that way of talking, but when two men are just fighting, the strong man mostly gets on top with doing good hard pounding, and the man that's getting all that pounding, he mostly never likes it so far as I have been able yet to see it, and I don't see much difference what kind of noble way they are made of when they ain't got any kind of business to get together there to be fighting. That certainly is the only way I ever see it happen right, Melanctha, whenever I happen to be anywhere I can be looking." "That's because you never can see anything that ain't just so simple, Jeff, with everybody, the way you always think it. It do make all the difference the kind of way anybody is made to do things game Jeff Campbell." "Maybe Melanctha, I certainly never say no you ain't right, Melanctha. I just been telling it to you all straight, Melanctha, the way I always see it. Perhaps if you run around where you ain't got any business, and you stand up very straight and say, I am so brave, nothing can ever ever hurt me, maybe nothing will ever hurt you then Melanctha. I never have seen it do so. I never can say truly any differently to you Melanctha, but I always am ready to be learning from you, Melanctha. And perhaps when somebody cuts into you real hard, with a brick he is throwing, perhaps you never will do any hollering then, Melanctha. I certainly don't ever say no, Melanctha to you, I only say that ain't the way yet I ever see it happen when I had a chance to be there looking."

They sat there together, quiet by the fire, and they did not seem to feel very loving.

"I certainly do wonder," Melanctha said dreamily, at last breaking into their long unloving silence. "I certainly do wonder why always it happens to me I care for anybody who ain't no ways good enough for me ever to be thinking to respect him."

Jeff looked at Melanctha. Jeff got up then and walked a little up and down the room, and then he came back, and his face was set and dark and he was very quiet to her.

"Oh dear, Jeff, sure, why you look so solemn now to me. Sure Jeff I never am meaning anything real by what I just been saying. What was I just been saying Jeff to you. I only certainly was just thinking how everything always was just happening to me."

Jeff Campbell sat very still and dark, and made no answer.

"Seems to me, Jeff you might be good to me a little tonight when my head hurts so, and I am so tired with all the hard work I have been doing, thinking, and I always got so many things to be a trouble to me, living like I do with nobody ever who can help me. Seems to me you might be good to me Jeff to-night, and not get angry, every little thing I am ever saying to you."

"I certainly would not get angry ever with you, Melanctha, just because you say things to me. But now I certainly been thinking you really mean what you have been just then saying to me." "But you say all the time to me Jeff, you ain't no ways good enough in your loving to me, you certainly say to me all the time you ain't no ways good or understanding to me." "That certainly is what I say to you always, just the way I feel it to you Melanctha always, and I got it right in me to say it, and I have got a right in me to be very strong and feel it, and to be always sure to believe it, but it ain't right for you Melanctha to feel it. When you feel it so Melanctha, it does certainly make everything all wrong with our loving. It makes it so I certainly never can bear to have it."

They sat there then a long time by the fire, very silent, and not loving, and never looking to each other for it. Melanctha was moving and twitching herself and very nervous with it. Jeff was heavy and sullen and dark and very serious in it.

"Oh why can't you forget I said it to you Jeff now, and I certainly am so tired, and my head and all now with it."

Jeff stirred, "All right Melanctha, don't you go make yourself sick now in your head, feeling so bad with it," and Jeff made himself do it, and he was a patient doctor again now with Melanctha when he felt her really having her head hurt with it. "It's all right now Melanctha darling, sure it is now I tell you. You just lie down now a little, dear one, and I sit here by the fire and just read awhile and just watch with you so I will be here ready, if you need me to give you something to help you resting." And then Jeff was a good doctor to her, and very sweet and tender with her, and Melanctha loved him to be there to help her, and then Melanctha fell asleep a little, and Jeff waited there beside her until he saw she was really sleeping, and then he went back and sat down by the fire.

And Jeff tried to begin again with his thinking, and he could not make it come clear to himself, with all his thinking, and he felt everything all thick and heavy and bad, now inside him, everything that he could not understand right, with all the hard work he made, with his thinking. And then he moved himself a little, and took a book to forget his thinking, and then as always, he loved it when he was reading, and then very soon he was deep in his reading, and so he forgot now for a little while that he never could seem to be very understanding.

And so Jeff forgot himself for awhile in his reading, and Melanctha was sleeping. And then Melanctha woke up and she was screaming. "Oh, Jeff, I thought you gone away for always from me. Oh, Jeff, never now go away no more from me. Oh, Jeff, sure, sure, always be just so good to me."

There was a weight in Jeff Campbell from now on, always with him, that he could never lift out from him, to feel easy. He always was trying not to have it in him and he always was trying not to let Melanctha feel it, with him, but it was always there inside him. Now Jeff Campbell always was serious, and dark, and heavy, and sullen, and he would often sit a long time with Melanctha without moving.

"You certainly never have forgiven to me, what I said to you that night, Jeff, now have you?" Melanctha asked him after a long silence, late one evening with him. "It ain't ever with me a question like forgiving, Melanctha, I got in me. It's just only what you are feeling for me, makes any difference to me. I ain't ever seen anything since in you, makes me think you didn't mean it right, what you said about not thinking now any more I was good, to make it right for you to be really caring so very much to love me."

"I certainly never did see no man like you, Jeff. You always wanting to have it all clear out in words always, what everybody is always feeling. I certainly don't see a reason, why I should always be explaining to you what I mean by what I am just saying. And you ain't got no feeling ever for me, to ask me what I meant, by what I was saying when I was so tired, that night. I never know anything right I was saying." "But you don't ever tell me now, Melanctha, so I really hear you say it, you don't mean it the same way, the way you said it to me." "Oh Jeff, you so stupid always to me and always just bothering with your always asking to me. And I don't never any way remember ever anything I been saying to you, and I am always my head, so it hurts me it half kills me, and my heart jumps so, sometimes I think I die so when it hurts me, and I am so blue always, I think sometimes I take something to just kill me, and I got so much to bother thinking always and doing, and I got so much to worry, and all that, and then you come and ask me what I mean by what I was just saying to you. I certainly don't know, Jeff, when you ask me. Seems to me, Jeff, sometimes you might have some kind of a right feeling to be careful to me." "You ain't got no right Melanctha Herbert," flashed out Jeff through his dark, frowning anger, "you certainly ain't got no right always to be using your being hurt and being sick, and having pain, like a weapon, so as to make me do things it ain't never right for me to be doing for you. You certainly ain't got no right to be always holding your pain out to show me." "What do you mean by them words, Jeff Campbell." "I certainly do mean them just like I am saying them, Melanctha. You act always, like I been responsible all myself for all our loving one another. And if it's anything anyway that ever hurts you, you act like as if it was me made you just begin it all with me. I ain't no coward, you hear me, Melanctha? I never put my trouble back on anybody, thinking that they made me. I certainly am right ready always, Melanctha, you certainly had ought to know me, to stand all my own trouble for me, but I tell you straight now, the way

I think it Melanctha, I ain't going to be as if I was the reason why you wanted to be loving, and to be suffering so now with me." "But ain't you certainly ought to be feeling it so, to be right, Jeff Campbell. Did I ever do anything but just let you do everything you wanted to me. Did I ever try to make you be loving to me. Did I ever do nothing except just sit there ready to endure your loving with me. But I certainly never, Jeff Campbell, did make any kind of way as if I wanted really to be having you for me."

Jeff stared at Melanctha. "So that's the way you say it when you are thinking right about it all, Melanctha. Well I certainly ain't got a word to say ever to you any more, Melanctha, if that's the way it's straight out to you now, Melanctha." And Jeff almost laughed out to her, and he turned to take his hat and coat, and go away now forever from her.

Melanctha dropped her head on her arms, and she trembled all over and inside her. Jeff stopped a little and looked very sadly at her. Jeff could not so quickly make it right for himself, to leave her.

"Oh, I certainly shall go crazy now, I certainly know that," Melanctha moaned as she sat there, all fallen and miserable and weak together.

Jeff came and took her in his arms, and held her. Jeff was very good then to her, but they neither of them felt inside all right, as they once did, to be together.

From now on, Jeff had real torment in him.

Was it true what Melanctha had said that night to him? Was it true that he was the one had made all this trouble for them? Was it true, he was the only one, who always had had wrong ways in him? Waking or sleeping Jeff now always had this torment going on inside him.

Jeff did not know now any more, what to feel within him. He did not know how to begin thinking out this trouble that must always now be bad inside him. He just felt a confused struggle and resentment always in him, a knowing, no, Melanctha was not right in what she had said that night to him, and then a feeling, perhaps he always had been wrong in the way he never could be understanding. And then would come strong to him, a sense of the deep sweetness in Melanctha's loving and a hating the cold slow way he always had to feel things in him.

Always Jeff knew, sure, Melanctha was wrong in what she had said that night to him, but always Melanctha had had deep feeling with him, always he was poor and slow in the only way he knew how to have any feeling. Jeff knew Melanctha was wrong, and yet he always had a deep doubt in him. What could he know, who had such slow feeling in him? What could he ever know, who always had to find his way with just thinking. What could he know, who had to be taught such a long time to learn about what was really loving? Jeff now always had this torment in him.

Melanctha was now always making him feel her way, strong whenever she was with him. Did she go on to do it just to show him, did she do it so now because she was no longer loving, did she do it so because that was her way to make him be really loving. Jeff never did know how it was that it all happened so to him.

Melanctha acted now the way she had said it always had been with them. Now it was always Jeff who had to do the asking. Now it was always Jeff who had to ask when would be the next time he should come to see her. Now always she was good and patient to him, and now always she was kind and loving with him, and always Jeff felt it was, that she was good to give him anything he ever asked or wanted, but never now any more for her own sake to make her happy in him. Now she did these things, as if it was just to please her Jeff Campbell who needed she should now have kindness for him. Always now he was the beggar, with them. Always now Melanctha gave it, not of her need, but from her bounty to him. Always now Jeff found it getting harder for him.

Sometimes Jeff wanted to tear things away from before him, always now he wanted to fight things and be angry with them, and always now Melanctha was so patient to him.

Now, deep inside him, there was always a doubt with Jeff, of Melanctha's loving. It was not a doubt yet to make him really doubting, for with that, Jeff never could be really loving, but always now he knew that something, and that not in him, something was wrong with their loving. Jeff Campbell could not know any right way to think out what was inside Melanctha with her loving, he could not use any way now to reach inside her to find if she was true in her loving, but now something had gone wrong between them, and now he never felt sure in him, the way once she had made him, that now at last he really had got to be understanding.

Melanctha was too many for him. He was helpless to find out the way she really felt now for him. Often Jeff would ask her, did she really love him. Always she said, "Yes Jeff, sure, you know that," and now instead of a full sweet strong love with it, Jeff only felt a patient, kind endurance in it.

Jeff did not know. If he was right in such a feeling, he certainly never any more did want to have Melanctha Herbert with him. Jeff Campbell hated badly to think Melanctha ever would give him love, just for his sake, and not because she needed it herself, to be with him. Such a way of loving would be very hard for Jeff to be enduring.

"Jeff what makes you act so funny to me. Jeff you certainly now are jealous to me. Sure Jeff, now I don't see ever why you be so foolish to look so to me." "Don't you ever think I can be jealous of anybody ever Melanctha, you hear me. It's just, you certainly don't ever understand me. It's just this way with me always now Melanctha. You love me, and I don't care anything what you do or what you ever been to anybody. You don't love me, then I don't care any more about what you ever do or what you ever be to anybody. But I never want you to be being good Melanctha to me, when it ain't your loving makes you need it. I certainly don't ever want to be having any of your kind of kindness to me. If you don't love me, I can stand it. All I never want to have is your being good to me from kindness. If you don't love me, then you and I certainly do quit right here Melanctha, all strong feeling, to be always living to each other. It certainly never is anybody I ever am thinking about when I am thinking with you Melanctha darling. That's the true way I am telling you Melanctha, always. It's only your loving me ever gives me anything to bother me Melanctha, so all you got to do, if you don't really love me, is just certainly to say so to me. I won't bother you more then than I can help to keep from it Melanctha. You certainly need never to be in any worry, never, about me Melanctha. You just tell me straight out Melanctha, real, the way you feel it. I certainly can stand it all right, I tell you true Melanctha. And I never will care to know why or nothing Melanctha. Loving is just living Melanctha to me, and if you don't really feel it now Melanctha to me, there ain't ever nothing between us then Melanctha, is there? That's straight and honest just the way I always feel it to you now Melanctha. Oh Melanctha, darling, do you love me? Oh Melanctha, please, please, tell me honest, tell me, do you really love me?"

"Oh you so stupid Jeff boy, of course I always love you. Always and always Jeff and I always just so good to you. Oh you so stupid Jeff and don't know when you got it good with me. Oh dear, Jeff I certainly am so tired Jeff to-night, don't you go be a bother to me. Yes I love you Jeff, how often you want me to tell you. Oh you so stupid Jeff, but yes I love you. Now I won't say it no more now tonight Jeff, you hear me. You just be good Jeff now to me or else I certainly get awful angry with you. Yes I love you, sure, Jeff, though you don't any way deserve it from me. Yes, yes I love you. Yes Jeff I say it till I certainly am very sleepy. Yes I love you now Jeff, and you certainly must stop asking me to tell you. Oh you great silly boy Jeff Campbell, sure I love you, oh you silly stupid, my own boy Jeff Campbell. Yes I love you and I certainly never won't say it one more time to-night Jeff, now you hear me."

Yes Jeff Campbell heard her, and he tried hard to believe her. He did not really doubt her but somehow it was wrong now, the way Melanctha said it. Jeff always now felt baffled with Melanctha. Something, he knew, was not right now in her. Something in her always now was making stronger the torment that was tearing every minute at the joy he once always had had with her.

Always now Jeff wondered did Melanctha love him. Always now he was wondering, was Melanctha right when she said, it was he had made all their beginning. Was Melanctha right when she said, it was he had the real responsibility for all the trouble they had and still were having now between them. If she was right, what a brute he always had been in his acting. If she was right, how good she had been to endure the pain he had made so bad so often for her. But no, surely she had made herself to bear it, for her own sake, not for his to make him happy. Surely he was not so twisted in all his long thinking. Surely he could remember right what it was had happened every day in their long loving. Surely he was not so poor a coward as Melanctha always seemed to be thinking. Surely, surely, and then the torment would get worse every minute in him.

One night Jeff Campbell was lying in his bed with his thinking, and night after night now he could not do any sleeping for his thinking. To-night suddenly he sat up in his bed, and it all came clear to him, and he pounded his pillow with his fist, and he almost shouted out alone there to him, "I ain't a brute the way Melanctha has been saying. It's all wrong the way I been worried thinking. We did begin fair, each not for the other but for ourselves, what we were wanting. Melanctha Herbert did it just like I did it, because she liked it bad enough to want to stand it. It's all wrong in me to think it any way except the way we really did it. I certainly don't know now whether she is now real and true in her loving. I ain't got any way ever to find out if she is real and true now always to me. All I know is I didn't ever make her to begin to be with me. Melanctha has got to stand for her own trouble, just like I got to stand for my own trouble. Each man has got to do it for himself when he is in real trouble. Melanctha, she certainly don't remember right when she says I made her begin and then I made her trouble. No by God, I ain't no coward nor a brute either ever to her. I been the way I felt it honest, and that certainly is all about it now between us, and everybody always has just got to stand for their own trouble. I certainly am right this time the way I see it." And Jeff lay down now, at last in comfort, and he slept, and he was free from his long doubting torment.

"You know Melanctha," Jeff Campbell began, the next time he was alone to talk a long time to Melanctha. "You know Melanctha, sometimes I think a whole lot about what you like to say so much about being game and never doing any hollering. Seems to me Melanctha, I certainly don't understand right what you mean by not hollering. Seems to me it certainly ain't only what comes right away when one is hit, that counts to be brave to be bearing, but all that comes later from your getting sick from the shock of being hurt once in a fight, and all that, and all the being taken care of for years after, and the suffering of your family, and all that, you certainly must stand and not holler, to be certainly really brave the way I understand it." "What you mean Jeff by your talking." "I mean, seems to me really not to holler, is to be strong not to show you ever have been hurt. Seems to me, to get your head hurt from your trouble and to show it,

ain't certainly no braver than to say, oh, oh, how bad you
hurt me, please don't hurt me mister. It just certainly seems
to me, like many people think themselves so game just to
stand what we all of us always just got to be standing, and
everybody stands it, and we don't certainly none of us like
it, and yet we don't ever most of us think we are so much
being game, just because we got to stand it."

·"I know what you mean now by what you are saying to
me now Jeff Campbell. You make a fuss now to me, because
I certainly just have stopped standing everything you like to
be always doing so cruel to me. But that's just the way always with you Jeff Campbell, if you want to know it. You
ain't got no kind of right feeling for all I always been forgiving to you." "I said it once for fun, Melanctha, but now I
certainly do mean it, you think you got a right to go where
you got no business, and you say, I am so brave nothing can
hurt me, and then something, like always, it happens to hurt
you, and you show your hurt always so everybody can see
it, and you say, I am so brave nothing did hurt me except he
certainly didn't have any right to, and see how bad I suffer,
but you never hear me make a holler, though certainly anybody got any feeling, to see me suffer, would certainly never
touch me except to take good care of me. Sometimes I certainly don't rightly see Melanctha, how much more game
that is than just the ordinary kind of holler." "No, Jeff Campbell, and made the way you is you certainly ain't likely ever
to be much more understanding." "No, Melanctha, nor you
neither. You think always, you are the only one who ever can
do any way to really suffer." "Well, and ain't I certainly always been the only person knows how to bear it. No, Jeff
Campbell, I certainly be glad to love anybody really worthy,
but I made so, I never seem to be able in this world to find
him." "No, and your kind of way of thinking, you certainly
Melanctha never going to any way be able ever to be finding of him. Can't you understand Melanctha, ever, how no

man certainly ever really can hold your love for long times together. You certainly Melanctha, you ain't got down deep loyal feeling, true inside you, and when you ain't just that moment quick with feeling, then you certainly ain't ever got anything more there to keep you. You see Melanctha, it certainly is this way with you, it is, that you ain't ever got any way to remember right what you been doing, or anybody else that has been feeling with you. You certainly Melanctha, never can remember right, when it comes what you have done, and what you think happens to you." "It certainly is all easy for you Jeff Campbell to be talking. You remember right, because you don't remember nothing till you get home with your thinking everything all over, but I certainly don't think much ever of that kind of way of remembering right, Jeff Campbell. I certainly do call it remembering right Jeff Campbell, to remember right just when it happens to you, so you have a right kind of feeling not to act the way you always been doing to me, and then you go home Jeff Campbell, and you begin with your thinking, and then it certainly is very easy for you to be good and forgiving with it. No, that ain't to me, the way of remembering Jeff Campbell, not as I can see it not to make people always suffer, waiting for you certainly to get to do it. Seems to me like Jeff Campbell, I never could feel so like a man was low and to be scorning of him, like that day in the summer, when you threw me off just because you got one of those fits of your remembering. No, Jeff Campbell, it's real feeling every moment when it's needed, that certainly does seem to me like real remembering. And that way, certainly, you don't never know nothing like what should be right Jeff Campbell. No Jeff, it's me that always certainly has had to bear it with you. It's always me that certainly has had to suffer, while you go home to remember. No you certainly ain't got no sense yet Jeff, what you need to make you really feeling. No, it certainly is me Jeff Campbell, that always has got to be re-

membering for us both, always. That's what's the true way
with us Jeff Campbell, if you want to know what it is I am
always thinking." "You is certainly real modest Melanctha,
when you do this kind of talking, you sure is Melanctha,"
said Jeff Campbell laughing. "I think sometimes Melanctha
I am certainly awful conceited, when I think sometimes I am
all out doors, and I think I certainly am so bright, and better
than most everybody I ever got anything now to do with, but
when I hear you talk this way Melanctha, I certainly do
think I am a real modest kind of fellow." "Modest!" said
Melanctha, angry, "Modest, that certainly is a queer thing
for you Jeff to be calling yourself even when you are laughing." "Well it certainly does depend a whole lot what you are
thinking with," said Jeff Campbell. "I never did use to think
I was so much on being real modest Melanctha, but now I
know really I am, when I hear you talking. I see all the time
there are many people living just as good as I am, though
they are a little different to me. Now with you Melanctha if
I understand you right what you are talking, you don't think
that way of no other one that you are ever knowing." "I certainly could be real modest too, Jeff Campbell," said
Melanctha, "If I could meet somebody once I could keep
right on respecting when I got so I was really knowing with
them. But I certainly never met anybody like that yet, Jeff
Campbell, if you want to know it." "No, Melanctha, and
with the way you got of thinking, it certainly don't look like
as if you ever will Melanctha, with your never remembering
anything only what you just then are feeling in you, and you
not understanding what any one else is ever feeling, if they
don't holler just the way you are doing. No Melanctha, I certainly don't see any ways you are likely ever to meet one, so
good as you are always thinking you be." "No, Jeff Campbell, it certainly ain't that way with me at all the way you say
it. It's because I am always knowing what it is I am wanting,
when I get it. I certainly don't never have to wait till I have

it, and then throw away what I got in me, and then come back and say, that's a mistake I just been making, it ain't that never at all like I understood it, I want to have, bad, what I didn't think it was I wanted. It's that way of knowing right what I am wanting, makes me feel nobody can come right with me, when I am feeling things, Jeff Campbell. I certainly do say Jeff Campbell, I certainly don't think much of the way you always do it, always never knowing what it is you are ever really wanting and everybody always got to suffer. No Jeff, I don't certainly think there is much doubting which is better and the stronger with us two, Jeff Campbell."

"As you will, Melanctha Herbert," cried Jeff Campbell, and he rose up, and he thundered out a black oath, and he was fierce to leave her now forever, and then with the same movement, he took her in his arms and held her.

"What a silly goose boy you are, Jeff Campbell," Melanctha whispered to him fondly.

"Oh yes," said Jeff, very dreary. "I never could keep really mad with anybody, not when I was a little boy and playing. I used most to cry sometimes, I couldn't get real mad and keep on a long time with it, the way everybody always did it. It's certainly no use to me Melanctha, I certainly can't ever keep mad with you Melanctha, my dear one. But don't you ever be thinking it's because I think you right in what you been just saying to me. I don't Melanctha really think it that way, honest, though I certainly can't get mad the way I ought to. No Melanctha, little girl, really truly, you ain't right the way you think it. I certainly do know that Melanctha, honest. You certainly don't do me right Melanctha, the way you say you are thinking. Good-by Melanctha, though you certainly is my own little girl for always." And then they were very good a little to each other, and then Jeff went away for that evening, from her.

Melanctha had begun now once more to wander. Melanctha did not yet always wander, but a little now she needed to begin to look for others. Now Melanctha Herbert began again to be with some of the better kind of black girls, and with them she sometimes wandered. Melanctha had not yet come again to need to be alone, when she wandered.

Jeff Campbell did not know that Melanctha had begun again to wander. All Jeff knew, was that now he could not be so often with her.

Jeff never knew how it had come to happen to him, but now he never thought to go to see Melanctha Herbert, until he had before, asked her if she could be going to have time then to have him with her. Then Melanctha would think a little, and then she would say to him, "Let me see Jeff, to-morrow, you was just saying to me. I certainly am awful busy you know Jeff just now. It certainly does seem to me this week Jeff, I can't always fix it. Sure I want to see you soon Jeff. I certainly Jeff got to do a little more now, I been giving so much time, when I had no business, just to be with you when you asked me. Now I guess Jeff, I certainly can't see you no more this week Jeff, the way I got to do things." "All right Melanctha," Jeff would answer and he would be very angry. "I want to come only just certainly as you want me now Melanctha." "Now Jeff you know I certainly can't be neglecting always to be with everybody just to see you. You come see me next week Tuesday Jeff, you hear me. I don't think Jeff I certainly be so busy, Tuesday." Jeff Campbell would then go away and leave her, and he would be hurt and very angry, for it was hard for a man with a great pride in himself, like Jeff Campbell, to feel himself no better than a beggar. And yet he always came as she said he should, on the day she had fixed for him, and always Jeff Campbell was not sure yet that he really understood what it was Melanctha wanted. Always Melanctha said to him, yes she loved him, sure he knew that. Always Melanctha said to him, she certainly did love him just the same as always, only sure he knew now she certainly did seem to be right busy with all she certainly now had to be doing.

Jeff never knew what Melanctha had to do now, that made her always be so busy, but Jeff Campbell never cared to ask Melanctha such a question. Besides Jeff knew Melanctha Herbert would never, in such a matter, give him any kind of a real answer. Jeff did not know whether it was that Melanctha did not know how to give a simple answer. And then how could he, Jeff, know what was important to her. Jeff Campbell always felt strongly in him, he had no right to interfere with Melanctha in any practical kind of a matter. There they had always, never asked each other any kind of question. There they had felt always in each other, not any right to take care of one another. And Jeff Campbell now felt less than he had ever, any right to claim to know what Melanctha thought it right that she should do in any of her ways of living. All Jeff felt a right in himself to question, was her loving.

Jeff learned every day now, more and more, how much it was that he could really suffer. Sometimes it hurt so in him, when he was alone, it would force some slow tears from him. But every day, now that Jeff Campbell, knew more how it could hurt him, he lost his feeling of deep awe that he once always had had for Melanctha's feeling. Suffering was not so much after all, thought Jeff Campbell, if even he could feel it so it hurt him. It hurt him bad, just the way he knew he once had hurt Melanctha, and yet he too could have it and not make any kind of a loud holler with it.

In tenderhearted natures, those that mostly never feel strong passion, suffering often comes to make them harder. When these do not know in themselves what it is to suffer, suffering is then very awful to them and they badly want to help everyone who ever has to suffer, and they have a deep reverence for anybody who knows really how to always suffer. But when it comes to them to really suffer, they soon

begin to lose their fear and tenderness and wonder. Why it
isn't so very much to suffer, when even I can bear to do it.
It isn't very pleasant to be having all the time, to stand it, but
they are not so much wiser after all, all the others just because they know too how to bear it.

Passionate natures who have always made themselves, to
suffer, that is all the kind of people who have emotions that
come to them as sharp as a sensation, they always get more
tender-hearted when they suffer, and it always does them
good to suffer. Tender-hearted, unpassionate, and comfortable natures always get much harder when they suffer, for so
they lose the fear and reverence and wonder they once had
for everybody who ever has to suffer, for now they know
themselves what it is to suffer and it is not so awful any
longer to them when they know too, just as well as all the
others, how to have it.

And so it came in these days to Jeff Campbell. Jeff knew
now always, way inside him, what it is to really suffer, and
now every day with it, he knew how to understand Melanctha better. Jeff Campbell still loved Melanctha Herbert and
he still had a real trust in her and he still had a little hope that
some day they would once more get together, but slowly,
every day, this hope in him would keep growing always
weaker. They still were a good deal of time together, but
now they never any more were really trusting with each
other. In the days when they used to be together, Jeff had felt
he did not know much what was inside Melanctha, but he
knew very well, how very deep always was his trust in her;
now he knew Melanctha Herbert better, but now he never
felt a deep trust in her. Now Jeff never could be really honest with her. He never doubted yet, that she was steady only
to him, but somehow he could not believe much really in
Melanctha's loving.

Melanctha Herbert was a little angry now when Jeff
asked her, "I never give nobody before Jeff, ever more than

one chance with me, and I certainly been giving you most a hundred Jeff, you hear me." "And why shouldn't you Melanctha, give me a million, if you really love me!" Jeff flashed out very angry. "I certainly don't know as you deserve that anyways from me, Jeff Campbell." "It ain't deserving, I am ever talking about to you Melanctha. It's loving, and if you are really loving to me you won't certainly never any ways call them chances." "Deed Jeff, you certainly are getting awful wise Jeff now, ain't you, to me." "No I ain't Melanctha, and I ain't jealous either to you. I just am doubting from the way you are always acting to me." "Oh yes Jeff, that's what they all say, the same way, when they certainly got jealousy all through them. You ain't got no cause to be jealous with me Jeff, and I am awful tired of all this talking now, you hear me."

Jeff Campbell never asked Melanctha any more if she loved him. Now things were always getting worse between them. Now Jeff never wanted to be honest to her, and now Jeff never had much to say to her.

Now when they were together, it was Melanctha always did most of the talking. Now she often had other girls there with her. Melanctha was always kind to Jeff Campbell but she never seemed to need to be alone now with him. She always treated Jeff, like her best friend, and she always spoke so to him and yet she never seemed now to very often want to see him.

Every day it was getting harder for Jeff Campbell. It was as if now, when he had learned to really love Melanctha, she did not need any more to have him. Jeff began to know this very well inside him.

Jeff Campbell did not know yet that Melanctha had begun again to wander. Jeff was not very quick to suspect Melanctha. All Jeff knew was, that he did not trust her to be now really loving to him.

Jeff was no longer now in any doubt inside him. He knew

very well now he really loved Melanctha. He knew now
very well she was not any more a real religion to him. Jeff
Campbell knew very well too now inside him, he did not really want Melanctha, now if he could no longer trust her,
though he loved her hard and really knew now what it was
to suffer.

Every day Melanctha Herbert was less and less near to
him. She always was very pleasant in her talk and to be with
him, but somehow now it never was any comfort to him.

Melanctha Herbert now always had a lot of friends
around her. Jeff Campbell never wanted to be with them.
Now Melanctha began to find it, she said it often to him, always harder to arrange to be alone now with him. Sometimes she would be late for him. Then Jeff always would try
to be patient in his waiting, for Jeff Campbell knew very
well how to remember, and he knew it was only right that he
should now endure this from her.

Then Melanctha began to manage often not to see him,
and once she went away when she had promised to be there
to meet him.

Then Jeff Campbell was really filled up with his anger.
Now he knew he could never really want her. Now he knew
he never any more could really trust her.

Jeff Campbell never knew why Melanctha had not come
to meet him. Jeff had heard a little talking now, about how
Melanctha Herbert had commenced once more to wander.
Jeff Campbell still sometimes saw Jane Harden, who always
needed a doctor to be often there to help her. Jane Harden always knew very well what happened to Melanctha. Jeff
Campbell never would talk to Jane Harden anything about
Melanctha. Jeff was always loyal to Melanctha. Jeff never
let Jane Harden say much to him about Melanctha, though
he never let her know that now he loved her. But somehow
Jeff did know now about Melanctha, and he knew about

some men that Melanctha met with Rose Johnson very often.

Jeff Campbell would not let himself really doubt Melanctha, but Jeff began to know now very well, he did not want her. Melanctha Herbert did not love him ever, Jeff knew it now, the way he once had thought that she could feel it. Once she had been greater for him than he had thought he could ever know how to feel it. Now Jeff had come to where he could understand Melanctha Herbert. Jeff was not bitter to her because she could not really love him, he was bitter only that he had let himself have a real illusion in him. He was a little bitter too, that he had lost now, what he had always felt real in the world, that had made it for him always full of beauty, and now he had not got this new religion really, and he had lost what he before had to know what was good and had real beauty.

Jeff Campbell was so angry now in him, because he had begged Melanctha always to be honest to him. Jeff could stand it in her not to love him, he could not stand it in her not to be honest to him.

Jeff Campbell went home from where Melanctha had not met him, and he was sore and full of anger in him.

Jeff Campbell could not be sure what to do, to make it right inside him. Surely he must be strong now and cast this loving from him, and yet, was he sure he now had real wisdom in him. Was he sure that Melanctha Herbert never had had a real deep loving for him. Was he sure Melanctha Herbert never had deserved a reverence from him. Always now Jeff had this torment in him, but always now he felt more that Melanctha never had real greatness for him.

Jeff waited to see if Melanctha would send any word to him. Melanctha Herbert never sent a line to him.

At last Jeff wrote his letter to Melanctha. "Dear Melanctha, I certainly do know you ain't been any way sick this last week when you never met me right the way you promised, and never sent me any word to say why you acted a way you certainly never could think was the right way you should do it to me. Jane Harden said she saw you that day and you went out walking with some people you like now to be with. Don't be misunderstanding me now any more Melanctha. I love you now because that's my slow way to learn what you been teaching, but I know now you certainly never had what seems to me real kind of feeling. I don't love you Melanctha any more now like a real religion, because now I know you are just made like all us others. I know now no man can ever really hold you because no man can ever be real to trust in you, because you mean right Melanctha, but you never can remember, and so you certainly never have got any way to be honest. So please you understand me right now Melanctha, it never is I don't know how to love you. I do know now how to love you, Melanctha, really. You sure do know that, Melanctha, in me. You certainly always can trust me. And so now Melanctha, I can say to you certainly real honest with you, I am better than you are in my right kind of feeling. And so Melanctha, I don't never any more want to be a trouble to you. You certainly make me see things Melanctha, I never any other way could be knowing. You been very good and patient to me, when I was certainly below you in my right feeling. I certainly never have been near so good and patient to you ever any way Melanctha, I certainly know that Melanctha. But Melanctha, with me, it certainly is, always to be good together, two people certainly must be thinking each one as good as the other, to be really loving right Melanctha. And it certainly must never be any kind of feeling, of one only taking, and one only just giving, Melanctha, to me. I know you certainly don't really ever understand me now Melanctha, but that's no matter. I certainly do know what I am feeling now with you real Melanctha. And so good-by now for good Melanctha. I say I can never ever really trust you real Melanctha, that's only just certainly from your way of not being ever equal in your feeling to anybody real, Melanctha, and your way never to know right how to remember. Many ways I really trust you deep Melanctha, and I certainly do feel deep all the good sweetness you certainly got real in you Melanctha. It's only just in your loving me Melanctha. You never can be equal to me and that I certainly never can bear any more to have it. And so now Melanctha, I always be your friend, if you need me, and now we never see each other any more to talk to."

And then Jeff Campbell thought and thought, and he could never make any way for him now, to see it different, and so at last he sent this letter to Melanctha.

And now surely it was all over in Jeff Campbell. Surely now he never any more could know Melanctha. And yet, perhaps Melanctha really loved him. And then she would know how much it hurt him never any more, any way, to see her, and perhaps she would write a line to tell him. But that was a foolish way for Jeff ever to be thinking. Of course Melanctha never would write a word to him. It was all over now for always, everything between them, and Jeff felt it a real relief to him.

For many days now Jeff Campbell only felt it as a relief in him. Jeff was all locked up and quiet now inside him. It was all settling down heavy in him, and these days when it was sinking so deep in him, it was only the rest and quiet of not fighting that he could really feel inside him. Jeff Campbell could not think now, or feel anything else in him. He had no beauty nor any goodness to see around him. It was a dull, pleasant kind of quiet he now had inside him. Jeff almost began to love this dull quiet in him, for it was more nearly being free for him than anything he had known in him since Melanctha Herbert first had moved him. He did not find it a real rest yet for him, he had not really conquered what had been working so long in him, he had not learned to see beauty and real goodness yet in what had happened to

him, but it was rest even if he was sodden now all through
him. Jeff Campbell liked it very well, not to have fighting always going on inside him.

And so Jeff went on every day, and he was quiet, and he
began again to watch himself in his working; and he did not
see any beauty now around him, and it was dull and heavy
always now inside him, and yet he was content to have gone
so far in keeping steady to what he knew was the right way
for him to come back to, to be regular, and see beauty in
every kind of quiet way of living, the way he had always
wanted it for himself and for all the colored people. He
knew he had lost the sense he once had of joy all through
him, but he could work, and perhaps he would bring some
real belief back into him about the beauty that he could not
now any more see around him.

And so Jeff Campbell went on with his working, and he
staid home every evening, and he began again with his reading, and he did not do much talking, and he did not seem to
himself to have any kind of feeling.

And one day Jeff thought perhaps he really was forgetting, one day he thought he could soon come back and be
happy in his old way of regular and quiet living.

Jeff Campbell had never talked to any one of what had
been going on inside him. Jeff Campbell liked to talk and he
was honest, but it never came out from him, anything he was
ever really feeling, it only came out from him, what it was
that he was always thinking. Jeff Campbell always was very
proud to hide what he was really feeling. Always he blushed
hot to think things he had been feeling. Only to Melanctha
Herbert, had it ever come to him, to tell what it was that he
was feeling.

And so Jeff Campbell went on with this dull and sodden,
heavy, quiet always in him, and he never seemed to be able
to have any feeling. Only sometimes he shivered hot with
shame when he remembered some things he once had been

feeling. And then one day it all woke up, and was sharp in him.

Dr. Campbell was just then staying long times with a sick man who might soon be dying. One day the sick man was resting. Dr. Campbell went to the window to look out a little, while he was waiting. It was very early now in the southern springtime. The trees were just beginning to get the little zigzag crinkles in them, which the young buds always give them. The air was soft and moist and pleasant to them. The earth was wet and rich and smelling for them. The birds were making sharp fresh noises all around them. The wind was very gentle and yet urgent to them. And the buds and the long earthworms, and the negroes, and all the kinds of children, were coming out every minute farther into the new spring, watery, southern sunshine.

Jeff Campbell too began to feel a little his old joy inside him. The sodden quiet began to break up in him. He leaned far out of the window to mix it all up with him. His heart went sharp and then it almost stopped inside him. Was it Melanctha Herbert he had just seen passing by him? Was it Melanctha, or was it just some other girl, who made him feel so bad inside him? Well, it was no matter, Melanctha was there in the world around him, he did certainly always know that in him. Melanctha Herbert was always in the same town with him, and he could never any more feel her near him. What a fool he was to throw her from him. Did he know she did not really love him. Suppose Melanctha was now suffering through him. Suppose she really would be glad to see him. And did anything else he did, really mean anything now to him? What a fool he was to cast her from him. And yet did Melanctha Herbert want him, was she honest to him, had Melanctha ever loved him, and did Melanctha now suffer by him? Oh! Oh! Oh! and the bitter water once more rose up in him.

All that long day, with the warm moist young spring stirring in him, Jeff Campbell worked, and thought, and beat his breast, and wandered, and spoke aloud, and was silent, and was certain, and then in doubt and then keen to surely feel, and then all sodden in him; and he walked, and he sometimes ran fast to lose himself in his rushing, and he bit his nails to pain and bleeding, and he tore his hair so that he could be sure he was really feeling, and he never could know what it was right, he now should be doing. And then late that night he wrote it all out to Melanctha Herbert, and he made himself quickly send it without giving himself any time to change it.

"It has come to me strong to-day Melanctha, perhaps I am wrong the way I now am thinking. Perhaps you do want me badly to be with you. Perhaps I have hurt you once again the way I used to. I certainly Melanctha, if I ever think that really, I certainly do want bad not to be wrong now ever any more to you. If you do feel the way to-day it came to me strong may-be you are feeling, then say so Melanctha to me, and I come again to see you. If not, don't say anything any more ever to me. I don't want ever to be bad to you Melanctha, really. I never want ever to be a bother to you. I never can stand it to think I am wrong, really, thinking you don't want me to come to you. Tell me Melanctha, tell me honest to me, shall I come now any more to see you." "Yes" came the answer, from Melanctha, "I be home Jeff to-night to see you."

Jeff Campbell went that evening late to see Melanctha Herbert. As Jeff came nearer to her, he doubted that he wanted really to be with her, he felt that he did not know what it was he now wanted from her. Jeff Campbell knew very well now, way inside him, that they could never talk their trouble out between them. What was it Jeff wanted now to tell Melanctha Herbert? What was it that Jeff Campbell now could tell her? Surely he never now could learn to trust her. Surely Jeff knew very well all that Melanctha always had inside her. And yet it was awful, never any more to see her.

Jeff Campbell went in to Melanctha, and he kissed her, and he held her, and then he went away from her and he stood still and looked at her. "Well Jeff!" "Yes Melanctha!" "Jeff what was it made you act so to me?" "You know very well Melanctha, it's always I am thinking you don't love me, and you are acting to me good out of kindness, and then Melanctha you certainly never did say anything to me why you never came to meet me, as you certainly did promise to me you would that day I never saw you!" "Jeff don't you really know for certain, I always love you?" "No Melanctha, deed I don't know it in me. Deed and certain sure Melanctha, if I only know that in me, I certainly never would give you any bother." "Jeff, I certainly do love you more seems to me always, you certainly had ought to feel that in you." "Sure Melanctha?" "Sure Jeff boy, you know that." "But then Melanctha why did you act so to me?" "Oh Jeff you certainly been such a bother to me. I just had to go away that day Jeff, and I certainly didn't mean not to tell you, and then that letter you wrote came to me and something happened to me. I don't know right what it was Jeff, I just kind of fainted, and what could I do Jeff, you said you certainly never any more wanted to come and see me!" "And no matter Melanctha, even if you knew, it was just killing me to act so to you, you never would have said nothing to me?" "No of course, how could I Jeff when you wrote that way to me. I know how you was feeling Jeff to me, but I certainly couldn't say nothing to you." "Well Melanctha, I certainly know I am right proud too in me, but I certainly never could act so to you Melanctha, if I ever knew any way at all you ever really loved me. No Melanctha darling, you and me certainly don't feel much the same way ever. Any way Melanctha, I certainly do love you true Melanctha." "And I love you too Jeff, even though you don't never certainly seem to believe me." "No I certainly don't any way believe you Melanctha, even when you say it to me. I don't know Melanctha how, but sure I certainly do trust you, only I don't believe now ever in your really being loving to me. I certainly do know you trust me always Melanctha, only somehow it ain't ever all right to me. I certainly don't know any way otherwise Melanctha, how I can say it to you." "Well I certainly can't help you no ways any more Jeff Campbell, though you certainly say it right when you say I trust you Jeff now always. You certainly is the best man Jeff Campbell, I ever can know, to me. I never been always thinking it can be ever different to me." "Well you trust me then Melanctha, and I certainly love you Melanctha, and seems like to me Melanctha, you and me had ought to be a little better than we certainly ever are doing now to be together. You certainly do think that way, too, Melanctha to me. But may be you do really love me. Tell me, please, real honest now Melanctha darling, tell me so I really always know it in me, do you really truly love me?" "Oh you stupid, stupid boy, Jeff Campbell. Love you, what do you think makes me always to forgive you. If I certainly didn't always love you Jeff, I certainly never would let you be always being all the time such a bother to me the way you certainly Jeff always are to me. Now don't you dass ever any more say words like that ever to me. You hear me now Jeff, or I do something real bad sometime, so I really hurt you. Now Jeff you just be good to me. You know Jeff how bad I need it, now you should always be good to me!"

Jeff Campbell could not make an answer to Melanctha. What was it he should now say to her? What words could help him to make their feeling any better? Jeff Campbell knew that he had learned to love deeply, that, he always knew very well now in him, Melanctha had learned to be strong to be always trusting, that he knew too now inside him, but Melanctha did not really love him, that he felt always too strong for him. That fact always was there in him, and it always thrust itself firm, between them. And so this talk did not make things really better for them.

Jeff Campbell was never any more a torment to Melanctha, he was only silent to her. Jeff often saw Melanctha and he was very friendly with her and he never any more was a bother to her. Jeff never any more now had much chance to be loving with her. Melanctha never was alone now when he saw her.

Melanctha Herbert had just been getting thick in her trouble with Jeff Campbell, when she went to that church where she first met Rose, who later was married regularly to Sam Johnson. Rose was a good-looking, better kind of black girl, and had been brought up quite like their own child by white folks. Rose was living now with colored people. Rose was staying just then with a colored woman, who had known 'Mis' Herbert and her black husband and this girl Melanctha.

Rose soon got to like Melanctha Herbert and Melanctha now always wanted to be with Rose, whenever she could do it. Melanctha Herbert always was doing everything for Rose that she could think of that Rose ever wanted. Rose always liked to be with nice people who would do things for her. Rose had strong common sense and she was lazy. Rose liked Melanctha Herbert, she had such kind of fine ways in her. Then, too, Rose had it in her to be sorry for the subtle, sweet-natured, docile, intelligent Melanctha Herbert who always was so blue sometimes, and always had had so much trouble. Then, too, Rose could scold Melanctha, for Melanctha Herbert never could know how to keep herself from trouble, and Rose was always strong to keep straight, with her simple selfish wisdom.

But why did the subtle, intelligent, attractive, half white girl Melanctha Herbert, with her sweetness and her power and her wisdom, demean herself to do for and to flatter and to be scolded, by this lazy, stupid, ordinary, selfish black girl. This was a queer thing in Melanctha Herbert.

And so now in these new spring days, it was with Rose that Melanctha began again to wander. Rose always knew very well in herself what was the right way to do when you wandered. Rose knew very well, she was not just any common kind of black girl, for she had been raised by white folks, and Rose always saw to it that she was engaged to him when she had any one man with whom she ever always wandered. Rose always had strong in her the sense for proper conduct. Rose always was telling the complex and less sure Melanctha, what was the right way she should do when she wandered.

Rose never knew much about Jeff Campbell with Melanctha Herbert. Rose had now known about Melanctha Herbert when she had been almost all her time with Dr. Campbell.

Jeff Campbell did not like Rose when he saw her with Melanctha. Jeff would never, when he could help it, meet her. Rose did not think much about Dr. Campbell. Melanctha never talked much about him to her. He was not important now to be with her.

Rose did not like Melanctha's old friend Jane Harden when she saw her. Jane despised Rose for an ordinary, stupid, sullen black girl. Jane could not see what Melanctha could find in that black girl, to endure her. It made Jane sick to see her. But then Melanctha had a good mind, but she certainly never did care much to really use it. Jane Harden now really never cared any more to see Melanctha, though Melanctha still always tried to be good to her. And Rose, she hated that stuck up, mean speaking, nasty, drunk thing, Jane Harden. Rose did not see how Melanctha could bear to ever see her, but Melanctha always was so good to everybody, she never would know how to act to people the way they deserved that she should do it.

Rose did not know much about Melanctha, and Jeff Campbell and Jane Harden. All Rose knew about Melanctha was her old life with her mother and her father. Rose was always glad to be good to poor Melanctha, who had had such an awful time with her mother and her father, and now she was alone and had nobody who could help her. "He was a awful black man to you Melanctha, I like to get my hands on him so he certainly could feel it. I just would Melanctha, now you hear me."

Perhaps it was this simple faith and simple anger and simple moral way of doing in Rose, that Melanctha now found such a comfort to her. Rose was selfish and was stupid and was lazy, but she was decent and knew always what was the right way she should do, and what she wanted, and she certainly did admire how bright was her friend Melanctha Herbert, and she certainly did feel how very much it was she always suffered and she scolded her to keep her from more trouble, and she never was angry when she found some of the different ways Melanctha Herbert sometimes had to do it.

And so always Rose and Melanctha were more and more together, and Jeff Campbell could now hardly ever any more be alone with Melanctha.

Once Jeff had to go away to another town to see a sick man. "When I come back Monday Melanctha, I come Monday evening to see you. You be home alone once Melanctha to see me." "Sure Jeff, I be glad to see you!"

When Jeff Campbell came to his house on Monday there was a note there from Melanctha. Could Jeff come day after to-morrow, Wednesday? Melanctha was so sorry she had to go out that evening. She was awful sorry and she hoped Jeff would not be angry.

Jeff was angry and he swore a little, and then he laughed, and then he sighed. "Poor Melanctha, she don't know any way to be real honest, but no matter, I sure do love her and I be good if only she will let me."

Jeff Campbell went Wednesday night to see Melanctha. Jeff Campbell took her in his arms and kissed her. "I certainly am awful sorry not to see you Jeff Monday, the way I promised, but I just couldn't Jeff, no way I could fix it." Jeff looked at her and then he laughed a little at her. "You want me to believe that really now Melanctha. All right I believe it if you want me to Melanctha. I certainly be good to you to-night the way you like it. I believe you certainly did want to see me Melanctha, and there was no way you could fix it." "Oh Jeff dear," said Melanctha, "I sure was wrong to act so to you. It's awful hard for me ever to say it to you, I have been wrong in my acting to you, but I certainly was bad this time Jeff to you. It do certainly come hard to me to say it Jeff, but I certainly was wrong to go away from you the way I did it. Only you always certainly been so bad Jeff, and such a bother to me, and making everything always so hard for me, and I certainly got some way to do it to make it come back sometimes to you. You bad boy Jeff, now you hear me, and this certainly is the first time Jeff I ever yet said it to anybody, I ever been wrong, Jeff, you hear me!" "All right Melanctha, I sure do forgive you, cause it's certainly the first time I ever heard you say you ever did anything wrong the way you shouldn't," and Jeff Campbell laughed and kissed her, and Melanctha laughed and loved him, and they really were happy now for a little time together.

And now they were very happy in each other and then they were silent and then they became a little sadder and then they were very quiet once more with each other.

"Yes I certainly do love you Jeff!" Melanctha said and she was very dreamy. "Sure, Melanctha." "Yes Jeff sure, but not the way you are now ever thinking. I love you more and more seems to me Jeff always, and I certainly do trust you more and more always to me when I know you. I do love you Jeff, sure yes, but not the kind of way of loving you are ever thinking it now Jeff with me. I ain't got certainly no hot passion any more now in me. You certainly have killed all that kind of feeling now Jeff in me. You certainly do know that Jeff, now the way I am always, when I am loving with you. You certainly do know that Jeff, and that's the way you certainly do like it now in me. You certainly don't mind now Jeff, to hear me say this to you."

Jeff Campbell was hurt so that it almost killed him. Yes he certainly did know now what it was to have real hot love in him, and yet Melanctha certainly was right, he did not deserve she should ever give it to him. "All right Melanctha I ain't ever kicking. I always will give you certainly always everything you want that I got in me. I take anything you want now to give me. I don't say never Melanctha it don't hurt me, but I certainly don't say ever Melanctha it ought ever to be any different to me." And the bitter tears rose up in Jeff Campbell, and they came and choked his voice to be silent, and he held himself hard to keep from breaking.

"Good-night Melanctha," and Jeff was very humble to her. "Good-night Jeff, I certainly never did mean any way to hurt you. I do love you, sure Jeff every day more and more, all the time I know you." "I know Melanctha, I know, it's never nothing to me. You can't help it, anybody ever the way they are feeling. It's all right now Melanctha, you believe me, good-night now Melanctha, I got now to leave you, good-by Melanctha, sure don't look so worried to me, sure Melanctha I come again soon to see you." And then Jeff stumbled down the steps, and he went away fast to leave her.

And now the pain came hard and harder in Jeff Campbell, and he groaned, and it hurt him so, he could not bear it. And the tears came, and his heart beat, and he was hot and worn and bitter in him.

Now Jeff knew very well what it was to love Melanctha. Now Jeff Campbell knew he was really understanding. Now

Jeff knew what it was to be good to Melanctha. Now Jeff was good to her always.

Slowly Jeff felt it a comfort in him to have it hurt so, and to be good to Melanctha always. Now there was no way Melanctha ever had had to bear things from him, worse than he now had it in him. Now Jeff was strong inside him. Now with all the pain there was peace in him. Now he knew he was understanding, now he knew he had a hot love in him, and he was good always to Melanctha Herbert who was the one had made him have it. Now he knew he could be good, and not cry out for help to her to teach him how to bear it. Every day Jeff felt himself more a strong man, the way he once had thought was his real self, the way he knew it. Now Jeff Campbell had real wisdom in him, and it did not make him bitter when it hurt him, for Jeff knew now all through him that he was really strong to bear it.

And so now Jeff Campbell could see Melanctha often, and he was patient, and always very friendly to her, and every day Jeff Campbell understood Melanctha Herbert better. And always Jeff saw Melanctha could not love him the way he needed she should do it. Melanctha Herbert had no way she ever really could remember.

And now Jeff knew there was a man Melanctha met very often, and perhaps she wanted to try to have this man to be good, for her. Jeff Campbell never saw the man Melanctha Herbert perhaps now wanted. Jeff Campbell only knew very well that there was one. Then there was Rose that Melanctha now always had with her when she wandered.

Jeff Campbell was very quiet to Melanctha. He said to her, now he thought he did not want to come any more especially to see her. When they met, he always would be glad to see her, but now he never would go anywhere any more to meet her. Sure he knew she always would have a deep love in him for her. Sure she knew that. "Yes Jeff, I always trust you Jeff, I certainly do know that all right." Jeff Campbell said, all right he never could say anything to reproach her. She knew always that he really had learned all through him how to love her. "Yes, Jeff, I certainly do know that." She knew now she could always trust him. Jeff always would be loyal to her though now she never was any more to him like a religion, but he never could forget the real sweetness in her. That Jeff must remember always, though now he never can trust her to be really loving to any man for always, she never did have any way she ever could remember. If she ever needed anybody to be good to her, Jeff Campbell always would do anything he could to help her. He never can forget the things she taught him so he could be really understanding, but he never any more wants to see her. He be like a brother to her always, when she needs it, and he always will be a good friend to her. Jeff Campbell certainly was sorry never any more to see her, but it was good that they now knew each other really. "Good-by Jeff you always been very good always to me." "Good-by Melanctha you know you always can trust yourself to me." "Yes, I know, I know Jeff, really." "I certainly got to go now Melanctha, from you. I go this time, Melanctha really," and Jeff Campbell went away and this time he never looked back to her. This time Jeff Campbell just broke away and left her.

Jeff Campbell loved to think now he was strong again to be quiet, and to live regular, and to do everything the way he wanted it to be right for himself and all the colored people. Jeff went away for a little while to another town to work there, and he worked hard, and he was very sad inside him, and sometimes the tears would rise up in him, and then he would work hard, and then he would begin once more to see some beauty in the world around him. Jeff had behaved right and he had learned to have a real love in him. That was very good to have inside him.

Jeff Campbell never could forget the sweetness in Melanctha Herbert, and he was always very friendly to her, but they

never any more came close to one another. More and more
Jeff Campbell and Melanctha fell away from all knowing of
each other, but Jeff never could forget Melanctha. Jeff never
could forget the real sweetness she had in her, but Jeff never
any more had the sense of a real religion for her. Jeff always
had strong in him the meaning of all the new kind of beauty
Melanctha Herbert once had shown him, and always more
and more it helped him with his working for himself and for
all the colored people.

Melanctha Herbert, now that she was all through with
Jeff Campbell, was free to be with Rose and the new men
she met now.

Rose was always now with Melanctha Herbert. Rose
never found any way to get excited. Rose always was telling
Melanctha Herbert the right way she should do, so that she
would not always be in trouble. But Melanctha Herbert
could not help it, always she would find new ways to get excited.

Melanctha was all ready now to find new ways to be in
trouble. And yet Melanctha Herbert never wanted not to do
right. Always Melanctha Herbert wanted peace and quiet,
and always she could only find new ways to get excited.

"Melanctha," Rose would say to her, "Melanctha, I certainly have got to tell you, you ain't right to act so with that
kind of feller. You better just had stick to black men now,
Melanctha, you hear me what I tell you, just the way you always see me do it. They're real bad men, now I tell you
Melanctha true, and you better had hear to me. I been raised
by real nice kind of white folks, Melanctha, and I certainly
knows awful well, soon as ever I can see 'em acting, what is
a white man will act decent to you and the kind it ain't never
no good to a colored girl to ever go with. Now you know
real Melanctha how I always mean right good to you, and
you ain't got no way like me Melanctha, what was raised by
white folks, to know right what is the way you should be

acting with men. I don't never want to see you have bad
trouble come hard to you now Melanctha, and so you just
hear to me now Melanctha, what I tell you, for I knows it. I
don't say never certainly to you Melanctha, you never had
ought to have nothing to do ever with no white men, though
it ain't never to me Melanctha, the best kind of a way a colored girl can have to be acting, no I never do say to you
Melanctha, you hadn't never ought to be with white men,
though it ain't never the way I feel it ever real right for a decent colored girl to be always doing, but not never Melanctha, now you hear me, no not never no kind of white men
like you been with always now Melanctha when I see you.
You just hear to me Melanctha, you certainly had ought to
hear to me Melanctha, I say it just like I knows it awful well,
Melanctha, and I knows you don't know no better, Melanctha, how to act so, the ways I seen it with them kind of white
fellers, them as never can know what to do right by a decent
girl they have ever got to be with them. Now you hear to me
Melanctha, what I tell you."

And so it was Melanctha Herbert found new ways to be
in trouble. But it was not very bad this trouble, for these
white men Rose never wanted she should be with, never
meant very much to Melanctha. It was only that she liked it
to be with them, and they knew all about fine horses, and it
was just good to Melanctha, now a little, to feel real reckless
with them. But mostly it was Rose and other better kind of
colored girls and colored men with whom Melanctha Herbert now always wandered.

It was summer now and the colored people came out into
the sunshine, full blown with the flowers. And they shone in
the streets and in the fields with their warm joy, and they
glistened in their black heat, and they flung themselves free
in their wide abandonment of shouting laughter.

It was very pleasant in some ways, the life Melanctha

Herbert now led with Rose and all the others. It was not always that Rose had to scold her.

There was not anybody of all these colored people, excepting only Rose, who ever meant much to Melanctha Herbert. But they all liked Melanctha, and the men all liked to see her do things, she was so game always to do anything anybody ever could do, and then she was good and sweet to do anything anybody ever wanted from her.

These were pleasant days then, in the hot southern negro sunshine, with many simple jokes and always wide abandonment of laughter. "Just look at that Melanctha there a running. Don't she just go like a bird when she is flying. Hey Melanctha there, I come and catch you, hey Melanctha, I put salt on your tail to catch you," and then the man would try to catch her, and he would fall full on the earth and roll in an agony of wide-mouthed shouting laughter. And this was the kind of way Rose always liked to have Melanctha do it, to be engaged to him, and to have a good warm nigger time with colored men, not to go about with that kind of white man, never could know how to act right, to any decent kind of girl they could ever get to be with them.

Rose, always more and more, liked Melanctha Herbert better. Rose often had to scold Melanctha Herbert, but that only made her like Melanctha better. And then Melanctha always listened to her, and always acted every way she could to please her. And then Rose was so sorry for Melanctha, when she was so blue sometimes, and wanted somebody should come and kill her.

And Melanctha Herbert clung to Rose in the hope that Rose could save her. Melanctha felt the power of Rose's selfish, decent kind of nature. It was so solid, simple, certain to her. Melanctha clung to Rose, she loved to have her scold her, she always wanted to be with her. She always felt a solid safety in her. Rose always was, in her way, very good to let Melanctha be loving to her. Melanctha never had any way she could really be a trouble to her. Melanctha never had any way that she could ever get real power, to come close inside to her. Melanctha was always very humble to her. Melanctha was always ready to do anything Rose wanted from her. Melanctha needed badly to have Rose always willing to let Melanctha cling to her. Rose was a simple, sullen, selfish, black girl, but she had a solid power in her. Rose had strong the sense of decent conduct, she had strong the sense for decent comfort. Rose always knew very well what it was she wanted, and she knew very well what was the right way to do to get everything she wanted, and she never had any kind of trouble to perplex her. And so the subtle intelligent attractive half white girl Melanctha Herbert loved and did for, and demeaned herself in service to this coarse, decent, sullen, ordinary, black, childish Rose and now this unmoral promiscuous shiftless Rose was to be married to a good man of the negroes, while Melanctha Herbert with her white blood and attraction and her desire for a right position was perhaps never to be really regularly married. Sometimes the thought of how all her world was made filled the complex, desiring Melanctha with despair. She wondered often how she could go on living when she was so blue. Sometimes Melanctha thought she would just kill herself, for sometimes she thought this would be really the best thing for her to do.

Rose was now to be married to a decent good man of the negroes. His name was Sam Johnson, and he worked as a deck hand on a coasting steamer, and he was very steady, and he got good wages.

Rose first met Sam Johnson at church, the same place where she had met Melanctha Herbert. Rose liked Sam when she saw him, she knew he was a good man and worked hard and got good wages, and Rose thought it would be very nice and very good now in her position to get really, regularly married.

Sam Johnson liked Rose very well and he always was ready to do anything she wanted. Sam was a tall, square shouldered, decent, a serious, straightforward, simple, kindly, colored workman. They got on very well together, Sam and Rose, when they were married. Rose was lazy, but not dirty, and Sam was careful but not fussy. Sam was a kindly, simple, earnest, steady workman, and Rose had good common decent sense in her, of how to live regular, and not to have excitements, and to be saving so you could be always sure to have money, so as to have everything you wanted.

It was not very long that Rose knew Sam Johnson, before they were regularly married. Sometimes Sam went into the country with all the other young church people, and then he would be a great deal with Rose and with her Melanctha Herbert. Sam did not care much about Melanctha Herbert. He liked Rose's ways of doing, always better. Melanctha's mystery had no charm for Sam ever. Sam wanted a nice little house to come to when he was tired from his working, and a little baby all his own he could be good to. Sam Johnson was ready to marry as soon as ever Rose wanted he should do it. And so Sam Johnson and Rose one day had a grand real wedding and were married. Then they furnished completely, a little red brick house and then Sam went back to his work as deck hand on a coasting steamer.

Rose had often talked to Sam about how good Melanctha was and how much she always suffered. Sam Johnson never really cared about Melanctha Herbert, but he always did almost everything Rose ever wanted, and he was a gentle, kindly creature, and so he was very good to Rose's friend Melanctha. Melanctha Herbert knew very well Sam did not like her, and so she was very quiet, and always let Rose do the talking for her. She only was very good to always help Rose, and to do anything she ever wanted from her, and to be very good and listen and be quiet whenever Sam had anything to say to her. Melanctha liked Sam Johnson, and all her life Melanctha loved and wanted good and kind and considerate people, and always Melanctha loved and wanted people to be gentle to her, and always she wanted to be regular, and to have peace and quiet in her, and always Melanctha could only find new ways to be in trouble. And Melanctha needed badly to have Rose, to believe her, and to let her cling to her. Rose was the only steady thing Melanctha had to cling to and so Melanctha demeaned herself to be like a servant, to wait on, and always to be scolded, by this ordinary, sullen black, stupid, childish woman.

Rose was always telling Sam he must be good to poor Melanctha. "You know Sam," Rose said very often to him, "You certainly had ought to be very good to poor Melanctha, she always do have so much trouble with her. You know Sam how I told you she had such a bad time always with that father, and he was awful mean to her always that awful black man, and he never took no kind of care ever to her, and he never helped her when her mother died so hard, that poor Melanctha. Melanctha's ma you know Sam, always was just real religious. One day Melanctha was real little, and she heard her ma say to her pa, it was awful sad to her, Melanctha had not been the one the Lord had took from them stead of the little brother who was dead in the house there from fever. That hurt Melanctha awful when she heard her ma say it. She never could feel it right, and I don't no ways blame Melanctha, Sam, for not feeling better to her ma always after, though Melanctha, just like always she is, always was real good to her ma after, when she was so sick, and died so hard, and nobody never to help Melanctha do it, and she just all alone to do everything without no help come to her no way, and that ugly awful black man she have for a father never all the time come near her. But that's always the way Melanctha is just doing Sam, the way I been telling to you. She always is being just so good to everybody and nobody ever there to thank her for it. I never did see nobody ever Sam, have such bad luck, seems to me always with them, like that poor Melanctha always has it, and she always so good with it, and never no murmur in her, and never no complaining from her, and just never saying nothing with it. You be real good to her Sam, now you hear me, now you and me is married right together. He certainly was an awful black man to her Sam, that father she had, acting always just like a brute to her and she so game and never to tell anybody how it hurt her. And she so sweet and good always to do anything anybody ever can be wanting. I don't see Sam how some men can be to act so awful. I told you Sam, how once Melanctha broke her arm bad and she was so sick and it hurt her awful and he never would let no doctor come near to her and he do some things so awful to her, she don't never want to tell nobody how bad he hurt her. That's just the way Sam with Melanctha always, you never can know how bad it is, it hurts her. You hear me Sam, you always be real good to her now you and me is married right to each other."

And so Rose and Sam Johnson were regularly married, and Rose sat at home and bragged to all her friends how nice it was to be married really to a husband.

Rose did not have Melanctha to live with her, now Rose was married. Melanctha was with Rose almost as much as ever but it was a little different now their being together.

Rose Johnson never asked Melanctha to live with her in the house, now Rose was married. Rose liked to have Melanctha come all the time to help her, Rose liked Melanctha to be almost always with her, but Rose was shrewd in her simple selfish nature, she did not ever think to ask Melanctha to live with her.

Rose was hard headed, she was decent, and she always knew what it was she needed. Rose needed Melanctha to be with her, she liked to have her help her, the quick, good Melanctha to do for the slow, lazy, selfish, black girl, but

Rose could have Melanctha to do for her and she did not need her to live with her.

Sam never asked Rose why she did not have her. Sam always took what Rose wanted should be done for Melanctha, as the right way he should act toward her.

It could never come to Melanctha to ask Rose to let her. It never could come to Melanctha to think that Rose would ask her. It would never ever come to Melanctha to want it, if Rose should ask her, but Melanctha would have done it for the safety she always felt when she was near her. Melanctha Herbert wanted badly to be safe now, but this living with her, that, Rose would never give her. Rose had strong the sense for decent comfort, Rose had strong the sense for proper conduct, Rose had strong the sense to get straight always what she wanted, and she always knew what was the best thing she needed, and always Rose got what she wanted.

And so Rose had Melanctha Herbert always there to help her, and she sat and was lazy and she bragged and she complained a little and she told Melanctha how she ought to do, to get good what she wanted like she Rose always did it, and always Melanctha was doing everything Rose ever needed. "Don't you bother so, doing that Melanctha, I do it or Sam when he comes home to help me. Sure you won't mind lifting it Melanctha? You is very good Melanctha to do it, and when you go out Melanctha, you stop and get some rice to bring me to-morrow when you come in. Sure you won't forget Melanctha. I never see anybody like you Melanctha to always do things so nice for me." And then Melanctha would do some more for Rose, and then very late Melanctha would go home to the colored woman where she lived now.

And so though Melanctha still was so much with Rose Johnson, she had times when she could not stay there. Melanctha now could not really cling there. Rose had Sam, and Melanctha more and more lost the hold she had had there.

Melanctha Herbert began to feel she must begin again to look and see if she could find what it was she had always wanted. Now Rose Johnson could no longer help her.

And so Melanctha Herbert began once more to wander and with men Rose never thought it was right she should be with.

One day Melanctha had been very busy with the different kinds of ways she wandered. It was a pleasant late afternoon at the end of a long summer. Melanctha was walking along, and she was free and excited. Melanctha had just parted from a white man and she had a bunch of flowers he had left with her. A young buck, a mulatto, passed by and snatched them from her. "It certainly is real sweet in you sister, to be giving me them pretty flowers," he said to her.

"I don't see no way it can make them sweeter to have with you," said Melanctha. "What one man gives, another man had certainly just as much good right to be taking." "Keep your old flowers then, I certainly don't never want to have them." Melanctha Herbert laughed at him and took them. "No, I didn't nohow think you really did want to have them. Thank you kindly mister, for them. I certainly always do admire to see a man always so kind of real polite to people." The man laughed, "You ain't nobody's fool I can say for you, but you certainly are a damned pretty kind of girl, now I look at you. Want men to be polite to you? All right, I can love you, that's real polite now, want to see me try it." "I certainly ain't got no time this evening just only left to thank you. I certainly got to be real busy now, but I certainly always will admire to see you." The man tried to catch and stop her, Melanctha Herbert laughed and dodged so that he could not touch her. Melanctha went quickly down a side street near her and so the man for that time lost her.

For some days Melanctha did not see any more of her

mulatto. One day Melanctha was with a white man and they saw him. The white man stopped to speak to him. Afterwards Melanctha left the white man and she then soon met him. Melanctha stopped to talk to him. Melanctha Herbert soon began to like him.

Jem Richards, the new man Melanctha had begun to know now, was a dashing kind of fellow, who had to do with fine horses and with racing. Sometimes Jem Richards would be betting and would be good and lucky, and be making lots of money. Sometimes Jem would be betting badly, and then he would not be having any money.

Jem Richards was a straight man. Jem Richards always knew that by and by he would win again and pay it, and so Jem mostly did win again, and then he always paid it.

Jem Richards was a man other men always trusted. Men gave him money when he lost his, for they all knew Jem Richards would win again, and when he did win they knew, and they were right, that he would pay it.

Melanctha Herbert all her life had always loved to be with horses. Melanctha liked it that Jem knew all about fine horses. He was a reckless man was Jem Richards. He knew how to win out, and always all her life, Melanctha Herbert loved successful power.

Melanctha Herbert always liked Jem Richards better. Things soon began to be very strong between them.

Jem was more game even than Melanctha. Jem always had known what it was to have real wisdom. Jem had always all his life been understanding.

Jem Richards made Melanctha Herbert come fast with him. He never gave her any time with waiting. Soon Melanctha always had Jem with her. Melanctha did not want anything better. Now in Jem Richards, Melanctha found everything she had ever needed to content her.

Melanctha was now less and less with Rose Johnson. Rose did not think much of the way Melanctha now was

going. Jem Richards was all right, only Melanctha never had
no sense of the right kind of way she should be doing. Rose
often was telling Sam now, she did not like the fast way
Melanctha was going. Rose told it to Sam, and to all the girls
and men, when she saw them. But Rose was nothing just
then to Melanctha. Melanctha Herbert now only needed Jem
Richards to be with her.

And things were always getting stronger between Jem
Richards and Melanctha Herbert. Jem Richards began to
talk now as if he wanted to get married to her. Jem was deep
in his love now for her. And as for Melanctha, Jem was all
the world now to her. And so Jem gave her a ring, like white
folks, to show he was engaged to her, and would by and by
be married to her. And Melanctha was filled full with joy to
have Jem so good to her.

Melanctha always loved to go with Jem to the races. Jem
had been lucky lately with his betting, and he had a swell
turn-out to drive in, and Melanctha looked very handsome
there beside him.

Melanctha was very proud to have Jem Richards want
her. Melanctha loved it the way Jem knew how to do it.
Melanctha loved Jem and loved that he should want her. She
loved it too, that he wanted to be married to her. Jem
Richards was a straight decent man, whom other men always looked up to and trusted. Melanctha needed badly a
man to content her.

Melanctha's joy made her foolish. Melanctha told everybody about how Jem Richards, that swell man who owned
all those fine horses and was so game, nothing ever scared
him, was engaged to be married to her, and that was the ring
he gave her.

Melanctha let out her joy very often to Rose Johnson.
Melanctha had begun again now to go there.

Melanctha's love for Jem made her foolish. Melanctha

had to have some one always now to talk to and so she went often to Rose Johnson.

Melanctha put all herself into Jem Richards. She was mad and foolish in the joy she had there.

Rose never liked the way Melanctha did it. "No Sam I don't say never Melanctha ain't engaged to Jem Richards the way she always says it, and Jem he is all right for that kind of a man he is, though he do think himself so smart and like he owns the earth and everything he can get with it, and he sure gave Melanctha a ring like he really meant he should be married right soon with it, only Sam, I don't ever like it the way Melanctha is going. When she is engaged to him Sam, she ain't not right to take on so excited. That ain't no decent kind of a way a girl ever should be acting. There ain't no kind of a man going stand that, not like I knows men Sam, and I sure does know them. I knows them white and I knows them colored, for I was raised by white folks, and they don't none of them like a girl to act so. That's all right to be so when you is just only loving, but it ain't no ways right to be acting so when you is engaged to him, and when he says, all right he get really regularly married to you. You see Sam I am right like I am always and I knows it. Jem Richards, he ain't going to the last to get real married, not if I knows it right, the way Melanctha now is acting to him. Rings or anything ain't nothing to them, and they don't never do no good for them, when a girl acts foolish like Melanctha always now is acting. I certainly will be right sorry Sam, if Melanctha has real bad trouble come now to her, but I certainly don't no ways like it Sam the kind of way Melanctha is acting to him. I don't never say nothing to her Sam. I just listens to what she is saying always, and I thinks it out like I am telling to you Sam but I don't never say nothing no more now to Melanctha. Melanctha didn't say nothing to me about that Jem Richards till she was all liked finished with him, and I never did like it Sam, much, the

way she was acting, not coming here never when she first
ran with those men and met him. And I didn't never say
nothing to her, Sam, about it, and it ain't nothing ever to me,
only I don't never no more want to say nothing to her, so I
just listens to what she got to tell like she wants it. No Sam,
I don't never want to say nothing to her. Melanctha just got
to go her own way, not as I want to see her have bad trouble
ever come hard to her, only it ain't in me never Sam, after
Melanctha did so, ever to say nothing more to her how she
should be acting. You just see Sam like I tell you, what way
Jem Richards will act to her, you see Sam I just am right like
I always am when I knows it."

Melanctha Herbert never thought she could ever again be
in trouble. Melanctha's joy had made her foolish.

And now Jem Richards had some bad trouble with his
betting. Melanctha sometimes felt now when she was with
him that there was something wrong inside him. Melanctha
knew he had had trouble with his betting but Melanctha
never felt that that could make any difference to them.

Melanctha once had told Jem, sure he knew she always
would love to be with him, if he was in jail or only just a
beggar. Now Melanctha said to him, "Sure you know Jem
that it don't never make any kind of difference you're having any kind of trouble, you just try me Jem and be game,
don't look so worried to me. Jem sure I know you love me
like I love you always, and it's all I ever could be wanting
Jem to me, just your wanting me always to be with you. I get
married Jem to you soon ever as you can want me, if you
once say it Jem to me. It ain't nothing to me ever, anything
like having any money Jem, why you look so worried to
me."

Melanctha Herbert's love had surely made her mad and
foolish. She thrust it always deep into Jem Richards and
now that he had trouble with his betting, Jem had no way
that he ever wanted to be made to feel it. Jem Richards never

could want to marry any girl while he had trouble. That was no way a man like him should do it. Melanctha's love had made her mad and foolish, she should be silent now and let him do it. Jem Richards was not a kind of man to want a woman to be strong to him, when he was in trouble with his betting. That was not the kind of a time when a man like him needed to have it.

Melanctha needed so badly to have it, this love which she had always wanted, she did not know what she should do to save it. Melanctha saw now, Jem Richards always had something wrong inside him. Melanctha soon dared not ask him. Jem was busy now, he had to sell things and see men to raise money. Jem could not meet Melanctha now so often.

It was lucky for Melanctha Herbert that Rose Johnson was coming now to have her baby. It had always been understood between them, Rose should come and stay then in the house where Melanctha lived with an old colored woman, so that Rose could have the Doctor from the hospital near by to help her, and Melanctha there to take care of her the way Melanctha always used to do it.

Melanctha was very good now to Rose Johnson. Melanctha did everything that any woman could, she tended Rose, and she was patient, submissive, soothing and untiring, while the sullen, childish, cowardly, black Rosie grumbled, and fussed, and howled, and made herself to be an abomination and like a simple beast.

All this time Melanctha was always being every now and then with Jem Richards. Melanctha was beginning to be stronger with Jem Richards. Melanctha was never so strong and sweet and in her nature as when she was deep in trouble, when she was fighting so with all she had, she could not do any foolish thing with her nature.

Always now Melanctha Herbert came back again to be nearer to Rose Johnson. Always now Melanctha would tell

all about her troubles to Rose Johnson. Rose had begun now
a little again to advise her.

Melanctha always told Rose now about the talks she had
with Jem Richards, talks where they neither of them liked
very well what the other one was saying. Melanctha did not
know what it was Jem Richards wanted. All Melanctha
knew was, he did not like it when she wanted to be good
friends and get really married, and then when Melanctha
would say, "all right, I never wear your ring no more Jem,
we ain't not any more to meet ever like we ever going to get
really regular married," then Jem did not like it either. What
was it Jem Richards really wanted?

Melanctha stopped wearing Jem's ring on her finger.
Poor Melanctha, she wore it on a string she tied around her
neck so that she could always feel it, but Melanctha was
strong now with Jem Richards, and he never saw it. And
sometimes Jem seemed to be awful sorry for it, and sometimes he seemed kind of glad of it. Melanctha never could
make out really what it was Jem Richards wanted.

There was no other woman yet to Jem, that Melanctha
knew, and so she always trusted that Jem would come back
to her, deep in his love, the way once he had had it and had
made all the world like she once had never believed anybody could really make it. But Jem Richards was more game
than Melanctha Herbert. He knew how to fight to win out,
better. Melanctha really had already lost it, in not keeping
quiet and waiting for Jem to do it.

Jem Richards was not yet having better luck in his betting. He never before had had such a long time without some
good coming to him in his betting. Sometimes Jem talked as
if he wanted to go off on a trip somewhere and try some
other place for luck with his betting. Jem Richards never
talked as if he wanted to take Melanctha with him.

And so Melanctha sometimes was really trusting, and
sometimes she was all sick inside her with her doubting.

What was it Jem really wanted to do with her? He did not
have any other woman, in that Melanctha could be really
trusting, and when she said no to him, no she never would
come near him, now he did not want to have her, then Jem
would change and swear, yes sure he did want her, now and
always right here near him, but he never now any more said
he wanted to be married soon to her. But then Jem Richards
never would marry a girl, he said that very often, when he
was in this kind of trouble, and now he did not see any way
he could get out of his trouble. But Melanctha ought to wear
his ring, sure she knew he never had loved any kind of
woman like he loved her. Melanctha would wear the ring a
little while, and then they would have some more trouble,
and then she would say to him, no she certainly never would
any more wear anything he gave her, and then she would
wear it on the string so nobody could see it but she could always feel it on her.

Poor Melanctha, surely her love had made her mad and
foolish.

And now Melanctha needed always more and more to be
with Rose Johnson, and Rose had commenced again to advise her, but Rose could not help her. There was no way now
that anybody could advise her. The time when Melanctha
could have changed it with Jem Richards was now all past
for her. Rose knew it, and Melanctha too, she knew it, and it
almost killed her to let herself believe it.

The only comfort Melanctha ever had now was waiting
on Rose till she was so tired she could hardly stand it. Always Melanctha did everything Rose ever wanted. Sam
Johnson began now to be very gentle and a little tender to
Melanctha. She was so good to Rose and Sam was so glad
to have her there to help Rose and to do things and to be a
comfort to her.

Rose had a hard time to bring her baby to its birth and
Melanctha did everything that any woman could.

The baby though it was healthy after it was born did not live long. Rose Johnson was careless and negligent and self-ish and when Melanctha had to leave for a few days the baby died. Rose Johnson had liked her baby well enough and per-haps she just forgot it for a while, anyway the child was dead and Rose and Sam were very sorry, but then these things came so often in the negro world in Bridgepoint that they neither of them thought about it very long. When Rose had become strong again she went back to her house with Sam. And Sam Johnson was always now very gentle and kind and good to Melanctha who had been so good to Rose in her bad trouble.

Melanctha Herbert's troubles with Jem Richards were never getting any better. Jem always now had less and less time to be with her. When Jem was with Melanctha now he was good enough to her. Jem Richards was worried with his betting. Never since Jem had first begun to make a living had he ever had so much trouble for such a long time to-gether with his betting. Jem Richards was good enough now to Melanctha but he had not much strength to give her. Melanctha could never any more now make him quarrel with her. Melanctha never now could complain of his treat-ment of her, for surely, he said it always by his actions to her, surely she must know how a man was when he had trou-ble on his mind with trying to make things go a little better.

Sometimes Jem and Melanctha had long talks when they neither of them liked very well what the other one was say-ing, but mostly now Melanctha could not make Jem Richards quarrel with her, and more and more, Melanctha could not find any way to make it right to blame him for the trouble she now always had inside her. Jem was good to her, and she knew, for he told her, that he had trouble all the time now with his betting. Melanctha knew very well that for her it was all wrong inside Jem Richards, but Melanctha had now no way that she could really reach him.

Things between Melanctha and Jem Richards were now never getting any better. Melanctha now more and more needed to be with Rose Johnson. Rose still liked to have Melanctha come to her house and do things for her, and Rose liked to grumble to her and to scold her and to tell Melanctha what was the way Melanctha always should be doing so she could make things come out better and not always be so much in trouble. Sam Johnson in these days was always very good and gentle to Melanctha. Sam was now beginning to be very sorry for her.

Jem Richards never made things any better for Melanctha. Often Jem would talk so as to make Melanctha almost certain that he never any more wanted to have her. Then Melanctha would get very blue, and she would say to Rose, sure she would kill herself, for that certainly now was the best way she could do.

Rose Johnson never saw it the least bit that way. "I don't see Melanctha why you should talk like you would kill yourself just because you're blue. I'd maybe kill somebody else but I'd never kill myself. If I ever killed myself, Melanctha it'd be by accident and if I ever killed myself by accident, Melanctha, I'd be awful sorry. And that certainly is the way you should feel it Melanctha, now you hear me, not just talking foolish like you always do. It certainly is only your way just always being foolish makes you all that trouble to come to you always now, Melanctha, and I certainly right well knows that. You certainly never can learn no way Melanctha ever with all I certainly been telling to you, ever since I know you good, that it ain't never no way like you do always is the right way you be acting ever and talking, the way I certainly always have seen you do so Melanctha always. I certainly am right Melanctha, about them ways you have to do it, and I knows it; but you certainly never can noways learn to act right Melanctha, I certainly do know that, I certainly do my best Melanctha to help you with it

only you certainly never do act right Melanctha, not to nobody ever, I can see it. You never act right by me Melanctha
no more than by everybody. I never say nothing to you
Melanctha when you do so, for I certainly never do like it
when I just got to say it to you, but you just certainly done
with that Jem Richards you always say wanted real bad to be
married to you, just like I always said to Sam you certainly
was going to do it. And I certainly am real kind of sorry like
for you Melanctha, but you certainly had ought to have
come to see me to talk to you, when you first was engaged
to him so I could show you, and now you got all this trouble
come to you Melanctha like I certainly know you always
catch it. It certainly ain't never Melanctha I ain't real sorry
to see trouble come so hard to you, but I certainly can see
Melanctha it all is always just the way you always be having it in you not never to do right. And now you always talk
like you just kill yourself because you are so blue, that certainly never is Melanctha, no kind of a way for any decent
kind of a girl to do."

Rose had begun to be strong now to scold Melanctha and
she was impatient very often with her, but Rose could now
never any more be a help to her. Melanctha Herbert never
could know now what it was right she should do. Melanctha
always wanted to have Jem Richards with her and now he
never seemed to want her, and what could Melanctha do.
Surely she was right now when she said she would just kill
herself, for that was the only way now she could do.

Sam Johnson always, more and more, was good and gentle to Melanctha. Poor Melanctha, she was so good and
sweet to do anything anybody ever wanted, and Melanctha
always liked it if she could have peace and quiet, and always
she could only find new ways to be in trouble. Sam often
said this now to Rose about Melanctha.

"I certainly don't never want Sam to say bad things about
Melanctha, for she certainly always do have most awful

kind of trouble come hard to her, but I never can say I like it real right Sam the way Melanctha always has to do it. It's now just the same with her like it is always she has got to do it, now the way she is with that Jem Richards. He certainly now don't never want to have her but Melanctha she ain't got no right kind of spirit. No Sam I don't never like the way any more Melanctha is acting to him, and then Sam, she ain't never real right honest, the way she always should do it. She certainly just don't kind of never Sam tell right what way she is doing with it. I don't never like to say nothing Sam no more to her about the way she always has to be acting. She always say, yes all right Rose, I do the way you say it, and then Sam she don't never noways do it. She certainly is right sweet and good, Sam, is Melanctha, nobody ever can hear me say she ain't always ready to do things for everybody any way she ever can see to do it, only Sam some ways she never does act real right ever, and some ways, Sam, she ain't ever real honest with it. And Sam sometimes I hear awful kind of things she been doing, some girls know about her how she does it, and sometimes they tell me what kind of ways she has to do it, and Sam it certainly do seem to me like more and more I certainly am awful afraid Melanctha never will come to any good. And then Sam, sometimes, you hear it, she always talk like she kill herself all the time she is so blue, and Sam that certainly never is no kind of way any decent girl ever had ought to do. You see Sam, how I am right like I always is when I knows it. You just be careful, Sam, now you hear me, you be careful Sam sure, I tell you, Melanctha more and more I see her I certainly do feel Melanctha no way is really honest. You be careful, Sam now, like I tell you, for I knows it, now you hear to me, Sam, what I tell you, for I certainly always is right, Sam, when I knows it."

At first Sam tried a little to defend Melanctha, and Sam always was good and gentle to her, and Sam liked the ways

Melanctha had to be quiet to him, and to always listen as if she was learning, when she was there and heard him talking, and then Sam liked the sweet way she always did everything so nicely for him; but Sam never liked to fight with anybody ever, and surely Rose knew best about Melanctha and anyway Sam never did really care much about Melanctha. Her mystery never had had any interest for him. Sam liked it that she was sweet to him and that she always did everything Rose ever wanted that she should be doing, but Melanctha never could be important to him. All Sam ever wanted was to have a little house and to live regular and to work hard and to come home to his dinner, when he was tired with his working and by and by he wanted to have some children all his own to be good to, and so Sam was real sorry for Melanctha, she was so good and so sweet always to them, and Jem Richards was a bad man to behave so to her, but that was always the way a girl got it when she liked that kind of a fast fellow. Anyhow Melanctha was Rose's friend, and Sam never cared to have anything to do with the kind of trouble always came to women, when they wanted to have men, who never could know how to behave good and steady to their women.

And so Sam never said much to Rose about Melanctha. Sam was always very gentle to her, but now he began less and less to see her. Soon Melanctha never came any more to the house to see Rose and Sam never asked Rose anything about her.

Melanctha Herbert was beginning now to come less and less to the house to be with Rose Johnson. This was because Rose seemed always less and less now to want her, and Rose would not let Melanctha now do things for her. Melanctha was always humble to her and Melanctha always wanted in every way she could to do things for her. Rose said no, she guessed she do that herself like she likes to have it better. Melanctha is real good to stay so long to help her, but Rose guessed perhaps Melanctha better go home now, Rose don't need nobody to help her now, she is feeling real strong, not like just after she had all that trouble with the baby, and then Sam, when he comes home for his dinner he likes it when Rose is all alone there just to give him his dinner. Sam always is so tired now, like he always is in the summer, so many people always on the steamer and they make so much work so Sam is real tired now, and he likes just to eat his dinner and never have people in the house to be a trouble to him.

Each day Rose treated Melanctha more and more as if she never wanted Melanctha any more to come there to the house to see her. Melanctha dared not ask Rose why she acted in this way to her. Melanctha badly needed to have Rose always there to save her. Melanctha wanted badly to cling to her and Rose had always been so solid for her. Melanctha did not dare to ask Rose if she now no longer wanted her to come and see her.

Melanctha now never any more had Sam to be gentle to her. Rose always sent Melanctha away from her before it was time for Sam to come home to her. One day Melanctha had stayed a little longer, for Rose that day had been good to let Melanctha begin to do things for her. Melanctha then left her and Melanctha met Sam Johnson who stopped a minute to speak kindly to her.

The next day Rose Johnson would not let Melanctha come in to her. Rose stood on the steps, and there she told Melanctha what she thought now of her.

"I guess Melanctha it certainly ain't no ways right for you to come here no more just to see me. I certainly don't Melanctha no ways like to be a trouble to you. I certainly think Melanctha I get along better now when I don't have nobody like you are, always here to help me, and Sam he do so good now with his working, he pay a little girl something to come every day to help me. I certainly do think Melanctha I don't never want you no more to come here just to see me." "Why Rose, what I ever done to you, I certainly don't think you is right Rose to be so bad now to me." "I certainly don't noways Melanctha Herbert think you got any right ever to be complaining the way I been acting to you. I certainly never do think Melanctha Herbert, you hear to me, nobody ever been more patient to you than I always been to like you, only Melanctha, I hear more things now so awful bad about you, everybody always is telling to me what kind of a way you always have been doing so much, and me always so good to you, and you never no ways, knowing how to be honest to me. No Melanctha it ain't ever in me, not to want you to have good luck come to you, and I like it real well Melanctha when you some time learn how to act the way it is decent and right for a girl to be doing, but I don't no ways ever like it the kind of things everybody tell me now about you. No Melanctha, I can't never any more trust you. I certainly am real sorry to have never any more to see you, but there ain't no other way, I ever can be acting to you. That's all I ever got any more to say to you now Melanctha." "But Rose, deed; I certainly don't know, no more than the dead, nothing I ever done to make you act so to me. Anybody say anything bad about me Rose, to you, they just a pack of liars to you, they certainly is Rose, I tell you true. I certainly never done nothing I ever been ashamed to tell you. Why you act so bad to me Rose. Sam he certainly don't think ever like you do, and Rose I always do everything I can, you ever want me to do for you." "It ain't never no use standing there talking, Melanctha Herbert. I just can tell it to you, and Sam, he don't know nothing about women ever the way they can be acting. I certainly am very sorry Melanctha, to have to act so now to you, but I certainly can't do no other way with you, when you do things always so bad, and everybody is talking so about you. It ain't no use to you to stand there and say it different to me Melanctha. I certainly am al-

ways right Melanctha Herbert, the way I certainly always
have been when I knows it, to you. No Melanctha, it just is,
you never can have no kind of a way to act right; the way a
decent girl has to do, and I done my best always to be telling
it to you Melanctha Herbert, but it don't never do no good
to tell nobody how to act right; they certainly never can
learn when they ain't got no sense right to know it, and you
never have no sense right Melanctha to be honest, and I ain't
never wishing no harm to you ever Melanctha Herbert, only
I don't never want any more to see you come here. I just say
to you now, like I always been saying to you, you don't
know never the right way, any kind of decent girl has to be
acting, and so Melanctha Herbert, me and Sam, we don't
never any more want you to be setting your foot in my house
here Melanctha Herbert, I just tell you. And so you just go
along now, Melanctha Herbert, you hear me, and I don't
never wish no harm to come to you."

Rose Johnson went into her house and closed the door
behind her. Melanctha stood like one dazed, she did not
know how to bear this blow that almost killed her. Slowly
then Melanctha went away without even turning to look behind her.

Melanctha Herbert was all sore and bruised inside her,
Melanctha had needed Rose always to believe her, Melanctha needed Rose always to let her cling to her, Melanctha
wanted badly to have somebody who could make her always
feel a little safe inside her, and now Rose had sent her from
her. Melanctha wanted Rose more than she had ever wanted
all the others. Rose always was so simple, solid, decent, for
her. And now Rose had cast her from her. Melanctha was
lost, and all the world went whirling in a mad weary dance
around her.

Melanctha Herbert never had any strength alone ever to
feel safe inside her. And now Rose Johnson had cast her
from her, and Melanctha could never any more be near her.

Melanctha Herbert knew now, way inside her, that she was lost, and nothing any more could ever help her.

Melanctha went that night to meet Jem Richards who had promised to be at the old place to meet her. Jem Richards was absent in his manner to her. By and by he began to talk to her, about the trip he was going to take soon, to see if he could get some luck back in his betting. Melanctha trembled, was Jem too now going to leave her. Jem Richards talked some more then to her, about the bad luck he always had now, and how he needed to go away to see if he could make it come out any better.

Then Jem stopped, and then he looked straight at Melanctha.

"Tell me Melanctha right and true, you don't care really nothing more about me now Melanctha," he said to her.

"Why you ask me that, Jem Richards," said Melanctha.

"Why I ask you that Melanctha, God Almighty, because I just don't give a damn now for you any more Melanctha. That the reason I was asking."

Melanctha never could have for this an answer. Jem Richards waited and then he went away and left her.

Melanctha Herbert never again saw Jem Richards. Melanctha never again saw Rose Johnson, and it was hard to Melanctha never any more to see her. Rose Johnson had worked in to be the deepest of all Melanctha's emotions.

"No, I don't never see Melanctha Herbert no more now," Rose would say to anybody who asked her about Melanctha. "No, Melanctha she never comes here no more now, after we had all that trouble with her acting so bad with them kind of men she liked so much to be with. She don't never come to no good Melanctha Herbert don't, and me and Sam don't want no more to see her. She didn't do right ever the way I told her. Melanctha just wouldn't, and I always said it to her, if she don't be more kind of careful, the way she always had to be acting, I never did want no more she should come here in my house no more to see me. I ain't no ways ever against any girl having any kind of a way, to have a good time like she wants it, but not that kind of a way Melanctha always had to do it. I expect some day Melanctha kill herself, when she act so bad like she do always, and then she get so awful blue. Melanctha always says that's the only way she ever can think it a easy way for her to do. No, I always am real sorry for Melanctha, she never was no just common kind of nigger, but she don't never know now with all the time I always was telling it to her, no she never no way could learn, what was the right way she should do. I certainly don't never want no kind of harm to come bad to Melanctha, but I certainly do think she will most kill herself some time, the way she always say it would be easy way for her to do. I never see nobody ever could be so awful blue."

But Melanctha Herbert never really killed herself because she was so blue, though often she thought this would be really the best way for her to do. Melanctha never killed herself, she only got a bad fever and went into the hospital where they took good care of her and cured her.

When Melanctha was well again, she took a place and began to work and to live regular. Then Melanctha got very sick again, she began to cough and sweat and be so weak she could not stand to do her work.

Melanctha went back to the hospital, and there the Doctor told her she had the consumption, and before long she would surely die. They sent her where she would be taken care of, a home for poor consumptives, and there Melanctha stayed until she died.

THE GENTLE LENA

LENA was patient, gentle, sweet and german. She had been a servant for four years and had liked it very well.

Lena had been brought from Germany to Bridgepoint by a cousin and had been in the same place there for four years.

This place Lena had found very good. There was a pleasant, unexacting mistress and her children, and they all liked Lena very well.

There was a cook there who scolded Lena a great deal but Lena's german patience held no suffering and the good incessant woman really only scolded so for Lena's good.

Lena's german voice when she knocked and called the family in the morning was as awakening, as soothing, and as appealing, as a delicate soft breeze in midday, summer. She stood in the hallway every morning a long time in her unexpectant and unsuffering german patience calling to the young ones to get up. She would call and wait a long time and then call again, always even, gentle, patient, while the young ones fell back often into that precious, tense, last bit of sleeping that gives a strength of joyous vigor in the young, over them that have come to the readiness of middle age, in their awakening.

Lena had good hard work all morning, and on the pleasant, sunny afternoons she was sent out into the park to sit and watch the little two year old girl baby of the family.

The other girls, all them that make the pleasant, lazy crowd, that watch the children in the sunny afternoons out in the park, all liked the simple, gentle, german Lena very well. They all, too, liked very well to tease her, for it was so easy to make her mixed and troubled, and all helpless, for she could never learn to know just what the other quicker girls meant by the queer things they said.

The two or three of these girls, the ones that Lena always sat with, always worked together to confuse her. Still it was pleasant, all this life for Lena.

The little girl fell down sometimes and cried, and then Lena had to soothe her. When the little girl would drop her hat, Lena had to pick it up and hold it. When the little girl was bad and threw away her playthings, Lena told her she could not have them and took them from her to hold until the little girl should need them.

It was all a peaceful life for Lena, almost as peaceful as a pleasant leisure. The other girls, of course, did tease her, but then that only made a gentle stir within her.

Lena was a brown and pleasant creature, brown as blonde races often have them brown, brown, not with the yellow or the red or the chocolate brown of sun burned countries, but brown with the clear color laid flat on the light toned skin beneath, the plain, spare brown that makes it right to have been made with hazel eyes, and not too abundant straight, brown hair, hair that only later deepens itself into brown from the straw yellow of a german childhood.

Lena had the flat chest, straight back and forward falling shoulders of the patient and enduring working woman, though her body was now still in its milder girlhood and work had not yet made these lines too clear.

The rarer feeling that there was with Lena, showed in all the even quiet of her body movements, but in all it was the strongest in the patient, old-world ignorance, and earth made pureness of her brown, flat, soft featured face. Lena had eyebrows that were a wondrous thickness. They were black, and spread, and very cool, with their dark color and their beauty, and beneath them were her hazel eyes, simple and human, with the earth patience of the working, gentle, german woman.

Yes it was all a peaceful life for Lena. The other girls, of course, did tease her, but then that only made a gentle stir within her.

"What you got on your finger Lena," Mary, one of the girls she always sat with, one day asked her. Mary was good natured, quick, intelligent and Irish.

Lena had just picked up the fancy paper made accordion that the little girl had dropped beside her, and was making it squeak sadly as she pulled it with her brown, strong, awkward finger.

"Why, what is it, Mary, paint?" said Lena, putting her finger to her mouth to taste the dirt spot.

"That's awful poison Lena, don't you know?" said Mary, "that green paint that you just tasted."

Lena had sucked a good deal of the green paint from her finger. She stopped and looked hard at the finger. She did not know just how much Mary meant by what she said.

"Ain't it poison, Nellie, that green paint, that Lena sucked just now," said Mary. "Sure it is Lena, it's real poison, I ain't foolin' this time anyhow."

Lena was a little troubled. She looked hard at her finger where the paint was, and she wondered if she had really sucked it.

It was still a little wet on the edges and she rubbed it off a long time on the inside of her dress, and in between she wondered and looked at the finger and thought, was it really poison that she had just tasted.

"Ain't it too bad, Nellie, Lena should have sucked that," Mary said.

Nellie smiled and did not answer. Nellie was dark and

thin, and looked Italian. She had a big mass of black hair that she wore high up on her head, and that made her face look very fine.

Nellie always smiled and did not say much, and then she would look at Lena to perplex her.

And so they all three sat with their little charges in the pleasant sunshine a long time. And Lena would often look at her finger and wonder if it was really poison that she had just tasted and then she would rub her finger on her dress a little harder.

Mary laughed at her and teased her and Nellie smiled a little and looked queerly at her.

Then it came time, for it was growing cooler, for them to drag together the little ones, who had begun to wander, and to take each one back to its own mother. And Lena never knew for certain whether it was really poison, that green stuff that she had tasted.

During these four years of service, Lena always spent her Sundays out at the house of her aunt, who had brought her four years before to Bridgepoint.

This aunt, who had brought Lena, four years before, to Bridgepoint, was a hard, ambitious, well meaning, german woman. Her husband was a grocer in the town, and they were very well to do. Mrs. Haydon, Lena's aunt, had two daughters who were just beginning as young ladies, and she had a little boy who was not honest and who was very hard to manage.

Mrs. Haydon was a short, stout, hard built, german woman. She always hit the ground very firmly and compactly as she walked. Mrs. Haydon was all a compact and well hardened mass, even to her face, reddish and darkened from its early blonde, with its hearty, shiny, cheeks, and doubled chin well covered over with the uproll from her short, square neck.

The two daughters, who were fourteen and fifteen,

looked like unkneaded, unformed mounds of flesh beside her.

The elder girl, Mathilda, was blonde, and slow, and simple, and quite fat. The younger, Bertha, who was almost as tall as her sister, was dark, and quicker, and she was heavy, too, but not really fat.

These two girls the mother had brought up very firmly. They were well taught for their position. They were always both well dressed, in the same kinds of hats and dresses, as is becoming in two german sisters. The mother liked to have them dressed in red. Their best clothes were red dresses, made of good heavy cloth, and strongly trimmed with braid of a glistening black. They had stiff, red felt hats, trimmed with black velvet ribbon, and a bird. The mother dressed matronly, in a bonnet and in black, always sat between her two big daughters, firm, directing, and repressed.

The only weak spot in this good german woman's conduct was the way she spoiled her boy, who was not honest and who was very hard to manage.

The father of this family was a decent, quiet, heavy, and uninterfering german man. He tried to cure the boy of his bad ways, and make him honest, but the mother could not make herself let the father manage, and so the boy was brought up very badly.

Mrs. Haydon's girls were now only just beginning as young ladies, and so to get her niece, Lena, married, was just then the most important thing that Mrs. Haydon had to do.

Mrs. Haydon had four years before gone to Germany to see her parents, and had taken the girls with her. This visit had been for Mrs. Haydon most successful, though her children had not liked it very well.

Mrs. Haydon was a good and generous woman, and she patronized her parents grandly, and all the cousins who came from all about to see her. Mrs. Haydon's people were of the middling class of farmers. They were not peasants, and they lived in a town of some pretension, but it all seemed very poor and smelly to Mrs. Haydon's american born daughters.

Mrs. Haydon liked it all. It was familiar, and then here she was so wealthy and important. She listened and decided, and advised all of her relations how to do things better. She arranged their present and their future for them, and showed them how in the past they had been wrong in all their methods.

Mrs. Haydon's only trouble was with her two daughters, whom she could not make behave well to her parents. The two girls were very nasty to all their numerous relations. Their mother could hardly make them kiss their grandparents, and every day the girls would get a scolding. But then Mrs. Haydon was so very busy that she did not have time to really manage her stubborn daughters.

These hard working, earth-rough german cousins were to these american born children, ugly and dirty, and as far below them as were italian or negro workmen, and they could not see how their mother could ever bear to touch them, and then all the women dressed so funny and were worked all rough and different.

The two girls stuck up their noses at them all, and always talked in English to each other about how they hated all these people and how they wished their mother would not do so. The girls could talk some German, but they never chose to use it.

It was her eldest brother's family that most interested Mrs. Haydon. Here there were eight children, and out of the eight, five of them were girls.

Mrs. Haydon thought it would be a fine thing to take one of these girls back with her to Bridgepoint and get her well started. Everybody liked that she should do so, and they were all willing that it should be Lena.

Lena was the second girl in her large family. She was at

this time just seventeen years old. Lena was not an important daughter in the family. She was always sort of dreamy
and not there. She worked hard and went very regularly at
it, but even good work never seemed to bring her near.

Lena's age just suited Mrs. Haydon's purpose. Lena
could first go out to service, and learn how to do things, and
then, when she was a little older, Mrs. Haydon could get her
a good husband. And then Lena was so still and docile, she
would never want to do things her own way. And then, too,
Mrs. Haydon, with all her hardness had wisdom, and she
could feel the rarer strain there was in Lena.

Lena was willing to go with Mrs. Haydon. Lena did not
like her german life very well. It was not the hard work but
the roughness that disturbed her. The people were not gentle, and the men when they were glad were very boisterous,
and would lay hold of her and roughly tease her. They were
good people enough around her, but it was all harsh and
dreary for her.

Lena did not really know that she did not like it. She did
not know that she was always dreamy and not there. She did
not think whether it would be different for her away off
there in Bridgepoint. Mrs. Haydon took her and got her different kinds of dresses, and then took her with them to the
steamer. Lena did not really know what it was that had happened to her.

. Mrs. Haydon, and her daughters, and Lena traveled second class on the steamer. Mrs. Haydon's daughters hated
that their mother should take Lena. They hated to have a
cousin, who was to them, little better than a nigger, and then
everybody on the steamer there would see her. Mrs. Haydon's daughters said things like this to their mother, but she
never stopped to hear them, and the girls did not dare to
make their meaning very clear. And so they could only go on
hating Lena hard, together. They could not stop her from
going back with them to Bridgepoint.

Lena was very sick on the voyage. She thought, surely before it was over that she would die. She was so sick she could not even wish that she had not started. She could not eat, she could not moan, she was just blank and scared, and sure that every minute she would die. She could not hold herself in, nor help herself in her trouble. She just staid where she had been put, pale, and scared, and weak, and sick, and sure that she was going to die.

Mathilda and Bertha Haydon had no trouble from having Lena for a cousin on the voyage, until the last day that they were on the ship, and by that time they had made their friends and could explain.

Mrs. Haydon went down every day to Lena, gave her things to make her better, held her head when it was needful, and generally was good and did her duty by her.

Poor Lena had no power to be strong in such trouble. She did not know how to yield to her sickness nor endure. She lost all her little sense of being in her suffering. She was so scared, and then at her best, Lena, who was patient, sweet and quiet, had not self-control, nor any active courage.

Poor Lena was so scared and weak, and every minute she was sure that she would die.

After Lena was on land again a little while, she forgot all her bad suffering. Mrs. Haydon got her the good place, with the pleasant unexacting mistress, and her children, and Lena began to learn some English and soon was very happy and content.

All her Sundays out Lena spent at Mrs. Haydon's house. Lena would have liked much better to spend her Sundays with the girls she always sat with, and who often asked her, and who teased her and made a gentle stir within her, but it never came to Lena's unexpectant and unsuffering german nature to do something different from what was expected of her, just because she would like it that way better. Mrs. Hay-

don had said that Lena was to come to her house every other
Sunday, and so Lena always went there.

Mrs. Haydon was the only one of her family who took
any interest in Lena. Mr. Haydon did not think much of her.
She was his wife's cousin and he was good to her, but she
was for him stupid, and a little simple, and very dull, and
sure some day to need help and to be in trouble. All young
poor relations, who were brought from Germany to Bridgepoint were sure, before long, to need help and to be in trouble.

The little Haydon boy was always very nasty to her. He
was a hard child for any one to manage, and his mother
spoiled him very badly. Mrs. Haydon's daughters as they
grew older did not learn to like Lena any better. Lena never
knew that she did not like them either. She did not know that
she was only happy with the other quicker girls, she always
sat with in the park, and who laughed at her and always
teased her.

Mathilda Haydon, the simple, fat, blonde, older daughter
felt very badly that she had to say that this was her cousin
Lena, this Lena who was little better for her than a nigger.
Mathilda was an overgrown, slow, flabby, blonde, stupid, fat
girl, just beginning as a woman; thick in her speech and dull
and simple in her mind, and very jealous of all her family
and of other girls, and proud that she could have good
dresses and new hats and learn music, and hating very badly
to have a cousin who was a common servant. And then
Mathilda remembered very strongly that dirty nasty place
that Lena came from and that Mathilda had so turned up her
nose at, and where she had been made so angry because her
mother scolded her and liked all those rough cow-smelly
people.

Then, too, Mathilda would get very mad when her
mother had Lena at their parties, and when she talked about
how good Lena was, to certain german mothers in whose

sons, perhaps, Mrs. Haydon might find Lena a good husband. All this would make the dull, blonde, fat Mathilda very angry. Sometimes she would get so angry that she would, in her thick, slow way, and with jealous anger blazing in her light blue eyes, tell her mother that she did not see how she could like that nasty Lena; and then her mother would scold Mathilda, and tell her that she knew her cousin Lena was poor and Mathilda must be good to poor people.

Mathilda Haydon did not like relations to be poor. She told all her girl friends what she thought of Lena, and so the girls would never talk to Lena at Mrs. Haydon's parties. But Lena in her unsuffering and unexpectant patience never really knew that she was slighted. When Mathilda was with her girls in the street or in the park and would see Lena, she always turned up her nose and barely nodded to her, and then she would tell her friends how funny her mother was to take care of people like that Lena, and how, back in Germany, all Lena's people lived just like pigs.

The younger daughter, the dark, large, but not fat, Bertha Haydon, who was very quick in her mind, and in her ways, and who was the favourite with her father, did not like Lena, either. She did not like her because for her Lena was a fool and so stupid, and she would let those Irish and Italian girls laugh at her and tease her, and everybody always made fun of Lena, and Lena never got mad, or even had sense enough to know that they were all making an awful fool of her.

Bertha Haydon hated people to be fools. Her father, too, thought Lena was a fool, and so neither the father nor the daughter ever paid any attention to Lena, although she came to their house every other Sunday.

Lena did not know how all the Haydons felt. She came to her aunt's house all her Sunday afternoons that she had out, because Mrs. Haydon had told her she must do so. In the same way Lena always saved all of her wages. She never thought of any way to spend it. The german cook, the good

woman who always scolded Lena, helped her to put it in the
bank each month, as soon as she got it. Sometimes before it
got into the bank to be taken care of, somebody would ask
Lena for it. The little Haydon boy sometimes asked and
would get it, and sometimes some of the girls, the ones Lena
always sat with, needed some more money; but the german
cook, who always scolded Lena, saw to it that this did not
happen very often. When it did happen she would scold
Lena very sharply, and for the next few months she would
not let Lena touch her wages, but put it in the bank for her
on the same day that Lena got it.

So Lena always saved her wages, for she never thought
to spend them, and she always went to her aunt's house for
her Sundays because she did not know that she could do
anything different.

Mrs. Haydon felt more and more every year that she had
done right to bring Lena back with her, for it was all coming
out just as she had expected. Lena was good and never
wanted her own way, she was learning English, and saving
all her wages, and soon Mrs. Haydon would get her a good
husband.

All these four years Mrs. Haydon was busy looking
around among all the german people that she knew for the
right man to be Lena's husband, and now at last she was
quite decided.

The man Mrs. Haydon wanted for Lena was a young
german-american tailor, who worked with his father. He was
good and all the family were very saving, and Mrs. Haydon
was sure that this would be just right for Lena, and then too,
this young tailor always did whatever his father and his
mother wanted.

This old german tailor and his wife, the father and the
mother of Herman Kreder, who was to marry Lena Mainz,
were very thrifty, careful people. Herman was the only child
they had left with them, and he always did everything they

wanted. Herman was now twenty-eight years old, but he had never stopped being scolded and directed by his father and his mother. And now they wanted to see him married.

Herman Kreder did not care much to get married. He was a gentle soul and a little fearful. He had a sullen temper, too. He was obedient to his father and his mother. He always did his work well. He often went out on Saturday nights and on Sundays, with other men. He liked it with them but he never became really joyous. He liked to be with men and he hated to have women with them. He was obedient to his mother, but he did not care much to get married.

Mrs. Haydon and the elder Kreders had often talked the marriage over. They all three liked it very well. Lena would do anything that Mrs. Haydon wanted, and Herman was always obedient in everything to his father and his mother. Both Lena and Herman were saving and good workers and neither of them ever wanted their own way.

The elder Kreders, everybody knew, had saved up all their money, and they were hard, good german people, and Mrs. Haydon was sure that with these people Lena would never be in any trouble. Mr. Haydon would not say anything about it. He knew old Kreder had a lot of money and owned some good houses, and he did not care what his wife did with that simple, stupid Lena, so long as she would be sure never to need help or to be in trouble.

Lena did not care much to get married. She liked her life very well where she was working. She did not think much about Herman Kreder. She thought he was a good man and she always found him very quiet. Neither of them ever spoke much to the other. Lena did not care much just then about getting married.

Mrs. Haydon spoke to Lena about it very often. Lena never answered anything at all. Mrs. Haydon thought, perhaps Lena did not like Herman Kreder. Mrs. Haydon could not believe that any girl not even Lena, really had no feeling about getting married.

Mrs. Haydon spoke to Lena very often about Herman. Mrs. Haydon sometimes got very angry with Lena. She was afraid that Lena, for once, was going to be stubborn, now when it was all fixed right for her to be married.

"Why you stand there so stupid, why don't you answer, Lena," said Mrs. Haydon one Sunday, at the end of a long talking that she was giving Lena about Herman Kreder, and about Lena's getting married to him.

"Yes ma'am," said Lena, and then Mrs. Haydon was furious with this stupid Lena. "Why don't you answer with some sense, Lena, when I ask you if you don't like Herman Kreder. You stand there so stupid and don't answer just like you ain't heard a word what I been saying to you. I never see anybody like you, Lena. If you going to burst out at all, why don't you burst out sudden instead of standing there so silly and don't answer. And here I am so good to you, and find you a good husband so you can have a place to live in all your own. Answer me, Lena, don't you like Herman Kreder? He is a fine young fellow, almost too good for you, Lena, when you stand there so stupid and don't make no answer. There ain't many poor girls that get the chance you got now to get married."

"Why, I do anything you say, Aunt Mathilda. Yes, I like him. He don't say much to me, but I guess he is a good man, and I do anything you say for me to do."

"Well then Lena, why you stand there so silly all the time and not answer when I asked you."

"I didn't hear you say you wanted I should say anything to you. I didn't know you wanted me to say nothing. I do whatever you tell me it's right for me to do. I marry Herman Kreder, if you want me."

And so for Lena Mainz the match was made.

Old Mrs. Kreder did not discuss the matter with her Herman. She never thought that she needed to talk such things over with him. She just told him about getting married to Lena Mainz who was a good worker and very saving and never wanted her own way, and Herman made his usual little grunt in answer to her.

Mrs. Kreder and Mrs. Haydon fixed the day and made all the arrangements for the wedding and invited everybody who ought to be there to see them married.

In three months Lena Mainz and Herman Kreder were to be married.

Mrs. Haydon attended to Lena's getting all the things that she needed. Lena had to help a good deal with the sewing. Lena did not sew very well. Mrs. Haydon scolded because Lena did not do it better, but then she was very good to Lena, and she hired a girl to come and help her. Lena still stayed on with her pleasant mistress, but she spent all her evenings and Sundays with her aunt and all the sewing.

Mrs. Haydon got Lena some nice dresses. Lena liked that very well. Lena liked having new hats even better, and Mrs. Haydon had some made for her by a real milliner who made them very pretty.

Lena was nervous these days, but she did not think much about getting married. She did not know really what it was, that, which was always coming nearer.

Lena liked the place where she was with the pleasant mistress and the good cook, who always scolded, and she liked the girls she always sat with. She did not ask if she would like being married any better. She always did whatever her aunt said and expected, but she was always nervous when she saw the Kreders with their Herman. She was excited and she liked her new hats, and everybody teased her and every day her marrying was coming nearer, and yet she did not really know what it was, this that was about to happen to her.

Herman Kreder knew more what it meant to be married

and he did not like it very well. He did not like to see girls
and he did not want to have to have one always near him.
Herman always did everything that his father and his mother
wanted and now they wanted that he should be married.

Herman had a sullen temper; he was gentle and he never
said much. He liked to go out with other men, but he never
wanted that there should be any women with them. The men
all teased him about getting married. Herman did not mind
the teasing but he did not like very well the getting married
and having a girl always with him.

Three days before the wedding day, Herman went away
to the country to be gone over Sunday. He and Lena were to
be married Tuesday afternoon. When the day came Herman
had not been seen or heard from.

The old Kreder couple had not worried much about it.
Herman always did everything they wanted and he would
surely come back in time to get married. But when Monday
night came, and there was no Herman, they went to Mrs.
Haydon to tell her what had happened.

Mrs. Haydon got very much excited. It was hard enough
to work so as to get everything all ready, and then to have
that silly Herman go off that way, so no one could tell what
was going to happen. Here was Lena and everything all
ready, and now they would have to make the wedding later
so that they would know that Herman would be sure to be
there.

Mrs. Haydon was very much excited, and then she could
not say much to the old Kreder couple. She did not want to
make them angry, for she wanted very badly now that Lena
should be married to their Herman.

At last it was decided that the wedding should be put off
a week longer. Old Mr. Kreder would go to New York to
find Herman, for it was very likely that Herman had gone
there to his married sister.

Mrs. Haydon sent word around, about waiting until a

week from that Tuesday, to everybody that had been invited, and then Tuesday morning she sent for Lena to come down to see her.

Mrs. Haydon was very angry with poor Lena when she saw her. She scolded her hard because she was so foolish, and now Herman had gone off and nobody could tell where he had gone to, and all because Lena always was so dumb and silly. And Mrs. Haydon was just like a mother to her, and Lena always stood there so stupid and did not answer what anybody asked her, and Herman was so silly too, and now his father had to go and find him. Mrs. Haydon did not think that any old people should be good to their children. Their children always were so thankless, and never paid any attention, and older people were always doing things for their good. Did Lena think it gave Mrs. Haydon any pleasure, to work so hard to make Lena happy, and get her a good husband, and then Lena was so thankless and never did anything that anybody wanted. It was a lesson to poor Mrs. Haydon not to do things any more for anybody. Let everybody take care of themselves and never come to her with any troubles; she knew better now than to meddle to make other people happy. It just made trouble for her and her husband did not like it. He always said she was too good, and nobody ever thanked her for it, and there Lena was always standing stupid and not answering anything anybody wanted. Lena could always talk enough to those silly girls she liked so much, and always sat with, but who never did anything for her except to take away her money, and here was her aunt who tried so hard and was so good to her and treated her just like one of her own children and Lena stood there, and never made any answer and never tried to please her aunt, or to do anything that her aunt wanted. "No, it ain't no use your standin' there and cryin', now, Lena. It's too late now to care about that Herman. You should have cared some before, and then you wouldn't have to stand there and cry now, and be a disappointment to me, and then I get scolded by my husband for taking care of everybody, and nobody ever thankful. I am glad you got the sense to feel sorry now, Lena, anyway, and I try to do what I can to help you out in your trouble, only you don't deserve to have anybody take any trouble for you. But perhaps you know better next time. You go home now and take care you don't spoil your clothes and that new hat, you had no business to be wearin' that this morning, but you ain't got no sense at all, Lena. I never in my life see anybody be so stupid."

Mrs. Haydon stopped and poor Lena stood there in her hat, all trimmed with pretty flowers, and the tears coming out of her eyes, and Lena did not know what it was that she had done, only she was not going to be married and it was a disgrace for a girl to be left by a man on the very day she was to be married.

Lena went home all alone, and cried in the street car.

Poor Lena cried very hard all alone in the street car. She almost spoiled her new hat with her hitting it against the window in her crying. Then she remembered that she must not do so.

The conductor was a kind man and he was very sorry when he saw her crying. "Don't feel so bad, you get another feller, you are such a nice girl," he said to make her cheerful. "But Aunt Mathilda said now, I never get married," poor Lena sobbed out for her answer. "Why you really got trouble like that," said the conductor. "I just said that now to josh you. I didn't ever think you really was left by a feller. He must be a stupid feller. But don't you worry, he wasn't much good if he could go away and leave you, lookin' to be such a nice girl. You just tell all your trouble to me, and I help you." The car was empty and the conductor sat down beside her to put his arm around her, and to be a comfort to her. Lena suddenly remembered where she was, and if she did things like that her aunt would scold her. She moved away from the man into the corner. He laughed. "Don't be scared," he said, "I wasn't going to hurt you. But you just keep up your spirit. You are a real nice girl, and you'll be sure to get a real good husband. Don't you let nobody fool you. You're all right and I don't want to scare you."

The conductor went back to his platform to help a passenger get on the car. All the time Lena stayed in the street car, he would come in every little while and reassure her, about her not to feel so bad about a man who hadn't no more sense than to go away and leave her. She'd be sure yet to get a good man, she needn't be so worried, he frequently reassured her.

He chatted with the other passenger who had just come in, a very well dressed old man, and then with another who came in later, a good sort of a working man, and then another who came in, a nice lady, and he told them all about Lena's having trouble, and it was too bad there were men who treated a poor girl so badly. And everybody in the car was sorry for poor Lena and the workman tried to cheer her, and the old man looked sharply at her, and said she looked like a good girl, but she ought to be more careful and not to be so careless, and things like that would not happen to her, and the nice lady went and sat beside her and Lena liked it, though she shrank away from being near her.

So Lena was feeling a little better when she got off the car, and the conductor helped her, and he called out to her, "You be sure you keep up a good heart now. He wasn't no good that feller and you were lucky for to lose him. You'll get a real man yet, one that will be better for you. Don't you be worried, you're a real nice girl as I ever see in such trouble," and the conductor shook his head and went back into his car to talk it over with the other passengers he had there.

The german cook, who always scolded Lena, was very angry when she heard the story. She never did think Mrs. Haydon would do so much for Lena, though she was always

talking so grand about what she could do for everybody. The
good german cook always had been a little distrustful of her.
People who always thought they were so much never did really do things right for anybody. Not that Mrs. Haydon
wasn't a good woman. Mrs. Haydon was a real, good, german woman, and she did really mean to do well by her niece
Lena. The cook knew that very well, and she had always
said so, and she always had liked and respected Mrs. Haydon, who always acted very proper to her, and Lena was so
backward, when there was a man to talk to, Mrs. Haydon did
have hard work when she tried to marry Lena. Mrs. Haydon
was a good woman, only she did talk sometimes too grand.
Perhaps this trouble would make her see it wasn't always so
easy to do, to make everybody do everything just like she
wanted. The cook was very sorry now for Mrs. Haydon. All
this must be such a disappointment, and such a worry to her,
and she really had always been very good to Lena. But Lena
had better go and put on her other clothes and stop with all
that crying. That wouldn't do nothing now to help her, and
if Lena would be a good girl, and just be real patient, her
aunt would make it all come out right yet for her. "I just tell
Mrs. Aldrich, Lena, you stay here yet a little longer. You
know she is always so good to you, Lena, and I know she let
you, and I tell her all about that stupid Herman Kreder. I got
no patience, Lena, with anybody who can be so stupid. You
just stop now with your crying, Lena, and take off them
good clothes and put them away so you don't spoil them
when you need them, and you can help me with the dishes
and everything will come off better for you. You see if I ain't
right by what I tell you. You just stop crying now Lena
quick, or else I scold you."

Lena still choked a little and was very miserable inside
her but she did everything just as the cook told her.

The girls Lena always sat with were very sorry to see her
look so sad with her trouble. Mary the Irish girl sometimes

got very angry with her. Mary was always very hot when she talked of Lena's aunt Mathilda, who thought she was so grand, and had such stupid, stuck up daughters. Mary wouldn't be a fat fool like that ugly tempered Mathilda Haydon, not for anything anybody could ever give her. How Lena could keep on going there so much when they all always acted as if she was just dirt to them, Mary never could see. But Lena never had any sense of how she should make people stand round for her, and that was always all the trouble with her. And poor Lena, she was so stupid to be sorry for losing that gawky fool who didn't ever know what he wanted and just said "ja" to his mamma and his papa, like a baby, and was scared to look at a girl straight, and then sneaked away the last day like as if somebody was going to do something to him. Disgrace, Lena talking about disgrace! It was a disgrace for a girl to be seen with the likes of him, let alone to be married to him. But that poor Lena, she never did know how to show herself off for what she was really. Disgrace to have him go away and leave her. Mary would just like to get a chance to show him. If Lena wasn't worth fifteen like Herman Kreder, Mary would just eat her own head all up. It was a good riddance Lena had of that Herman Kreder and his stingy, dirty parents, and if Lena didn't stop crying about it,—Mary would just naturally despise her.

Poor Lena, she knew very well how Mary meant it all, this she was always saying to her. But Lena was very miserable inside her. She felt the disgrace it was for a decent german girl that a man should go away and leave her. Lena knew very well that her aunt was right when she said the way Herman had acted to her was a disgrace to everyone that knew her. Mary and Nellie and the other girls she always sat with were always very good to Lena but that did not make her trouble any better. It was a disgrace the way Lena had been left, to any decent family, and that could never be made any different to her.

And so the slow days wore on, and Lena never saw her Aunt Mathilda. At last on Sunday she got word by a boy to go and see her Aunt Mathilda. Lena's heart beat quick for she was very nervous now with all this that had happened to her. She went just as quickly as she could to see her Aunt Mathilda.

Mrs. Haydon quick, as soon as she saw Lena, began to scold her for keeping her aunt waiting so long for her, and for not coming in all the week to see her, to see if her aunt should need her, and so her aunt had to send a boy to tell her. But it was easy, even for Lena, to see that her aunt was not really angry with her. It wasn't Lena's fault, went on Mrs. Haydon, that everything was going to happen all right for her. Mrs. Haydon was very tired taking all this trouble for her, and when Lena couldn't even take trouble to come and see her aunt, to see if she needed anything to tell her. But Mrs. Haydon really never minded things like that when she could do things for anybody. She was tired now, all the trouble she had been taking to make things right for Lena, but perhaps now Lena heard it she would learn a little to be thankful to her. "You get all ready to be married Tuesday, Lena, you hear me," said Mrs. Haydon to her. "You come here Tuesday morning and I have everything all ready for you. You wear your new dress I got you, and your hat with all them flowers on it, and you be very careful coming you don't get your things all dirty, you so careless all the time, Lena, and not thinking, and you act sometimes you never got no head at all on you. You go home now, and you tell your Mrs. Aldrich that you leave her Tuesday. Don't you go forgetting now, Lena, anything I ever told you what you should do to be careful. You be a good girl, now Lena. You get married Tuesday to Herman Kreder." And that was all Lena ever knew of what had happened all this week to Herman Kreder. Lena forgot there was anything to know about it. She was really to be married Tuesday, and her Aunt

Mathilda said she was a good girl, and now there was no disgrace left upon her.

Lena now fell back into the way she always had of being always dreamy and not there, the way she always had been, except for the few days she was so excited, because she had been left by a man the very day she was to have been married. Lena was a little nervous all these last days, but she did not think much about what it meant for her to be married.

Herman Kreder was not so content about it. He was quiet and was sullen and he knew he could not help it. He knew now he just had to let himself get married. It was not that Herman did not like Lena Mainz. She was so good as any other girl could be for him. She was a little better perhaps than other girls he saw, she was so very quiet, but Herman did not like to always have to have a girl around him. Herman had always done everything that his mother and his father wanted. His father had found him in New York, where Herman had gone to be with his married sister.

Herman's father when he had found him coaxed Herman a long time and went on whole days with his complaining to him, always troubled but gentle and quite patient with him, and always he was worrying to Herman about what was the right way his boy Herman should always do, always whatever it was his mother ever wanted from him, and always Herman never made him any answer.

Old Mr. Kreder kept on saying to him, he did not see how Herman could think now, it could be any different. When you make a bargain you just got to stick right to it, that was the only way old Mr. Kreder could ever see it, and saying you would get married to a girl and she got everything all ready, that was a bargain just like one you make in business and Herman he had made it, and now Herman he would just have to do it, old Mr. Kreder didn't see there was any other way a good boy like his Herman had, to do it. And then too that Lena Mainz was such a nice girl and Herman hadn't ought to really give his father so much trouble and make him pay out all that money, to come all the way to New York just to find him, and they both lose all that time from their working, when all Herman had to do was just to stand up, for an hour, and then he would be all right married, and it would be all over for him, and then everything at home would never be any different to him.

And his father went on; there was his poor mother saying always how her Herman always did everything before she ever wanted, and now just because he got notions in him, and wanted to show people how he could be stubborn, he was making all this trouble for her, and making them pay all that money just to run around and find him. "You got no idea Herman, how bad mama is feeling about the way you been acting Herman," said old Mr. Kreder to him. "She says she never can understand how you can be so thankless Herman. It hurts her very much you been so stubborn, and she find you such a nice girl for you, like Lena Mainz who is always just so quiet and always saves up all her wages, and she never wanting her own way at all like some girls are always all the time to have it, and your mama trying so hard, just so you could be comfortable Herman to be married, and then you act so stubborn Herman. You like all young people Herman, you think only about yourself, and what you are just wanting, and your mama she is thinking only what is good for you to have, for you in the future. Do you think your mama wants to have a girl around to be a bother, for herself, Herman. It's just for you Herman she is always thinking, and she talks always about how happy she will be, when she sees her Herman married to a nice girl, and then when she fixed it all up so good for you, so it never would be any bother to you, just the way she wanted you should like it, and you say yes all right, I do it, and then you go away like this and act stubborn, and make all this trouble everybody to take for you, and we spend money, and I got to travel all

round to find you. You come home now with me Herman
and get married, and I tell your mama she better not say anything to you about how much it cost me to come all the way
to look for you—Hey Herman," said his father coaxing,
"Hey, you come home now and get married. All you got to
do Herman is just to stand up for an hour Herman, and then
you don't never to have any more bother to it—Hey Herman!—you come home with me to-morrow and get married. Hey Herman."

Herman's married sister liked her brother Herman, and
she had always tried to help him, when there was anything
she knew he wanted. She liked it that he was so good and always did everything that their father and their mother
wanted, but still she wished it could be that he could have
more his own way, if there was anything he ever wanted.

But now she thought Herman with his girl was very
funny. She wanted that Herman should be married. She
thought it would do him lots of good to get married. She
laughed at Herman when she heard the story. Until his father
came to find him, she did not know why it was Herman had
come just then to New York to see her. When she heard the
story she laughed a good deal at her brother Herman and
teased him a good deal about his running away, because he
didn't want to have a girl to be all the time around him.

Herman's married sister liked her brother Herman, and
she did not want him not to like to be with women. He was
good, her brother Herman, and it would surely do him good
to get married. It would make him stand up for himself
stronger. Herman's sister always laughed at him and always
she would try to reassure him. "Such a nice man as my
brother Herman acting like as if he was afraid of women.
Why the girls all like a man like you Herman, if you didn't
always run away when you saw them. It do you good really
Herman to get married, and then you got somebody you can
boss around when you want to. It do you good Herman to

get married, you see if you don't like it, when you really done it. You go along home now with papa, Herman and get married to that Lena. You don't know how nice you like it Herman when you try once how you can do it. You just don't be afraid of nothing, Herman. You good enough for any girl to marry, Herman. Any girl be glad to have a man like you to be always with them Herman. You just go along home with papa and try it what I say, Herman. Oh you so funny Herman, when you sit there, and then run away and leave your girl behind you. I know she is crying like anything Herman for to lose you. Don't be bad to her Herman. You go along home with papa now and get married Herman. I'd be awful ashamed Herman, to really have a brother didn't have spirit enough to get married, when a girl is just dying for to have him. You always like me to be with you Herman. I don't see why you say you don't want a girl to be all the time around you. You always been good to me Herman, and I know you always be good to that Lena, and you soon feel just like as if she had always been there with you. Don't act like as if you wasn't a nice strong man, Herman. Really I laugh at you Herman, but you know I like awful well to see you real happy. You go home and get married to that Lena, Herman. She is a real pretty girl and real nice and good and quiet and she make my brother Herman very happy. You just stop your fussing now with Herman, papa. He go with you to-morrow papa, and you see he like it so much to be married, he make everybody laugh just to see him be so happy. Really truly, that's the way it will be with you Herman. You just listen to me what I tell you Herman." And so his sister laughed at him and reassured him, and his father kept on telling what the mother always said about her Herman, and he coaxed him and Herman never said anything in answer, and his sister packed his things up and was very cheerful with him, and she kissed him, and then she laughed and then she kissed him, and his father went and bought the tickets for the train, and at last late on Sunday he brought Herman back to Bridgepoint with him.

It was always very hard to keep Mrs. Kreder from saying what she thought, to her Herman, but her daughter had written her a letter, so as to warn her not to say anything about what he had been doing, to him, and her husband came in with Herman and said, "Here we are come home mama, Herman and me, and we are very tired it was so crowded coming," and then he whispered to her. "You be good to Herman, mama, he didn't mean to make us so much trouble," and so old Mrs. Kreder, held in what she felt was so strong in her to say to her Herman. She just said very stiffly to him, "I'm glad to see you come home to-day, Herman." Then she went to arrange it all with Mrs. Haydon.

Herman was now again just like he always had been, sullen and very good, and very quiet, and always ready to do whatever his mother and his father wanted. Tuesday morning came, Herman got his new clothes on and went with his father and his mother to stand up for an hour and get married. Lena was there in her new dress, and her hat with all the pretty flowers, and she was very nervous for now she knew she was really very soon to be married. Mrs. Haydon had everything all ready. Everybody was there just as they should be and very soon Herman Kreder and Lena Mainz were married.

When everything was really over, they went back to the Kreder house together. They were all now to live together, Lena and Herman and the old father and the old mother, in the house where Mr. Kreder had worked so many years as a tailor, with his son Herman always there to help him.

Irish Mary had often said to Lena she never did see how Lena could ever want to have anything to do with Herman Kreder and his dirty stingy parents. The old Kreders were to an Irish nature, a stingy, dirty couple. They had not the free-hearted, thoughtless, fighting, mud bespattered, ragged,

peat-smoked cabin dirt that irish Mary knew and could forgive and love. Theirs was the german dirt of saving, of being
dowdy and loose and foul in your clothes so as to save them
and yourself in washing, having your hair greasy to save it
in the soap and drying, having your clothes dirty, not in freedom, but because so it was cheaper, keeping the house close
and smelly because so it cost less to get it heated, living so
poorly not only so as to save money but so they should never
even know themselves that they had it, working all the time
not only because from their nature they just had to and because it made them money but also that they never could be
put in any way to make them spend their money.

This was the place Lena now had for her home and to her
it was very different than it could be for an irish Mary. She
too was german and was thrifty, though she was always so
dreamy and not there. Lena was always careful with things
and she always saved her money, for that was the only way
she knew how to do it. She never had taken care of her own
money and she never had thought how to use it.

Lena Mainz had been, before she was Mrs. Herman
Kreder, always clean and decent in her clothes and in her
person, but it was not because she ever thought about it or
really needed so to have it, it was the way her people did in
the german country where she came from, and her Aunt
Mathilda and the good german cook who always scolded,
had kept her on and made her, with their scoldings, always
more careful to keep clean and to wash real often. But there
was no deep need in all this for Lena and so, though Lena
did not like the old Kreders, though she really did not know
that, she did not think about their being stingy dirty people.

Herman Kreder was cleaner than the old people, just because it was his nature to keep cleaner, but he was used to
his mother and his father, and he never thought that they
should keep things cleaner. And Herman too always saved
all his money, except for that little beer he drank when he

went out with other men of an evening the way he always liked to do it, and he never thought of any other way to spend it. His father had always kept all the money for them and he always was doing business with it. And then too Herman really had no money, for he always had worked for his father, and his father had never thought to pay him.

And so they began all four to live in the Kreder house together, and Lena began soon with it to look careless and a little dirty, and to be more lifeless with it, and nobody ever noticed much what Lena wanted, and she never really knew herself what she needed.

The only real trouble that came to Lena with their living all four there together, was the way old Mrs. Kreder scolded. Lena had always been used to being scolded, but this scolding of old Mrs. Kreder was very different from the way she ever before had had to endure it.

Herman, now he was married to her, really liked Lena very well. He did not care very much about her but she never was a bother to him being there around him, only when his mother worried and was nasty to them because Lena was so careless, and did not know how to save things right for them with their eating, and all the other ways with money, that the old woman had to save it.

Herman Kreder had always done everything his mother and his father wanted but he did not really love his parents very deeply. With Herman it was always only that he hated to have any struggle. It was all always all right with him when he could just go along and do the same thing over every day with his working, and not to hear things, and not to have people make him listen to their anger. And now his marriage, and he just knew it would, was making trouble for him. It made him hear more what his mother was always saying, with her scolding. He had to really hear it now because Lena was there, and she was so scared and dull always when she heard it. Herman knew very well with his mother,

it was all right if one ate very little and worked hard all day
and did not hear her when she scolded, the way Herman always had done before they were so foolish about his getting
married and having a girl there to be all the time around him,
and now he had to help her so the girl could learn too, not to
hear it when his mother scolded, and not to look so scared,
and not to eat much, and always to be sure to save it.

Herman really did not know very well what he could do
to help Lena to understand it. He could never answer his
mother back to help Lena, that never would make things any
better for her, and he never could feel in himself any way to
comfort Lena, to make her strong not to hear his mother, in
all the awful ways she always scolded. It just worried Herman to have it like that all the time around him. Herman did
not know much about how a man could make a struggle with
a mother, to do much to keep her quiet, and indeed Herman
never knew much how to make a struggle against any one
who really wanted to have anything very badly. Herman all
his life never wanted anything so badly, that he would really
make a struggle against any one to get it. Herman all his life
only wanted to live regular and quiet, and not talk much and
to do the same way every day like every other with his
working. And now his mother had made him get married to
this Lena and now with his mother making all that scolding,
he had all this trouble and this worry always on him.

Mrs. Haydon did not see Lena now very often. She had
not lost her interest in her niece Lena, but Lena could not
come much to her house to see her, it would not be right,
now Lena was a married woman. And then too Mrs. Haydon
had her hands full just then with her two daughters, for she
was getting them ready to find them good husbands, and
then too her own husband now worried her very often about
her always spoiling that boy of hers, so he would be sure to
turn out no good and be a disgrace to a german family, and
all because his mother always spoiled him. All these things

were very worrying now to Mrs. Haydon, but still she
wanted to be good to Lena, though she could not see her
very often. She only saw her when Mrs. Haydon went to call
on Mrs. Kreder or when Mrs. Kreder came to see Mrs. Haydon, and that never could be very often. Then too these days
Mrs. Haydon could not scold Lena, Mrs. Kreder was always
there with her, and it would not be right to scold Lena when
Mrs. Kreder was there, who had now the real right to do it.
And so her aunt always said nice things now to Lena, and
though Mrs. Haydon sometimes was a little worried when
she saw Lena looking sad and not careful, she did not have
time just then to really worry much about it.

Lena now never any more saw the girls she always used
to sit with. She had no way now to see them and it was not
in Lena's nature to search out ways to see them, nor did she
now ever think much of the days when she had been used to
see them. They never any of them had come to the Kreder
house to see her. Not even Irish Mary had ever thought to
come to see her. Lena had been soon forgotten by them.
They had soon passed away from Lena and now Lena never
thought any more that she had ever known them.

The only one of her old friends who tried to know what
Lena liked and what she needed, and who always made
Lena come to see her, was the good german cook who had
always scolded. She now scolded Lena hard for letting herself go so, and going out when she was looking so untidy. "I
know you going to have a baby Lena, but that's no way for
you to be looking. I am ashamed most to see you come and
sit here in my kitchen, looking so sloppy and like you never
used to Lena. I never see anybody like you Lena. Herman is
very good to you, you always say so, and he don't treat you
bad even though you don't deserve to have anybody good to
you, you so careless all the time, Lena, letting yourself go
like you never had anybody tell you what was the right way
you should know how to be looking. No, Lena, I don't see

no reason you should let yourself go so and look so untidy Lena, so I am ashamed to see you sit there looking so ugly, Lena. No Lena that ain't no way ever I see a woman make things come out better, letting yourself go so every way and crying all the time like as if you had real trouble. I never wanted to see you marry Herman Kreder, Lena, I knew what you got to stand with that old woman always, and that old man, he is so stingy too and he don't say things out but he ain't any better in his heart than his wife with her bad ways, I know that Lena, I know they don't hardly give you enough to eat, Lena, I am real sorry for you Lena, you know that Lena, but that ain't any way to be going round so untidy Lena, even if you have got all that trouble. You never see me do like that Lena, though sometimes I got a headache so I can't see to stand to be working hardly, and nothing comes right with all my cooking, but I always see Lena, I look decent. That's the only way a german girl can make things come out right Lena. You hear me what I am saying to you Lena. Now you eat something nice Lena, I got it all ready for you, and you wash up and be careful Lena and the baby will come all right to you, and then I make your Aunt Mathilda see that you live in a house soon all alone with Herman and your baby, and then everything go better for you. You hear me what I say to you Lena. Now don't let me ever see you come looking like this any more Lena, and you just stop with that always crying. You ain't got no reason to be sitting there now with all that crying, I never see anybody have trouble it did them any good to do the way you are doing, Lena. You hear me Lena. You go home now and you be good the way I tell you Lena, and I see what I can do. I make your Aunt Mathilda make old Mrs. Kreder let you be till you get your baby all right. Now don't you be scared and so silly Lena. I don't like to see you act so Lena when really you got a nice man and so many things really any girl should be grateful to be having. Now you go home Lena to-day and you do the way I say, to you, and I see what I can do to help you."

"Yes Mrs. Aldrich," said the good german woman to her mistress later, "Yes Mrs. Aldrich that's the way it is with them girls when they want so to get married. They don't know when they got it good Mrs. Aldrich. They never know what it is they're really wanting when they got it, Mrs. Aldrich. There's that poor Lena, she just been here crying and looking so careless so I scold her, but that was no good that marrying for that poor Lena, Mrs. Aldrich. She do look so pale and sad now Mrs. Aldrich, it just break my heart to see her. She was a good girl was Lena, Mrs. Aldrich, and I never had no trouble with her like I got with so many young girls nowadays, Mrs. Aldrich, and I never see any girl any better to work right than our Lena, and now she got to stand it all the time with that old woman Mrs. Kreder. My! Mrs. Aldrich, she is a bad old woman to her. I never see Mrs. Aldrich how old people can be so bad to young girls and not have no kind of patience with them. If Lena could only live with her Herman, he ain't so bad the way men are, Mrs. Aldrich, but he is just the way always his mother wants him, he ain't got no spirit in him, and so I don't really see no help for that poor Lena. I know her aunt, Mrs. Haydon, meant it all right for her Mrs. Aldrich, but poor Lena, it would be better for her if her Herman had stayed there in New York that time he went away to leave her. I don't like it the way Lena is looking now, Mrs. Aldrich. She looks like as if she don't have no life left in her hardly, Mrs. Aldrich, she just drags around and looks so dirty and after all the pains I always took to teach her and to keep her nice in her ways and looking. It don't do no good to them, for them girls to get married Mrs. Aldrich, they are much better when they only know it, to stay in a good place when they got it, and keep on regular with their working. I don't like it the way Lena looks now Mrs. Aldrich. I wish I knew some way to help that poor Lena, Mrs. Aldrich, but she is a bad old woman, that old Mrs. Kreder, Herman's mother. I speak to Mrs. Haydon real soon, Mrs. Aldrich, I see what we can do now to help that poor Lena."

These were really bad days for poor Lena. Herman always was real good to her and now he even sometimes tried to stop his mother from scolding Lena. "She ain't well now mama, you let her be now you hear me. You tell me what it is you want she should be doing, I tell her. I see she does it right just the way you want it mama. You let be, I say now mama, with that always scolding Lena. You let be, I say now, you wait till she is feeling better." Herman was getting really strong to struggle, for he could see that Lena with that baby working hard inside her, really could not stand it any longer with his mother and the awful ways she always scolded.

It was a new feeling Herman now had inside him that made him feel he was strong to make a struggle. It was new for Herman Kreder really to be wanting something, but Herman wanted strongly now to be a father, and he wanted badly that his baby should be a boy and healthy. Herman never had cared really very much about his father and his mother, though always, all his life, he had done everything just as they wanted, and he had never really cared much about his wife, Lena, though he always had been very good to her, and had always tried to keep his mother off her, with the awful way she always scolded, but to be really a father of a little baby, that feeling took hold of Herman very deeply. He was almost ready, so as to save his baby from all trouble, to really make a strong struggle with his mother and with his father, too, if he would not help him to control his mother.

Sometimes Herman even went to Mrs. Haydon to talk all this trouble over. They decided then together, it was better to wait there all four together for the baby, and Herman could

make Mrs. Kreder stop a little with her scolding, and then
when Lena was a little stronger, Herman should have his
own house for her, next door to his father, so he could always be there to help him in his working, but so they could
eat and sleep in a house where the old woman could not control them and they could not hear her awful scolding.

And so things went on, the same way, a little longer. Poor
Lena was not feeling any joy to have a baby. She was scared
the way she had been when she was so sick on the water.
She was scared now every time when anything would hurt
her. She was scared and still and lifeless, and sure that every
minute she would die. Lena had no power to be strong in
this kind of trouble, she could only sit still and be scared,
and dull, and lifeless, and sure that every minute she would
die.

Before very long, Lena had her baby. He was a good,
healthy little boy, the baby. Herman cared very much to have
the baby. When Lena was a little stronger he took a house
next door to the old couple, so he and his own family could
eat and sleep and do the way they wanted. This did not seem
to make much change now for Lena. She was just the same
as when she was waiting with her baby. She just dragged
around and was careless with her clothes and all lifeless, and
she acted always and lived on just as if she had no feeling.
She always did everything regular with the work, the way
she always had had to do it, but she never got back any spirit
in her. Herman was always good and kind, and always
helped her with her working. He did everything he knew to
help her. He always did all the active new things in the
house and for the baby. Lena did what she had to do the way
she always had been taught it. She always just kept going
now with her working, and she was always careless, and
dirty, and a little dazed, and lifeless. Lena never got any better in herself of this way of being that she had had ever since
she had been married.

Mrs. Haydon never saw any more of her niece, Lena. Mrs. Haydon had now so much trouble with her own house, and her daughters getting married, and her boy, who was growing up, and who always was getting so much worse to manage. She knew she had done right by Lena. Herman Kreder was a good man, she would be glad to get one so good, sometimes, for her own daughters, and now they had a home to live in together, separate from the old people, who had made their trouble for them. Mrs. Haydon felt she had done very well by her niece, Lena, and she never thought now she needed any more to go and see her. Lena would do very well now without her aunt to trouble herself any more about her.

The good german cook who had always scolded, still tried to do her duty like a mother to poor Lena. It was very hard now to do right by Lena. Lena never seemed to hear now what anyone was saying to her. Herman was always doing everything he could to help her. Herman always, when he was home, took good care of the baby. Herman loved to take care of his baby. Lena never thought to take him out or to do anything she didn't have to.

The good cook sometimes made Lena come to see her. Lena would come with her baby and sit there in the kitchen, and watch the good woman cooking, and listen to her sometimes a little, the way she used to, while the good german woman scolded her for going around looking so careless when now she had no trouble, and sitting there so dull, and always being just so thankless. Sometimes Lena would wake up a little and get back into her face her old, gentle, patient, and unsuffering sweetness, but mostly Lena did not seem to hear much when the good german woman scolded. Lena always liked it when Mrs. Aldrich her good mistress spoke to her kindly, and then Lena would seem to go back and feel herself to be like she was when she had been in service. But mostly Lena just lived along and was careless in her clothes, and dull, and lifeless.

By and by Lena had two more little babies. Lena was not so much scared now when she had the babies. She did not seem to notice very much when they hurt her, and she never seemed to feel very much now about anything that happened to her.

They were very nice babies, all these three that Lena had, and Herman took good care of them always. Herman never really cared much about his wife, Lena. The only things Herman ever really cared for were his babies. Herman always was very good to his children. He always had a gentle, tender way when he held them. He learned to be very handy with them. He spent all the time he was not working, with them. By and by he began to work all day in his own home so that he could have his children always in the same room with him.

Lena always was more and more lifeless and Herman now mostly never thought about her. He more and more took all the care of their three children. He saw to their eating right and their washing, and he dressed them every morning, and he taught them the right way to do things, and he put them to their sleeping, and he was now always every minute with them. Then there was to come to them, a fourth baby. Lena went to the hospital near by to have the baby. Lena seemed to be going to have much trouble with it. When the baby was come out at last, it was like its mother lifeless. While it was coming, Lena had grown very pale and sicker. When it was all over Lena had died, too, and nobody knew just how it had happened to her.

The good german cook who had always scolded Lena, and had always to the last day tried to help her, was the only one who ever missed her. She remembered how nice Lena had looked all the time she was in service with her, and how her voice had been so gentle and sweet-sounding, and how she always was a good girl, and how she never had to have any trouble with her, the way she always had with all the other girls who had been taken into the house to help her. The good cook sometimes spoke so of Lena when she had time to have a talk with Mrs. Aldrich, and this was all the remembering there now ever was of Lena.

Herman Kreder now always lived very happy, very gentle, very quiet, very well content alone with his three children. He never had a woman any more to be all the time around him. He always did all his own work in his house, when he was through every day with the work he was always doing for his father. Herman always was alone, and he always worked alone, until his little ones were big enough to help him. Herman Kreder was very well content now and he always lived very regular and peaceful, and with every day just like the next one, always alone now with his three good, gentle children.

TENDER
BUTTONS

OBJECTS

A CARAFE, THAT IS A BLIND GLASS.

A kind in glass and a cousin, a spectacle and nothing strange a single hurt color and an arrangement in a system to pointing. All this and not ordinary, not unordered in not resembling. The difference is spreading.

GLAZED GLITTER.

Nickel, what is nickel, it is originally rid of a cover.

The change in that is that red weakens an hour. The change has come. There is no search. But there is, there is that hope and that interpretation and sometime, surely any is unwelcome, sometime there is breath and there will be a sinecure and charming very charming is that clean and cleansing. Certainly glittering is handsome and convincing.

There is no gratitude in mercy and in medicine. There can be breakages in Japanese. That is no programme. That is no color chosen. It was chosen yesterday, that showed spitting and perhaps washing and polishing. It certainly showed no obligation and perhaps if borrowing is not natural there is some use in giving.

A SUBSTANCE IN A CUSHION.

The change of color is likely and a difference a very little difference is prepared. Sugar is not a vegetable.

Callous is something that hardening leaves behind what will be soft if there is a genuine interest in there being present as many girls as men. Does this change. It shows that dirt is clean when there is a volume.

A cushion has that cover. Supposing you do not like to change, supposing it is very clean that there is no change in appearance, supposing that there is regularity and a costume is that any the worse than an oyster and an exchange. Come to season that is there any extreme use in feather and cotton. Is there not much more joy in a table and more chairs and very likely roundness and a place to put them.

A circle of fine card board and a chance to see a tassel.

What is the use of a violent kind of delightfulness if there is no pleasure in not getting tired of it. The question does not come before there is a quotation. In any kind of place there is a top to covering and it is a pleasure at any rate there is some venturing in refusing to believe nonsense. It shows what use there is in a whole piece if one uses it and it is extreme and very likely the little things could be dearer but in any case there is a bargain and if there is the best thing to do is to take it away and wear it and then be reckless be reckless and resolved on returning gratitude.

Light blue and the same red with purple makes a change. It shows that there is no mistake. Any pink shows that and very likely it is reasonable. Very likely there should not be a finer fancy present. Some increase means a calamity and this is the best preparation for three and more being together. A little calm is so ordinary and in any case there is sweetness and some of that.

A seal and matches and a swan and ivy and a suit.

A closet, a closet does not connect under the bed. The

band if it is white and black, the band has a green string. A sight a whole sight and a little groan grinding makes a trimming such a sweet singing trimming and a red thing not a round thing but a white thing, a red thing and a white thing.

The disgrace is not in carelessness nor even in sewing it comes out out of the way.

What is the sash like. The sash is not like anything mustard it is not like a same thing that has stripes, it is not even more hurt than that, it has a little top.

A BOX.

Out of kindness comes redness and out of rudeness comes rapid same question, out of an eye comes research, out of selection comes painful cattle. So then the order is that a white way of being round is something suggesting a pin and is it disappointing, it is not, it is so rudimentary to be analysed and see a fine substance strangely, it is so earnest to have a green point not to red but to point again.

A PIECE OF COFFEE.

More of double.

A place in no new table.

A single image is not splendor. Dirty is yellow. A sign of more in not mentioned. A piece of coffee is not a detainer. The resemblance to yellow is dirtier and distincter. The clean mixture is whiter and not coal color, never more coal color than altogether.

The sight of a reason, the same sight slighter, the sight of a simpler negative answer, the same sore sounder, the intention to wishing, the same splendor, the same furniture.

The time to show a message is when too late and later there is no hanging in a blight.

A not torn rose-wood color. If it is not dangerous then a pleasure and more than any other if it is cheap is not cheaper. The amusing side is that the sooner there are no fewer the more certain is the necessity dwindled. Supposing that the case contained rose-wood and a color. Supposing that there was no reason for a distress and more likely for a number, supposing that there was no astonishment, is it not necessary to mingle astonishment.

The settling of stationing cleaning is one way not to shatter scatter and scattering. The one way to use custom is to use soap and silk for cleaning. The one way to see cotton is to have a design concentrating the illusion and the illustration. The perfect way is to accustom the thing to have a lining and the shape of a ribbon and to be solid, quite solid in standing and to use heaviness in morning. It is light enough in that. It has that shape nicely. Very nicely may not be exaggerating. Very strongly may be sincerely fainting. May be strangely flattering. May not be strange in everything. May not be strange to.

DIRT AND NOT COPPER.

Dirt and not copper makes a color darker. It makes the shape so heavy and makes no melody harder.

It makes mercy and relaxation and even a strength to spread a table fuller. There are more places not empty. They see cover.

NOTHING ELEGANT.

A charm a single charm is doubtful. If the red is rose and there is a gate surrounding it, if inside is let in and there places change then certainly something is upright. It is earnest.

MILDRED'S UMBRELLA.

A cause and no curve, a cause and loud enough, a cause and extra a loud clash and an extra wagon, a sign of extra, a sac a small sac and an established color and cunning, a slender grey and no ribbon, this means a loss a great loss a restitution.

A METHOD OF A CLOAK.

A single climb to a line, a straight exchange to a cane, a desperate adventure and courage and a clock, all this which is a system, which has feeling, which has resignation and success, all makes an attractive black silver.

A RED STAMP.

If lilies are lily white if they exhaust noise and distance and even dust, if they dusty will dirt a surface that has no extreme grace, if they do this and it is not necessary it is not at all necessary if they do this they need a catalogue.

A BOX.

A large box is handily made of what is necessary to replace any substance. Suppose an example is necessary, the plainer it is made the more reason there is for some outward recognition that there is a result.

A box is made sometimes and them to see to see to it neatly and to have the holes stopped up makes it necessary to use paper.

A custom which is necessary when a box is used and taken is that a large part of the time there are three which have different connections. The one is on the table. The two are on the table. The three are on the table. The one, one is the same length as is shown by the cover being longer. The other is different there is more cover that shows it. The other is different and that makes the corners have the same shade the eight are in singular arrangement to make four necessary.

Lax, to have corners, to be lighter than some weight, to indicate a wedding journey, to last brown and not curious, to be wealthy, cigarettes are established by length and by doubling.

Left open, to be left pounded, to be left closed, to be circulating in summer and winter, and sick color that is grey that is not dusty and red shows, to be sure cigarettes do measure an empty length sooner than a choice in color.

Winged, to be winged means that white is yellow and pieces pieces that are brown are dust color if dust is washed off, then it is choice that is to say it is fitting cigarettes sooner than paper.

An increase why is an increase idle, why is silver cloister, why is the spark brighter, if it is brighter is there any result, hardly more than ever.

A PLATE.

An occasion for a plate, an occasional resource is in buying and how soon does washing enable a selection of the same thing neater. If the party is small a clever song is in order.

Plates and a dinner set of colored china. Pack together a string and enough with it to protect the centre, cause a considerable haste and gather more as it is cooling, collect more trembling and not any even trembling, cause a whole thing to be a church.

A sad size a size that is not sad is blue as every bit of blue is precocious. A kind of green a game in green and nothing flat nothing quite flat and more round, nothing a particular color strangely, nothing breaking the losing of no little piece.

A splendid address a really splendid address is not shown by giving a flower freely, it is not shown by a mark or by wetting.

Cut cut in white, cut in white so lately. Cut more than any other and show it. Show it in the stem and in starting and in evening coming complication.

A lamp is not the only sign of glass. The lamp and the cake are not the only sign of stone. The lamp and the cake and the cover are not the only necessity altogether.

A plan a hearty plan, a compressed disease and no coffee, not even a card or a change to incline each way, a plan that has that excess and that break is the one that shows filling.

A SELTZER BOTTLE.

Any neglect of many particles to a cracking, any neglect of this makes around it what is lead in color and certainly discolor in silver. The use of this is manifold. Supposing a certain time selected is assured, suppose it is even necessary, suppose no other extract is permitted and no more handling is needed, suppose the rest of the message is mixed with a very long slender needle and even if it could be any black border, supposing all this altogether made a dress and suppose it was actual, suppose the mean way to state it was occasional, if you suppose this in August and even more melodiously, if you suppose this even in the necessary incident of there certainly being no middle in summer and winter, suppose this and an elegant settlement a very elegant settlement is more than of consequence, it is not final and sufficient and substituted. This which was so kindly a present was constant.

A LONG DRESS.

What is the current that makes machinery, that makes it crackle, what is the current that presents a long line and a necessary waist. What is this current.

What is the wind, what is it.

Where is the serene length, it is there and a dark place is not a dark place, only a white and red are black, only a yellow and green are blue, a pink is scarlet, a bow is every color. A line distinguishes it. A line just distinguishes it.

A RED HAT.

A dark grey, a very dark grey, a quite dark grey is monstrous ordinarily, it is so monstrous because there is no red in it. If red is in everything it is not necessary. Is that not an argument for any use of it and even so is there any place that is better, is there any place that has so much stretched out.

A BLUE COAT.

A blue coat is guided guided away, guided and guided away, that is the particular color that is used for that length and not any width not even more than a shadow.

A PIANO.

If the speed is open, if the color is careless, if the selection of a strong scent is not awkward, if the button holder is held by all the waving color and there is no color, not any color. If there is no dirt in a pin and there can be none scarcely, if there is not then the place is the same as up standing.

This is no dark custom and it even is not acted in any such a way that a restraint is not spread. That is spread, it shuts and it lifts and awkwardly not awkwardly the centre is in standing.

A CHAIR.

A widow in a wise veil and more garments shows that shadows are even. It addresses no more, it shadows the stage and learning. A regular arrangement, the severest and the most preserved is that which has the arrangement not more than always authorised.

A suitable establishment, well housed, practical, patient and staring, a suitable bedding, very suitable and not more particularly than complaining, anything suitable is so necessary.

A fact is that when the direction is just like that, no more, longer, sudden and at the same time not any sofa, the main action is that without a blaming there is no custody.

Practice measurement, practice the sign that means that really means a necessary betrayal, in showing that there is wearing.

Hope, what is a spectacle, a spectacle is the resemblance between the circular side place and nothing else, nothing else.

To choose it is ended, it is actual and more than that it has it certainly has the same treat, and a seat all that is practiced and more easily much more easily ordinarily.

Pick a barn, a whole barn, and bend more slender accents than have ever been necessary, shine in the darkness necessarily.

Actually not aching, actually not aching, a stubborn bloom is so artificial and even more than that, it is a spectacle, it is a binding accident, it is animosity and accentuation.

If the chance to dirty diminishing is necessary, if it is why is there no complexion, why is there no rubbing, why is there no special protection.

A FRIGHTFUL RELEASE.

A bag which was left and not only taken but turned away was not found. The place was shown to be very like the last time. A piece was not exchanged, not a bit of it, a piece was left over. The rest was mismanaged.

A PURSE.

A purse was not green, it was not straw color, it was hardly seen and it had a use a long use and the chain, the chain was never missing, it was not misplaced, it showed that it was open, that is all that it showed.

A MOUNTED UMBRELLA.

What was the use of not leaving it there where it would hang what was the use if there was no chance of ever seeing it come there and show that it was handsome and right in the way it showed it. The lesson is to learn that it does show it, that it shows it and that nothing, that there is nothing, that there is no more to do about it and just so much more is there plenty of reason for making an exchange.

A CLOTH.

Enough cloth is plenty and more, more is almost enough for that and besides if there is no more spreading is there plenty of room for it. Any occasion shows the best way.

MORE.

An elegant use of foliage and grace and a little piece of white cloth and oil.

Wondering so winningly in several kinds of oceans is the reason that makes red so regular and enthusiastic. The reason that there is more snips are the same shining very colored rid of no round color.

A NEW CUP AND SAUCER.

Enthusiastically hurting a clouded yellow bud and saucer, enthusiastically so is the bite in the ribbon.

OBJECTS.

Within, within the cut and slender joint alone, with sudden equals and no more than three, two in the centre make two one side.

If the elbow is long and it is filled so then the best example is all together.

The kind of show is made by squeezing.

EYE GLASSES.

A color in shaving, a saloon is well placed in the centre of an alley.

A CUTLET.

A blind agitation is manly and uttermost.

CARELESS WATER.

No cup is broken in more places and mended, that is to say a plate is broken and mending does do that it shows that culture is Japanese. It shows the whole element of angels and orders. It does more to choosing and it does more to that ministering counting. It does, it does change in more water.

Supposing a single piece is a hair supposing more of them are orderly, does that show that strength, does that show that joint, does that show that balloon famously. Does it.

A PAPER.

A courteous occasion makes a paper show no such occasion and this makes readiness and eyesight and likeness and a stool.

A DRAWING.

The meaning of this is entirely and best to say the mark, best to say it best to show sudden places, best to make bitter, best to make the length tall and nothing broader, anything between the half.

WATER RAINING.

Water astonishing and difficult altogether makes a meadow and a stroke.

COLD CLIMATE.

A season in yellow sold extra strings makes lying places.

MALACHITE.

The sudden spoon is the same in no size. The sudden spoon is the wound in the decision.

AN UMBRELLA.

Coloring high means that the strange reason is in front not more in front behind. Not more in front in peace of the dot.

A PETTICOAT.

A light white, a disgrace, an ink spot, a rosy charm.

A WAIST.

A star glide, a single frantic sullenness, a single financial grass greediness.

Object that is in wood. Hold the pine, hold the dark, hold in the rush, make the bottom.

A piece of crystal. A change, in a change that is remarkable there is no reason to say that there was a time.

A woolen object gilded. A country climb is the best disgrace, a couple of practices any of them in order is so left.

A TIME TO EAT.

A pleasant simple habitual and tyrannical and authorised and educated and resumed and articulate separation. This is not tardy.

A LITTLE BIT OF A TUMBLER.

A shining indication of yellow consists in there having been more of the same color than could have been expected when all four were bought. This was the hope which made the six and seven have no use for any more places and this necessarily spread into nothing. Spread into nothing.

A FIRE.

What was the use of a whole time to send and not send if there was to be the kind of thing that made that come in. A letter was nicely sent.

A HANDKERCHIEF.

A winning of all the blessings, a sample not a sample because there is no worry.

RED ROSES.

A cool red rose and a pink cut pink, a collapse and a sold hole, a little less hot.

IN BETWEEN.

In between a place and candy is a narrow foot-path that shows more mounting than anything, so much really that a calling meaning a bolster measured a whole thing with that. A virgin a whole virgin is judged made and so between curves and outlines and real seasons and more out glasses and a perfectly unprecedented arrangement between old ladies and mild colds there is no satin wood shining.

COLORED HATS.

Colored hats are necessary to show that curls are worn by an addition of blank spaces, this makes the difference between single lines and broad stomachs, the least thing is lightening, the least thing means a little flower and a big delay a big delay that makes more nurses than little women really little women. So clean is a light that nearly all of it shows pearls and little ways. A large hat is tall and me and all custard whole.

A FEATHER.

A feather is trimmed, it is trimmed by the light and the bug and the post, it is trimmed by little leaning and by all sorts of mounted reserves and loud volumes. It is surely cohesive.

A BROWN.

A brown which is not liquid not more so is relaxed and yet there is a change, a news is pressing.

A LITTLE CALLED PAULINE.

A little called anything shows shudders.

Come and say what prints all day. A whole few watermelon. There is no pope.

No cut in pennies and little dressing and choose wide soles and little spats really little spices.

A little lace makes boils. This is not true.

Gracious of gracious and a stamp a blue green white bow a blue green lean, lean on the top.

If it is absurd then it is leadish and nearly set in where there is a tight head.

A peaceful life to arise her, noon and moon and moon. A letter a cold sleeve a blanket a shaving house and nearly the best and regular window.

Nearer in fairy sea, nearer and farther, show white has lime in sight, show a stitch of ten. Count, count more so that thicker and thicker is leaning.

I hope she has her cow. Bidding a wedding, widening received treading, little leading mention nothing.

Cough out cough out in the leather and really feather it is not for.

Please could, please could, jam it not plus more sit in when.

A SOUND.

Elephant beaten with candy and little pops and chews all bolts and reckless reckless rats, this is this.

A TABLE.

A table means does it not my dear it means a whole steadiness. Is it likely that a change.

A table means more than a glass even a looking glass is tall. A table means necessary places and a revision a revision

of a little thing it means it does mean that there has been a
stand, a stand where it did shake.

SHOES.

To be a wall with a damper a stream of pounding way and
nearly enough choice makes a steady midnight. It is pus.

A shallow hole rose on red, a shallow hole in and in this
makes ale less. It shows shine.

A DOG.

A little monkey goes like a donkey that means to say that
means to say that more sighs last goes. Leave with it. A little monkey goes like a donkey.

A WHITE HUNTER.

A white hunter is nearly crazy.

A LEAVE.

In the middle of a tiny spot and nearly bare there is a nice
thing to say that wrist is leading. Wrist is leading.

SUPPOSE AN EYES.

Suppose it is within a gate which open is open at the hour
of closing summer that is to say it is so.

All the seats are needing blackening. A white dress is in
sign. A soldier a real soldier has a worn lace a worn lace of
different sizes that is to say if he can read, if he can read he
is a size to show shutting up twenty-four.

Go red go red, laugh white.

Suppose a collapse in rubbed purr, in rubbed purr get.

Little sales ladies little sales ladies little saddles of mutton.

Little sales of leather and such beautiful beautiful, beautiful beautiful.

A SHAWL.

A shawl is a hat and hurt and a red balloon and an under coat and a sizer a sizer of talks.

A shawl is a wedding, a piece of wax a little build. A shawl.

Pick a ticket, pick it in strange steps and with hollows. There is hollow hollow belt, a belt is a shawl.

A plate that has a little bobble, all of them, any so.

Please a round it is ticket.

It was a mistake to state that a laugh and a lip and a laid climb and a depot and a cultivator and little choosing is a point it.

BOOK.

Book was there, it was there. Book was there. Stop it, stop it, it was a cleaner, a wet cleaner and it was not where it was wet, it was not high, it was directly placed back, not back again, back it was returned, it was needless, it put a bank, a bank when, a bank care.

Suppose a man a realistic expression of resolute reliability suggests pleasing itself white all white and no head does that mean soap. It does not so. It means kind wavers and little chance to beside beside rest. A plain.

Suppose ear rings, that is one way to breed, breed that. Oh chance to say, oh nice old pole. Next best and nearest a pillar. Chest not valuable, be papered.

Cover up cover up the two with a little piece of string and hope rose and green, green.

Please a plate, put a match to the seam and really then really then, really then it is a remark that joins many many lead games. It is a sister and sister and a flower and a flower and a dog and a colored sky a sky colored grey and nearly that nearly that let.

PEELED PENCIL, CHOKE.

Rub her coke.

IT WAS BLACK, BLACK TOOK.

Black ink best wheel bale brown.

Excellent not a hull house, not a pea soup, no bill no care, no precise no past pearl pearl goat.

THIS IS THIS DRESS, AIDER.

Aider, why aider why whow, whow stop touch, aider whow, aider stop the muncher, muncher munchers.

A jack in kill her, a jack in, makes a meadowed king, makes a to let.

FOOD

ROASTBEEF; MUTTON; BREAKFAST;
SUGAR; CRANBERRIES; MILK; EGGS;
APPLE; TAILS; LUNCH; CUPS; RHUBARB;
SINGLE FISH; CAKE; CUSTARD; POTATOES;
ASPARAGUS; BUTTER; END OF SUMMER;
SAUSAGES; CELERY; VEAL; VEGETABLE;
COOKING; CHICKEN; PASTRY; CREAM;
CUCUMBER; DINNER; DINING; EATING;
SALAD; SAUCE; SALMON; ORANGE; COCOA
AND CLEAR SOUP AND ORANGES AND OAT-
MEAL; SALAD DRESSING AND AN
ARTICHOKE; A CENTRE IN A TABLE.

ROASTBEEF.

In the inside there is sleeping, in the outside there is reddening, in the morning there is meaning, in the evening there is feeling. In the evening there is feeling. In feeling anything is resting, in feeling anything is mounting, in feeling there is resignation, in feeling there is recognition, in feeling there is recurrence and entirely mistaken there is pinching. All the standards have steamers and all the curtains have bed linen and all the yellow has discrimination and all the circle has circling. This makes sand.

Very well. Certainly the length is thinner and the rest, the round rest has a longer summer. To shine, why not shine, to shine, to station, to enlarge, to hurry the measure all this means nothing if there is singing, if there is singing then there is the resumption.

The change the dirt, not to change dirt means that there is no beefsteak and not to have that is no obstruction, it is so easy to exchange meaning, it is so easy to see the difference. The difference is that a plain resource is not entangled with thickness and it does not mean that thickness shows such cutting, it does mean that a meadow is useful and a cow absurd. It does not mean that there are tears, it does not mean that exudation is cumbersome, it means no more than a memory, a choice and a reëstablishment, it means more than any escape from a surrounding extra. All the time that there is use there is use and any time there is a surface there is a surface, and every time there is an exception there is an exception and every time there is a division there is a dividing. Any time there is a surface there is a surface and every time there is a suggestion there is a suggestion and every time there is silence there is silence and every time that is languid there is that there then and not oftener, not always, not particular, tender and changing and external and central and surrounded and singular and simple and the same and the surface and the circle and the shine and the succor and the white and the same and the better and the red and the same and the centre and the yellow and the tender and the better, and altogether.

Considering the circumstances there is no occasion for a reduction, considering that there is no pealing there is no occasion for an obligation, considering that there is no outrage there is no necessity for any reparation, considering that there is no particle sodden there is no occasion for deliberation. Considering everything and which way the turn is tending, considering everything why is there no restraint, considering everything what makes the place settle and the plate distinguish some specialties. The whole thing is not understood and this is not strange considering that there is no education, this is not strange because having that certainly does show the difference in cutting, it shows that when there is turning there is no distress.

In kind, in a control, in a period, in the alteration of pigeons, in kind cuts and thick and thin spaces, in kind ham and different colors, the length of leaning a strong thing outside not to make a sound but to suggest a crust, the principal taste is when there is a whole chance to be reasonable, this does not mean that there is overtaking, this means nothing precious, this means clearly that the chance to exercise is a social success. So then the sound is not obtrusive. Suppose it is obtrusive suppose it is. What is certainly the desertion is not a reduced description, a description is not a birthday.

Lovely snipe and tender turn, excellent vapor and slender butter, all the splinter and the trunk, all the poisonous darkening drunk, all the joy in weak success, all the joyful tenderness, all the section and the tea, all the stouter symmetry.

Around the size that is small, inside the stern that is the middle, besides the remains that are praying, inside the between that is turning, all the region is measuring and melting is exaggerating.

Rectangular ribbon does not mean that there is no eruption it means that if there is no place to hold there is no place to spread. Kindness is not earnest, it is not assiduous it is not revered.

Room to comb chickens and feathers and ripe purple, room to curve single plates and large sets and second silver, room to send everything away, room to save heat and distemper, room to search a light that is simpler, all room has no shadow.

There is no use there is no use at all in smell, in taste, in teeth, in toast, in anything, there is no use at all and the respect is mutual.

Why should that which is uneven, that which is resumed, that which is tolerable why should all this resemble a smell, a thing is there, it whistles, it is not narrower, why is there no obligation to stay away and yet courage, courage is everywhere and the best remains to stay.

If there could be that which is contained in that which is felt there would be a chair where there are chairs and there would be no more denial about a clatter. A clatter is not a smell. All this is good.

The Saturday evening which is Sunday is every week

day. What choice is there when there is a difference. A regulation is not active. Thirstiness is not equal division.

Anyway, to be older and ageder is not a surfeit nor a suction, it is not dated and careful, it is not dirty. Any little thing is clean, rubbing is black. Why should ancient lambs be goats and young colts and never beef, why should they, they should because there is so much difference in age.

A sound, a whole sound is not separation, a whole sound is in an order.

Suppose there is a pigeon, suppose there is.

Looseness, why is there a shadow in a kitchen, there is a shadow in a kitchen because every little thing is bigger.

The time when there are four choices and there are four choices in a difference, the time when there are four choices there is a kind and there is a kind. There is a kind. There is a kind. Supposing there is a bone, there is a bone. Supposing there are bones. There are bones. When there are bones there is no supposing there are bones. There are bones and there is that consuming. The kindly way to feel separating is to have a space between. This shows a likeness.

Hope in gates, hope in spoons, hope in doors, hope in tables, no hope in daintiness and determination. Hope in dates.

Tin is not a can and a stove is hardly. Tin is not necessary and neither is a stretcher. Tin is never narrow and thick.

Color is in coal. Coal is outlasting roasting and a spoonful, a whole spoon that is full is not spilling. Coal any coal is copper.

Claiming nothing, not claiming anything, not a claim in everything, collecting claiming, all this makes a harmony, it even makes a succession.

Sincerely gracious one morning, sincerely graciously

trembling, sincere in gracious eloping, all this makes a furnace and a blanket. All this shows quantity.

Like an eye, not so much more, not any searching, no compliments.

Please be the beef, please beef, pleasure is not wailing. Please beef, please be carved clear, please be a case of consideration.

Search a neglect. A sale, any greatness is a stall and there is no memory, there is no clear collection.

A satin sight, what is a trick, no trick is mountainous and the color, all the rush is in the blood.

Bargaining for a little, bargain for a touch, a liberty, an estrangement, a characteristic turkey.

Please spice, please no name, place a whole weight, sink into a standard rising, raise a circle, choose a right around, make the resonance accounted and gather green any collar.

To bury a slender chicken, to raise an old feather, to surround a garland and to bake a pole splinter, to suggest a repose and to settle simply, to surrender one another, to succeed saving simpler, to satisfy a singularity and not to be blinder, to sugar nothing darker and to read redder, to have the color better, to sort out dinner, to remain together, to surprise no sinner, to curve nothing sweeter, to continue thinner, to increase in resting recreation to design string not dimmer.

Cloudiness what is cloudiness, is it a lining, is it a roll, is it melting.

The sooner there is jerking, the sooner freshness is tender, the sooner the round it is not round the sooner it is withdrawn in cutting, the sooner the measure means service, the sooner there is chinking, the sooner there is sadder than salad, the sooner there is none do her, the sooner there is no choice, the sooner there is a gloom freer, the same sooner and more sooner, this is no error in hurry and in pressure and in opposition to consideration.

A recital, what is a recital, it is an organ and use does not strengthen valor, it soothes medicine.

A transfer, a large transfer, a little transfer, some transfer, clouds and tracks do transfer, a transfer is not neglected.

Pride, when is there perfect pretence, there is no more than yesterday and ordinary.

A sentence of a vagueness that is violence is authority and a mission and stumbling and also certainly also a prison. Calmness, calm is beside the plate and in way in. There is no turn in terror. There is no volume in sound.

There is coagulation in cold and there is none in prudence. Something is preserved and the evening is long and the colder spring has sudden shadows in a sun. All the stain is tender and lilacs really lilacs are disturbed. Why is the perfect reëstablishment practiced and prized, why is it composed. The result the pure result is juice and size and baking and exhibition and nonchalance and sacrifice and volume and a section in division and the surrounding recognition and horticulture and no murmur. This is a result. There is no superposition and circumstance, there is hardness and a reason and the rest and remainder. There is no delight and no mathematics.

MUTTON.

A letter which can wither, a learning which can suffer and an outrage which is simultaneous is principal.

Student, students are merciful and recognised they chew something.

Hate rests that is solid and sparse and all in a shape and largely very largely. Interleaved and successive and a sample of smell all this makes a certainty a shade.

Light curls very light curls have no more curliness than soup. This is not a subject.

Change a single stream of denting and change it hurriedly, what does it express, it expresses nausea. Like a very strange likeness and pink, like that and not more like that than the same resemblance and not more like that than no middle space in cutting.

An eye glass, what is an eye glass, it is water. A splendid specimen, what is it when it is little and tender so that there are parts. A centre can place and four are no more and two and two are not middle.

Melting and not minding, safety and powder, a particular recollection and a sincere solitude all this makes a shunning so thorough and so unrepeated and surely if there is anything left it is a bone. It is not solitary.

Any space is not quiet it is so likely to be shiny. Darkness very dark darkness is sectional. There is a way to see in onion and surely very surely rhubarb and a tomato, surely very surely there is that seeding. A little thing in is a little thing.

Mud and water were not present and not any more of either. Silk and stockings were not present and not any more of either. A receptacle and a symbol and no monster were present and no more. This made a piece show and was it a kindness, it can be asked was it a kindness to have it warmer, was it a kindness and does gliding mean more. Does it.

Does it dirty a ceiling. It does not. Is it dainty, it is if prices are sweet. Is it lamentable, it is not if there is no undertaker. Is it curious, it is not when there is youth. All this makes a line, it even makes makes no more. All this makes cherries. The reason that there is a suggestion in vanity is due to this that there is a burst of mixed music.

A temptation any temptation is an exclamation if there are misdeeds and little bones. It is not astonishing that bones mingle as they vary not at all and in any case why is a bone outstanding, it is so because the circumstance that does not make a cake and character is so easily churned and cherished.

Mouse and mountain and a quiver, a quaint statue and pain in an exterior and silence more silence louder shows salmon a mischief intender. A cake, a real salve made of mutton and liquor, a specially retained rinsing and an established cork and blazing, this which resignation influences and restrains, restrains more altogether. A sign is the specimen spoken.

A meal in mutton, mutton, why is lamb cheaper, it is cheaper because so little is more. Lecture, lecture and repeat instruction.

BREAKFAST.

A change, a final change includes potatoes. This is no authority for the abuse of cheese. What language can instruct any fellow.

A shining breakfast, a breakfast shining, no dispute, no practice, nothing, nothing at all.

A sudden slice changes the whole plate, it does so suddenly.

An imitation, more imitation, imitation succeed imitations.

Anything that is decent, anything that is present, a calm and a cook and more singularly still a shelter, all these show the need of clamour. What is the custom, the custom is in the centre.

What is a loving tongue and pepper and more fish than there is when tears many tears are necessary. The tongue and the salmon, there is not salmon when brown is a color, there is salmon when there is no meaning to an early morning being pleasanter. There is no salmon, there are no teacups, there are the same kind of mushes as are used as stomachers by the eating hopes that makes eggs delicious. Drink is likely to stir a certain respect for an egg cup and more water melon than was ever eaten yesterday. Beer is neglected and cocoanut is famous. Coffee all coffee and a sample of soup all soup these are the choice of a baker. A white cup means a wedding. A wet cup means a vacation. A strong cup means an especial regulation. A single cup means a capital arrangement between the drawer and the place that is open.

Price a price is not in language, it is not in custom, it is not in praise.

A colored loss, why is there no leisure. If the persecution is so outrageous that nothing is solemn is there any occasion for persuasion.

A grey turn to a top and bottom, a silent pocketful of much heating, all the pliable succession of surrendering makes an ingenious joy.

A breeze in a jar and even then silence, a special anticipation in a rack, a gurgle a whole gurgle and more cheese than almost anything, is this an astonishment, does this incline more than the original division between a tray and a talking arrangement and even then a calling into another room gently with some chicken in any way.

A bent way that is a way to declare that the best is all together, a bent way shows no result, it shows a slight restraint, it shows a necessity for retraction.

Suspect a single buttered flower, suspect it certainly, suspect it and then glide, does that not alter a counting.

A hurt mended stick, a hurt mended cup, a hurt mended article of exceptional relaxation and annoyance, a hurt mended, hurt and mended is so necessary that no mistake is intended.

What is more likely than a roast, nothing really and yet it is never disappointed singularly.

A steady cake, any steady cake is perfect and not plain, any steady cake has a mounting reason and more than that it has singular crusts. A season of more is a seasonthat is instead. A season of many is not more a season than most.

Take no remedy lightly, take no urging intently, take no separation leniently, beware of no lake and no larder.

Burden the cracked wet soaking sack heavily, burden it so that it is an institution in fright and in climate and in the best plan that there can be.

An ordinary color, a color is that strange mixture which makes, which does make which does not make a ripe juice, which does not make a mat.

A work which is a winding a real winding of the cloaking of a relaxing rescue. This which is so cool is not dusting, it is not dirtying in smelling, it could use white water, it could use more extraordinarily and in no solitude altogether. This which is so not winsome and not widened and really not so dipped as dainty and really dainty, very dainty, ordinarily, dainty, a dainty, not in that dainty and dainty. If the time is determined, if it is determined and there is reunion there is reunion with that then outline, then there is in that a piercing shutter, all of a piercing shouter, all of a quite weather, all of a withered exterior, all of that in most violent likely.

An excuse is not dreariness, a single plate is not butter, a single weight is not excitement, a solitary crumbling is not only martial.

A mixed protection, very mixed with the same actual intentional unstrangeness and riding, a single action caused necessarily is not more a sign than a minister.

Seat a knife near a cage and very near a decision and more nearly a timely working cat and scissors. Do this temporarily and make no more mistake in standing. Spread it all and arrange the white place, does this show in the house, does it not show in the green that is not necessary for that color, does it not even show in the explanation and singularly not at all stationary.

SUGAR.

A violent luck and a whole sample and even then quiet.

Water is squeezing, water is almost squeezing on lard. Water, water is a mountain and it is selected and it is so practical that there is no use in money. A mind under is exact and so it is necessary to have a mouth and eye glasses.

A question of sudden rises and more time than awfulness is so easy and shady. There is precisely that noise.

A peck a small piece not privately overseen, not at all not a slice, not at all crestfallen and open, not at all mounting and chaining and evenly surpassing, all the bidding comes to tea.

A separation is not tightly in worsted and sauce, it is so kept well and sectionally.

Put it in the stew, put it to shame. A little slight shadow and a solid fine furnace.

The teasing is tender and trying and thoughtful.

The line which sets sprinkling to be a remedy is beside the best cold.

A puzzle, a monster puzzle, a heavy choking, a neglected Tuesday.

Wet crossing and a likeness, any likeness, a likeness has blisters, it has that and teeth, it has the staggering blindly and a little green, any little green is ordinary.

One, two and one, two, nine, second and five and that.

A blaze, a search in between, a cow, only any wet place, only this tune.

Cut a gas jet uglier and then pierce pierce in between the next and negligence. Choose the rate to pay and pet pet very much. A collection of all around, a signal poison, a lack of languor and more hurts at ease.

A white bird, a colored mine, a mixed orange, a dog.

Cuddling comes in continuing a change.

A piece of separate outstanding rushing is so blind with open delicacy.

A canoe is orderly. A period is solemn. A cow is accepted.

A nice old chain is widening, it is absent, it is laid by.

CRANBERRIES.

Could there not be a sudden date, could there not be in the present settlement of old age pensions, could there not be by a witness, could there be.

Count the chain, cut the grass, silence the noon and murder flies. See the basting undip the chart, see the way the kinds are best seen from the rest, from that and untidy.

Cut the whole space into twenty-four spaces and then and then is there a yellow color, there is but it is smelled, it is then put where it is and nothing stolen.

A remarkable degree of red means that, a remarkable exchange is made.

Climbing altogether in when there is a solid chance of soiling no more than a dirty thing, coloring all of it in steadying is jelly.

Just as it is suffering, just as it is succeeded, just as it is moist so is there no countering.

MILK.

A white egg and a colored pan and a cabbage showing settlement, a constant increase.

A cold in a nose, a single cold nose makes an excuse. Two are more necessary.

All the goods are stolen, all the blisters are in the cup.

Cooking, cooking is the recognition between sudden and nearly sudden very little and all large holes.

A real pint, one that is open and closed and in the middle is so bad.

Tender colds, seen eye holders, all work, the best of change, the meaning, the dark red, all this and bitten, really bitten.

Guessing again and golfing again and the best men, the very best men.

MILK.

Climb up in sight climb in the whole utter needles and a guess a whole guess is hanging. Hanging hanging.

EGGS.

Kind height, kind in the right stomach with a little sudden mill.

Cunning shawl, cunning shawl to be steady.

In white in white handkerchiefs with little dots in a white belt all shadows are singular they are singular and procured and relieved.

No that is not the cow's shame and a precocious sound, it is a bite.

Cut up alone the paved way which is harm. Harm is old boat and a likely dash.

APPLE.

Apple plum, carpet steak, seed clam, colored wine, calm seen, cold cream, best shake, potato, potato and no no gold work with pet, a green seen is called bake and change sweet is bready, a little piece a little piece please.

A little piece please. Cane again to the presupposed and

ready eucalyptus tree, count out sherry and ripe plates and little corners of a kind of ham. This is use.

TAILS.

Cold pails, cold with joy no joy.

A tiny seat that means meadows and a lapse of cuddles with cheese and nearly bats, all this went messed. The post placed a loud loose sprain. A rest is no better. It is better yet. All the time.

LUNCH.

Luck in loose plaster makes holy gauge and nearly that, nearly more states, more states come in town light kite, blight not white.

A little lunch is a break in skate a little lunch so slimy, a west end of a board line is that which shows a battle beneath so that necessity is a silk under wear. That is best wet. It is so natural, and why is there flake, there is flake to explain exhaust.

A real cold hen is nervous is nervous with a towel with a spool with real beads. It is mostly an extra sole nearly all that shaved, shaved with an old mountain, more than that bees more than that dinner and a bunch of likes that is to say the hearts of onions aim less.

Cold coffee with a corn a corn yellow and green mass is a gem.

CUPS.

A single example of excellence is in the meat. A bent stick is surging and might all might is mental. A grand clothes is searching out a candle not that wheatly not that by more than an owl and a path. A ham is proud of co-coanut.

A cup is neglected by being all in size. It is a handle and meadows and sugar any sugar.

A cup is neglected by being full of size. It shows no shade, in come little wood cuts and blessing and nearly not that not with a wild bought in, not at all so polite, not nearly so behind.

Cups crane in. They need a pet oyster, they need it so hoary and nearly choice. The best slam is utter. Nearly be freeze.

Why is a cup a stir and a behave. Why is it so seen.

A cup is readily shaded, it has in between no sense that is to say music, memory, musical memory.

Peanuts blame, a half sand is holey and nearly.

RHUBARB.

Rhubarb is susan not susan not seat in bunch toys not wild and laughable not in little places not in neglect and vegetable not in fold coal age not please.

SINGLE FISH.

Single fish single fish single fish egg-plant single fish sight.

A sweet win and not less noisy than saddle and more ploughing and nearly well painted by little things so.

Please shade it a play. It is necessary and beside the large sort is puff.

Every way oakly, please prune it near. It is so found.

It is not the same.

CAKE.

Cake cast in went to be and needles wine needles are such.

This is today. A can experiment is that which makes a

town, makes a town dirty, it is little please. We came back. Two bore, bore what, a mussed ash, ash when there is tin. This meant cake. It was a sign.

Another time there was extra a hat pin sought long and this dark made a display. The result was yellow. A caution, not a caution to be.

It is no use to cause a foolish number. A blanket stretch a cloud, a shame, all that bakery can tease, all that is beginning and yesterday yesterday we had it met. It means some change. No some day.

A little leaf upon a scene an ocean any where there, a bland and likely in the stream a recollection green land. Why white.

CUSTARD.

Custard is this. It has aches, aches when. Not to be. Not to be narrowly. This makes a whole little hill.

It is better than a little thing that has mellow real mellow. It is better than lakes whole lakes, it is better than seeding.

POTATOES.

Real potatoes cut in between.

POTATOES.

In the preparation of cheese, in the preparation of crackers, in the preparation of butter, in it.

ROAST POTATOES.

Roast potatoes for.

ASPARAGUS.

Asparagus in a lean in a lean to hot. This makes it art and it is wet wet weather wet weather wet.

BUTTER.

Boom in boom in, butter. Leave a grain and show it, show it. I spy.

It is a need it is a need that a flower a state flower. It is a need that a state rubber. It is a need that a state rubber is sweet and sight and a swelled stretch. It is a need. It is a need that state rubber.

Wood a supply. Clean little keep a strange, estrange on it.

Make a little white, no and not with pit, pit on in within.

END OF SUMMER.

Little eyelets that have hammer and a check with stripes between a lounge, in wit, in a rested development.

SAUSAGES.

Sausages in between a glass.

There is read butter. A loaf of it is managed. Wake a question. Eat an instant, answer.

A reason for bed is this, that a decline, any decline is poison, poison is a toe a toe extractor, this means a solemn change. Hanging.

No evil is wide, any extra in leaf is so strange and singular a red breast.

CELERY.

Celery tastes tastes where in curled lashes and little bits and mostly in remains.

A green acre is so selfish and so pure and so enlivened.

VEAL.

Very well very well, washing is old, washing is washing.

Cold soup, cold soup clear and particular and a principal a principal question to put into.

VEGETABLE.

What is cut. What is cut by it. What is cut by it in.

It was a cress a crescent a cross and an unequal scream, it was upslanting, it was radiant and reasonable with little ins and red.

News. News capable of glees, cut in shoes, belike under pump of wide chalk, all this combing.

WAY LAY VEGETABLE.

Leaves in grass and mow potatoes, have a skip, hurry you up flutter.

Suppose it is ex a cake suppose it is new mercy and leave charlotte and nervous bed rows. Suppose it is meal. Suppose it is sam.

COOKING.

Alas, alas the pull alas the bell alas the coach in china, alas the little put in leaf alas the wedding butter meat, alas the receptacle, alas the back shape of mussle, mussle and soda.

CHICKEN.

Pheasant and chicken, chicken is a peculiar third.

CHICKEN.

Alas a dirty word, alas a dirty third alas a dirty third, alas a dirty bird.

CHICKEN.

Alas a doubt in case of more go to say what it is cress. What is it. Mean. Potato. Loaves.

CHICKEN.

Stick stick call then, stick stick sticking, sticking with a chicken. Sticking in an extra succession, sticking in.

CHAIN-BOATS.

Chain-boats are merry, are merry blew, blew west, carpet.

PASTRY.

Cutting shade, cool spades and little last beds, make violet, violet when.

CREAM.

In a plank, in a play sole, in a heated red left tree there is shut in specs with salt be where. This makes an eddy. Necessary.

CREAM.

Cream cut. Any where crumb. Left hop chambers.

CUCUMBER.

Not a razor less, not a razor, ridiculous pudding, red and relet put in, rest in a slender go in selecting, rest in, rest in in white widening.

DINNER.

Not a little fit, not a little fit sun sat in shed more mentally.

Let us why, let us why weight, let us why winter chess, let us why way.

Only a moon to soup her, only that in the sell never never be the cocups nice be, shatter it they lay.

Egg ear nuts, look a bout. Shoulder. Let it strange, sold in bell next herds.

It was a time when in the acres in late there was a wheel that shot a burst of land and needless are niggers and a sample sample set of old eaten butterflies with spoons, all of it to be are fled and measure make it, make it, yet all the one in that we see where shall not it set with a left and more so, yes there add when the longer not it shall the best in the way when all be with when shall not for there with see and chest how for another excellent and excellent and easy easy excellent and easy express e c, all to be nice all to be no so. All to be no so no so. All to be not a white old chat churner. Not to be any example of an edible apple in.

DINING.

Dining is west.

EATING.

Eat ting, eating a grand old man said roof and never never re soluble burst, not a near ring not a bewildered neck, not really any such bay.

Is it so a noise to be is it a least remain to rest, is it a so old say to be, is it a leading are been. Is it so, is it so, is it so, is it so is it so is it so.

Eel us eel us with no no pea no pea cool, no pea cool cooler, no pea cooler with a land a land cost in, with a land cost in stretches.

Eating he heat eating he heat it eating, he heat it heat eating. He heat eating.

A little piece of pay of pay owls owls such as pie, bolsters.

Will leap beat, willie well all. The rest rest oxen occasion occasion to be so purred, so purred how.

It was a ham it was a square come well it was a square remain, a square remain not it a bundle, not it a bundle so is a grip, a grip to shed bay leave bay leave draught, bay leave draw cider in low, cider in low and george. George is a mass.

EATING.

It was a shame it was a shame to stare to stare and double and relieve relieve be cut up show as by the elevation of it and out out more in the steady where the come and on and the all the shed and that.

It was a garden and belows belows straight. It was a pea, a pea pour it in its not a succession, not it a simple, not it a so election, election with.

SALAD.

It is a winning cake.

SAUCE.

What is bay labored what is all be section, what is no much. Sauce sam in.

SALMON.

It was a peculiar bin a bin found in beside.

ORANGE.

Why is a feel oyster an egg stir. Why is it orange centre.

A show at tick and loosen loosen it so to speak sat.

It was an extra leaker with a see spoon, it was an extra licker with a see spoon.

ORANGE.

A type oh oh new new not no not knealer knealer of old show beefsteak, neither neither.

ORANGES.

Build is all right.

ORANGE IN.

Go lack go lack use to her.
Cocoa and clear soup and oranges and oat-meal.
Whist bottom whist close, whist clothes, woodling.
Cocoa and clear soup and oranges and oat-meal.
Pain soup, suppose it is question, suppose it is butter, real is, real is only, only excreate, only excreate a no since.

A no, a no since, a no since when, a no since when since, a no since when since a no since when since, a no since, a no since when since, a no since, a no, a no since a no since, a no since, a no since.

SALAD DRESSING AND AN ARTICHOKE.

Please pale hot, please cover rose, please acre in the red stranger, please butter all the beef-steak with regular feel faces.

SALAD DRESSING AND AN ARTICHOKE.

It was please it was please carriage cup in an ice-cream, in an ice-cream it was too bended bended with scissors and all this time. A whole is inside a part, a part does go away, a hole is red leaf. No choice was where there was and a second and a second.

A CENTRE IN A TABLE.

It was a way a day, this made some sum. Suppose a cod liver a cod liver is an oil, suppose a cod liver oil is tunny, suppose a cod liver oil tunny is pressed suppose a cod liver oil tunny pressed is china and secret with a bestow a bestow reed, a reed to be a reed to be, in a reed to be.

Next to me next to a folder, next to a folder some waiter, next to a foldersome waiter and re letter and read her. Read her with her for less.

ROOMS

Act so that there is no use in a centre. A wide action is not a width. A preparation is given to the ones preparing. They do not eat who mention silver and sweet. There was an occupation.

A whole centre and a border make hanging a way of dressing. This which is not why there is a voice is the remains of an offering. There was no rental.

So the tune which is there has a little piece to play. And the exercise is all there is of a fast. The tender and true that makes no width to hew is the time that there is question to adopt.

To begin the placing there is no wagon. There is no change lighter. It was done. And then the spreading, that was not accomplishing that needed standing and yet the time was not so difficult as they were not all in place. They had no change. They were not respected. They were that, they did it so much in the matter and this showed that that settlement was not condensed. It was spread there. Any change was in the ends of the centre. A heap was heavy. There was no change.

Burnt and behind and lifting a temporary stone and lifting more than a drawer.

The instance of there being more is an instance of more. The shadow is not shining in the way there is a black line.

The truth has come. There is a disturbance. Trusting to a
baker's boy meant that there would be very much exchanging and anyway what is the use of a covering to a door.
There is a use, they are double.

If the centre has the place then there is distribution. That
is natural. There is a contradiction and naturally returning
there comes to be both sides and the centre. That can be seen
from the description.

The author of all that is in there behind the door and that
is entering in the morning. Explaining darkening and ex-
pecting relating is all of a piece. The stove is bigger. It was
of a shape that made no audience bigger if the opening is as-
sumed why should there not be kneeling. Any force which is
bestowed on a floor shows rubbing. This is so nice and
sweet and yet there comes the change, there comes the time
to press more air. This does not mean the same as disap-
pearance.

A little lingering lion and a Chinese chair, all the handsome cheese which is stone, all of it and a choice, a choice
of a blotter. If it is difficult to do it one way there is no place
of similar trouble. None. The whole arrangement is established. The end of which is that there is a suggestion, a suggestion that there can be a different whiteness to a wall. This
was thought.

A page to a corner means that the shame is no greater
when the table is longer. A glass is of any height, it is higher,
it is simpler and if it were placed there would not be any
doubt.

Something that is an erection is that which stands and
feeds and silences a tin which is swelling. This makes no di-
version that is to say what can please exaltation, that which
is cooking.

A shine is that which when covered changes permission.
An enclosure blends with the same that is to say there is

blending. A blend is that which holds no mice and this is not because of a floor it is because of nothing, it is not in a vision.

A fact is that when the place was replaced all was left that was stored and all was retained that would not satisfy more than another. The question is this, is it possible to suggest more to replace that thing. This question and this perfect denial does make the time change all the time.

The sister was not a mister. Was this a surprise. It was. The conclusion came when there was no arrangement. All the time that there was a question there was a decision. Replacing a casual acquaintance with an ordinary daughter does not make a son.

It happened in a way that the time was perfect and there was a growth of a whole dividing time so that where formerly there was no mistake there was no mistake now. For instance before when there was a separation there was waiting, now when there is separation there is the division between intending and departing. This made no more mixture than there would be if there had been no change.

A little sign of an entrance is the one that made it alike. If it were smaller it was not alike and it was so much smaller that a table was bigger. A table was much bigger, very much bigger. Changing that made nothing bigger, it did not make anything bigger littler, it did not hinder wood from not being used as leather. And this was so charming. Harmony is so essential. Is there pleasure when there is a passage, there is when every room is open. Every room is open when there are not four, there were there and surely there were four, there were two together. There is no resemblance.

A single speed, the reception of table linen, all the wonder of six little spoons, there is no exercise.

The time came when there was a birthday. Every day was no excitement and a birthday was added, it was added on Monday, this made the memory clear, this which was a speech showed the chair in the middle where there was copper.

Alike and a snail, this means Chinamen, it does there is no doubt that to be right is more than perfect there is no doubt and glass is confusing it confuses the substance which was of a color. Then came the time for discrimination, it came then and it was never mentioned it was so triumphant, it showed the whole head that had a hole and should have a hole it showed the resemblance between silver.

Startling a starving husband is not disagreeable. The reason that nothing is hidden is that there is no suggestion of silence. No song is sad. A lesson is of consequence.

Blind and weak and organised and worried and betrothed and resumed and also asked to a fast and always asked to consider and never startled and not at all bloated, this which is no rarer than frequently is not so astonishing when hair brushing is added. There is quiet, there certainly is.

No eye-glasses are rotten, no window is useless and yet if air will not come in there is a speech ready, there always is and there is no dimness, not a bit of it.

All along the tendency to deplore the absence of more has not been authorised. It comes to mean that with burning there is that pleasant state of stupefication. Then there is a way of earning a living. Who is a man.

A silence is not indicated by any motion, less is indicated by a motion, more is not indicated it is enthralled. So sullen and so low, so much resignation, so much refusal and so much place for a lower and an upper, so much and yet more silence, why is not sleeping a feat why is it not and when is there some discharge when. There never is.

If comparing a piece that is a size that is recognised as not a size but a piece, comparing a piece with what is not recognised but what is used as it is held by holding, comparing these two comes to be repeated. Suppose they are put together, suppose that there is an interruption, supposing that beginning again they are not changed as to position, suppose all this and suppose that any five two of whom are not separating suppose that the five are not consumed. Is there an exchange, is there a resemblance to the sky which is admitted to be there and the stars which can be seen. Is there. That was a question. There was no certainty. Fitting a failing meant that any two were indifferent and yet they were all connecting that, they were all connecting that consideration. This did not determine rejoining a letter. This did not make letters smaller. It did.

The stamp that is not only torn but also fitting is not any symbol. It suggests nothing. A sack that has no opening suggests more and the loss is not commensurate. The season gliding and the torn hangings receiving mending all this shows an example, it shows the force of sacrifice and likeness and disaster and a reason.

The time when there is not the question is only seen when there is a shower. Any little thing is water.

There was a whole collection made. A damp cloth, an oyster, a single mirror, a manikin, a student, a silent star, a single spark, a little movement and the bed is made. This shows the disorder, it does, it shows more likeness than anything else, it shows the single mind that directs an apple. All the coats have a different shape, that does not mean that they differ in color, it means a union between use and exercise and a horse.

A plain hill, one is not that which is not white and red and green, a plain hill makes no sunshine, it shows that without a disturber. So the shape is there and the color and the outline and the miserable centre. It is not very likely that there is a centre, a hill is a hill and no hill is contained in a pink tender descender.

A can containing a curtain is a solid sentimental usage. The trouble in both eyes does not come from the same symmetrical carpet, it comes from there being no more disturbance than in little paper. This does show the teeth, it shows color.

A measure is that which put up so that it shows the length has a steel construction. Tidiness is not delicacy, it does not destroy the whole piece, certainly not it has been measured and nothing has been cut off and even if that has been lost there is a name, no name is signed and left over, not any space is fitted so that moving about is plentiful. Why is there so much resignation in a package, why is there rain, all the same the chance has come, there is no bell to ring.

A package and a filter and even a funnel, all this together makes a scene and supposing the question arises is hair curly, is it dark and dusty, supposing that question arises, is brushing necessary, is it, the whole special suddenness commences then, there is no delusion.

A cape is a cover, a cape is not a cover in summer, a cape is a cover and the regulation is that there is no such weather. A cape is not always a cover, a cape is not a cover when there is another, there is always something in that thing in establishing a disposition to put wetting where it will not do more harm. There is always that disposition and in a way there is some use in not mentioning changing and in establishing the temperature, there is some use in it as establishing all that lives dimmer freer and there is no dinner in the middle of anything. There is no such thing.

Why is a pale white not paler than blue, why is a connection made by a stove, why is the example which is mentioned not shown to be the same, why is there no adjustment between the place and the separate attention. Why is there a choice in gamboling. Why is there no necessary dull stable, why is there a single piece of any color, why is there that sensible silence. Why is there the resistance in a mixture, why is there no poster, why is there that in the window, why is there no suggester, why is there no window, why is there no oyster closer. Why is there a circular diminisher, why is there a bather, why is there no scraper, why is there a dinner, why is there a bell ringer, why is there a duster, why is there a section of a similar resemblance, why is there that scissor.

South, south which is a wind is not rain, does silence choke speech or does it not.

Lying in a conundrum, lying so makes the springs restless, lying so is a reduction, not lying so is arrangeable.

Releasing the oldest auction that is the pleasing some still renewing.

Giving it away, not giving it away, is there any difference. Giving it away. Not giving it away.

Almost very likely there is no seduction, almost very likely there is no stream, certainly very likely the height is penetrated, certainly certainly the target is cleaned. Come to sit, come to refuse, come to surround, come slowly and age is not lessening. The time which showed that was when there was no eclipse. All the time that resenting was removal all that time there was breadth. No breath is shadowed, no breath is painstaking and yet certainly what could be the use of paper, paper shows no disorder, it shows no desertion.

Why is there a difference between one window and another, why is there a difference, because the curtain is shorter. There is no distaste in beefsteak or in plums or in gallons of milk water, there is no defiance in original piling up over a roof, there is no daylight in the evening, there is none there empty.

A tribune, a tribune does not mean paper, it means nothing more than cake, it means more sugar, it shows the state of lengthening any nose. The last spice is that which shows the whole evening spent in that sleep, it shows so that walking is an alleviation, and yet this astonishes everybody the distance is so sprightly. In all the time there are three days, those are not passed uselessly. Any little thing is a change that is if nothing is wasted in that cellar. All the rest of the chairs are established.

A success, a success is alright when there are there rooms and no vacancies, a success is alright when there is a package, success is alright anyway and any curtain is wholesale. A curtain diminishes and an ample space shows varnish.

One taste one tack, one taste one bottle, one taste one fish, one taste one barometer. This shows no distinguishing sign when there is a store.

Any smile is stern and any coat is a sample. Is there any use in changing more doors than there are committees. This question is so often asked that squares show that they are blotters. It is so very agreeable to hear a voice and to see all the signs of that expression.

Cadences, real cadences, real cadences and a quiet color. Careful and curved, cake and sober, all accounts and mixture, a guess at anything is righteous, should there be a call there would be a voice.

A line in life, a single line and a stairway, a rigid cook, no cook and no equator, all the same there is higher than that another evasion. Did that mean shame, it meant memory. Looking into a place that was hanging and was visible looking into this place and seeing a chair did that mean relief, it did, it certainly did not cause constipation and yet there is a melody that has white for a tune when there is straw color. This shows no face.

Star-light, what is star-light, star-light is a little light that is not always mentioned with the sun, it is mentioned with the moon and the sun, it is mixed up with the rest of the time.

Why is the name changed. The name is changed because in the little space there is a tree, in some space there are no trees, in every space there is a hint of more, all this causes the decision.

Why is there education, there is education because the two tables which are folding are not tied together with a ribbon, string is used and string being used there is a necessity for another one and another one not being used to hearing shows no ordinary use of any evening and yet there is no disgrace in looking, none at all. This came to separate when there was simple selection of an entire pre-occupation.

A curtain, a curtain which is fastened discloses mourning, this does not mean sparrows or elocution or even a whole preparation, it means that there are ears and very often much more altogether.

Climate, climate is not southern, a little glass, a bright winter, a strange supper an elastic tumbler, all this shows that the back is furnished and red which is red is a dark color. An example of this is fifteen years and a separation of regret.

China is not down when there are plates, lights are not ponderous and incalculable.

Currents, currents are not in the air and on the floor and in the door and behind it first. Currents do not show it plainer. This which is mastered has so thin a space to build it all that there is plenty of room and yet is it quarreling, it is not and the insistence is marked. A change is in a current and there is no habitable exercise.

A religion, almost a religion, any religion, a quintal in religion, a relying and a surface and a service in indecision and a creature and a question and a syllable in answer and more counting and no quarrel and a single scientific statement and no darkness and no question and an earned administration and a single set of sisters and an outline and no blisters and the section seeing yellow and the centre having spelling and no solitude and no quaintness and yet solid quite so solid and the single surface centred and the question in the placard and the singularity, is there a singularity, and the singularity, why is there a question and the singularity why is the surface outrageous, why is it beautiful why is it not when there is no doubt, why is anything vacant, why is not disturbing a centre no virtue, why is it when it is and why is it when it is and there is no doubt, there is no doubt that the singularity shows.

A climate, a single climate, all the time there is a single climate, any time there is a doubt, any time there is music that is to question more and more and there is no politeness, there is hardly any ordeal and certainly there is no table-cloth.

This is a sound and obligingness more obligingness leads to a harmony in hesitation.

A lake a single lake which is a pond and a little water any water which is an ant and no burning, not any burning, all this is sudden.

A canister that is the remains of furniture and a looking-glass and a bed-room and a larger size, all the stand is shouted and what is ancient is practical. Should the resemblance be so that any little cover is copied, should it be so that yards are measured, should it be so and there be a sin, should it be so then certainly a room is big enough when it is so empty and the corners are gathered together.

The change is mercenary that settles whitening the coloring and serving dishes where there is metal and making yellow any yellow every color in a shade which is expressed in a tray. This is a monster and awkward quite awkward and the little design which is flowered which is not strange and yet has visible writing, this is not shown all the time but at once, after that it rests where it is and where it is in place. No change is not needed. That does show design.

Excellent, more excellence is borrowing and slanting very slanting is light and secret and a recitation and emigration. Certainly shoals are shallow and nonsense more nonsense is sullen. Very little cake is water, very little cake has that escape.

Sugar any sugar, anger every anger, lover sermon lover, centre no distractor, all order is in a measure.

Left over to be a lamp light, left over in victory, left over in saving, all this and negligence and bent wood and more even much more is not so exact as a pen and a turtle and even, certainly, and even a piece of the same experience as more.

To consider a lecture, to consider it well is so anxious and so much a charity and really supposing there is grain and if a stubble every stubble is urgent, will there not be a chance of legality. The sound is sickened and the price is purchased and golden what is golden, a clergyman, a single tax, a currency and an inner chamber.

Checking an emigration, checking it by smiling and certainly by the same satisfactory stretch of hands that have more use for it than nothing, and mildly not mildly a correction, not mildly even a circumstance and a sweetness and a serenity. Powder, that has no color, if it did have would it be white.

A whole soldier any whole soldier has no more detail than any case of measles.

A bridge a very small bridge in a location and thunder, any thunder, this is the capture of reversible sizing and more indeed more can be cautious. This which makes monotony careless makes it likely that there is an exchange in principle and more than that, change in organization.

This cloud does change with the movements of the moon and the narrow the quite narrow suggestion of the building. It does and then when it is settled and no sounds differ then comes the moment when cheerfulness is so assured that there is an occasion.

A plain lap, any plain lap shows that sign, it shows that there is not so much extension as there would be if there were more choice in everything. And why complain of more, why complain of very much more. Why complain at all when it is all arranged that as there is no more opportunity and no more appeal and not even any more clinching that certainly now some time has come.

A window has another spelling, it has "f" all together, it lacks no more then and this is rain, this may even be something else, at any rate there is no dedication in splendor. There is a turn of the stranger.

Catholic to be turned is to venture on youth and a section of debate, it even means that no class where each one over fifty is regular is so stationary that there are invitations.

A curving example makes righteous finger-nails. This is the only object in secretion and speech.

To being the same four are no more than were taller. The rest had a big chair and a surveyance a cold accumulation of nausea, and even more than that, they had a disappointment.

Nothing aiming is a flower, if flowers are abundant then they are lilac, if they are not they are white in the centre.

Dance a clean dream and an extravagant turn up, secure the steady rights and translate more than translate the authority, show the choice and make no more mistakes than yesterday.

This means clearness, it means a regular notion of exercise, it means more than that, it means liking counting, it means more than that, it does not mean exchanging a line.

Why is there more craving than there is in a mountain. This does not seem strange to one, it does not seem strange to an echo and more surely is in there not being a habit. Why is there so much useless suffering. Why is there.

Any wet weather means an open window, what is attaching eating, anything that is violent and cooking and shows weather is the same in the end and why is there more use in something than in all that.

The cases are made and books, back books are used to secure tears and church. They are even used to exchange black slippers. They can not be mended with wax. They show no need of any such occasion.

A willow and no window, a wide place stranger, a wideness makes an active centre.

The sight of no pussy cat is so different that a tobacco zone is white and cream.

A lilac, all a lilac and no mention of butter, not even bread and butter, no butter and no occasion, not even a silent resemblance, not more care than just enough haughty.

A safe weight is that which when it pleases is hanging. A safer weight is one more naughty in a spectacle. The best game is that which is shiny and scratching. Please a pease and a cracker and a wretched use of summer.

Surprise, the only surprise has no occasion. It is an ingredient and the section the whole section is one season.

A pecking which is petting and no worse than in the same morning is not the only way to be continuous often.

A light in the moon the only light is on Sunday. What was the sensible decision. The sensible decision was that notwithstanding many declarations and more music, not even notwithstanding the choice and a torch and a collection, notwithstanding the celebrating hat and a vacation and even more noise than cutting, notwithstanding Europe and Asia and being overbearing, not even notwithstanding an elephant and a strict occasion, not even withstanding more cultivation and some seasoning, not even with drowning and with the ocean being encircling, not even with more likeness and any cloud, not even with terrific sacrifice of pedestrianism and a special resolution, not even more likely to be pleasing. The care with which the rain is wrong and the green is wrong and the white is wrong, the care with which there is a chair and plenty of breathing. The care with which there is incredible justice and likeness, all this makes a magnificent asparagus, and also a fountain.

SELECTED BIBLIOGRAPHY

Works by Gertrude Stein

Three Lives, 1908
Tender Buttons, 1915
Geography and Plays, 1923
The Making of Americans, 1925
Useful Knowledge, 1928
Acquaintance with Description, 1929
Ten Portraits, 1930
Lucy Church Amiably, 1930
Before Flowers of Friendship Faded, 1931
How to Write, 1931
Operas and Plays, 1932
Matisse, Picasso, and Gertrude Stein, 1932
The Autobiography of Alice B. Toklas, 1933
Four Saints in Three Acts: an opera, 1934
Portraits and Prayers, 1934
Lectures in America, 1935
Narration, 1936
Everybody's Autobiography, 1937
Picasso, 1938
The World Is Round, 1939
Paris France, 1940
Ida, 1941
Wars I Have Seen, 1945
In Savoy Yes Is for a Very Young Man: a play, 1946
Brewsie and Willie, 1946

Four in America, 1947
Mother of Us All: an opera, 1947
Blood on The Dining Room Floor, 1948
First Reader, and Three Plays, Carl Van Vechten, ed., 1948
Last Operas and Plays, Carl Van Vechten, ed., 1949
Things As They Are, 1950
Two: Gertrude Stein & Her Brother, 1951
Mrs. Reynolds, 1952
Five Earlier Novelettes, 1952
Bee Time Vine, 1953

Biography and Criticism

Bridgman, Richard. *Gertrude Stein in Pieces.* New York: Oxford University Press, 1970.

Brinnin, John Malcolm. *The Third Rose: Gertrude Stein and Her World.* Boston: Little, Brown, 1959.

Copeland, Carolyn F. *Language and Time and Gertrude Stein.* Iowa City: University of Iowa Press, 1976.

DeKoven, Marianne. *A Different Language: Gertrude Stein's Experimental Writing.* Madison: University of Wisconsin Press, 1983.

Doane, Janice L. *Silence and Narrative: The Early Novels of Gertrude Stein.* Westport, CT: Greenwood Press, 1986.

Grohn, Judy. *Really Reading Gertrude Stein.* Freedom, CA: The Crowning Press, 1989.

Hobhouse, Janet. *Everybody Who Was Anybody: A Biography of Gertrude Stein.* New York: Doubleday, 1989.

Hoffman, Frederick J. *Gertrude Stein.* Minneapolis: University of Minnesota Press, 1961.

——. *Critical Essays on Gertrude Stein*. Boston: G. K. Hall, 1986.

Meese, Elizabeth. "Gertrude Stein and Me: A Revolution in the Letter." In *Sem/Erotics Theorizing Lesbian Writing*. New York: New York University Press, 1992.

Mellow, James R. *Charmed Circle: Gertrude Stein and Company*. New York: Avon, 1975.

Newton, Esther. "Alice-Hunting." In *Butch/Femme: Inside Lesbian Gender*, ed. Sally Munt. London: Cassell, 1998.

Souhami, Diana. *Gertrude and Alice*. San Francisco: Pandora/HarperCollins, 1991.

Sprigge, Elizabeth. *Gertrude Stein: Her Life and Work*. New York: Harper, 1957.

Stewart, Allegra. *Gertrude Stein and the Present*. Cambridge, MA: Harvard University Press, 1967.

Sutherland, Donald. *Gertrude Stein: A Biography of Her Work*. Westport, CT: Greenwood Press, 1972.

Walker, Jayne L. *The Making of a Modernist: Gertrude from* Three Lives *to* Tender Buttons. Amherst: University of Massachusetts Press, 1984.

Classic Writing by American Women

THE AWAKENING: & SELECTED STORIES
Kate Chopin 524489
Published in 1899, *The Awakening*'s portrayal of a woman, stifled by the bonds of her marriage, who discovers the power of her own sexuality, shocked the popular taste of the day. It remains "as pertinent as any fiction." —*New York Times*

TWENTY YEARS AT HULL HOUSE *Jane Addams* 527399
At a time when America was filled with a fear of foreigners, Jane Addams lived and worked among the immigrant sweatshop toilers, the unwed mothers, the aged, and sick, to show them in practice what others merely preached: the true concept of American Democracy.

MY ANTONIA *Willa Cather* 525795
This magnificent tale, full of Cather's descriptions of the Nebraskan grasslands, tells of a woman coming of age in the early days of the twentieth century. Passionate, beautiful, and strong enough to work the fields, Antonia comes to embody the spirit of the American frontier.

THREE BY FLANNERY O'CONNOR 525140
Flannery O'Conner's strong, fiercely comic, powerful fiction has won unanimous critical acclaim. No other writer has captured the Southern rhythm, the throb of humor, hysteria and passion so well. Here in one volume are *Wise Blood, Everything That Rises Must Converge,* and *The Violent Bear It Away,* three works that helped establish her reputation as one of America's most original and provocative writers.

To order call: 1-800-788-6262

READ THE TOP 25 SIGNET CLASSICS